SHARKS ARE SCARY
AREN'T THEY?

SHARKS ARE SCARY
AREN'T THEY?

CHRISTINE EDWARDS

The Book Guild Ltd

First published in Great Britain in 2023 by
The Book Guild Ltd
Unit E2 Airfield Business Park,
Harrison Road, Market Harborough,
Leicestershire. LE16 7UL
Tel: 0116 2792299
www.bookguild.co.uk
Email: info@bookguild.co.uk
Twitter: @bookguild

Typeset in 11pt Minion Pro

Printed and bound in Great Britain by CMP UK

ISBN 978 1915352 613

British Library Cataloguing in Publication Data.
A catalogue record for this book is available from the British Library.

For Gareth
and
all those who seek to protect sharks and our oceans.

PROLOGUE

Words. There are thousands of them. Over 172,000 according to The Oxford English Dictionary. We all use them. I do. You do. When we are alone. When we are silent. Our heads are full of them. Eyes open. Eyes shut. Words swirl in and out of our minds. Our days, dreams and daydreams are filled with them.

So, let's take a word. Any word. Like pizza. Yes, pizza. That's a word. What thoughts does this word evoke? What feelings? What images pop into your head? A whole pizza? One slice? Maybe a pizza with your favourite topping. Cheese. Tomato. Mushroom. Ham. Pineapple. Yuk! Pineapple. I know how I feel when I think about that revolting fruit. So, do you like pizza or hate it? Reading the word, can you smell it? Can you remember the taste it makes when you pop it in your mouth, and it melts on your tongue? Are you hungry by any chance and craving a slice? You might feel the need to pop this book down and go and have some. If you do, do.

The point I'm trying to make is that words are powerful. They shape our thoughts and our feelings.

Let's take another word. Night. Reading that word, is your night a sky full of stars? Twinkling. Sparkly. Light. Exciting night.

Or dark? Full of fear. Black. Midnight. Scary night. Do you relish the night-time or are you fearful of it?

Another word. Clown. Now what can you see? What are you thinking? How do you feel? Are clowns funny? Do their face paint and coloured clothing fill you with joy or fear? When clowns chase each other with buckets of confetti pretending it's water before inevitably tripping, tipping the contents over an unsuspecting victim, is that hilarious? Does it make you smile? Or are you as nervous and wary of these colourful entertainers as I am? Actually, it's more than that, they terrify me. My head fills with words, with questions. Who is under the make-up? Why the huge red smiley mouth? Who does that? Clowns. I know what I'd like to do if one ran at me with a bucket. I'd turn the hose on them and spray them from head to toe with freezing cold water! Yes, I would! That would teach them.

Pizza. Night. Clowns. Three words. Words make us think thoughts and feel feelings. When your eyes first fell on this book, you may have noticed the word sharks running down the spine. Sharks. Now that's a word guaranteed to conjure emotion. How does the word make you feel? Do you like sharks? Do they scare you? Have you seen one swimming in depressing circles in a dreaded aquarium or in a documentary or film? I have, many times. Then there's the music. Music accompanies the shark, always, without exception, intense, powerful music. The relentless rhythm serves to embellish atmosphere, an unstoppable pulse beating beneath the melody reminiscent of an imminent attack by the shark itself. There was a time when I'd never seen a shark with my own eyes, in the flesh, always through someone else's fearful, fault-finding eyes. Let's investigate the word a little deeper. Shark. It has a sharp, cutting, deadly ring to it. Look the word up in a dictionary and it suggests attack. Shark. Fish. A large fish that has sharp teeth and a pointed fin on its back. A great white shark. A man-eating shark. Look it up in a thesaurus. Shark: A person who preys on others.

A dishonest person, someone who persuades other people to pay inflated prices for an item or service. People needing a place to live can often find themselves at the mercy of local property sharks. Sharks. Even bad people are described as sharks! A group of sharks is called a herd, gam, school, frenzy, or shiver. Do those last two words sound pleasant? Frenzy suggests attack and shiver suggests scared. They must have been chosen by someone harbouring an intense dislike for this fish, maybe the same person who coined murder for crows.

I never used to fear sharks. No. Not back then. Nervous maybe but not scared. I remember my dad taking Greg and I to Connah's Quay swimming baths on Friday evenings. Younger brothers can be extremely annoying! I'm left with two memories from those nights, the first is Greg tugging at my leg under the water. My imagination told me it was a shark sinking its teeth into me. My heart would jump and skip a beat. It made me nervous, and he knew it. My incessant squealing made him laugh. Eating fish and chips on the way home in the back of Dad's precious green Morris Minor 1000 Traveller (complete with its ash wood frame) is the other memory. Steamy windows and chippy smells, the happy memory from those innocent days oh so long ago. A time before sharks consumed my mind. Back then, my head was full of playtimes, friends, homework, riding my bike, playing football, and building dens with Greg amongst the poplar trees at the bottom of our long garden in Chester. Oh, and our fish finger, pea and mashed potato teas, the reward for running the full length of Hoole Lane to get home from school. I could never get home quick enough. My haste was not prompted by the desire to attack my homework, far from it, I ran home to watch television and to tuck into my tea from a tray on my lap! Depending on the day it was either an episode of *Skippy the Bush Kangaroo*; *Daktari* with Clarence the cross-eyed lion; *Belle and Sebastian* – the adventures of a boy and his Pyrenean mountain dog; *Marine Boy* – A cartoon about a boy who chewed oxygum enabling him to breathe underwater or my favourite, *Flipper* – the dolphin that swam faster than lightning. There's a pattern here which I've only just realised!

I loved music too, still do. Show me a child that doesn't. There was only one band in the world for me back then. In the May of 1963, Lenny the Lion, a furry papier mâché puppet with a golf ball for a nose, appeared in an episode of a music programme, *Pops with Lenny* and introduced thousands of children to the Beatles. Wow. I loved them. The Fab Four. They were indeed fabulous. Fabulous and gorgeous. All of them! Hearing them singing 'From Me To You' that day and I was hooked.

So that was me. Happy most of the time, content, without a care in the world. I loved the sea and holidays beside it. I remember diving through waves and swimming without armbands for the first time. This changed. By the time I waved goodbye to my teenage years, I feared the sea and the sharks that roamed there. The fear bit me without warning and I remember the moment they sank their teeth into me and sent shivers down my spine.

What changes can change again.

Jane.

ANYTIME, ANYWHERE

The fin cut through the surface revealing little about the size of the shark below. It was cruising leisurely, turning this way and that, fully in control, steady. Its stout grey body and pointed snout enabled this magnificent specimen to move with ease. Slight adjustments to pectoral, dorsal and tail fins took him down into the depths one minute then back up to the surface moments later. This master of the seas was on a mission.

Marco and Sonja had been in the bay since two, on the beach and in the water. Marco was holding his daughter with outstretched arms playfully threatening her with a dunking. Her young toes brushed the watery surface before being relentlessly whisked up into the air. She'd squeal with delight, pulling her feet up in the vain attempt of keeping them out, too young to realise that being immersed was a predictable inevitability. She would be plunged, waist deep into the cooling sea every time. In truth they both loved this pastime. He loved her. Her auburn curls, her smile, the way she called him 'Papa.' Everything. Most of all, he loved being her father. The past three years had been the best of his life. He kissed her tanned forehead, spun her round then dropped her again with a resounding splash!

The shark was moving effortlessly, slipping through the water in silence. This male was four metres (4m) in length, a solitary hunter who had spent the day patrolling down in the depths, just off the coast, meandering curiously. He hadn't eaten since last night and was ready to feast. The fading sunlight danced on the water. His hunger would soon have to be satisfied.

Marco held Sonja up out of the water, her tiny frame momentarily blocking out the tired sun. These Saturday beach afternoons had become a regular occurrence since Estefania had to work. Nia, as Marco affectionately called her, was the other love of his life. They'd met when Marco, originally from Madrid, was on a backpacking gap year in Columbia, her homeland. He'd spent five days trekking through dense jungles along the Inca Trail to reach 'The Lost City' or 'Ciudad Perdida' as it's known locally. Having completed the trek, his group found themselves drinking beer in a bar in Santa Marta where Nia worked as a server. He'd been mesmerised by her from the second he saw her. He couldn't help but stare; she was beautiful. Her long brown hair flowed behind her as she moved quickly between the tables. When she stood next to him and placed his beer down, their eyes met, and he knew. Luckily for him, she knew too and within a three-week whirlwind romance they left Columbia together to set up home here by the sea. It had been tough for both leaving the closeness of their families, but they were a family now and this was their home.

Never once had Marco resented this father-daughter time, in fact, he looked forward to it. The disappointment when Nia's boss at the sea front café rang to tell her things were quiet so she needn't come in was palpable. The sea was calmer now. These late summer afternoons had become the perfect time to teach Sonja to swim. Who needs a pool when you live near the ocean?

Sonja was wearing her new swim vest, its snug fit and floats helped to keep her head out of the water when she was lying on her tummy. With his hand cradling her belly, Marco gently moved her backwards and forwards through the water. She gleefully kicked her legs and splashed her arms. When these beach days had started a year ago, she couldn't swim a stroke. Now she was moving with more control and purpose. She used her hands and feet to 'swim to Papa.' The inflatable ball they'd been playing with earlier on the beach bobbed gently in the shallows. Marco palmed it into the air where it danced on the breeze before landing slightly ahead of her flailing arms. This ball had coaxed her and was undoubtedly the main reason she attempted to propel herself along. Another being Marco's perseverance and encouraging words – 'get the ball, bring it to Papa.' Both parents believed it to be the best present they'd ever bought for her. Sonja doggy paddled in the direction of the elusive ball, the breeze thwarting her efforts, keeping it at bay. No matter how hard she tried, the ball remained just beyond her reaching fingertips. Determined, she persisted until Marco discretely lifted it back into the air, flicking it over her head. Being a water baby was something both he and Nia strived for. Sonja had to be able to swim living so close to the ocean.

The shark entered the bay at 17:27 on that beautiful summer afternoon. He could sense something. Smell it. There was something he wanted. Within seconds he had located it. Prey was present. All living things emit an electrical pulse and he had locked onto one. Yes, this was what he wanted. The hunter was hunting. The hunted knew nothing. The shark moved with more urgency. With a flick of the tail, he made a sudden sharp turn following vibrations in the water. He was closing in.

Marco let Sonja retrieve the ball enough times to keep her interested in the chase. He grabbed the ball and swam further out into the blue. The sun was making longer shadows now. The ripples danced with golden sparkles. Marco sighed. Life was good. The strengthening breeze gave him a chill. He knew it was one more swim then home. He watched as she swam towards him. Beaming, calling 'Papa, Papa.' He would often find himself staring at her and feeling overwhelmed with emotion.

'Come on sweetie, swim to Papa.' She was close, swimming faster. Marco turned and gave three big kicks further out and away from her. This swim would be her longest yet, my word he would have a tale to tell Nia tonight! One more kick for luck.

The shark was speeding up. Faster. Moving with ghost-like silence. Determined. Closing in. Streamlined. The torpedo-like torso propelled him efficiently through the water. This invisible predator would strike from below any second now. Who knows at what point a victim of a shark attack understands their fate? This particular juvenile had no idea. A splash ahead. A flicker at the surface. Seconds later, impact. The strike. Jaws jut forward revealing rows of razor-sharp teeth. The kill. There is no thrashing. No suffering. Job done. Fed. Satisfied.

Marco turned. Panic set in. 'Sonja!' He lunged for her. Quick. He must help her. He grabbed at her, his nervous fingers pulling at her vest. She had rolled almost all the way over this time. He scrabbled and managed to lift her just as her face submerged.

'Sonja, Sonja! Papa's here!' First came the spluttering and coughing then the rapid blinking of saltwater tears. Marco held her close to his chest and soothed her. He felt guilty for taking his eyes off her and was already determined to take more care next week. He strained every emotional muscle in his body not to shoot out of the water with her. He knew he needed to calm her so she would remember their afternoon in the sea positively. Retreating to the beach they changed, packed up their belongings and started on the short walk along the beach back to the car park.

'Look darling the sun is going to be gone soon, wave bye-bye, we'll see it tomorrow.'

One fish would not see the morning sun. The fish the shark had singled out. The prey the shark had hunted. The fish that had satisfied the shark's hunger. The fish had no warning. He suffered a deadly attack from a silent assassin. The shark exited the bay at 18:03 as father and daughter reached the car. The short journey home would take ten minutes. They never even knew the shark was there. The shark never came for them. Never hunted them. Never would.

'That's enough for tonight lad, now get some shut-eye, we're off tomorra. Get ya eyes shut and get to sleep.'

The boy's father closed the book. He carved his way through the usual bedroom floor clutter to the door, a perilous journey only the brave dared to tread. Flicking the switch, he stepped out. Light from the landing streamed across the room then, seconds later, the room was plunged into darkness as the door clicked shut, only to open again immediately.

'Happy birthday lad. Now, I mean it, we've got one heck of a ways to go in't morning. Sleep well Sharkbite!'

The boy breathed quickly. He wrestled with the urge to move, lying there long enough for his father to reach the bottom of the stairs. After the telltale creak from that last well-trodden step, he could wait no longer. He slid out from under the duvet, crept on silent tiptoes to the door, cautiously opening it a crack before diving back into the safety of his bed. The sliver of yellow was just enough for him to make out familiar shapes and treasured objects in his room, but he still pulled the duvet up over his head. Nervous fingers scrabbled under the pillow to find the torch that lived there and the comic he'd snaffled away earlier. Spiderman was going to save him tonight, watch over him, be there to protect him from those dreams that flooded in to haunt his sleep. He was sure they would seep in later. He always hoped that the last thing he thought about would float in his dreams. It worked some of the time. Some parents tuck their children into bed and tell stories that soothe their little ones enabling them to calmly drift into an imaginary land of sleep-inducing make-believe. Oh, how the boy longed for his dad to be one of those and tell him stories like he used to. Maybe it was a boy thing, but his father's night-time tales were few and far between and chosen to provoke or tease. The look on the boy's face was of someone struggling to fight back the tears. Palms sweating, white faced, Charlie started to read.

CHARLIE PARKER

I launch myself off the top step. My bare feet land in soft sand. The door smashes into the handle-shaped groove in the side of our caravan and slams shut behind me. I'm the first one out. I can hear Mam yelling for me; she hates us banging the door. It's early – eight o'clock. I can feel the sun on my face and the sand is warm. I'm *never* up this early at home. At home I sleep till midday or later unless it's a school day and I have to get up. Today is different. Today is the first day. The first day of my holiday. The holiday I've been looking forward to since the beginning of the summer term: the seaside.

I'll stand here a bit and wriggle my toes in the sand. I love not wearing shoes. I love the sand under my feet. Mam says I've not liked wearing shoes since I was a baby, or socks for that matter. It didn't matter where I was or what we were doing I would rip my shoes and socks off! She says I chucked so many out the pram they could have filled a shop! If I didn't have to, I'd never wear shoes. Socks are even worse. I hate the feeling of trapped toes. I feel like I can't breathe in socks, it's like touching cotton wool – yuk! The first thing I do after riding my bike home from school and slamming the front door is kick off both shoes. They lie in the hall, wherever they happen to fall, until I am forced to put them on again the next morning when I trudge back out to school. I'm always barefooted at home and my feet are normally dirty. I don't care and luckily me mam and dad don't either. All weekend, whether I'm in my bedroom or in the back garden chucking a ball for Pepper, my feet are shoe and sock free!

We arrived at the caravan site yesterday, just before the sun set. It's called 'Sea View' and our pitch is on the top of the hill with the best views, 'spectacular' me mam calls it. I stare at the horizon. The water in the distance looks dark and dingy and I can feel goosebumps run up my arms and down the back of my neck. The tiny, almost invisible hairs on my arms stand up on end. It makes me shiver. From where I'm standing, I can see the sea lapping onto the shore below. I listen hard but can't hear the waves. I've stood here when it's been crashing in. The only sounds breaking my peace are the screeches from the scavenging gulls soaring in the sky above me. Harsh screeches. Dad says they're 'intelligent, resourceful and inquisitive creatures.' I don't agree. I don't like them at all, not since they dive-bombed me and my ice cream at the impressionable age of five. Seven years ago that was, but I still hate them with a passion. Thieving, greedy, attackers-of-children is what I call them. This is not the only thing me and Dad don't agree on!

My eyes drift down along the beach. It's empty. It's never busy here. The only people who use our beach are the people who stay at the site and a few locals. Today it's deserted. Totally deserted. I think about that word for a minute. Deserted. Empty. No one. Just the sand and the dunes. Deserted. Like a desert. Makes me smile. Our beach is a deserted desert. We have our very own desert on the east coast of England. The only difference between our desert and the deserts of Africa is that most days ours are windswept, freezing and lashed with rain. I imagine camels instead of donkeys trotting along our beach. Shame, we don't have either. I remember a morning two years ago, there was an old bloke trudging along in a howling gale. Only he knows why! He wasn't even walking a dog! Dad reckoned it was perfect kite flying weather. Wrong! I couldn't get it off the ground but me dad did. It went straight up, wobbled about for thirty seconds before crashing back to earth like a rocket, point first, at a million miles an hour and took the geezer out. Weird how things like that happen. He couldn't have hit him if he'd tried. The bloke lay there for a bit and then me dad had to take him to A&E. He needed five stitches. Dad drove him home and got him some fish and chips to make it up to him. He was well chuffed with that. Not seen him since, probably terrified we might bump into him again!

I'm Charlie by the way. I'm twelve. It was my birthday yesterday. I'm not your average twelve-year-old, whatever that is! Some people call me quirky. I overheard our neighbour, Mrs Bean, say this once and it worried me enough to ask the folks what it meant. Dad said something like, 'Worry not Charlie lad, we love ya, we love who ya are, we think you're cute lad, there ain't nothing wrong with being different son! Ya are who ya are and ya are a bit of a social misfit but an all-round good egg.' Mam smiled, hugged me, and said, 'The plate with the chip in it has the more interesting story!' I didn't understand what on earth they were on about but strangely I thought that being quirky was a good thing and anyway, at least I'm not named after a small green vegetable! Yuk! Beans! The only ones I like are Henry J Heinz's orange baked beans that come out of a tin. One of his fifty-seven varieties. I used to wonder why he put a fifty-seven on the tin and found out it was Henry's lucky number. I don't have a lucky number. Hats are my lucky thing and I have an impressive collection that I insist on wearing whenever I step outside our front door. Even on a school day. Little do the outside world know but I wear them inside too as soon as I crawl out of bed. My hair is longer than other boys my age which seems to stress a lot of my older relatives. Yeah, I'm Charlie, a quirky kid!

Otherwise, I'm fairly ordinary as boys go. I'm vegetarian. We all are. I play the guitar. I love crackers and cheese and looking up at the stars. I ride my bike. I collect things – small things. Bugs, butterflies, and buttercups. Leaves, shells, and stones. Over the years my pockets have been home to lots of treasures. When I was younger worms and centipedes would wriggle in my pocket's murky depths staying hidden until I went to bed. Then they'd wriggle in the pocket on my bedroom floor until they were rescued by me mam. She'd do her nut and shout, 'Charlie not again!' Mam says I'm *painfully* shy. I don't think I am, I'm just fussy who I talk to! I like school but prefer my bedroom. I love animals. Dogs, cats, and goats. Mam goes to goat yoga; I went with her once. Goats everywhere. Goats are great! I love jungle animals, creepy crawlies, toads and frogs, fish… well not all fish but more of that later.

Mam and Dad love animals. Even before I can remember, the stories that filled my head at night-time were of giraffes, elephants, lions, and tigers. My eyes closed, my head would drop and sink into my pillow, and I'd drift off peacefully. Mam and Dad hoped the stories they shared would fill my days and dreams with a love of all things nature. It worked. Before I could walk, even before I grew to love her, my Auntie Elle had painted a collage on one of the walls in my playroom. A hippo, frog, tiger, lion, zebra, rabbit, and a ladybird made their home there hiding in huge green leaves. I loved spending time in my jungle.

I love words. I juggle them in my head. I love the sound some words make. My favourite ones are onomatopoeic words. It took me ages to learn how to say that. Words that sound like what they're describing, like crack, howl and snap, said with a loud 'p.' The longest onomatopoeic word is in some book called *Ulysses* by James Joyce – 'tattarrattat.' I love that word. Not reading the book though. Mam studied it at school and told me it's about 'the

Blooms' and it's blooming boring! I've loved words even before I knew what they were. I started speaking in sentences soon after my first birthday, earlier than most children learn to talk! Mam and Dad put it down to all the stories they told me at bedtime. Yeah, it couldn't be that I'm a genius could it, no! Had to be down to them. I guess most parents read to their kids so I must be more intelligent than most! That's what I tell my little brothers anyway. Mam and Dad went to town on the sounds, the quack, the moo, the cluck, and the roar. I guess most parents do that too, but I remember loving it. I still do. I love reading, writing, quizzes, crosswords, word facts and games. Words intrigue me.

The sun is warm today and a welcome change. It rains here a lot but not as much as at home. Today the sky is blue. No cumulus clouds in sight. They're my favourite sort of cloud. Fluffy, white, cauliflower-shaped clouds that change into faces or impersonate animals. It's quieter here than at home too. I like that. I like peace and quiet more than most kids. Dad says I'm an old soul. Sort of thing I would expect from him.

Our house is on the A57 next to a new roundabout on the outskirts of Sheffield. It used to be fields of green and colourful blossom, not tarmac and roads. Our air is full of pollution not pollen, just grey exhaust fumes! The roundabout is rammed most of the time. It's great to get away from the screeching brakes, police sirens, and the irritating horn honking! Mam calls it a 'complete nuisance' and Dad says it's a 'pain in the neck'. Well, he doesn't actually say the word 'neck', the word he uses begins with an 'a', but our mam says we're not allowed to repeat it! I don't break this rule. Our roundabout only goes quiet at the end of the day when the last car leaves the city and drives off down the road. Traffic noise fades away and peace reigns until the first car arrives at the roundabout the next morning when it all starts again. Our roundabout is lovely and big, there are five roads that go from it and two are dual carriageways. It has a steep grassy bank all round which is covered in daffodils in the spring and there are twenty-five trees on there. The tallest is a silver birch which the council planted smack in the middle. Also, there are loads of bushes on there that get flattened two or three times a month by joyriders in stolen cars trying to escape from the plod. Dad gets cross every time he hears a joyrider racing down our road. He shouts at them from inside our lounge, 'Got more intelligent socks than you idiots.' Brave man me dad. After one chase a police car ended up on the roundabout and took out a tree. I didn't understand why my folks found it so hilarious until I discovered it was a copper beech! The coppers were okay, the copper beech didn't fare so well! Mam says that daffodils can take a real bashing and still come back, 'resilient little things' she calls them. No matter how squashed they are they always bounce back. She says that's the reason she sometimes calls me 'flower'! Our roundabout would be a great place to play and climb but me and my brothers are banned from going there and that's another rule we *all* obey. We're not stupid!

Mam and Dad have been coming here to escape the noise and hustle and bustle for years, even before I was born. They get all silly and start giggling like kids when they talk about the good old days. I don't know what went on but it's something secret they won't tell. I told me dad I thought he'd proposed here but he told me not to believe it, me mam had asked him! I'm none the wiser. Probably never know. Maybe he did ask her, and she turned him down!

I think they'd have chosen to live up here if it weren't for their jobs. They met at university in Middlesbrough. Weird they ended up there. Dad is Sheffield born and bred. Mam is from Chester. She studied economics and her first job was in one of the universities in Sheffield. Not sure what she did but it had something to do with timetables. Dad told me that when people asked her if she enjoyed her job, she would take a large breath and accompany the out breath by shrugging her shoulders saying, 'It's a nightmare but a job's a job!' She never talked like she liked it. Then one day, before

I was born, he told me she came home early and never went back. She's always been my stay-at-home mam. I loved that. I love her. Dad does something with computers. No idea what but it involves logistics. That's a cool word, I had to look it up. Dad's the person that gets lorry loads of potatoes delivered from the wholesaler to the supermarket. Not sure which one, maybe Morrisons. Mam started working part-time at Tesco. She is on that desk when you first walk in. First line of defence she calls it. Dad says she's not paid enough to take the abuse. She seems happy. Dad used to travel down the M1 from Sheffield to Derby every day and he was beyond thrilled when they told him he could work from home. He's a sarcastic one me dad, thinks he's funny.

I've been coming here since before I can remember, before my first birthday and every year since. Almost every holiday. We've even squeezed in the odd weekend. We come here whatever the weather. We've had rain, wind, and sun. In every strength and combination. But no snow. Well, no snow yet! The torrential rain we had here last February felt worse than any snow I've ever been in. It was blinding. It doesn't make much difference to me, it can rain, or the sun can shine, it's my favourite place. But over time, things are changing. It's changed and still is. Thinking of this makes me sad. I sigh.

I look along the beach. It curves round the bay in the distance in the shape of the letter C. Our bay. My bay. The sand follows the grassy headland out to sea and at the end where the land meets the sea there's no sand just boulders. The beach is long and wide, even when the tide comes in it's still wide and the sand is soft and yellow. Smooth sand is great for my feet. The sort of sand you can run on without stubbing your toes on something sharp. There are pebbles, shells, driftwood, and the dreaded litter. There's always litter. I hate it. Why do people leave litter? I don't get it! Paper, beer cans and bottles and the dreaded plastic. People take stuff to the beach for a day out and then leave rubbish behind when they go home. It spoils it for everyone else! And it's not us kids either but we get the bad press! I've seen loads of grown-ups chucking stuff out of car windows outside our house. They get to our roundabout, open the window and out it goes. They don't even care that someone can see them from a garden or the car behind. Cigarette butts are the worst, they drive me mam bonkers. Butts have got plastic in them called *cellulose acetate.* It takes ages for that stuff to decompose, decades. The butts will probably last longer than the people smoking them especially if they end up in our front garden! Nobody weeds that! Mam won't touch the front or back garden. She says there's no point and anyway she's going for the wildflower meadow look! We get crisp packets, chocolate wrappers, McDonald's bags, Starbucks cups and lids blowing around in there too. Once, Mam found a flip-flop on the rockery and it was the final straw. She made us go out round the streets litter picking and she yelled at anyone who dropped anything, even a baby got an ear bashing for dropping his dummy. Dad gets mad about the amount of chewing gum on the pavements. If one of us stands on some and he finds it stuck on the mats of his red Ford C-Max car we have to steer well clear!

I used to think the litter on our beach was dropped by accident by people leaving in a hurry, probably when it starts raining. But there are strange people, weird folk I can't get my head round, who drop things on purpose. They just don't care. The rubbish they leave behind on our beach lies there or blows around until it is grabbed by the sea. I think there is something poetic about the sea carrying our litter for a while, giving it a good wash, and then dumping it back for someone to find. Poetic, I love that word. I find it moving that the sea cleans our rubbish. Shame the fish have to suffer it. Even people who go fishing leave rubbish. I've found loads of nets and lines on the beach. They should know better! The ocean is *not* a bin! Plastic rubbish is the scourge of the seas. I think there should be more people like me, who don't drop litter in the first place and who can be bothered to pick other people's rubbish up and chuck it away properly. It's not rocket science. I have a brown leather satchel that goes everywhere with me. Everything I need is inside it, notebooks, pens, sweets, mementos I pick up along the way and a string bag for litter. Yep, I pick up litter wherever I go, just can't stand it.

My hands dig deep into the pockets of my favourite blue shorts as I scrunch my toes. I love the feeling of the sand between my toes. I'm going to take my time this morning. I take a deep breath. Then slowly breathe out. I do this a few times. My fingers touch something in the secret pocket inside my pocket. Mam forgets to check this pocket so things can stay in there for a while. It's the pebble I found last week. Pebbles have to have something special about them for me to pick them up. This one is super smooth, an unusual oval shape and has a circular hole at the narrow end. It makes me remember. I unzip my secret pocket, take it out and pop it in my satchel. Who knows, I might need the pocket for something else this week.

Funny how an object can take you back to the moment you found it. I picked this pebble up on a walk or I should say route march over the moors. In case you didn't know, it always rains in Yorkshire, and on that afternoon the heavens opened. Dad went off like a whippet, hood pulled over his head and Pepper, our black and tan cocker spaniel, was running loyally at his side. The rest of us were left behind, struggling to keep up. I couldn't wait to get back to the car. Eric was last. He's always at the back, everyone's shadow. The rain was coming down in rods, felt like someone was whacking me in the face with a rose bush. It was impossible to open my eyes but running with your eyes closed has never been a good idea. It was inevitable one of us would fall over and yep, it was me! I landed face first in the mud. Great! I lay there and didn't know whether to laugh or cry. I hadn't hurt myself, well my pride maybe. I sat there and wiped my eyes. I don't recommend wiping your eyes with fingers covered in mud either! I couldn't see and blinked out grit-filled tears. Mam knelt next to me and used the cuff of her wet jumper to wipe away the layer of stinky mud from my eyes and as I picked myself up my hand found my pebble. The moment needed a souvenir, so I picked it up and popped it in my pocket where it's been hiding ever since. We were drenched. Halfway home me dad stopped the car and treated us to pasty and chips which we ate like we'd never seen food. There's something to be said about how great food tastes when you're cold, wet through and huddled together in a steamed-up car going home from the moors. Yep, that was the best idea me dad had that day!

I live in these shorts. I couldn't care less what I look like in them. I wear clothes that are functional. Clothes I can throw on. At home, on holiday, in any season, you'll always find me in shorts and a T-shirt. Any T-shirt. Plain or with a motif on it. I don't care. The T-shirt I'm modelling today is red with a polar bear sitting on the front wearing a pair of sunglasses and underneath it says solar bear. Hilarious!

There's a bit of a breeze. Sand blows in my eyes and through my fringe. Grandpa says it's too long for boys my age and it's about time I got it cut but at least I've got hair! I have to take my cap off and shake away sand, and I run my hand through my hair, moving the fringe out of my eyes. Cap back on and the fringe blows straight back. Same routine, cap off, hair moved, cap on. I do this a lot. Preferable to getting it cut, that's never gonna happen. I wriggle my toes again and scrunch them. I hear shouting from the caravan, and it makes me run. They're on their way. I race over the grass towards the path to go down the hill. I know where I'm going. I've been there many times before, ever since I started tottering on tiny feet. I'm not tottering now. Now I'm sprinting as fast as my legs will carry me, well as fast as the thick sand on the path will let them. I'm going to get down first. Harry and Eric will be rushing to catch me. Racing, I race my brothers all the time. They'll scope the path at the top looking for me, scanning to find me as I zigzag down. It won't take Harry long to spot me. There it goes, the door bangs open and shuts again. I can hear him.

'Charlie, Charlie, wait for me!'

I stop and look back up the hill. I'm halfway down and yep, they're on their way. I'm not going to wait for them. No way. I turn on my heels and run faster, the slope of the hill helps. Their little legs won't catch me. I'm competitive, I admit it, but I am the eldest, older than Harry by four years and nearly ten years older than Eric. I'll beat them both. I know I will. I have to. I've got a great head start. Harry probably couldn't care less who won. He's more chilled than me and Eric's little legs are never going to be quick enough. I'm still going to run though. Near the bottom my feet sink by the heel into the thicker sand, and it slows me down a bit but not enough for them to catch me. Winning feels good. When they get to the bottom, they won't follow me anyway. They'll go onto the beach. I used to go there but not anymore. No, I go the other way over the stones onto the rocks. This makes me feel sad. Things haven't always been like that. Five years ago, when it was just Harry and me, we'd bomb down to the beach. We'd run as fast as we could for as far as we could, me shouting 'Hurry up Harry, come on, hurry up!' I'd shout it again and again and he would run until he couldn't take another step. When we went walking with Dad, he started shouting it too. Both of us must have shouted it hundreds of times and it stuck. Dad has called him, 'Hurry up Harry' ever since. His little legs took two or three steps to each one of mine, so I suppose it's not surprising he was tired. He'd bend over puffing, hands on knees to steady himself. We would then scour the beach looking for something special while we got our breath back. Over the years I've found and collected the usual things you'd expect to find on a beach, bits of wood, shells, rocks, and pebbles. The shelves in my bedroom are weighed down with them. Each object reminds me of a different day and why I picked it up and popped it in my pocket. Our best find was a chain made of gold. Real gold. It caused much excitement and squealing. It was a broken bracelet but to us it was pirate treasure! I remember Mam and Dad spent the rest of the day with their heads buried in their books while us two intrepid explorers spent the afternoon hunting for more. That was the day a metal detector went to the top of my Christmas list!

Dad has pet names for all of us. He calls me mam tangerine, tan for short. At first, I thought he was being sarcastic because her skin is really pale and then I thought it was about her ginger hair and freckles. I only found out a few years ago that the name started after they had visited the orangutan sanctuary in Sabah, Borneo, in their gap year. Mam fell in love with them and me dad too, I mean that was when she knew she loved me dad. They've been together ever since.

Harry and I used to be inseparable. At home or on holiday, we'd spend every waking hour together, playing, laughing, arguing, doing all the things that big and little brothers do. At the seaside we'd be on the beach waiting for Mam and Dad to come out of the caravan and come down. They've always taken ages to pack the bags trying to make sure they put in everything we need for a day on the beach. It takes them ages to walk down with it all too. Fingers crossed they packed well because when they forget stuff, I get the short straw and have to go back and get it. It's only when the folks set foot on the beach we're allowed in the sea. Putting even one toe in the water before that is a big no no. It was and will always be a serious family rule. A rule that can't be broken, unlike other rules like not eating sweets before tea, everyone breaks that! When Mam and Dad got to the beach Harry and I would race over to where they were setting up camp for the day, chuck our tops off, empty our pockets and boom, we were in the sea jumping the waves. We were in and out of the water all day. I got to be a strong swimmer. I'd swim with me dad and we'd dive through the waves. Who doesn't love doing that? That was then but that has changed. Things are different now. No more swimming for me.

I'm down. I've reached the bottom of the hill. Yessss. I'm the champion, championes, championes, ole, ole, ole. I sing these words over and over. Love them. I stand with my arms up impersonating the legend that is Usain Bolt. My brothers aren't even halfway down. 'Boom!!!' I shout it loud enough for them to hear. Yeah, I feel good. I watch them. Harry is standing with his hands on his hips waiting for Eric as usual. I can hear him shouting for him to get a move on and I can tell he's niggled. Well, he should get up earlier like me then shouldn't he! It's going to take them ages. Eric's got his football with him which will slow him down more. His ball is one of those cheap plastic ones that flies everywhere except where you aim it. More junk that will eventually end up in a landfill pit somewhere until the end of time! Call me cynical! Kicking, throwing, and stopping to pick up his ball takes forever. Harry waits until Eric gets to him then he takes off to wait at the next bend. He has to stop and start all the way down. That's why I'm up and out before them. Can't be bothered with that. Harry wipes the back of his hand across his forehead. It's hot work minding our 'Shadow'. Harry's cheeks are rosy red already and the day hasn't even started. He always catches the sun and burns no matter how much factor fifty Mam puts on him. Eric picks his ball up, drops it and kicks it back up the hill! Harry is doing his nut! Eric will take all day at this rate. He loves that ball. Mam and Dad have drilled us both to look out for Eric. Another rule we mustn't break. Eric's annoying most of the time, poking his nose in where he's not wanted then bursting into tears when we won't let him join in with our games or play with our toys. But we love him. I stare at them a bit then look up. From where I'm standing, I can see a campervan in the pitch next to ours which I've never seen here before but I do know an old VW camper when I see one. Adam, my best mate's dad has got one but his is green and this one's dark blue. The site isn't big, I cycled it with Harry and counted the pitches and there are only thirty-two. Ours is before the end, next to the biggest caravan that belongs to Nicki and Steve. Mam says we get the same pitch every time for being their best customers. The sun is shining on our back window. Our table is under that window. The heart of the place, me mam calls it. The place we sit for meals, play board games, cards and where she likes to sit, red wine in hand, watching the sunset. The 'triple-decker bunk bed' runs down one side and the toilet cubicle with miniscule sink is at the bottom of the bed wedged into a space that's too small for them to fit comfortably. It's a squeeze in there for me so don't know how Mam and Dad cope! The kitchen is on the other side with the sink and cooker squeezed between two small worktops, where all the meals are prepared, and copious cups of tea are made. I love saying that 'copious cups, copious cups'. It's something Grandma says a lot. She drives over to our house a couple of times a month from Kingsley in Cheshire. The minute she walks in the door she shouts, 'Get that kettle on I'm going to need copious cups of tea to get over that journey on the Snake Pass, it's a veritable nightmare!' Built by Thomas Telford in 1821, the Snake Pass is twenty-five miles of road that joins Manchester and Sheffield. She hates it, torture she calls it. Me dad tells her she'd be better off slugging brandy! Everything else we need, like plates, bowls, pots, pans, knives, spoons, and forks are stashed in the cupboards and drawers that run the length of the kitchen, up near the ceiling and under the surfaces. Every nook and cranny is used. Caravans are great, it all goes in somewhere. Clothes and toys are crammed under the beds. The kitchen ends at the door about halfway along. A sofa doubles up as a double bed and takes up the rest of the space under the windows down both sides and along the far end. There are a couple of small tables in the corners and that's it, our caravan. Dad made the curtains. Mam made the cushions and throws. They go on about it being their labour of love then they giggle a lot. I think they knew when they bought the caravan that we would use it a lot, so it had to be right. They've told me ever since I was a nipper that we couldn't afford holidays abroad, so the caravan was going to be it. Now there are five of us we definitely can't and anyway we're not leaving Pepper behind. Truth is me dad hates flying so none of us are going on a plane anytime soon! Our caravan is warm and toasty when nights are cold or storms hit, which is most days up here! Shoes have to come off at the door, suits me. It's drummed into us boys to keep our caravan clean and tidy. It's our home from home and we do love it. Nicki and Steve's caravan is bigger than ours and arranged in a different way, but it still feels cosy, all caravans do. They have been coming here for the first two weeks of the summer holidays for as long as I can remember. Nicki is an infant teacher so has no option but to come when school breaks up. Bet she loves being next to us three boys! When they first got their caravan, they must have rattled around in it. Now they've got two children, four-year-old Molly and Toby who's three. Mam and Dad are friends with Nicki and Steve. The four of them sit outside after tea, drinking and chatting, 'putting the world to rights' they call it. They talk about everything and nothing while us five play until late. It normally ends up with me dad and Steve drinking whisky and talking about fishing and Nicki and Mam moaning about them! They are always laughing though. I love the days and evenings here; they seem longer than at home and we all talk more.

Ah, there she is. Mam's out, weighed down with bags. I can tell they're heavy, she's taking her time coming down the steps and yep, she has to put them straight onto the floor. There's me dad too, he's stepping down with exaggerated knee bends, trying to avoid tripping over Pepper who's all over the place. She's off, nose to the floor, sniffing in the dunes in the beach-grass. The beach is Pepper's idea of paradise. The smells must be fantastic. Dad's carrying bags too and wearing his red and grey rucksack. His rucksack-backpack is what he calls it. Try saying that quickly. Rucksack-backpack. Rucksack-backpack. None of us are brave enough to ferret around in there. He keeps his stash of digestives, ready salted crisps, a can of his favourite Stones bitter and a multipack of Tunnocks.

Tunnocks made by Thomas Tunnock, what a cracking name, and his biscuits aren't bad either.

I only ate breakfast half an hour ago but seeing those bags makes me feel hungry. When I woke up this morning Mam and Dad were already in the kitchen making the picnic. They spent last week shopping till they dropped, and the food is stashed in every space: the fridge, freezer and cupboards are well and truly stocked, you couldn't fit anything else in if you tried. The caravan has to be full of food because we eat a picnic on the beach every lunch (unless it rains) and a meal in the caravan every night. The only time we don't do that is when we drive along the coast to the fish and chip shop in the village for 'Fishy Fry-day'. At home or on holiday, 'Fishy Fry-day' happens every Friday. We call it that even though none of us eat fish. Mam says her favourite 'Fishy Fry-days' are when she has them with 'Fizzy Fridays' – half-price Prosecco from The Horseshoe, our local pub back home. Mam says we shouldn't do it every Friday, we should keep it for special occasions, after 'Cider Thursday' and before 'Stout Saturday'! She's hilarious me mam! Mam and Dad are creatures of habit. We always go to the chip shop in the village. We eat cheese pasties and chips covered in tons of salt and vinegar and wrapped in sheets of newspaper. When we're on holiday we like to sit on the same bench by the harbour surrounded by bobbing boats, screaming seagulls and baskets of fish. The smell of fish is everywhere, you can't escape it. It really is a 'Fishy Fry-day'. Our cheesy chip fingers are licked clean and washed down with cans of pop and cones of ice cream. Rain or shine that is our routine.

They're all on the way down. I'm not waiting for any of them. I'm getting off the beach and going to the pebbles. It's not easy walking on pebbles and stones with bare feet. My arms flap up and down like a seagull as I jerk across this painful floor. Every time I go to put my feet down, I know it's going to hurt. I grimace even before the pain hits. I'm looking for the smooth pebbles, but those sneaky knife-edged ones just love stabbing my feet. I have to take more time. I am moving like a thief, slow and steady, like Fagin from *Oliver Twist* by Charles Dickens. Thinking of this makes me remember the end-of-term party last weekend. Me dad – Dad dancing! He looked sick... not! I think I look like him right now. Grown-ups shouldn't floss! Actually, kids shouldn't floss either. Worst dance ever! Not far now. This is the worst bit. I have to cross the pavement of pebbles or the 'pebbles of doom' I call them, to get to the boulders and then to the rocks. The boulders are like a road going out to sea before turning and going along the coast. It might look like a road, but no car would ever drive on it. The surface is uneven with huge gaps between the stones. There, I've made it. My feet are grateful to be standing on a massive boulder big enough for four to stand on. The sea came in and went back out before breakfast but luckily for me, the sun was up before I was and has already dried the stones. Slippery boulders are dangerous and the boulders near the sea are wet which makes them look black. The ones around where I'm standing are all the shades of grey. The tides wash in and out with a force that will not stop. Nothing will ever stop it. It's a bit like the force in *Star Wars*. I like to think of the sea as the earth's force, surrounding us and invading the land, day and night. Last night, as we slept in our caravan, the water washed over the stones and back out to sea again. Mam told me the boulders were put there years ago to protect the shore from wearing away and to help secure the homes and the lives of the people who live here. I really appreciate the protective boulders. No matter how hard the waves try to eat away at our hill they'll be kept at bay. Mam reckons without the boulder barrier the hill would have worn away a long time ago and the caravan park would've crashed into the sea. I had a few bad dreams when I first heard that, something that's not unusual for me. Whenever we arrive here the first thing I do is check the boulders are still there protecting our hill. I always feel relieved to see them and am thankful for the kind people who put them there. I step from boulder to boulder, heading towards the sea. I walk carefully on steady feet until I reach the rocks. Most of the rocks are smooth but some have sharp edges. It's dangerous here; there are gaps, holes and cracks between the rocks and I don't want to fall on the slippery seaweed that's dotted about, I could disappear forever, never to be seen again! When the sea rushed in and out last night not all the water made it back and got trapped to make rock pools. I'm nearly where I want to be. Five more steps and I'll be there. The sea is about three or four metres ahead of me. I put my arms up above my head. Boom, I've made it. Buzzingggg! I sit down.

JANE JONES

Sipping coffee outside in morning sunshine with a view to the horizon is a thing to be celebrated. Breathing air infused with scents of the sea the icing on the cake. I would say it was my idea of perfection only bettered were the beverage champagne! Anyone living in England comes to expect inclement weather in every season so today has started well. My Jamaican Blue Mountain coffee is hitting the spot. Grown in the eastern region of Jamaica, the jewel in the Caribbean Sea, this silky smooth beverage transports me back to those tropical climes and an island bursting with sunshine. My current view overlooks the North Sea, considerably cooler and less romantic, but glorious, nonetheless. I love coffee. One mug is never enough. It's only after a second mug hits the spot that my blood starts pumping and I'm ready for the day. Oh, and it has to be real coffee, those instant granules in a jar are a poor imitation, might as well make gravy for the taste they provide, dishwater, revolting stuff! Coffee holds such an important part in my daily diet that I had a bean to cup machine installed in my recently purchased retirement present to myself, my pride and joy, my VW camper van or Dory, as I affectionately call her. I chose to name her after the famous palette surgeon fish from the film, *Finding Dory* not only because they are similar in colour. In the film, Dory becomes separated from her parents and before being reunited with them she has exciting adventures, discovers unfamiliar places, and befriends a host of underwater creatures. Like her, I too intend to explore, have adventures, and make memories that will last forever, unlike poor Dory who could hardly remember a thing! I celebrated my sixty-second birthday in December and bought the camper. I've bought myself a present on my birthday for as long as I can remember. Over the years I've treated myself to exotic holidays, a moped, a red Mazda MX-5, a set of golf clubs and oak flooring for my lounge, amongst other things! All luxurious gifts that I'd longed and saved up for ensuring my birthdays were never disappointing. Retiring was a key moment in my life, so I decided the same rule applied, hence Dory. The rush of youth shot through my veins the moment I turned the key in the ignition and drove her off the forecourt. I'd done it and could now embark on the journey into the next chapter of my life. I'm still young at heart and full of fun, who wants to spend time around a grumpy pensioner? My friends and family certainly don't and I'm intending on spending considerably more time with them once I return home.

I have never and will never be a morning person so imagine my frustration when sunlight streamed through my poor excuse for curtains to wake me at the unearthly hour of 04:55! Seagulls soaring and squabbling above my camper made sure I didn't fall back to sleep! I lay there, heart and mind racing, eyes open, eyes shut, desperately trying to adjust to the sunlight piercing my brain. I felt more tired this morning than I had before going to bed! Last night I'd wrongly predicted that the journey from home in Birmingham to Northumberland would have resulted in me sleeping soundly till noon! Only now does hindsight inform me that my decision to drive up here yesterday was a bad one! The journey can only be described as tortuous, seven hours of battling my way through traffic jam after traffic jam on all routes north! Lorries, caravans, accidents, roadworks and then to rub salt into the wound the last leg had to be on the dreaded A1! At 660 kilometres (km), (410 miles), it is home to what must be the longest traffic queue in the UK! Luckily for me I only needed to tackle a quarter of that, but the traffic was stationary for two hours! Two! It seemed as if everyone had chosen to evacuate Birmingham at precisely the same time, on the same day and head in precisely the same direction. Don't get me wrong, I love Birmingham, the much maligned second city but I was desperate to escape it for a while. Drivers know from bitter experience that Friday traffic is never good, but it had completely slipped my mind that the day I'd chosen to begin the rest of my life, was the same day schools closed their doors and padlocked their gates for the summer! I was one amongst thousands of families streaming out of towns and cities to head for the coast. What a wonderful feeling of relief to lift the tension as I turned into the first B road since leaving home. I could have cried. Arriving at my destination minutes later and I couldn't believe my luck as I was directed to my glorious pitch with its breathtaking view of the sea. It made the ordeal worthwhile.

Living up to its name, 'Sea View' awarded a wonderful first impression. A quick stroll round to explore the site and soothe stiff limbs served to whet my appetite, not stopping to eat on route I was famished. An hour later I'd devoured garlic prawns, a Lebanese fattoush salad, crusty bread smothered in salted butter, all washed down with a cold glass of Sancerre sitting outside under a fading sun. A beautiful end to a stressful day! I called Mum, something I do every day, to tell her of my journey. The little she contributed to the conversation spoke volumes for the pain she was unsuccessfully trying to hide. She doesn't like it when I go away, we live eighty-four miles apart and only see each other once a month but knowing I'm away, she misses me. She hated me flying overseas but as that's a thing of the past those worries of hers will ease. We were saying our goodbyes when a caravan pulled up and started reversing into the pitch next to mine. I was tired and in no mood to make pleasant conversation with strangers so ended the call and scarpered inside.

Arriving here had been the culmination of a dream that had been twinkling away in the recesses of my mind for years. I'd reached the difficult decision to retire earlier than anticipated after life dealt me some particularly unpleasant cards. Plucking up the courage to venture away on my own, it was to Northumberland, the northernmost county in England, I'd chosen to head to first, a place where I feel emotionally safe. Home to a famous wall and steeped in a maritime history, Northumberland benefits from sixty-four miles of stunning coastline with over thirty magnificent beaches. The county holds wonderful memories for me. Benji, a dear friend I'd met years ago in Fiji, lives in Newcastle upon Tyne and over the years we've spent many days there together. Returning home and I'd share photos on social media sites of castles, seafront markets and beaches. Friends were astounded by the beauty of the place, the place I affectionately refer to as England's greatest secret! Proud of my computer skills, I found and booked the caravan site online, not wanting to rely on Benji's kindness or outstay any welcome. Being independent also means I can control departure dates and times.

Today is the first day and it will start by the sea. I eventually rolled out of bed at 06:00 and for the past 40 minutes have been sitting in front of my van enjoying the view. It's so peaceful here. Clouds are scudding across a sky of endless blue. Having to suffer years of ear-piercing screeching as part of my job, I often find silence can be deafening, overwhelmingly so, but not today. I sip the last dregs of coffee and peel a grapefruit. My doctor suggested eating a grapefruit with breakfast every morning, the enzymes are supposed to help lower my blood pressure. The fruit has become an essential, potentially life-saving segment in my daily diet, and I've grown to like them! If I'm sounding like a creature of habit, I am!

I'm unsure whether my routines are a result of years of precision working or a character trait inherited from one or both parents. I just know what I like. You do when you reach my age! Sharp juices hit the mouth causing my taste buds to explode, the sour sensation forcing cheek and lip muscles to tense. I have no choice but to suck a sharp intake of breath through clenched teeth, an audible hiss the result. Red, white, and pink grapefruit varieties are imported into the UK from citrus-growing countries around the globe, notably the United States. Any variety can be bitter, acidic, or sweet and you never know what you're going to get until the juices ooze over your tongue. Having a sweet pink grapefruit last time does not guarantee you'll get the same next time. Sneaky little things, grapefruits, but I like them.

As I stare over the miles of empty sea my eyes are drawn to a single triangular sail appearing over the horizon, when my peace is shattered by loud voices erupting from the caravan next to me. My van is neatly sandwiched between two caravans, and one obviously houses children! Now don't get me wrong, I like children but does anyone who's not given birth to one really want to be so close to any, especially on a holiday? Be honest! The number of voices squealing away suggests there's more than one! Over the years I treated hundreds of youngsters. Parents attending for six monthly check-ups were encouraged to bring their little ones along, they could familiarise themselves with the surgery and to me of course. If they were lucky, they'd even get a ride in the chair! Introducing young children this way proved successful and often resulted in them becoming my easiest clients. After appointments, colleagues often rewarded children with a lollipop or sweet something which didn't sit well with me. I saw it as a sneaky way of getting them back into the chair for further treatment! My young patients left with a more perfect smile and an 'I'm a star patient', 'I love my dentist' or 'I've had a whale of a time' sticker stuck on their coat! Well-meaning parents would render their marginally anxious child a quivering wreck with the unnecessary and misguided, 'Don't worry she won't hurt you!' Reassuring words were the kiss of death, the seed firmly planted for the rot to set in! Excuse the pun. My intention had always been to heal, never to hurt. I gained a wonderful reputation for giving injections or removing teeth without children or adults feeling a thing and I'm proud of that. Yes, I like children but I'm off before this noisy cohort come out.

Fifteen minutes later and I'd tidied my bits and pieces away, prepared a packed lunch, thrown my essentials into a rucksack and beach bag, locked the van and set off to the beach with a newly found spring in my step. I'm smiling. I'm happy. Fresh air and sunshine are underrated cures for worries and woes and are certainly helping this retired dentist put her best foot forward this morning. The black-capped, red-billed Arctic terns give shrill warning calls from above. Similar in most respects to other seabirds it's their markings, size and call which make them easy to distinguish. Hearing their calls reminds me of a visit to the Farne Islands a few years ago. It was June. Remember the month. Don't ever forget it. June!

The Farne Islands are a small group of islands owned by the National Trust lying in the North Sea, 3.21km (2 miles) off the Northumberland coast between Seahouses to the south and Bamburgh to the north. Thousands of terns fly to the Farne Islands to nest every year. The nesting season begins in May and each bird produces in the region of three eggs, the chicks hatch twenty-two days later and become fledglings in June and July. Visiting the islands in June and you're guaranteed to see terns with chicks, but you're guaranteed far more than that!

Benji drove north along the coast; an hour later and we'd arrived in Seahouses, a fishing village shaped by the traditions of those who'd gone before. We parked in a huge car park, disproportionately large for a population of 1800 and it didn't take long for me to understand why! Tourists spilled onto roads from overcrowded pavements, hundreds of them, eating fish and chips, browsing in gift shops, and crammed onto benches sucking ice lollies. Seeing women queuing at a small building made my heart sink, this was the only public toilet in the village and the line snaked beyond the roundabout away down the hill, I would have to wait! Holidaymakers, day trippers and seasoned photographers were milling about in the streets with locals scurrying amongst the irritating throng in their pursuance of daily routines! We purchased boat tickets from the Billy Sheil's booth in the centre of Seahouses and wandered past women at the back of the toilet train hopping about in desperation regretting that last tea or lager! We headed down to the harbour through quaint side streets lined with picturesque cottages and their colourful pots of summer flowers, to buy an island ticket from an overly charming volunteer working in the National Trust trailer nestled by the harbour wall. Donning a flowery frock and hat combo fashionable fifty years ago, she reminded me of the middle-aged social climber, Margot Leadbetter, the intimidating character famously portrayed by Penelope Keith in, *The Good Life*, a television series from the 1970s. If you're too young to know who she was, then imagine your most patronising teacher and you'll get the idea. Handing me my ticket, she refused to let go and clung onto it as she irritatingly tried to sell me a cap. She was astounded when I refused, shaking her head she broke into fits of laughter and in her best condescending tone pronounced, 'On your head be it, don't say I didn't warn you!' I should have known then. I found out soon enough. We mingled amongst the tourists to board a boat and once all passengers were safely ensconced, headed out of the harbour and out to sea. The journey was made all the more exciting by puffin and seal spotting, there are thousands of them living in this region and they made for an exciting spectacle. Puffins launched themselves from cliffs to hunt herring in the water beneath our hull and grey seals bathed on rocks or dived for fish, every now and then popping up for a breather before disappearing back down. Disembarking at the jetty, we were immediately greeted by feisty terns protecting their eggs and chicks with firm pecks to our heads. The terns build their nests on the ground, on grass, stone, or sand and ideally under the protection of bushes. Due to the huge number of birds' nests you had to be careful where you put your feet! Stepping too close and they would warn you off. Dive-bombing terns! There was nothing you could do to avoid them! You had to walk past them. A cap! I needed a cap! A cap! Poppycock! Margot should have sold me a builder's hat! It was terrifying. I spent the two-hour excursion running the gauntlet of terns and hiding in the souvenir shop with the other chickens! My day was complete when a particularly large cormorant sought me out from the crowd and christened me from head to toe in excrement, pungent, white excrement, thick, pungent, white excrement which refuses to wash off no matter how many times you wash it! My red cagoule was splattered. Great! Hilariously funny for the hundreds lucky enough to witness the drama and thank God it wasn't them but not so for those sitting next to me on the boat ride back to the mainland! It wasn't the sea making them sick! I have since become the butt of many a poo joke, again, please excuse the pun!

Every year terns migrate from pole to pole, flying anywhere between one and two million miles in their lifetime. Impressive hey, especially when you think that astronauts would have to fly to the moon and back three times in their rockets or shuttles to do the same. Terns don't have to be awake when they're flying either, they can sleep and glide! Experiencing one of nature's finest spectacles was a privilege, terns are certainly impressive birds, and I will return to the Farne Islands, just not in June!

As I near the bottom of the path the sound of the sea starts to drown out the squawking birds. Living in Birmingham in the Midlands some fifteen miles from Lindley Hall Farm, Fenny Drayton, Leicestershire, the geographical centre of England, it should come as no surprise that I relish opportunities to be by the sea. Weston-super-Mare is arguably our closest beach but even on a good day the drive can take two hours. The wonderful M5, a roadwork nightmare! I intend to take full advantage of this empty beach so stroll to the end to stretch tired legs. My back and hips, well all of me really, feel stiff after suffering through my traffic ordeal yesterday and of course my sleeping arrangements are far from ideal. It's definitely no fun getting old and I've no choice but to get used to it. Walking helps. I flick off my flip-flops and scrunch and stretch my fatigued feet in the carpet of soft sand. My senses stir and I'm transported back to another beach, a beach in Indonesia, a beach of golden sand that I walked upon three years ago. My feet sank to just below the knee, an unusually beautiful sinking feeling! But I must not think about Indonesia, no, not Indonesia, not this morning, not yet. I must focus on the here and now. At the end of the beach, I'll retrace my footsteps. The sea is calling me, whispering in my ear; I ignore it, so it starts shouting my name. The urge to be in the water is overwhelming. Ripples wash up the sand. I dip my toes in the water. Blimey it's cold. It doesn't seem to matter how many warm or hot days we have in England; the temperature of the water feels the same, cold. Depending on the region, sea temperatures in the British Isles range from 6 to 10 Celsius during winter months and 15 to 20 Celsius during the summer. That's cold. There will be no swimming for me this trip. Disappointment rushes through my veins. No, I must not let this in, not today. Right, come on Jane, pull yourself together! Time to find somewhere to sit, read and relax. There's not a soul in sight but being presented with an empty beach makes the decision surprisingly difficult. Decisions, decisions. I spy rocks on the other side of the path I came down earlier. Yes, find a natural seat on the rocks, a beach holds too many memories for my first day; day two will be my beach day! Crossing the pebbles and stones in flip-flops, offering at best inadequate protection, proves challenging.

Stepping gingerly over the pebbles, my soles and toes are at the mercy of these insensitive blighters. They must love me, no matter how vigorously I shake my feet, they won't leave. A pebble falls out but three take their chance to jump in! Relief washes over me when I finally arrive at the larger stones. Should have worn my old surf shoes, not that I've ever surfed of course but I purchased them for precisely this moment. My decision to leave them at home was foolish. The sturdy soles and the stretchy uppers would have offered more protection during these painful minutes. Hey ho onwards I go. Crossing the boulders, I arrive on the rocks. That's when the putrid stench of rotting seaweed hits me, the smelly algae is scattered around the edges of the rock pools, and I'm not the only one to smell it. Flies buzz around the piles seemingly enjoying the pong, I don't! I spy a flat stone at the base of the hill, a cracking spot to spend the day, escape the smell and it's far enough from where the sea is crashing against the rocks to avoid showers of salt spray. I've found a good spot where I'll remain dry and seaweed stench free. Searching for the yacht I spied earlier, I find myself disappointed that it must have chosen to disappear back over the horizon, sailing to pastures new, oh how I wish they'd taken me with them. Must stay positive and appreciate the here and now. Time for a few deep breaths. Air enters my nose, fills my lungs and after holding it there for a little while I consciously choose to push it out of my mouth. Ten of these and a feeling of calm washes over me and a smile creeps across my face. I've only gone and done it. I'm here. Hours were spent in the planning, the route, the number of days I'd spend at each destination, the food, the cost of fuel, everything! Everything except the one thing I couldn't plan for, how I'd feel when I arrived! At this precise moment, the world looks good. My hands and shoulders aren't faring so well, weighed down by bags heavy enough to rub sore strap marks and almost cut off the blood supply to the tips of my fingers! I'm relieved to be rid of them but wouldn't be without them, they're full of paraphernalia needed to help me get through the day. Fingers crossed I've remembered everything! I certainly don't intend heading back up the hill for anything. I'm spending the day reading so at the very least I need to be comfortable. In the weeks before leaving I'd downloaded enough thrillers and historical fiction onto my kindle to keep me busy till Christmas. I intend losing myself in the lot! A welcome freshness whistles over the stones as I make myself comfortable. Yes, this is perfect. Or is it? My peace is shattered once again by youthful cries, this time from above.

'Charlie, Charlie, wait for me.'

Glancing over my shoulder I see a boy, presumably the Charlie in question, standing halfway down the path waiting for a couple of younger boys, more than likely, his brothers. Charlie, a name to warm the soul and conjure a memory from childhood, a time when life was easy, and joy filled my heart. My parents gifted me a teddy on the day I was born, a soft golden-coloured bear that seemed real, with brown embroidered eyes, a small snout and stitched nose and mouth. It was stuffed with wool and had four realistic paws. I remember holding him, looking into his eyes, and loving him. According to Mum, I named him Charlie as soon as I could speak. He's 62 years, 7 months, and 17 days old and I've loved him all my life, still do! When my nephew, Ed, was born seventeen years ago, I made the difficult decision to gift Charlie to him and remember the day as if it were yesterday. Rosie, my youngest sister, was recuperating in the hospital. Giving birth had proved challenging, common for a first-time mum and she needed plenty of rest. It was with mixed emotions that I navigated my way through those dimly lit corridors, flowers in one hand my beloved bear in the other. Knowing who I was about to meet and what I was about to do was overwhelming. Seeing Rosie holding her beautiful boy and the tears flowed down my cheeks. She handed Ed to me and the moment I looked into his eyes it was love at first sight, we bonded immediately. I loved him. I bequeathed him my bear and although it was the right thing to do and I'd do it again, I continue to feel the loss! If life had been different and I'd had a child of my own, I would have named him or her Charlie, not Charles or Charlotte, Charlie. The boy on the path is wearing a red T-shirt and blue shorts, clothing making him easy to distinguish against the yellow and green terrain of the hill. He's wearing a cap over long carrot curls that brush his shoulders. His choice of cap is an interesting one, like me, he's clearly not a fan of modern sporty versions. Memories of my grandfather spring to mind, digging through clods of clay in his beloved vegetable garden, wearing black hobnail boots, grey trousers held up with braces over a pristinely white shirt, topped off with his tweed newsboy cap with its stiff peak. I never saw him in anything else. According to Grandma, white shirts and grey trousers were the full extent of his wardrobe, the only other clothing hanging in there were two black suits he wore for special occasions, funerals, and weddings. Coloured braces were his only flamboyance. His clothes take me back to younger days when we would stay at their house. The upstairs was cold, and I got up in the night to run to the toilet, on my way back to bed Grandma's door was open a crack. We weren't allowed in her room, but I couldn't resist sneaking a peek and was shocked to see her getting ready for bed wearing lacy bloomers past her shins. I spied a chamber pot under the bed; it was white with an ornate handle. At the time I couldn't believe the size of this giant cup and remember thinking that Grandma must love tea! Now that I know what it's used for, I certainly wouldn't want to drink out of it! Funny how a boy in a hat can take you back and release memories you don't remember you still have!

My grandparents hail from Carrog in Denbighshire, North Wales and being Welsh, we called Grandma, *Nain*, and Grandpa, *Taid*. It was in M&S in Foregate Street, Chester back in the 1960s when I was trying on some clothes and a woman in the adjoining cubicle called out for her *nain*! Couldn't believe my ears, there was more than one! I loved my *nain*. Sunflowers remind me of her. She spoke of her love for this happy plant and what she said I'll never forget. 'Sunflowers get their energy from the sun, on sunny days they face the sun, on cold dark days they turn to face each other. We should all be a bit more sunflower.' I miss her kind ways.

Didn't really get to know *Taid*, he died when I was eight but thinking of him and I'm reminded of two anecdotes, one is quite lovely and involves me, the other not so and involves my poor father.

The first. *Taid* loved his garden and the wildlife that frequented his beloved borders, developing a particular fondness for ladybirds, lucky ladybirds is how he referred to them. As a four-year-old he would sit me on his knee and sing his ladybird song, well I thought it was his, found out much later of course that it was written in 1744 by some unknown person and consequently belongs to everyone. 'Ladybird ladybird fly away home, your house is on fire and your children are gone, all except one and her name is Ann, and she hid under the frying pan!' Whenever a ladybird lands on me, I blow it away, make a wish, sing his song and hear his voice. Lovely. The loveliness of ladybirds.

The second. My father told me of a time his parents took him to a café in Bala, a village close to their home, eating out was a rare treat so my dad was understandably excited. They sat down and ordered sandwiches, cake, and ice cream. My father's dream dessert was, still is, the knickerbocker glory, that delicious mix of ice cream, meringue, fruit, and cream. He couldn't believe his luck at the size of the dessert placed on the table in front of him, it was the biggest knickerbocker glory he'd ever seen, crowned with a cherry on the top. Dad chose to save the cherry to eat last and struggled to avoid giving in to temptation. When he was finally ready for his crowning glory and reached for the cherry, *Taid* tapped his hand away and popped the treasured fruit into his own mouth swallowing it whole. Then turning to my distraught father smugly pronounced, 'That will teach you my lad, never save the best till last!' My father never forgot that cherry and it took him a long time to forgive his father. He took this as a lesson for life, to enjoy what you have when you have it! I never truly understood what it meant. I do now!

It's funny how seeing the boy in the cap evokes memories. The boy and my grandfather, generations apart, styling similar fashions is strangely comforting. For the life of me though I will never understand why anyone would dig in a white shirt!

I was wrong, the boy is not waiting but sprinting down to the bottom of the hill. Please, please let them leave me well alone and disappear down the beach. Delving into my rucksack I retrieve my kindle and barely finish typing the password when the not so dulcet tones of singing bombard my ears. Charlie is on the beach and has chosen to mark the event by blasting out the words to a football song or some equally irritating jingle and he's waving his arms about like a fool! Wonderful! A resounding, 'boom,' cuts the quiet. For goodness sake, why doesn't he shut up? Two adults, likely the boys' parents, are starting down with a dog in tow. It just gets better! I have a sneaky feeling this lot will prove to be a noisy bunch and I intend to steer well clear of the lot of them. The boys' voices sound vaguely familiar. God forbid they are my noisy neighbours! Just when everything was going so well! My plans may have to change and force me to leave Northumberland sooner than anticipated. Hey ho, being here was only ever going to be where my adventure started, how long I stay is ultimately up to me. My road trip will eventually take me further north around the Scottish coastline, down the west coast into England, hugging the sea into north Wales, continuing along coast roads into England to Land's End and along the south coast before finally returning home from somewhere near Norwich. I intend making this a trip to remember, discovering the delights Britain's coastal villages and towns have to offer. I'd spoken of making this journey many times and in mad moments had even considered walking or cycling the route. That would be a tough task, too tough for me, hence the camper. I had intended putting this trip on hold until my foreign travels had ceased, when I was too old to fly which, I'd anticipated to be sometime in my late seventies or early eighties. I'd know the day. I'd step off a long-haul flight and wouldn't be able to face boarding another; travelling to exotic climes is exciting but can be tough on older bones. Even at my age I ache more and for longer than I used to, but I never could have foreseen that it would all come crashing down and end at the tender age of sixty-one! The end arrived within a month of retiring, an unfortunate and unwelcome coincidence. Written in bold capitals at the top of my 'bucket list of dreams' was to spend more time in Indonesia, the Philippines, Australia and Ecuador. My head seems heavy and falls, tears follow. The tissue from my pocket has been waiting for this moment and successfully dabs the wet drops away. Tissues have taken up permanent residence in my pockets. As a child I was prone to sniffles and colds. I still am. With all the emotional upheaval of late I'm careful to have a suitable supply of tissues with me at all times. This is the very thing I'd feared would happen, crying and feeling overwhelmed by it all. It's a commonly held belief that the most stressful times of life are getting married, divorced, suffering from illness, moving house, changing jobs, retirement, and the death of a loved one. Within the past ten months I've struggled with not one, not two but three from that list, one indirectly. Life has been a roller coaster of late, with ups and more than my fair share of downs, I've been through a whole fairground ride of emotions and I'm numb!

A flicker catches my eye. The boy Charlie is moving across the rocks in front of me. What's he doing? Where's he going? He's closer now and he's younger than I thought, nearer eleven or twelve, he's tall for his age. I watch him navigate the rocks, he moves with purpose, he seems to know where he's heading, me thinks he's been here before. I've never met him, but I know him to be brave, he must be, anyone who walks over pebbles barefooted has to be brave. Oh wonderful, now he's shouting. My eyes burn a hole in the back of his head. Please let him turn and catch me glaring, it might encourage him to shut up! He sits down and falls quiet. The only sounds remaining are from the sea hitting the rocks and the seagulls struggling against the wind swirling at the base of the hill. Peace. Long may it reign.

THE ROCK POOL MEETING

I love dangling my feet in the rock pool. My rock pool. The water is cold. The tides come in and out every twelve hours. The sea shoots over the rocks and falls into the cracks and gaps to make pools. Any fish and creatures in the water fall into the gaps too. Some of the gaps are massive, if I fell in one, I might never be seen again. When the water drops in it pushes other fish and creatures out. It's a cycle. I didn't understand what it meant until Dad told me to think about the wheel on my bike. What goes round comes round. A cycle. Like a wheel. I got it after that. That was one of his good days. He's not always been a pain! The fish and creatures go where the water goes and can end up in another pool or fall back into the sea to freedom. It's weird, my rock pool stays the same, but it changes too. I think about what it must be like to be a creature living in there. Bet it's scary or maybe it's exciting. I don't know but it's got to be tough. There are lots of pools here. Mine's the biggest. It's got sharp edges all the way round except in one bit and that's where I sit. From my stone seat I can look at the sea and splash my legs. I've never been in it but if I did, I could stand in the middle with my arms stretched out and my hands wouldn't touch the sides. The water would come as high as my chin. When we're here on holiday I come here every day but not in the evenings and never at night, it's too dangerous. Mam and Dad have drummed it into us that we must never ever underestimate the power of the sea.

I stare into my pool. The water is still and flat like glass. I look down and see a face looking back at me. I smile at the face and the face smiles too. My teeth sparkle. I have had to wear stainless-steel braces for two years. The orthodontist who fitted them, Mr Payne, yep that really is his name, said it was almost criminal to cover up such perfectly white teeth but as they were not perfectly straight it had to be done. Dad had to stick his nose in, 'What's the point, they'll all need filling, when I were a nipper me dentist made me have a few and I told him I'd rather have a gob full of gold than a winter wonderland of white!' Mr Payne ignored him and told me the brace was due to overcrowding. When I heard him say that I thought he meant our house. Dad took the mick out of me for a long time after that, he still does. I've noticed more people with perfect names for the jobs they do. I had a reception teacher called Mrs Muddle, Mrs Blood was in charge of first aid and Mr Hedges was our caretaker, you couldn't make it up could you? My dentist and orthodontist tell me my teeth are strong and healthy which they put down to drinking water, no soft drinks, only water and the odd cup of tea, Yorkshire tea. In our house, when it's tea it has to be Yorkshire. Dad won't drink any other brew. He took me to have the last check-up and when Mr Payne complimented me on my choice of drinks, me dad couldn't help himself. 'Can't be water can it, ya know what water does to the bottom of boats!' Hardly surprising, but him snorting in the surgery at his own joke got a dry response! Funniest man I know, me dad! Not! I take my cap off. The freckled-faced, ginger-haired boy in the water does the same. I'm happy with the face looking back at me. Long eyelashes, brown eyes, and strong cheekbones, I think I look all right.

Here they come. I can hear Eric screaming. Harry is running down the beach with Pepper in tow. Eric is dragging behind and crying as usual. He's like a tap is our Eric, one minute bawling his eyes out, the next laughing his head off. Never known a kid turn it on and off like him. Anything me or Harry do can set him off. First, he sulks and frowns, then his bottom lip comes out, after that he screams and stamps about the place! It doesn't matter who started it or whose fault it is, Harry and me get the same from Mam and Dad. 'Play nicely with your brother Charlie, for goodness sake Harry, let him join in!' We don't even start it most of the time. He can be very annoying. I love our dog, Pepper. Most people think we called her that after salt and pepper, but they'd be wrong. Her full name is Sgt Pepper, sergeant, as in *Sgt. Pepper's Lonely Hearts Club Band*. Dad and I are massive Beatles fans. Dad always wanted a dog so Pepper's really his. Mam's not a dog person. She didn't want one but eventually caved. Now none of us would be without her. The sea is noisy down here. Good I can't hear Eric. They're way down the beach now anyway.

I look back in my pool. What will I find in here today? Other holidays I've found snails, periwinkles, limpets, shells, anemones, crabs, barnacles, and fish, lots of fish. Creatures that live in rock pools are strong, they have to be. They hunt and they're hunted. I've sat here a lot and have learnt to appreciate them. I wonder if they worry about stuff like I do, like where they might end up after the next high tide. I lift the strap of my satchel over my head and put it down on the stone next to me. I undo the two buckles and take out the notebook and pencil that live there. When I'm here I make notes, draw sketches, write poems, and knock out a few songs. I want to remember the crazy creatures and unusual critters that I find and keep a record for next time. I love finding stuff I haven't seen before. I'm happy here. It's my happy place. I like being on my own. I never used to, but I do now. I have to.

A busy fly buzzes over the water, darting in straight lines to make triangles just above the surface. I watch it for a bit. Flies do this a lot, zoom about in straight lines. Flies are weird. Seagulls squawk from somewhere behind me, I don't trust them, so I better check where they are. My heart jumps. A woman is sitting there, behind me. I've never seen anyone here before. I look away but sneak another look. Her hair is white. She's wearing a black T-shirt and black shorts. Her dark clothes make her hair look really white. I've never seen anyone with hair that white except Father Christmas, but her hair is much shorter than his and straight! I look back in my pool. I spy a small brown crab with thick front claws. It's hiding under an open anemone waiting for something to go past. I've only seen this species a few times. I open my notebook and flick through the pages. That's it. Here it is. The same crab was here last May. I suppose it might not be the same crab, but it looks the same but bigger. I drew it, looked it up and wrote porcelain crab underneath. I turn to the next clean page and write today's date. Next to number one I make a note of the crab. I write anemone next to number two. I watch the crab for a bit. It's moving slowly and even though I know where it is, it's hard to spot when you blink or if you look away. The colour camouflages it. I watch the crab for a bit then me dad starts yelling!

The boy has proved a welcome distraction ensuring the kindle in my lap remains unread. Sitting and watching the day wander by is something we all do to some degree and I'm enjoying witnessing the innocent joys of a child lost in his own little world before the burdens of life inevitably weigh him down! Rock pool watching can be fun, you never know what you'll see or find in a natural aquarium but him here alone makes me wonder why he isn't on the beach playing with his brothers. Maybe he prefers his own company or needs time away from his younger brothers. Siblings can be irritating, something I could relate to being the eldest of four siblings. Four! It will always be four. I can't help but remember how things used to be and sadness seeps in and a sigh slips out. I stare over at his brothers.

Both boys are haring up and down the beach like lunatics. The older of the two is seven or eight years of age and slim, hardly surprising racing about like that, he's burning calories with every step. Only wish I had half his energy. Sarah, my sister and middle child in our family, would jump to his defence and proclaim him the victim of middle child syndrome. His physical and emotional development suitably scarred and stunted by stress due to his position or rather lack of it within the family. Firstborn children are historically privileged, youngest children indulged, leaving the middle child with nothing! Sarah claims to have suffered the same and might have a point; she's tiny. Many years ago, when Rosie and I were talking about embarking on a diet, Sarah asked if she could join in and do it too. Incredulous she'd even contemplate such a thing considering she probably weighed the same as two of my legs and one of Rosie's! We made a joke that Rosie and I would be eating celery and cress whilst Sarah tucked into a plate of doughnuts! We laughed it off over fish and chips! We enjoy our time together and laugh a lot; love does that. Sarah has the best laugh of anyone I know, it's an enchantingly sweet expression of the joy she exudes. She always manages to brighten even the darkest of days. Rosie and I never did diet and Sarah ate chips and doughnuts without a care remaining stick thin! I adore my sisters even the one with the middle child syndrome! Middle child syndrome aside, the boy on the beach seems gloriously happy, they both do. He's wearing a white cotton T-shirt, brightly patterned Bermuda shorts and white pumps. For goodness sake, who dresses their child in white! Red hair and faces sprinkled with freckles is obviously a family trait. The little guy is stockier and dressed in what I can only describe as hand-me-downs, his blue T-shirt and matching shorts are at best one, maybe two sizes, too big for him. Poor little fellow! The parents, weighed down with provisions, are making slow but steady progress down the hill. They don't seem old enough to have three children, a sure sign that I'm getting old. Arriving at the bottom, the boy's father calls over to Charlie, but the boy fails to respond, either not hearing or choosing to ignore him. I heard him as clear as a bell, so I presume it's the latter. The cocker spaniel chases the boys as they throw off their T-shirts and sprint into the shallows. The father is making his way over to speak with Charlie, time for my Jo Nesbo thriller. I manage five lines before being startled by a voice beside me.

'How do, me name's Matt, I'm Charlie's dad, that lad o'er there. Thought I'd better check he ain't bugging ya.' I look up and am surprised to be greeted by this thirty-something man who's extending his hand out to me. We shake hands. He oozes warmth and charm which disarms me.

'Hi, I'm Jane. Jane Jones. Pleased to meet you.'

When introducing myself to strangers I feel the need to add, 'Jane, without the y, plain Jane.' Sadly, I'm blessed with two plain names, there's nothing exciting or romantic about either however Jones bothers me less as it connects me with my Welsh ancestors. Saying that, Ed was conducting research for a school project and discovered that we're 49% Irish, go figure! I'm disappointed not to have been bequeathed a middle name, my choice would have been Elizabeth, Margaret or Katherine, a touch of the royal would have suited me and jazzed things up a little. Yes, Jane Jones is a plain name and there's nothing plain about me!

We exchange the usual pleasantries, and he makes to go but stops, glances over to his son then leans in and whispers, 'Nah then, how about ya join us tonight. It was Charlie's birthday yesterday, the lad's twelve and he's a good kid. We're going to have a bit of a party later. Come and fill ya boots and have a beer or wine if ya like. Tan, I mean Sam, me other half, she drinks wine by the bucket load, it'll be a great crack. It'll be me and the wife, Hurry up Harry and Shadow o'er there on the beach, they're mine too and the couple from the caravan at the end, Steve and Nicki, with their two little uns, doo dah and wot not.' He pauses before calling over to his son, 'Now then lad, don't ya be annoying this fine lady here will ya, keep it down hey!' The boy couldn't fail to hear that, and the boy shot his father a glare. Undeterred, Matt continues, 'That's ours up there,' indicating the caravan in the pitch next to mine. I knew it! My next-door neighbours, three boys! Lucky me! I bury a groan but a tiny tut escaped, hopefully he didn't hear it.

Wonderful teeth are a prerequisite for a dentist, a mouth of gaps and gums is hardly a showcase of your dental abilities! An older colleague of mine with a shocking set of gnashers, reminiscent of the character Sloth, from the cult film, *The Goonies*, struggled to understand why his clientele were dwindling. How he couldn't put two and two together was beyond me. Even the few teeth clinging on to life were rotten and crooked! My teeth are good, not so my ears! An ear for accents escapes me. Matt's Yorkshire lilt was difficult to decipher, him whispering and speaking fast didn't help. I'm relieved when he goes to sit with his son. Watching them is touching, the importance of family. My family mean everything, the cliché, 'blood is thicker than water', defines me. I stare out to the horizon lost in contemplation. Moments later and Matt's heading back to the beach.

'See ya later Jane, enjoy ya book, ta-ra!'

The kindness of strangers. I close my eyes in the vain attempt of holding back the tears welling within. Why do we close our eyes when we cry? We close them to dream, kiss and pray too. Maybe closing the eyes shuts out the world, shielding us from outside distractions and goes some way in protecting our soul. The exceptional and the special are not seen, you don't see love or loss you feel them. My head, neck and shoulders weigh heavy. The purpose of the road trip was to leave the pain behind; this is going to take longer than I'd hoped.

I was surprised to see me dad talking to the woman back there. He always comes to check on me. He's told me not to bug her. He said her name's Jane. Wish he'd trust me a bit. I'm not a little kid anymore. At least he's stopped trying to persuade me to go back to the beach. He used to do that all the time. My brothers are jumping in the waves. I used to love doing that. I don't do any of it anymore. Mam's lying on her towel reading a book. Dad's back on the beach. He'll play in the sea with Harry and Eric in a bit. I pick up my notebook, flick through the pages and look in the pool. A blenny shoots out of his hidey hole and lies on a rock about halfway down. I'm going to sketch it. I saw a small one last time. This is bigger, suppose it could be the same one but grown a bit. It's dark orange, about 10cm long and thin. I like them. They have big heads and big eyes like me! It doesn't take long to sketch the body; the head will take longer. I forgot about Jane and sneak a peek. She's crying! I look away. I'm a bit embarrassed. I don't want her to see me looking. I'll have another look in a bit. I wait a bit. I look again. Yep, she's still crying! I feel bad. I don't like seeing grown-ups cry. What's making her sad? Dad was talking to her, and she was okay. He probably made her cry! He makes me sad all the time! I don't know. Back to my blenny. Can't see him, he's gone. Tom. I'll call him Tom, he's a tompot blenny! Found him, he's perched on his two side fins and propping himself up like he's about to do a sit-up! His mouth is open like he's trying to say something. He's got a frill on his back. It looks like it was cut out of the lace curtains in the caravan. It's even the same colour. I'll finish my picture. One more look at Jane. Oh no, she's not good. What do I do? Should I do anything? I don't know. I'm going to ask if she's okay. Mam tells us we should care about people. If someone's sad we should look out for them. Maybe she's hurt herself then I'll go and get me mam. She's not a stranger, me dad said she was okay. He was wrong, she's not okay, is she? Me dad's wrong a lot of the time!

For goodness sake, I've cried enough. It's got to stop. My heart's pounding so hard it hurts, physical pain caused by emotional pain. Crying has helped relieve some of the pressure I've been harbouring. I've cried more lately than in all the years of my life, well that's how it feels. I need to have a strong word with myself and pull myself together. Sighing, I slide the switch on my kindle, read three lines when a pair of bare feet appear at my side.

'Are you okay?'

I look up. Now it's the boy's turn to keep me from my book.

'Yes, I'm fine thank you.' My words don't have the desired effect, he just stands there! He shuffles on his feet. Resigned, I slide the switch on my kindle and the screen goes black.

SHARKS ARE SCARY AREN'T THEY?

I avert my gaze and am taken aback when he continues to probe. 'Are you sure you're okay? You were crying!'

The gentleness of his tone is engaging. I can feel his eyes boring into me and have no option but to reluctantly meet his stare. My mind's racing. I don't want to talk about it. I haven't talked about it with friends or family and certainly don't intend discussing my inner turmoil with this boy. I'm racking my brain contemplating what to say and consider fobbing him off with, 'Oh it's nothing I've got something in my eye,' or 'I'm just a little under the weather but honestly I'm okay,' he will then walk away, and I can get back to my kindle. This young boy couldn't possibly understand the impact recent events have made on my life, how things have changed and will never change back.

In the years before retiring, I'd compiled a wish list, dreams that I would tick off during my senior years. The crumpled paper on which they are written is lying at the bottom of my recycle bin waiting to be thrown out with the rest of the rubbish when I return home. As I approached my sixties I looked forward to and was excited by the opportunities that would come my way, not anymore, now I see a blank canvas. Apart from this trip nothing is decided, and all my plans have gone. Many would relish this clean slate and see it as an opportunity to take a fresh start, to create new opportunities, to take risks, not me. At the very top of my list, I'd written 'Retire and Go'. The last words at the bottom of a lengthy list were 'Road Trip in Camper Van'. The rest of the list is no more! What comes next is anyone's guess! These are the private thoughts bouncing around my brain so what I say next surprises me. 'Yes Charlie. Yes. I admit I'm sad but it's more than that. I'm devastated. Truly devastated and will never get over it. You're too young to understand the cause of my pain or the depths of my distress. You see it's the sharks!' He says nothing and simply stares back at me. You see I was right; he can't understand. I can barely understand it. It was only just then as I was saying it that it became clear to me, and I mean right at that precise moment the words spilled out of my mouth. That was the first time since my life began spiralling out of control that the realisation dawned, the depths of my angst. I look at him. Not sure what I was expecting him to do or say next but nodding frantically and grinning like a Cheshire cat was definitely not what I had in mind! Cheeky blighter!

'Yeah, I know. Sharks are scary aren't they?'

He spoke with the kind of excitement you feel when you're told you've come into money or won a prize. I mention the word sharks and he jumps to the obvious conclusion. Before giving me the chance to respond he elaborates to press home his point.

'Lots of people are scared of sharks. You're not the only one. Sharks are scary. I can't stand them either. That's why I'm over here. That's why I stay on the rocks. I can't go in the sea anymore. Don't be sad. Sharks are scary aren't they? They are!'

He stands there waiting for me to agree with him, but I can't. Irritated at my lack of response he repeats his question but this time with more conviction.

'Sharks are scary aren't they?'

He's misunderstood. I force a smile, shake my head, and deliver my reply with a soft authority. 'No. Sorry Charlie but no. Sharks are not scary.' I wait a moment for that to sink in then begin to elaborate. 'No Charlie, no they're not. I'm afraid you've got it wrong and misunderstand. Sharks are not scary. That's not why I'm crying.' Tears well up in my eyes and when there's no room left they overflow and roll down my cheeks. Time for my tissue, again! 'I'm sorry Charlie, I can't help it. I'm just desperately sad. I miss them. I love them and know I'll never swim with them in the oceans again. It breaks my heart. Sharks make my heart sing; they strike music to my soul, and I'll spend the rest of my life missing them.' Strange to speak about this with a boy, a stranger I've only just met. Our awkward interaction and my latest revelation have caused his smile to fade. Seemingly embarrassed at being corrected he bows his head, slides his hands in his pockets and shuffles on his feet. I take this as him itching to go but he surprises me when he mumbles something about not understanding. I take a moment. What did he say just now? Sharks scare him. They keep him out of the water!

He suffers from galeophobia, derived from the Greek words, *galeos*, meaning shark and *phobos*, meaning fear. I remember struggling with the same crippling affliction for decades, being so afraid that even dipping my toes in the sea was a step too far! The fear was very real. Sharks consumed my mind, swimming in the watery depths of my imagination. I understand the impact such a fear can have. Unlike poor Charlie, I was sixteen before sharks sank their teeth into me. Childhood nerves were an irrelevance, minor irritations played out with my brother in a pool, not serious or impacting. During family jaunts to the baths Greg would pretend to be a shark to taunt me, sneaking up from behind or below and delight in making me jump. Irritating, as brothers often are, but it wasn't until the June of 1975 after visiting the cinema to see *Jaws* with a friend, that my nerves were shredded, and the fear took hold! Walking out

124 minutes later and the damage was done! That film blighted my life for three decades! Going into the sea became something I used to do. Steven Spielberg, the director, has a lot to answer for. I wonder how many others had holidays or days to the seaside ruined after watching that man-eating great white attacking the inhabitants of the fictional island of Amity in New England, USA and don't get me started on John Williams' hauntingly stunning musical score. I gripped the arms of my cinema seat so tightly my knuckles turned white. After a particularly brutal attack carefully choreographed crowds charged from the sea as the great white disappeared towards the open ocean. The curtains closed. Unfortunately, it wasn't the end of the film! Back in the day films were on reels which required changing during the showing, hence the intermission. Cue for the uniformed usherettes to saunter down to the screen and sell ice creams. Tucking into my choc ice, my mind was racing in the hopes of finding a suitable excuse to leave, time sped by and before I knew it the second half was underway. Now don't get me wrong, the film was good, terrifyingly so and tremendously successful, a watershed moment for film and for me too as it happened. Pre-film, family days to the beach had been gloriously wonderful. Venturing into the sea was a daily occurrence and we'd play in there for hours without a care in the world. Dad was an amazing swimmer and loved the sea. I'll be forever grateful that he taught me to swim and for a childhood of happy seaside memories. I'm relieved the film wasn't produced until 1975, if I'd seen it earlier my happiest memories would undoubtedly have been different. Hardly surprising but my thoughts now turn to my brother. I miss him. I'm going to miss him for the rest of my life! He left us nine months ago. Closing my eyes, I can see him running through the overgrown thicket of nettles, fruit bushes and damson trees at the bottom of our long garden in Chester. He's wearing blue shorts, a blue and white striped T-shirt, black pumps and sporting a beautiful smile. His face, voice and smile are what I miss most! Memories play like film clips and are the only way to see and hear

him. Death is cruel! I want to let the pictures roll but in hushed tones and with tears in his eyes, Charlie speaks.

'I used to love the sea. Me and Harry jumped the waves. My favourite thing was diving through them. I can't do it now. I can't go in anymore. I'm scared!'

His fear is very real. Fears can take hold, they can grow and come to affect your life and harm your mental well-being. What can I do or say to this but reassure him, tell him that I used to feel the same but don't anymore? Time is a great healer and if it changed for me then it could for him. He'll get over it, harsh but true but the chances are he will and if he doesn't then he will learn to avoid situations where sharks are. Yes I think a little reassurance will suffice then that will be the end of the conversation, we'll say our goodbyes and he'll go back to his rock pool, and I'll return to my kindle. He obviously didn't get the memo and starts firing questions at me.

'I don't understand, what do you mean, how can you have been scared of them and now love them? How can you love sharks? They're scary! Where did you see them? Why won't you see them anymore? I don't get it. Sharks are scary!'

He falls quiet seemingly waiting for my response. Unbeknown to him, the most significant and delicate question was his last one. I'm not prepared to dive into that emotional baggage so take a moment on what to say. This is not going to be a quick fix. Maybe I do need to tell him how I conquered my fear; it might help him know such things are possible. After all, we're both here with time on our hands, it's the least I can do and will enable us to become better acquainted before attending his birthday surprise later. Deep down I know it's the kind thing to do but rather than answering his questions, I ask one of my own. 'Tell you what Charlie, how about you sit here with me for a little while and we can chat about it, or do you need to get back over there?' Unresponsive he stares blankly first at his family then back at his pool. I remain silent.

What's he thinking? More than likely, he's regretting coming over and contemplating how to make his escape! I don't have to wait much longer. Saying nothing, he forces a smile and turns to stroll back to his pool. Hey ho! He unexpectedly stops halfway, stands still then turns, heads back and plonks himself cross-legged on the rock in front of me. So here we are, two strangers, making time to talk. Only now do I worry what to say. Hearing about my experiences may be enough for him to take comfort that he's not alone. My emotional journey took me from nervous wreck to passionate advocate! Sharks swim through my mind twice a day, when I'm awake and when I'm asleep and they're no longer the stuff of nightmares, far from it, they soothe my soul to sleep.

Choosing to tell him of the great white from seventy-five may have been a mistake. I've looked into the eyes of enough children over the years to know a nervous child when I see one. Describing the bloodier scenes and his long eyelashes flicker over anxious eyes, widening as the intensity of the drama unfolded. Humming the two notes, E and F, played on the original score by a tubist, 'duh dum, duh dum', was certainly a step too far! They say the eyes are the window to the soul. Looking into those glistening brown eyes, searching beyond those watery pools of chocolate, dark shadows danced. With colour draining from his face, he closed his eyes and covered them with his hands. Time to lighten the mood, I'll tell him about what happened in the autumn a couple of years later and note to self, keep it upbeat!

'I was a dental student in Birmingham and had completed a particularly challenging set of exams at the end of my first year. Needing a holiday, Anne, a fellow student, and I chose to fly to Lindos, an enchanting town situated beneath an impressive acropolis on the Greek island of Rhodes. The trip would help us relax and recuperate; we were both exhausted. Trust me, exams never get any easier! There's plenty about Greece to love, the warm air that hits you the second you step off the plane, the architecture, and the endless sea views. Our hotel in Lindos was one of many whitewashed buildings lining the narrow back streets that wound down the hill from the monument above and was a seventy-minute drive from Diagoras Airport in Rhodes town. Unpacking took an hour, we then changed into our shorts and sun vests, donned our sunglasses, and headed to the beach smothered in Hawaiian Tropic, smelling of coconut and feeling fabulous. It was mid-morning. Lindos was quiet as we strolled down through narrow cobbled streets, still slumbering from the night before. Restaurant and bar staff busied themselves at tables strewn along the shaded frontages and in courtyard suntraps, all lovingly decorated with tropical plants in terracotta pots, where sun worshippers could justify that "one more for the road!". On our walk back later, we'd stop for a meal, something we'd do every night! In the evenings, those same streets were crowded with sunburnt tourists, music, singing and dancing, a wonderful Greek hullabaloo.' The word elicits a smile from this pensive boy. How sweet, it would appear he's enjoying my Greek tragedy! 'We browsed in a few of the small shops selling jewellery, leather bags, pottery and clothes, the usual traps to tempt the wealthy tourist! I didn't know it then, but I'd return home with a ceramic bowl complete with a vibrant aquamarine interior and a white fish painted into the base. Two grooves were cut into the brownish-red terracotta on the underside enabling it to be hung on a wall. Living in student digs my bowl was never destined for the wall. I continue to use it to this day for salads, pasta, and couscous. Whenever it appears on the table I'm taken down Greek memory lane! Walking down the hill that day, the sun on my face was liberating and hotter than any heat I'd experienced during an English summer, it felt good and so did I! I'd managed to see my way through a tricky year of anatomy, physiology and biochemistry and survived the flight, reasons to celebrate. I continue to be a nervous flier. Have you ever flown Charlie?'

'No and probably never will. Mam and Dad used to, but he hated it. He thought his head was going to explode. Mam said he couldn't cope with the pressure! After the planes crashed into the Twin Towers in 2001 he was done with it!'

'Perfectly understandable but there's a big wide world out there and if you want to see it then flying is something you simply have to do, it comes down to time and cost. Getting to far-flung places like Australia or Asia by train and boat would take longer than the holiday itself! It's simple mathematics. Maybe you'll fly when you're an adult, I hope you do, there's an awful lot to see. Anyway, better get on with my story or we'll be here all day! Where was I, oh yes, heading to the beach. Okay so I was in a joyous mood with no inkling of what was to come. Arriving at the bottom of the hill, we stepped out from between the shaded buildings into brilliant sunshine, an infinite sky of blue and the unwelcome stench of donkey poo from the sad beasts tethered together in lines. Despondent donkeys awaiting the burden of bone-idle tourists, returning from the beach or coaches with day trippers, wanting to view the monument without walking a step. Poor donkeys, it's criminal. Stepping onto the empty beach was a relief, a calm sun-drenched space awaiting the throngs of ouzo-soaked tourists yet to fall out of the beds they'd collapsed onto the night before. Music drifted on the breeze from a small shack on the sand, a beach bar selling Mythos, the local lager, on tap and by the can. Fresh fish, chips and toasties were served at driftwood tables under umbrellas woven by Georgios, basket maker and bar owner, Georgie we called him! We selected our spot for the day, changed into newly purchased bikinis revealing more of our white bodies, purchased a couple of cans of Mythos and headed into the sea to soothe stiff joints. Trust me, there's no better way of relieving travel stress than immersing oneself in a warm sea, under a hot sun, with a can of cold beer! First stop beach, second stop bar, third stop, sea! I'm convinced our oceans possess some miraculous, as yet undiscovered, healing properties, causing stress and worry to drift away on the tides, wash away whilst you lie there gloriously weightless. We ran in and I dived under, careful to hold my can up and out of the water. I've been caught out by that before! Warm waves washed over me. Flipping onto my back I kicked out towards the open ocean leaving Anne snorkelling in the shallows. A short time later, without warning, Anne shot towards me screaming for me to get out of the water. She was pointing behind me at a spot in the water I couldn't see. I can't put into words the terror that raced through my veins. Spinning round, sunlight bouncing off the water made it impossible for me to see below the surface. I hurtled for the sanctity of the beach as fast as my chaotically splashy strokes would let me. Crawling out I could already hear her chortling, her idea of a joke. Needless to say, I found the whole thing hysterically funny, not! Of course, we laughed about it later but secretly I knew I was in trouble. I made excuses not to go back in the sea after that and spent the rest of the week reading and sitting with Georgie; his bar became a haven. Anne's behaviour was disappointing to say the least. I'd confided in her, she knew how badly the film had affected me! Sharks were scary and I wasn't going to risk swimming in a foreign sea for fear of attack. That was then. I could not have envisaged sitting here today, over forty years later and speaking with you about it, hard to believe how things have changed. What you believe can't or won't change, can and does!'

I stop talking. His blank expression reveals nothing of his state of mind. I can't decide whether he's hanging on my every word or bored out of his brains, hard to read children sometimes, happy or sad, their faces are the same. Maybe the time has come for me to stop talking and for him to start. I'm intrigued to discover what caused his galeophobia, it must have started somewhere. Speaking softly, I send him an encouraging smile and ask him to tell me. The silence prevails which I'm determined not to fill. Crashing waves and screaming seagulls do not obliterate the deafening silence which has fallen between us. Time seems to stretch. Charlie says nothing. I say nothing. I continue to wait. He breaks first.

'They don't know I'm scared of sharks. I've not told them, none of them. When we come here I make excuses, so I don't have to go in the sea, like it's cold, I don't feel well or I'm going to check out my pool. It's hard coming up with new ones.' I feel a bit wobbly already. Can't believe I'm going to tell her about it. Don't even know her but her voice is soft, and I liked listening to her. Wish my music teacher, Miss Scott, talked to us like that. Scotty barks at us like we're a pack of dogs. When I found out her first name was Harmony I thought it was a joke! If I tell Jane about what happened to me she might be able to help but deep down I don't think she will. My shark thing is different from hers. It's stupid really. I've only told Nathan, the boy next door and regretted it the next day. I feel embarrassed about it but what can I do? Don't know what to say now. I'm sitting here chewing the inside of my cheek. Mam says I do it when I'm nervous. Be biting my nails next! Best if I look down, she can't catch my eye then. Teachers are good at catching eyes, that's how they get you, then the questions start. Spend half my life at school with my head down. Surprised teenagers don't have a reputation for bad necks! I hang my head in most lessons even when I know the answer. Other kids don't like me being right all the time. It's one of the things you do learn at school. She's not saying anything. My fingers fiddle in the cracks by my feet. 'It happened when I was eight, near here. It was chucking it down so the folks took us out for the day. They drove us to the aquarium down the coast a bit. Dad was looking after Harry most of the time. Mam sat down a lot. Think she might have been pregnant with Eric. She was tired and didn't feel well.'

I can barely hear his hushed tones above the sounds of the sea, but I am determined not to interrupt him.

'They let me go exploring on my own as long as they could see me. I went over to a big glass tank, it was massive, the sign on it said, 'Deep Ocean'. I could see lots of fish inside, some big ones. I put my arms on the glass. It was warm. I put my head on the glass. The floor was covered in sand and rocks. An octopus was in a hole. I could see one of his arms. A turtle swam up to the surface. Mam loves turtles. It's the turtle's fault. It was coming back down. I turned and shouted for her to come. To see the turtle with me. That's when it happened. I turned to look back in the tank. I turned to check on the turtle. But the turtle had… I couldn't see the… a shark was there. Next to my face. Looking at me. A shark!'

What a transformation! His body is tensing and he's raising his voice. His eyes flick from side to side as he divulges the details, seemingly in search of the shark itself. He's pointing and jerking his arms around, voice straining under the stress, he's becoming breathless.

'It was there. I forgot about the glass. It was looking right at me, and the mouth was open. I could see… I could see teeth. Tons of them. Sharp teeth. They were sharp, I could tell. It had dark eyes. Small and black. It was really close. It shook its head. It was attacking me. The face was long and pointy. Then it swam off and I could see how big it was. Then it came back. It moved fast. It came at me. But turned again. It kept swimming past looking at me. His tail was massive. He was big and grey and… and…'

I contemplate interrupting this wide-eyed worrier but he's speaking quickly and in mid-flow.

'I jumped and had a sort of panic. I got a shiver. I ran to me mam and dad. They hadn't seen it. I was puffing and panting and out of breath. I could feel my heart beating hard in my chest. I couldn't breathe. I couldn't. I put one hand over my heart and the other over my mouth. I was shaking. I pointed at the shark and said something, and I think it was pretty obvious I'd been spooked. Dad laughed and said, 'Some-*fin* tells me ya don't like him son,' and he kept saying it, 'Some-*fin*, some-*fin*, get it, do you get it?' After the holiday I went to play at Nathan's, and I told him, and he promised he wouldn't tell anyone, but he broke his promise and told my mates at school. They took the mick. We went to the library before afternoon break and Seb and Barney found books with pictures of sharks in them and they put them in front of me and all I could see were eyes and teeth. At playtime they ran up behind me shouting, 'shark' as loud as they could, showing me their teeth, screaming, and roaring and pretending to bite me and then they ran off. They kept coming back and doing it. That only lasted for a couple of weeks. The novelty wore off and they started teasing Oliver, a kid in our class. They caught him picking buttercups for his mam on his way home from school. He got grief for that for weeks. Felt bad for him but it got them off my back. But the damage was done, I was scared of sharks. I had my first shark nightmare a few days after that. We came here to the beach for a weekend not long after and I'd forgotten I was scared of sharks. I ran down to the sea like I always did but saw a dark shape in the water and something touched my leg. I panicked and got out as quick as I could. After I'd got out I looked and could only see seaweed but when I was in there it felt like a shark was under me and it was coming to get me. I haven't been in the sea since. I feel the same. Sometimes I can't even look at the sea.' That's it. She's the first adult I've told. I feel better. It wasn't hard, not really. I can't look at her. I look down and wait for her to say something. I feel like crying.

It must have taken a lot of courage for Charlie to open up to me. Now what do I say? How on earth do I respond to that? Words of wisdom would be good, let's hope I can find some! I understand how he feels, of course I do, I'd felt the same. Oh, great now he's snivelling, whatever I choose to say or do I'd better get on with it! Maybe it might help him to know how I conquered my fear and turned the corner, if nothing else, it may at least instil a sense of hope that he could do the same. I'll tell him about the time when I grabbed my fear by the proverbial throat and looked it in the eyes. I will tell him of Zanzibar.

THE HOOK THAT
REELED ME IN

'Over the years I've met up with Susie, another chum from dental school who, after qualifying, married Richard, a GP and moved to live in Dartmouth in Devon, on England's south coast. Thirteen years ago, during one of my annual pilgrimages to see her, she introduced me to a couple of friends, Andy, the local vet and Beth, his wife and business partner. The following September the four of them were planning the trip of a lifetime, a safari in Africa.'

Hearing those words and they elicit an immediate response from the boy, he lifts his head, and a smile emerges on his face, the topic had piqued his interest; I'd hooked him.

'Africa had been on my bucket list since seeing the film *Born Free*, at the impressionable age of eleven. In the film, Joy and George Adamson cared for Elsa, a young orphaned lioness before releasing her back into the Kenyan wilderness. Hearing the four of them chatting through their itinerary and I couldn't contain myself, blurting out how I'd love to tag along. Desperate to go but not be a nuisance, I assured them I'd bring a friend along and we'd keep out of their hair! Thankfully, they were delighted as advocates of the proverb, "the more the merrier"! You might be surprised but the friend I chose to invite was Anne, her humour continued to be questionable but her loyalty to me a redeeming feature. We had remained friends, she'd been my one constant companion as the years had ticked by, there for me when I needed her and that year I needed her to come with me to Africa.

'After landing at Jomo Kenyatta Airport, named after Kenya's first Prime Minister and President, we were transferred to the Muthaiga Club in Nairobi for a two-night stay. An oasis of tranquillity in an otherwise chaotic city, this exclusive club, founded in 1913, was originally frequented by British colonials. Our two-day stay was thanks to Richard's father who lived in Nairobi and a member of this picture-perfect retreat. Elegant buildings, beautiful gardens, manicured lawns, full English breakfasts, gin and tonics, and cups of tea combined to make it a quintessential home from home. Walking through the doors we seemed to step back in time and into a hotel unlike any other I've stayed in previously or since. Antiquated rules were the order of the day, use of mobile phones, laptops and cameras were restricted, dress codes enforced and the infamous, "men-only bar", which rose to prominence in *Out of Africa*, the film produced from the memoirs of Karen Blixen. Karen was a Danish author who lived on a farm in the foothills of the Ngong Hills along the Rift Valley to the south-west of Nairobe. Her book takes us on a journey of colonial life during the early twentieth century, having lived there for 17 years she knew the place intimately. Our short stay was the springboard that launched us into our African adventure.

'From Nairobi we travelled to the game reserve in a minivan, rust bucket more like, we were lucky to get there never mind survive a safari in that death trap. The sliding door only closed to halfway and a large pane in the rear window was missing, not scary in the slightest, we'd certainly be getting up close and personal with the animals! We were heading to Mara Camp 200 miles to the west in the Maasai Mara, a region named after the Maasai people who live amongst the swathes of grassy plains and rolling hills. *Mara*, meaning "spotted", refers to a landscape scattered with trees. The Maasai cut a striking figure in the shuka, their traditional red robes, a colour believed to scare lions. Thank goodness I'd packed my red cagoule! The journey had been expected to take six hours but took an excruciating nine! Treacherous main roads littered with potholes the size of moon craters, poor etiquette of other road users and police checks at every village were the least of our worries! The van was dangerous, and our driver's poor navigation skills and a love of back roads combined to make a bad situation worse! It didn't help that he chose to navigate a remote stretch of track at motorway speeds causing the back door to fly open and most of our luggage to fall out and bounce down the road! Our cries alerted the driver who remained oblivious to everything around him except his phone and the radio! Barely surviving his neck-throttling seat belts as he performed the emergency stop, we exploded out of the van to retrieve the bags in a race with locals emerging from the bush to claim their prizes!

'We were understandably relieved to arrive in one piece, something we celebrated at the bar. Not dying was a good way to start the safari! We settled into our tent, one of thirty neatly nestled along the banks of the Mara River. Our tent was roomy with space enough for two double beds, a tiled en-suite, shower, sink, hot and cold running water, and flushing toilet. It took glamping to a whole new level. Two gas lamps were our only light source once darkness fell, one between the beds the other in the bathroom. A wooden table and two chairs adorned the decking out front where we enjoyed a pot of tea and biscuits each morning, served by a Maasai warrior in full regalia. Two warriors escorted us to dinner and back again once the bar shut! Luxurious hotels around the world place a chocolate on your pillow at turndown, not in Kenya, two small hippos, carved from local soapstone stand on your pillow next to a note bearing the words, "Lala Salama", sleep safely. A lovely touch. Meals were eaten under canvas when it rained or outside on the banks of the river under the orange African sun. A campfire burned at night to ward off lions, a warming centrepiece where campers sat to share sightings and sing songs whilst enjoying an after-dinner drink or two!

'That first morning I woke to the patter of tiny monkey feet racing on the canvas above our heads, who needed an alarm clock? Half an hour later we stepped out into a torrential downpour but thanks to our protective awning were able to enjoy our morning cuppa whilst watching a giraffe, front legs awkwardly splayed, guzzling from a water hole close by. I continue to find it strange that the neck of a giraffe is long enough to reach high into the tree canopy to eat but too short for them to reach the ground comfortably to drink. Anne had forgotten to pack a rain jacket but luckily for her I'd packed a spare, my red cagoule, which I was delighted for her to wear. This was my idea of a joke Charlie, it stank, something I'll share with you another time but needless to say it was revenge for the Greek incident. She complained of an acrid stench following her round all day which gave me a wonderful sense of satisfaction. That cagoule didn't half pong! Like an elephant me, never forget!

'Leonard, our warrior guide, suggested we delay entering the park until after lunch and the promise of better weather. He wasn't wrong, as we swallowed our last few mouthfuls, the sun burst through the clouds with such an intensity as if an oven door had been thrown open. Thankfully, our van was deemed too dangerous and had been whisked off to a local garage for repair. We entered the park in a green open-topped jeep driven by Leonard. He looked the part in his khaki uniform, trousers, shirt, and leather boots, all topped off with a military-style peaked cap. It was surreal being out in the bush in an open-topped jeep. In those first few days I was fearful the animals would choose to jump in and join us! I actually never got used to that feeling of vulnerability and would have almost preferred our dodgy van; at least I could have hidden in the front seat. Leonard's attempts to reassure me fell on deaf ears when he suggested the animals wouldn't be interested but I should avoid looking them in the eyes! Not the best advice, during those early encounters I bowed my head and kept my eyes shut to avoid seeing anything!'

'Lions can jump 10m, I read it in my encyclopaedia. I don't get why they wouldn't jump in your jeep?'

'It's quite simple really Charlie, they don't view humans as prey and there's ample food in the bush to satisfy their hunger. Leonard's community live in the bush and wander through the wilderness on a daily basis. The only time they worry is when they come upon a lioness with cubs which she'd instinctively defend. Once I got my head round it I started to relax. Our dirt track of claggy red sand wound through thick vegetation and we spent time scanning for wildlife. The leaves were saturated from the rain and sparkled in the drying sun. Wet drops bounced sunlight into my eyes causing me to squint but no amount of glare could prevent me seeing the rear end of a fully grown elephant, eating in the long grass, less than an arm stretch away.' Charlie giggled. Good, I'd tickled his humour, not met a child yet who doesn't find rear end, bottom, or bum funny! 'What we came upon around the bend in the track can only be described as my, *Jurassic Park*, moment. In the film Alan Grant, played by New Zealand actor Sam Neill, sets eyes on the dinosaurs for the first time and is overcome with emotion, his legs give way, and he drops to the ground. The exact same thing happened to me, Leonard cut the engine and I sank to the floor of the jeep so mesmerised was I by the spectacle. The Mara River was meandering its way through vast green meadows awash with what can only be described as, a zoo full of animals. Imagine the scene Charlie. A herd of elephants were drinking at a pool nearby. The matriarch, quenching a particularly excessive thirst, sucked water into her trunk relentlessly which she then emptied into her mouth. The umpteen litres splashing into her stomach resounded like a waterfall. Birds sang in the canopies. A bloat of hippos bathed in the river watched over by crocodiles lazing log-like on muddy banks. Giraffes ate from mimosa and acacia trees, zebra grazed through the grasses and a rhino busied into the bush, her calf eagerly in tow. The beauty of observing wildlife wandering freely in their natural habit took my breath away and we'd see sights like this on a daily basis. The highlight of our stay was soaring across the skies at sunrise on a balloon safari, seeing the herds of animals from a different perspective. That required an early start, tiptoeing past tents of slumbering tourists well before dawn, our route lit by the moon and led by the guides. Boarding the balloon required a short nerve-wracking trek over the plains to be greeted by ten spear-wielding warriors, each one brandishing a flaming torch. Having them alongside went some way in placating my nerves. I was convinced we were being stalked by invisible creatures hiding in the undergrowth which would pounce at any moment! A short walk later and we arrived at an already inflated balloon. The warriors spread out to encircle the group as we took turns to clamber up a small stepladder and drop clumsily into the wicker basket. All aboard and the pilot fired the burners, the flames lit the darkness and warmed our expectant faces. Without warning we gently lifted off the ground and floated up to soar over the plains as the first rays of sunlight flickered across the sky. Floating silently, at the mercy of the breeze, in a wicker basket suspended under a chilli-red canopy, gave us a bird's-eye view of hundreds of migrating wildebeest. Arriving at the river they'd launch themselves off the steep banks and fall into the fast-flowing waters in their attempt of reaching more fertile grasslands on the other side. A treacherous journey if ever there was one, made all the more precarious by lion and hyena lying in wait hoping to pick off a young calf. Once the wildebeest arrive at the river they still need to escape the clutches of hungry crocodiles hiding in the shallows waiting on an early breakfast. Thankfully, the crocodiles didn't fare well that morning, unlike our group, who, after returning to earth with a painful thud, sat at tables decked with the finest cutlery and crockery to enjoy a champagne breakfast safe within the ring of protection of wonderful warriors. What a day!

'After a glorious three-week stay and countless encounters our safari came to an end, but our African adventure wasn't over, not by a long way. We took to the skies again but this time on a Kenya Airways flight bound for the exotic island of Zanzibar for a week of rest and recuperation. For me that meant lying on a sunbed, book in hand, sipping cocktails. That had been the intention, but it won't be the first time things don't turn out quite the way I predicted. The ninety-minute flight took us through the skies above Tanzania where I was lucky to be seated on the side of the plane offering spectacular views of Mount Kilimanjaro, the highest mountain in Africa. The holiday had already offered a feast of mouth-watering sights and I had no idea that in two days' time my life would change forever.

'I'd heard of Zanzibar, Africa's tropical paradise, but had no idea where it was or indeed anything about it other than it was the birth place of Freddie Mercury, one of the most talented singers to have ever lived and lead singer in British rock band Queen. This mystical island lies in the Indian Ocean some twenty miles off the coast of Tanzania, East Africa. Zanzibar, home to white beaches, shimmering turquoise waters, bustling streets and bazaars, spiced scents infusing everything they touch. The place conjures the magical and the mysterious. The colonial architecture of buildings protected by strong ornately carved doors in Stone Town, the old part of Zanzibar City, reminds us of a troubled past. Houses overlooking narrow streets summon spirits of the people who lived or travelled to trade here at the beginning of the eighteenth century. Wandering through intricate alleyways, sipping cocktails in a rooftop bar, and watching the sun fall from the sky was magical. Yes, I loved this tiny, yet intriguing city but it wasn't those characteristics that would change my life forever.

'Ocean Sunset, our beachfront hotel, was the perfect paradise. Eating breakfast outside under the African sunshine is enchanting, the smell of coffee, birdsong filtering the air, crusty bread still warm from the oven and eggs cooked the way you like, what's not to like? Plans for the day were agreed at breakfast. Day one and the six of us chose to explore Stone Town. Day two and we each wanted to do our own thing. Richard, Susie, Andy, and Anne wanted to stroll along the beach and explore local shops and markets, I couldn't think of anything worse so opted for a sunbed by the pool. Beth needed to attack an urgent email and would then join me by the pool fancying a swim. Finishing my fourth chapter and second cocktail, I noticed Beth disappearing inside a small, thatched building on the beach, reappearing twenty minutes later she headed my way. Apologising she announced she wouldn't be joining me after all, she'd opted to go scuba diving. I was shocked and couldn't hide my surprise. Beth had taken to the sport when she was twenty. The irony wasn't lost on me, we are the same age so when I was vowing never to venture into the sea again, she was learning to dive in it! She chatted for a while and although I heard every word, I couldn't take it in, my brain too consumed with visions of her under the water surrounded by sharks. I did hear her parting shot loud and clear, she asked if I wanted to join her and try a dive! I nearly choked on my margarita! She was left in no doubt, the idea was preposterous! We laughed, she wandered back to the dive centre, and I returned to the pages of my thriller. Thirty minutes later a group of six divers, including Beth, stepped out onto the beach all dressed in wetsuits cut to the knee, black booties and carrying their mask and fins. Wetsuits are made from neoprene, a synthetic rubber with bubbles of nitrogen trapped within the material which helps to keep you warm under the water, it can get cold down there. The group wandered down to the sea to board one of the wooden speedboats swaying in the shallows. Dive shop staff trudged back and forth carrying heavy scuba tanks to heave on board. The silver-coloured cylinders sparkled in the sunlight. I watched the boat cut through the water and speed out of the bay. I remember thinking how crazy they were to put themselves in harm's way, to go into the sea where sharks are, at best foolhardy, at worst deadly. Why would anyone stare death in the face or have it creep up behind them or rocket up from below! Thinking of it made me shiver. It took a while, but I eventually returned to drown myself in the dog-eared pages of my book and enjoy the solitude.

'Eating lunch by the pool watching a constant stream of boats whizzing in and out of the bay my attention was drawn to a slender twenty-something girl heading towards the pool, she was weighed down, a holdall hung over her shoulder, and she was carrying a scuba tank in each hand. Struggling, she awkwardly sidestepped between the sunbeds of glistening sun-worshippers, passing by close enough for me to see pearls of sweat running down her forehead and dripping into the corners of piercing blue eyes. She cut a striking figure, long blonde hair cascaded down to the small of her back, a red swimming costume and wetsuit pulled up waist high, the heat making it too hot to zip up fully. Undeterred and unable to stem the flow or wipe away the painful pools of salty tears those last few steps were made through gritted teeth. Squinting with a steely determination, she planted the tanks down on the tiles by the pool and wiped her brow with the back of her hand. Grabbing a towel from her bag she held it over her eyes until the pain subsided. She appeared to be waiting for someone and it became clear that she was preparing to teach a student in the pool, something I considered rather strange at the time. Her student arrived almost immediately, an elderly gentleman, who shook her hand and proceeded to fiddle nervously with the cord on his faded swim shorts, the original navy all but washed away in the decades since he splashed out on them. He was unsteady on his feet, apprehensive to be sure and didn't look in any way ready to take to the water, never mind in scuba gear! He wobbled as if he were going to fall so they moved to sit at a table where they proceeded to peruse a book. Remarkably he seemed in good spirits.

'Within the hour they'd slipped into their dive gear, and she'd helped him to manoeuvre to the shallow end and down the steps into the water, his movements clumsy and awkward, hampered by the tank on his back. The woman demonstrated skills which the man repeated. Initially he struggled to submerge but with the girl at his side and plenty of coaxing he eventually succeeded and before long began moving comfortably under the water. Occasionally the pair would ascend for a quick chat then sink back down. It was whilst I was watching them that things began to crystallise for me. It made sense to try a dive in the confines of a pool, skills can be taught and practised and in the event of a problem, getting out would be relatively easy. I hated to admit it, but it looked like fun. During the afternoon divers began returning to the resort to congregate and celebrate in the bar. I attributed their high spirits to them having had one too many at the joy of having survived the dive but eavesdropping revealed a different story. The excited exchanges were over photos and videos they'd captured on underwater cameras. This got me thinking. Somewhere in the region of forty divers went into the ocean that day and all made it out unharmed. None were attacked or eaten by a shark. Sharks were not the threat I'd considered them to be. How wrong I'd been and how many years I'd wasted crippled by my seemingly irrational fear.

'Divers study, take exams, train, and adhere to safe practices ensuring the vast majority dive a lifetime without encountering a life-threatening incident. I took a long hard look at myself that afternoon and became angry at what I saw. I'd allowed fear to take control of me. I decided it had to change and it was up to me to change it. I needed to find the strength to be strong! The same applies to you Charlie. Your parents, brothers, teachers and friends can support you but ultimately it's up to you.'

This feels like an appropriate moment to pause. I wait for him to say something, anything. The silence reaches that awkward stage, but he says nothing. 'Do you have good teachers Charlie? Can you talk to them?' He shrugs. Those young shoulders are carrying one heck of a burden. 'Charlie, as an adult I'm fairly confident, not a person prone to nerves or anxiety but when I was your age I had my own struggles, specifically fearful of the three d's, the dark, dogs and the dentist! Dentists genuinely scared me back then but look how that turned out! You see, I changed and if I can, you can. In truth, everyone is scared of something although admitting it proves more difficult for some. Being scared starts somewhere and both of us can pinpoint the precise moment our fear of sharks began. Knowing how it started is a good start!

'An ill-fitting door on the wardrobe in my bedroom held the key for my fear of the dark. My father attempted to repair it, but his carpentry skills were as faulty as the door itself! It never shut snugly after he mended it, meddled with it more like! The dark inside that wardrobe became increasingly threatening to me. I imagined all sorts living in there! Before settling down each night I had to jump out of bed many times to open and close that door, checking it was uninhabited and safe for me to give in to sleep. It was always empty of course but I still slept with a lamp on, still do on occasion.

'Dogs are now my friends but when you're five years old and your neighbour's six German shepherds vault over the hedge at the bottom of your garden and race at you full pelt, it's enough to terrify anyone, especially a little one. That ended well, a call from Mrs Rainford, their owner and they hurdled over me and jumped back. On another occasion I was delivering a jar of homemade gooseberry jam to Mrs Rainford on an errand for my mother. Walking down the path I could already hear the dogs barking inside. Who lets six dogs that size loose in a mid-terrace! A dog lover that's who! The front door was open but the glass door to the hall was shut.

Stepping into that porch to knock the door took courage. One of the dogs bounded down the hall to investigate and proceeded to launch himself through the glass. Standing there I was rooted to the spot in terror waiting for the blighter to bite. Luckily for me the explosion of shattering shards stopped him dead in his tracks and he skulked off tail between his legs. Mrs Rainford's dogs poured misery on an impressionable young girl which took ages to shake off! Needless to say, I never knocked on that door again.

'My first dental appointment got off to the wrong start when I spied a silver platter loaded with sharp instruments. The dentist made no attempt at small talk, plopped me in the chair and proceeded to stuff the tools of his trade into my mouth without putting me at my ease or explaining anything. Both he and the experience were horrid in equal measure, and he was rough to boot! It didn't help that he gave me gas at almost every appointment. I lost count of the number of times I vomited in my dad's Morris Minor on the way home! It was only after moving house and registering with a dentist that cared that my nerves improved. He replaced fear with trust. He was kind with soft, considerate hands.'

'It's funny you were scared of the dentist and then you were one. Same thing happened with sharks didn't it? You were scared of them and now you're sad you can't be with them. It's kinda the same isn't it?'

'Yes, you are correct which should tell you something...' I leave a poignant pause then add, 'Things can change! A handful of childhood incidents affected me, upset me, it's true but time is a glorious healer. Life changes as you grow. You have to know that you will change, in unknown ways but change you will. You can master your fears and not be ruled by them.' His expression was of someone deep in thought. I would love to know what's on his mind. It takes a while.

'What happened to Beth, did she come back safe?'

'Of course she did Charlie, and we sat together enjoying a beer while she extolled the virtues of diving in Zanzibar. I took the opportunity to confide how I felt about the whole "swimming in the sea thing" and my fear of sharks. She revealed that when she and Andy had first become acquainted he'd enjoyed diving but had lost the love. He blamed the loss of enthusiasm on his ears and not being able to equalise the pressure on the way down, which can be incredibly painful. Truth be known, he'd been harbouring a growing anxiety of deep water. I can't remember if it was what she said, how she said it or the amount of alcohol I'd imbibed but by the time we'd drunk our third beer I'd agreed to sign up for a dive in the pool the next morning and if that went well a dive in the ocean later that afternoon! I continue to be surprised at the decision I made that day, goodness knows how I plucked up the courage, but I did, didn't sleep much as a result though. Sharks swam in my dreams and spiralled into nightmares, dreams that began on that Greek island all those years ago! Since that day in Lindos, I'd find myself waking in the early hours feeling anxious, forehead sweating, palms clammy and heart pounding so hard it hurt. Over the years those dreams would strike without warning and were always the same, me drowning out on the high seas, chased into the darkest depths by a monster shark. The beast, closing in, mouth open revealing rows of flesh-tearing teeth intent on sinking into my thighs and taking my legs. The end of the dream and I'm miraculously saved and flop onto a deserted beach exhausted.

'That next morning, I was tired and convinced myself I wasn't doing the dives and disclosed my reservations to Anne over breakfast. She listened sympathetically but encouraged me to persevere. Her final words I'll never forget, 'You've been scared for more than half your life Jane, give yourself a break!' That did the trick! I decided to give the pool dive a go fully intending to back out of the ocean dive later without losing face; at least I could say I'd tried. The pool dive went better than expected. It was strangely comforting to be instructed by Hanna, the twenty-two-year-old Swede I'd observed teaching the previous afternoon. The scuba gear was heavier than I expected, movements above the water proved clumsy but underwater it was surprisingly comfortable. I loved being able to breathe underwater and that feeling of weightlessness was wonderful. That's when an extraordinary thing happened, one moment I was in the pool, the next boarding a boat full of divers and zipping out of the bay. I can offer no explanation other than being caught up in the moment. Hanna would be my guide, thank goodness, my life was in her hands, and I trusted her, I needed to. Hanna briefed me about what to expect, it was all a bit of a blur to be honest but the bit I did hear was the sea creatures to be wary of. Time was speeding too fast as we crossed those waters. Hanna's attempts at reassurance fell on deaf ears but her promise to stay by my side was encouraging. She taught me a couple of hand signals to help us communicate in the silent underwater world. She never mentioned sharks, neither did Beth so I didn't either but that didn't stop them swimming away in the recesses of my mind. Twenty minutes later and we were at the dive site, out in the open ocean, literally in the middle of nowhere. Final checks were made, and Beth's group rolled backwards over the side of the boat and into the water. They remained bobbing on the surface until their instructor gave the signal to descend, a thumb down, reminiscent of Caesar revealing the fate of a gladiator to a crowded amphitheatre in ancient Rome. Eerily they sank and disappeared beneath the waves. It was quiet. The captain, Hanna, and I were alone on the boat then it was my turn. The sun shone over the water making sparkles dance. It looked so inviting yet in my mind under the light was the dark, the deep and the danger. Fear began to take hold, my mouth was dry, my heart racing, and telltale knots grumbled in the pit of my stomach. The heat was intense. How I found the strength to stand up on the rocking boat in the gear, shuffle to the stern and make it down the ladder without falling beats me. Movements have to be slow and deliberate. Strange but it was with some relief that I entered those cooling waters. Once the reality of where I was hit, relief ebbed away almost as fast as it had arrived. My breathing was erratic, too fast. Hanna bobbed in front of me, her icy stare so strong I swear it pierced my soul. My doubts were no match for her strength and resolve. She told me to calm down and breathe slowly but I continued gulping air and hadn't even put the regulator in my mouth, continuing to breathe like that and the air in my tank wouldn't last long. The anxiety was overwhelming, I was on sensory overload. Hanna didn't pull any punches, unless I relaxed, I wasn't going down. I'd come so far and the thought of not going was worse than going! I couldn't bear the thought of having to tell Beth I'd bottled out at the last minute. I had a strong word with myself, squeezed every ounce of strength I could muster and managed to calm down enough to regulate my breathing. I was as ready as I'd ever be! We signalled okay, a circle made with thumb and index finger and that was it!

'Hanna pressed a switch on my dive jacket, my "Buoyancy Control Device" (BCD), and the air began hissing out and we started to sink beneath the waves. A BCD contains an air bladder, dump valves, inflator hose, weight pockets and deflator button. It was completely alien to me, but Hanna had positioned herself in front of me and took charge of the pressing of buttons and the tightening of straps. She was the key; without her I doubt it would have been possible. We went down feet first. The worst part was when my eyes were at sea level affording me my last glimpse of the sky and I had to make that move to go under. I couldn't trust that I'd be able to breathe, so held my breath for fear the sea would rush in and flood my lungs. Hanna prevented my tentative bolt for the surface with a few reassuring nods, holding my arm and by staring into my eyes. Instinct kicked in and my body took a panicked gulp of air instantly filling my lungs, such a beautiful puff of life. Divers breathe through a regulator in the mouth, something I'd never given any thought to, yet in that moment I could think of nothing else. I wanted to get out, what on earth was I doing and BANG, that's when it happened.

'My eyes opened on another world, what I was seeing had all the appearance of another planet. Goosebumps ran over my body causing me to shiver. The water around me was a crystal-clear turquoise blue, the bluest water I'd ever seen, which still holds now. For the first time in my life, I was seeing with an absolute clarity. I was floating, breathing, and moving in a water wonderland of gorgeousness, an underwater heaven. Five metres below me the white sandy floor was dotted with coral reefs and fish of every size, shape, and colour you can imagine. I was in my very own aquarium, immersed in a kaleidoscope of colours and mosaic of habitats. I literally could not believe what my eyes were seeing. Hanna signalled okay, I nodded but wanted to scream, "This is amazing!" Okay! This was not okay. Okay implies mediocre, satisfactory, or not bad. This experience was so much more. Hanna pointed out an unusual fish, red and white with tentacles and feather-like spines. She'd mentioned this particular species at the briefing, a lionfish, showing me her clenched fist told me it was dangerous and not to touch it. She didn't need to tell me twice, it was poisonous. She'd made it abundantly clear; divers shouldn't touch anything of the underwater world, we are there as observers, nothing more. The reality of where I was kicked in, nervously I reached for her hand. She held it and gave a couple of gentle reassuring squeezes. Simple acts of kindness during stressful times can make a massive difference. I felt more alive during that forty-minute dive than ever before. It's hard to put into words Charlie but everything was new to me, I'd never seen or experienced anything like it before. I was seeing the world, this underwater world, through different eyes, as if I were seeing it with my heart which doesn't really make sense but it's true. It touched me and moved me in seismic proportions and once seen and touched you can't un-see or un-feel it. The world completely changed for me in that moment. The world I'd known all my life had a whole other world around it, under it and I was in it, bathing in it, discovering it and sharing it for the very first time. Electric tingles ran through my body, and they are here now as I speak with you about it. For the first time in my life, I truly understood the meaning of awe and wonder. Diving, who knew, I was well and truly hooked.'

I stop to hold his gaze. 'Charlie, since Zanzibar I've made over a thousand dives in countries around the world but that one, my first one, I'll never forget. It changed everything; it changed my life.' Waiting for that to sink in I round off my tale with a cheery, 'Oh and a shark never got me!' I'm beaming, I can't help it, recollecting the experiences of my African adventure makes me incredibly happy and proud. Charlie stares at me, his eyes as wide as saucers, speechless and lost in a thoughtful silence and now a smile starts creeping over his face and if I'm not mistaken there's a newly found twinkle in his eyes.

'But if a shark had been there then it would have got you. You were just lucky.'

Cheeky but this boy is going to take more convincing!

SANDALS, SOCKS AND SUNBURNT SHINS

'Charlie, Charlie, snack time, come on.'

Mam's snacks normally involve chocolate. She forgot to shout me over once, it didn't go down well. I sulked for ages and made her feel right guilty. She felt so bad she gets me over for snacks and I get first goes! 'I've got to go. We're having snacks. I'll put my stuff away and I'll see you in a bit. Ta-ra.' I hope she's still here when I get back, I want her to tell me about the first time she saw a shark.

'Charlie come on, hurry up, they're melting.'

Yeah we're having chocolate. Takes a second to chuck the stuff in my satchel and I'm off to the beach. 'I liked your story. Thanks. Might see you later. Won't be long. See ya, bye.' The stupid pebbles of doom kill my feet. Can't wait to get on the sand. My feet will be happy too! A few more steps and yes, I've made it. The souls of my feet are safe. It's warm and I'm gagging for a drink. I race full pelt across the beach to our camp. Mam's put a towel down for me. She always does. Dad's putting the windbreak up. He puts one up even when there's no wind. He has to. There's no wind today. Well, a bit of a breeze but it doesn't matter he still has to put it up and it's his fault. Sand gets everywhere. It doesn't matter what you eat the grit gets in your teeth. Dad told us it takes millions of years for rocks, shells, and coral to break down into sand. He told us about the secret ingredient in sand. Thought he was being really clever, Sheffield's answer to Steve Backshall! Parrotfish bite coral. They crunch and grind it with their massive teeth. Teeth that look like a parrot's beak. They swallow the coral, not for food, it's the algae on the coral they want. The coral goes in, and they poo it out as sand. When us boys get sand in our mouth we can't spit it out quickly enough. Parrotfish poo, yuk! Dad regrets telling us about parrotfish. Us boys won't eat a thing on the beach unless the windbreak's up. That'll teach him! I kneel down and grab a rice crispy cake and my shark drinking bottle. Running in the sun makes me thirsty. I can hear the water going down my throat, bit like the elephant on Jane's safari. When I drink from this bottle it will be one more thing that reminds me of the aquarium incident. They think they're hilarious. My folks have this thing about buying me stuff with sharks on. I'm now the not-so-proud owner of shark pjs, slippers, T-shirts, a blue cap with teeth down the side and my new water bottle, it was a present yesterday. They watch me opening them and when I get to the shark present they both have this stupid grin, so I know it's the shark one before I rip the paper off! We snack and play with my cricket set, another present from yesterday. We take it in turns to bat and field. Pepper's always in the field, she's best at it. She runs to fetch the ball every time I whack it for six, something I do loads. Then we had a picnic. I love this time with the family, even with me dad. Playing on the beach and eating outside in the sunshine is great. After lunch me dad will go in the sea. He will shout for us to join him. There you go, he's up and off with Eric's ball shouting for us to play water polo. Harry and Eric are off to join him. I'm not. I'm staying put. I want to go with them. I want to so bad but can't. I'm not going in the sea. I look at me mam. She's staring at them. She's not taking her eyes off them, especially Eric. He's running along the sand at the edge of the sea. I look at her face, she is smiling. She loves them so much. I can't remember her looking at me like that, suppose she must have. Now I feel down. I'm going back. I make an excuse from my list of excuses and I'm off.

Jane's lying down. She looks like she's dozed off. I wanted to talk to her, to ask her to tell me about the first shark but I better not wake her up. I'll go and sit on my stone and check out the pool. Mam tells us it's the simple things in life we should care about. I think being here is what she means. I love it. Loved being in the sea more but there's nothing I can do about that. Boom, my feet go straight in the water. I start searching for crabs. All of a sudden Jane's standing next to me. Bloomin' heck, she nearly gave me a heart attack.

'Hi, mind if I join you. You like it here don't you, on the rocks I mean?'

'Yeah.' My stone seat is big enough for two or three, so I budge along a bit, and she sits down. She puts her feet in the water next to mine. I look at her but she's not looking at me. She's staring at them. Eric's taking it in turns to jump in and out of the water and Harry and me dad are diving through the waves. Harry's getting better at that, not as good as me but at this rate he soon will be. I don't want him to get better than me. It makes me angry. I don't get it, but it makes me sad at the same time. I'm up and down, up, and down. I'm fed up with it.

'You loved being in the sea didn't you?'

'Yeah.' I know it's a bit rude but what a stupid question. Think I was a bit blunt, but it makes me mad. I loved being in the sea, who doesn't? Why do adults ask such stupid questions? Kids love the sea. I'm not going to say anything now.

Snappy little fellow! He's changed his tune since returning from the beach. Children are such moody beings. Oh well, I'll say my goodbyes and return to my kindle. 'Okay Charlie I'll leave you to it. Have fun.' He pulls his legs out of the pool, crosses his arms over his reddening shins and rests his chin on top of his knees. 'I think you'd prefer me to leave you alone wouldn't you Charlie, hey?' The boy's eyes tentatively emerge from behind the fringe where they've been carefully concealed these past few minutes. Our eyes meet and he's quick to dip his head back down, the peak of his cap cleverly screening his face from the world. Gently rocking his slumped body, he speaks in hushed tones revealing an inner turmoil.

'Look. Look at them. Dad and Harry. I did that. It was fun. That used to be me, and I was better than Harry. Me and me dad used to have dive competitions and I'd win most of the time. Don't think he's even bothered we don't do it anymore. I was a great swimmer too. I'll never do it again. Stupid sharks!'

He'd barely spat the words out before bursting into tears and burying his head between his knees. I edge closer, the cold stone under my thighs causes me to shiver, caught in the quandary of what to do, hug him, find the right words, or do and say nothing and let the moment drift? I opt to try and find the right words. 'If you loved it once then you will again. Believe it and it will be. Do you want to Charlie? Mmm? Do you? Your family look like they're having fun together. Or are you resigned to your fate, to remain over here on your own? You don't have to answer me Charlie, only you truly know, and you have to ask yourself the question. If you prefer spending your holiday over here then come clean with your family and stop worrying about it but if you don't and the sea is a magnet pulling at you then you need to find the courage to address the issue. Burying your head in the proverbial sand won't help.' After an awkward silence I answer for him. 'You're longing to go in the sea aren't you? The answer lies within you waiting to be discovered, I'm not saying I can help you or know what you should do but if you want to then you'll find a way. Have you considered telling your parents?' Mention of his parents elicits a reaction, voice faltering, chin quivering, he whispers.

'Mmmm I do but it's impossible. It's too hard. I'm too scared. I don't want to talk about it anymore. Sorry.'

He chooses to change the subject, this time speaking with more confidence.

'What was it like when you saw a shark the first time? Did you see it coming? Were you scared?'

Mention of my first shark takes me back to Spain and that incredible day, shark number one, how could I ever forget it? I honestly thought I was a goner and would be singing alongside angels in a heavenly choir rather than swimming with one! My angel! Might not be prudent to tell him that! Twirling my toes in the pool, he follows suit and soon our feet create a whirling vortex in the water. Staring into the whirlpool, I'm reminded of the moment my life swirled full circle and turned in unexpected and powerful ways.

'It was amazing Charlie, my first shark encounter was in the cool waters of the Atlantic Ocean, 321km (200 miles), off the west coast of Africa, in Tenerife, the largest of Spain's Canary Islands. Two million British holidaymakers travel to Tenerife every year and a further 45,000, drawn by year-round sunshine, choose to make the island their home. The waters that wash up along the shores are teeming with the usual suspects, fish, rays, and turtles and the more unusual, dolphins and pilot whales. Beth relished sharing her diving exploits when we were in Zanzibar and how she'd learnt to dive in Tenerife. She fell in love with the place not long after falling in love with Andy. A year after becoming acquainted they'd made an impulsive decision to buy a holiday home there, settling for an apartment in Las Chafiras in the sunnier south, a quiet village in the foothills of Mount Teide. Andy hated British winters, Beth adored the sun and with only a four-hour flight from home, Tenerife was the logical choice. Their dream apartment, an attractive seven-minute drive from Reina Sofia Airport benefited from an outdoor pool, tapas restaurant, and lively bar. Best of all though was that it was off the beaten tourist track. Andy proposed to her there which only served to cement the island in their hearts for romantic getaways. Beth waxed lyrical about the beaches, the food, and the diving. Do you know anything about Tenerife, Charlie?'

'No but I've heard of it. My mate Seb's been there and told me he went to the top of a volcano in a cable car. He said the landscape around the volcano is like Mars, red rocks everywhere!'

'Your friend's not wrong. At 3718m, Mount Teide is Spain's highest peak, one of the largest volcanoes in the world and a UNESCO World Heritage Site. The surrounding terrain comprises landscapes the likes I've never seen before. Under the sea or up a mountain, this planet can continue to surprise us.

'We hadn't even arrived home from Zanzibar, and I'd accepted the invitation to join the pair of them in Tenerife a couple of months later with the sole purpose of learning to dive! My intention was to complete a beginner's course but if things didn't go well then what could be better than basking on a beach under a Spanish sun. Beth suggested that purchasing the handbook, *Open Water Diver*, by Drew Richardson, would help me, a text which comprehensively outlines dive procedures and skills. By the time November came round, I'd devoured every word. The nerves had well and truly kicked in and I had contemplated cancelling the trip a dozen times but am thrilled I didn't. It's far too easy to back out of things when you're nervous. If you can find a way to dig deep and accomplish something you find challenging, there's no greater feeling.

'The plane's wheels whisked us off before breakfast leaving behind a rain-soaked runway and lifting us up, up and away. Soaring across the skies we left home in an insufferable ten degrees Celsius and touched down, in time for lunch, in a simmering twenty-three. We spent the first four days relaxing on sun-drenched beaches, eating in the plethora of fish and tapas restaurants, drinking sangria by the jug, exploring quaint fishing villages, and browsing in local markets. Day five was dive day. I was as ready as I'd ever be, hadn't slept well which is hardly surprising hey? After an early breakfast we chose to tackle the longer route to Los Cristianos, driving along the dusty coast road, anything to delay the inevitable. Covered banana plantations line the roadside, canopies protecting Tenerife's main crop from the wind and sun and increasing humidity for these treasured plants on this parched Spanish island. Weaving in and out of picturesque bays for those eight miles did the trick, distracting me from the impending plunge but only until we pulled up at the dive centre. Luckily, my instructor Andres greeted us, and his bubbly personality instantly put me at ease. Skills were taught in the pool, and we chatted through questions. Being thoroughly prepared helped and gave me a new-found feeling of positivity. Sensing my anxieties, he emphasised the need to stay calm, to breathe slowly, to prepare methodically and to take my time. Diving and rushing about do not go together. The same rules apply in the water, finning slowly and avoiding erratic movements is the way to go. Doing this successfully and I'd conserve the air in my tank, be respectful to the underwater environment, have fun and stay safe. As a dentist, doing things slowly is something I could equate to. Rushing about when working in the mouth was never advisable, navigating into tiny holes and crevices with dental instruments is time-consuming if the work is to be done well. Slow but sure wins the race, as my clinical lecturer used to say. Slow was the way to go, I could handle that. Andres compared sucking the air from my tank to sipping the best of Spanish Rioja wines, something to be savoured, gulping and it's gone too soon. As a wine lover this analogy made perfect sense to me. Andres made no mention of sharks, neither did I but they were inevitably in my mind. He ran through the basic hand signals and taught me a couple of new ones. Divers the world over tend to use the same twenty or so signals although I've yet to meet a dive guide who didn't invent their own. Can be quite entertaining trying to work out what you're being told 30m below the waves. I've often thought how wonderful a universal sign language would be, allowing people of different nationalities to communicate from the get-go, what a marvellous aid to world peace that could be! That there isn't one suggests it's too difficult or impossible in a world where languages have their own quirks, regional variations, and cultural relevance. In Iceland, for example, there are forty-six words to describe snow. Even comparing countries with similar languages such as England and America, words can be misunderstood. Americans say chips we say crisps, they say elevator we say lift. Imagine the confusion when an American friend of mine went into a department store and asked a young female assistant to help him find pants. She proceeded to bring out an array of underpants in every size, shape and colour causing much embarrassment all round as all he'd wanted was trousers!

'Andres sketched the dive site on a whiteboard taking time to indicate the route we'd be taking, the depth and the sea life we could expect to see. As with any good briefing, I knew what to expect. Again, there was no mention of sharks. The kit was loaded into his rusty Citroen Berlingo, and we shot off a little further down the coast. The rocky landscape and stunning beaches were not enough to take my mind off the dive, the sea flashing by my window looking cold and uninviting. Nerves were tightening their grip; fear was taking hold. I could feel tension building in my neck muscles. Fifteen minutes later and Andres parked the van on the roadside next to a busy beach. We slipped into our wetsuits, BCD, and booties on the pavement at the back of the van, in full view of hundreds of sun-worshippers. I was relieved I'd put my costume on at home I can tell you! What a sight we must have made, waddling down the beach in full dive gear complete with scuba tank, carrying mask and fins, all under the glare of a watchful audience and a hot Spanish sun. Hilarious apparently, the throng of sunbathers broke out into fits of laughter, and we received a round of applause as we made it to the sea. Bobbing in the shallows we donned our mask and fins and were ready. There was a certain irony in that lot laughing at us and being oblivious to how utterly ridiculous they looked, overweight bodies squeezed into undersized swimming costumes, many sporting sandals and socks! A knotted handkerchief and the look would have been complete! The sports bars along the promenade were brimming with drinkers clad in football shirts singing rival chants. It's easy to spot the Brits abroad! Compared to them I didn't think we looked too bad!

'Andres taught me how to let air in and out of my BCD in the pool, inflating and deflating enables you to float and sink. I'd mastered the technique with relative ease but in the sea it took me ten minutes to pluck up the courage to deflate and sink beneath the waves. The assembled throng patiently waited to wave me off and we slowly disappeared under the water. I was genuinely hoping it wouldn't be the last I saw of them, however ridiculous I couldn't wait to see them again!

'Associating sharks with the deeper open ocean, I was relieved to know we intended diving no deeper than 6m. Andres led the way whilst Beth stayed at my side for moral support. Divers plan the dive and dive the plan. With no danger of bumping into a shark I managed to relax and enjoy my surroundings. The water glistened a warm blue on the surface, below it became a cold grey. My face was bitterly cold, the rest of my body enveloped in neoprene, surprisingly warm. Visibility, although crystal clear, revealed an underwater landscape devoid of corals and colour, certainly nothing as vibrant as the underwater world of Zanzibar. Cuboids of sizeable grey stone littered the seabed, the darkness of the sand added to make this a stark environment. Rather than swimming in a rich soup of sea life we were in a consommé of grey.

Everything was going to plan until Andres suddenly stopped. He changed direction slightly then hesitated. Turning to us he raised his hand showing us his palm, the signal to stop, followed by a thumb down telling us to descend a little deeper. Eleven metres down and he signalled for us to stop. Beth took hold of my arm in an attempt to reassure me. She'd made a good decision; my breathing had started to race. This hadn't been discussed during the briefing and I was feeling nervous but more nervously excited than scared. I tried to stay calm and as strange as it sounds I felt safe. Andres signalled for us to look at him, pointing his index and third finger towards his eyes then at his chest. He swam a short distance away and hung motionless just above the sandy floor next to a mound of sand. We watched and waited, for what I had no clue. Seconds later and slowly but surely the soft grains of sand gently cascaded to the floor to reveal my first shark! This was not how I thought a shark would present itself to me. A shark, 2m in length, gracefully lifted off the seabed, turned and slowly swam towards me. Had the regulator not been in my mouth I would have been doing a fish impression, open mouthed in shock. Time seemed to stand still. The shark continued in my direction moving effortlessly through the water. For a split second a scene from one of my nightmares flickered through my mind but I cut it short, there was already enough to be concentrating on. The shark was closing in, the metres ticked down five, four, three, two, one then it was level with me. I couldn't move. This majestic specimen slipped by without making a sound affording me a good look into those dark eyes before it disappeared down into the depths. Phew! Hovering there motionless in the water I was aware of how special that encounter had been, it was exhilarating leaving me quite overwhelmed. Andres told me later that it was an angel shark, also named sand devil. Whoever it was that named this species seemed to be in a quandary of biblical proportions, angel versus devil, good versus evil. For me it was simply beautiful, flat and grey with long side fins and eyes on the top of his head. It was a privilege to be in the company of such greatness. The fish wanted nothing more than to swim away. The last thing on that shark's mind was attacking me.

It had been hiding under the sand, eyes poking out, lying in wait to ambush an unsuspecting fish. It was not there for me, no, not to attack or eat me.'

'So, when the shark was coming at you, it was scary then not scary?'

He's fixated on the fear factor. 'Yes maybe initially a little scary but I was witnessing something extraordinary, a powerful fish moving with such ease through the water. You have to believe me Charlie it wasn't interested in me at all, not one juicy bit!'

'But when it swam out of sight were you worried it would come back and like sneak up behind you?'

'No, I stared after it desperately searching the darkness willing it to swim back wanting to see it one more time. It touched me, made my heart sing and once again I felt changed, a feeling washed through my body similar to when you are enthralled by an emotional piece of theatre, music, or film. Goosebumps run over your body, you cry and more than that, a spiritual awakening touches you. In that moment I felt alone with the shark, tearful and completely connected with the natural world and a fish I'd feared for decades. I've loved people and animals for as long as I can remember but when the shark entered my heart it was a love like never before. I'd found a peace I never knew existed. The rest of the dive went by in a blur, I do remember Andres showing me a seahorse, imagine that a huge powerful fish swims by then a tiny delicate one, and yes, a seahorse is a fish even though it looks more like a dragon! This lunar landscape taught me that looks can be deceiving and to see properly you have to look beyond.'

'But you must have been nervous the shark might come back. Come back for you. Weren't you?'

His tone suggests a growing frustration with my responses, he asks questions, hears what I'm saying but isn't listening to my answers, not my fault, the truth is the truth. 'No. Sorry Charlie but no. My senses were saturated trying to make sense of the alien underwater landscape there simply wasn't any room left in my mind for fear. It was exciting. I wanted that dive to last forever and kept telling myself to sip not gulp! By the end of the holiday, I'd mastered my breathing and buoyancy, no bashing into reefs by yours truly. The icing on the cake? I passed the course with flying colours; I was a diver. Boarding the plane home I'd completed nine dives, explored the underwater world of Tenerife, and ignited a passion that still burns today. Fancy that, I was a certified diver, something no one saw coming, especially me!'

I'd reached the end of my tale, my first shark. Charlie stares into his pool, his circling feet causing ripples in otherwise still waters. The pond into which his thoughts were plunging appeared devoid of life, anything trapped in there had long since disappeared into the haven of a nook or cranny to escape the whirlpool of tormenting toes. He says nothing. When he speaks, he chooses to change the subject.

PASSPORT TO FREEDOM

'I like writing. I write when I'm here. I write songs and poems. When I get home I add the music then me and my mates play them. I play the guitar and sing lead vocals. Mam tells everyone how talented I am. She's embarrassing but probably right! My songs start from things I do, places I visit and things I see or hear. I write my best stuff here.'

He pauses, the twinkle in his eyes has dimmed, seemingly losing their sparkle. Diving into his bag he pulls out a notepad and starts rifling through the pages. Peeking over his shoulder I see writing, drawings of fish, crabs, birds, and half-finished sketches. They're good. 'You have skills Charlie; you're a talented young man. Do you know what you want to do when you leave school?'

'No, not yet, maybe I'll be a rock star! I like English, maths, history, and art. I used to like music but can't stand my music teacher. All Ms Scott wants me to do is play music other people have written. Dad plays the guitar. He's in a band with some of his mates. They play in a few of our locals. Dad taught me to play ages ago. My songs are better than some of the noise our teacher makes us suffer!'

'A rock star, wow, would be one heck of a life but why not, others will, so why shouldn't you?' Ed, my seventeen-year-old nephew and his sister Lizzie, my thirteen-year-old niece are, without question, the most intelligent children on the planet. Any auntie will testify the same. It comes as a bit of a shock and a refreshing surprise to have a conversation with this young man speaking with a degree of eloquence and humour. The only other twelve-year-old I saw on any regular basis was Olivia Goldstein, my chewing gum queen. In the two years before retiring, she'd made numerous visits to the surgery for a prolonged course of treatment, a result of her insistence on chewing sugary gum and her parent's reluctance to stop her. On the most part the girl was monosyllabic, too busy chewing or lying open-mouthed in my dental chair, both make speaking a tad tricky! Children, particularly teenagers get a bad press but if Charlie's anything to go by and an example of the youth of today then the press are wrong, won't be the first time! 'Do you like school Charlie?'

'It's okay. I work hard most of the time. I've got some good mates. I don't like the homework, no one does do they, except the goody two shoes. If school isn't the place to relax and chill then home shouldn't be the place to do schoolwork! When I first got homework at secondary school I did it really well, but my standard slipped over time and by the end of the year I ended up scribbling it on bits of scrap paper ripped out of another school book just before the start of the lesson!'

He laughed; first time I'd seen him do that.

'Dr Wainwright was my science teacher last year and she made us take our workbook home after every lesson. Don't know why! Probably thought we'd read it when we tackled the homework. Fat chance! It was big and weighed a ton. What a waste of time schlepping it to and from school after every lesson and I kept forgetting to bring it back. She told me if I forgot it one more time I'd get detention. My table was right at the back of the class. Behind me was the equipment cupboard full of Bunsen burners and old revision guides. It was never locked so I hid my book in the back of that cupboard. I got away with it for five or six lessons. Every week she'd ask me, 'Mr Parker have you deigned to bring it this week?' Wainwright was good with the sarcasm. I pretended I wasn't sure. Thought I was being clever. Then one day the cupboard was locked and stayed locked for the next few lessons! I had to eventually ask her for a new book. A month later she marched up to me in the corridor and told me where she'd found my book. Smug she was. I said I'd no idea how it got in there, but something told me she was on to me! Shame science is compulsory. Can't wait to leave school and drop it.'

'You did well to escape punishment for that, in my day it would have been the cane or detention and I'm glad to say I never received either.' His story reignites a memory from my school days. 'Your mention of science reminds me of my teacher, Mrs Hanson, a chemistry graduate from Oxford University, undoubtedly clever but extremely unpopular to say the least. She was ineffective, unable to communicate with pupils with a lack of creativity in her teaching methods. She would preach to the blackboard whilst we laboriously copied her illegible scrawl. I often wondered if that really was the best she could do! She wasn't one of those inspirational teachers parents wished you had. Even the other teachers weren't fond of her! She was truly inept. In one particular lesson she attempted to demonstrate chemical change by mixing two liquids, no idea what they were or what the end result was supposed to be but the second the solutions came together, the plastic vending machine cup she'd used dissolved! It didn't stop there though, the solution hissed and started smoking then ate away at the surface of the desk! It was the lab technician who had to run in and save the day. Mrs Hanson lost the plot completely, started shouting and screaming at us until the technician escorted her from the room. It was nothing to do with any of us, but we got the brunt of her frustrations. In another lesson an incident occurred that saw her leaving the school for good, sad really but on the cards from the day she started. Clamps, beakers, pipettes, and Bunsen burners never saw the light of day, remaining forever locked in a cupboard confirming her complete lack of trust in our ability to perform even the most basic of experiments. Having said that, one pupil, Stuart McCabe, generally considered the most disruptive child in the school did manage to get his hands on a Bunsen burner and no one who witnessed him use it will ever forget it. He was naughty and incredibly intelligent, too clever by half and hated Mrs Hanson's lessons with a passion. He irritated her with his constant quips, and she irritated him with her constant put-downs. He once had the nerve to ask her what colour her hair had been before it turned "Brillo pad grey"! He sat outside the heads office for five days for that one, not that he was bothered! After serving his punishment he was allowed back into her lessons. On the very first one back he got his hands on her keys and secreted the Bunsen burner into his bag. He had a plan but waited until the board was awash of symbols, arrows, drawings, and notes. He surreptitiously rigged the burner hose to the tap in the sink at the back of the classroom, took aim and turned the tap on. Water shot out as if fired out of a jet wash, hitting the board with such force it erased everything and drenched Mrs Hanson and the children in the first three rows. Our bedraggled teacher screamed at us for ten minutes demanding that the culprit show themselves! She eventually managed to pin it on him. It was brilliant. I would never have had the courage to do such a thing. It takes guts to go against the grain. Anyway, that day went down in school folklore and people still talk about it to this day. They should have put his name on a plaque and stuck it on the lab wall for posterity.

'Listening to your antics with your homework and textbook, I'd say you're a risk-taker Charlie, channel that and you'll find the courage to fight your fear. Can you just give me a minute while I fetch my lunch from my bag?' Breakfast had been cut short, half a grapefruit and two coffees would normally be followed by toast, a bacon sandwich or fried egg, no wonder my stomach's letting me know it's time to eat! I'm looking forward to devouring my sandwich, flask of Darjeeling and packet of milk chocolate digestives. Settling back down I pour myself a cup of tea offering him the biscuits, no sooner open and he greedily tucks into a handful. If I'm not quick he'll devour the lot!

'Do you have school dinners or take a packed lunch?'

'School dinners! Not likely. School food is grim! Things are crispy when they're supposed to be soft and squidgy when they should be crunchy. Chips and beans are always cold in the middle, and I mean each individual chip or bean is cold. The dinner ladies, especially Mrs Dobson, hate their jobs, they must do, they're always grumpy. So no, I don't eat school dinners. The only school food I will eat is at break time when they sell boxes of cereal or packets of dried strawberries, they can't get that wrong!'

He's not wrong, school dinners have been grim since they came into being during the early part of the twentieth century. Some dinners I remember eating tasted as if they'd been cooked a hundred years ago! 'You have a way with words Charlie.'

'I like them. Mam says I've always been good with them. I like English. At school me and me mates change words, so the teachers won't have a clue what we are on about. We used to play "Bulldog", you know the game when the kids being bulldogs stand in the middle and the rest have to run from one side of the playground to the other without getting tagged and if you do get tagged then you're a bulldog too. The teachers banned it after complaints from namby-pamby parents who were upset their little precious was being chucked to the floor. It was only a game. So, we changed the name from "Bulldog" to "Tig 2", took the teachers ages to realise it was the same game and ban it again! We make up words too. Sometimes we talk in code to confuse them, things like, *hella dank*, *gorb*, and *lumby*, which mean, that's great, controversial, and sick. We've got loads more.'

'That's clever. Back in the day we enjoyed sneaking notes to each other under the desks! It was funny until the day my fifth-year maths teacher, the dreaded Mrs Harris, caught me and confiscated my jottings then for a reason only known to her, chose to read them to the class. She shouldn't have, I crushed her ability to teach algebra but then she crushed me. After she'd got the shouting and dressing-down out of her system, I stood in front of my classmates awaiting punishment, the offence was certainly worthy of detention or at worst a caning. Imagine my surprise to receive neither! Getting off the bus, I drifted through the estate as if floating on air, elated to have got away with my crime! The euphoria lasted precisely one second after setting foot into the kitchen. My mother greeted me with an icy stare and without saying a word gulped the entire contents of her sherry glass, placed it on the table, turned to me but said nothing. I stood there wishing she'd put me out of my misery, it was obvious she knew! Amontillado sherry, she was always sipping sherry when I got home from school. I wondered about that for years, why was she always sipping a sherry? I challenged her about it once and her answer still amuses me. 'Darling, I looked out of the window and could see the bus coming along the lane into the village and knew you'd be bounding through the door any minute so felt obliged to grab for the bottle!' When she finally broke the silence she sent me to my room. Horrible Harris had telephoned my mother and laid it on with a trowel. Waiting for my dad to arrive home from work was excruciating. Mr Serious gave me the usual spiel. 'What were you thinking young lady? Your grandfather was a headmaster! Your aunt taught maths for goodness sake! We come from a long line of educators. Your uncle still teaches chemistry! For goodness sake Jane, you should know better!' For the rest of the evening, I was confined to my room and forced to work on algebraic equation after algebraic equation. Five hours later, brain and hand sore, my evening meal was a bowl of lukewarm pea and ham soup. I crawled into bed hating algebra and pea and ham soup in equal measure. On reflection, I'd have preferred the cane!

'School days are supposed to be the best days of your life, a time to be young and carefree. Not for me, I couldn't wait to leave! My secondary school didn't have a sixth form, thank God, so anyone wanting to study for A levels had to leave and enrol at a college of further education, to say I was excited was an understatement. On my sixteenth birthday that all changed! The headteacher could not contain her joy at morning assembly announcing that my year group were the lucky ones and would be the first cohort allowed to stay on for sixth form! It felt like my life had ended and on my birthday too! A cruel present! Gutted doesn't describe the depths of how low I felt. I'd been looking forward to leaving school almost since the day I'd enrolled. My parents, on the other hand, were thrilled, working out they'd be quids in not having to fork out for the more expensive college costs. They could have afforded it, didn't bother them how upset I was. The school staff sensed our disappointment and set about placating us with incentives. As sixth formers we would become prefects, a role designed to raise our status and impress parents. As if policing younger pupils and being teachers' spies made up for being forced to stay at school! We were allocated a common room, a place to call our own where we could eat lunch, relax, study, and escape younger pupils, "plebs", we called them. To the staff it was a common room, to us it was a prison! The only incentive of any note was being allowed off the school premises at lunchtimes. Occasionally we didn't even go back!

Five students chose to stay on. The sixth and seventh didn't have a choice! My parents made the decision for me and no amount of pleading or promising to work harder at college succeeded in changing their minds. William Birch, we called him Billy, was mad as hell, he hated school and vowed that both the school and his parents would regret making him go back and oh my word, the school certainly did! On that first September morning, Mr Davies, our smug deputy head, marched into the room telling us we could have the honour of painting the room and making it our own. It was as if they were doing us a favour! A sneaky opportunity to get a shabby, disused room decorated with cheap labour more like! Nevertheless, the seven of us arranged to meet in the common room at noon the following Saturday, brushes in hand. Billy offered to provide the paint; apparently his dad had loads of tins in the garage. I'll never forget six of us walking along the corridor and opening the door to black and I mean newly painted pitch black! Even four fluorescent tubes buzzing away on the ceiling struggled to lighten the dark! We were in a black hole. The pocket-sized room took on the appearance of an object ogled down the wrong end of a telescope, shrunk to miniscule! Billy had taken it upon himself to arrive early and get the job done! Needless to say, Mr Davies was furious. No one liked it except Billy, we didn't, the teachers didn't, and the head hated it. That was it for Billy, the teachers set against him from that moment. He spent the next three weekends repainting the walls and ceiling under strict supervision, henceforth we bathed in magnolia. He had to do six coats to obliterate the black undercoat! He spent most of the first term suffering detentions and had more than his fair share of canings. It wasn't until much later that Billy had his revenge!

'Our lunchtime bolt for freedom became the highlight of the day, certainly for me. It felt wonderful being able to lord it over the rest of the school, even the teachers couldn't escape, their time taken up with marking, meetings, playground duties and supervising lunch in the hall, feeding time at the zoo more like! Who'd be a teacher? Each morning we'd plan our lunch-hour escapade. We had a reputation for hanging around the chip shop and newsagents in the arcade, meeting friends from the high school four streets away or looking cool and shaking our stuff in *Spin the Groove*, checking out the latest cassettes or top twenty single. Unbeknownst to us, Billy bought lunch at the chippy every day, chips, sausage and gravy or chips, sausage, and curry sauce.

A veritable fry fest. That was 190 days' worth of chips for the first year of sixth form and another 190 for the second, minus the odd days he spent at home as part of his punishment regime of course. Who'd have thought it, but Billy plotted his revenge from that very first day, a revenge that would only come to fruition eight years later. Polystyrene foam tiles covering the common room ceiling gave way, ironically collapsing on, the one and only, Mr Davies as he taught a politics lesson! The cause of the cave-in, 380 chip papers, plastic forks, mouldy half eaten sausages and polystyrene cups still holding their solidified remains of gravy and curry! Must have weighed a ton! Love to have been a fly on the wall that day!

'Success at school arguably improves your life choices, opens doors to better careers, a passport to freedom. Nobody would argue that a good education is paramount, whether taught at a school or indeed in the home but school offers so much more than that. When memories of subjects studied and lessons learned fade into a dim and distant past, it's the friendships, the first loves and the day-to-day incidents that remain and make you smile. My school days are remembered fondly, they took me to where I wanted to be. I hope they do the same for you Charlie.'

'I bet that room stank of chips. If we had polystyrene tiles in our school I'd cram loads of stuff up in the music room, the smellier the better! So, when did you decide to be a dentist then, was it at school or later on?'

'When I was about your age I thought I'd like to be a vet but couldn't reconcile how one could treat and cure animals when they are unable to communicate their ailments. You'd need to be telepathic! Where would you start? It troubled me enough to reconsider. Of course, I would have learned all I needed to know studying the veterinary science degree, but I was young.'

'So, after that did you want to be a dentist?'

'No, after that I aspired to be a doctor but once again doubts reared their ugly head and quashed that. Back then I thought doctors sat in a room all day writing prescriptions, I couldn't think of anything worse. Thinking back there are times it feels like an opportunity missed but I take heart from the fact that dentistry gave me a good living and anyway, there are similarities between the professions. It's an incredible gift to help people from a diagnosis through to successful treatment. The seed to becoming a dentist was planted during a routine dental appointment soon after my seventeenth birthday. I'd been treated by the same dentist for ten years and liked him. We had a conversation about career opportunities in the medical profession and he suggested giving dentistry some serious consideration. I distinctly remember telling him that I wasn't prepared to sit and stare in people's mouths all day, it was at that point he invited me to spend a week at his practice to discover what the profession was truly like.'

'But isn't being a dentist a lot about looking in people's mouths all day?'

'Yes it is but it's also so much more than that. Dentistry is a science but there are aspects of the subject, repairing and restoring teeth, which are similar to that of an artist, specifically a sculptor. Collaborating with my team of dental associates and hygienists we helped people, we eased their pain, we cured their dental and oral problems and strived to make them happy with their appearance. Nervous patients were supported, and careful interventions helped them conquer their fears. How something as small as a tooth can cause such distress never ceased to amaze me. You see, fear comes in all shapes and sizes. Facial disfigurement can be a challenging and frightening affliction for so many, using aesthetic dentistry, orthodontics, maxillofacial and oral surgery we managed to satisfy hundreds of patients, something I found incredibly rewarding. I had a wonderful career and I'm proud of my interventions.

'Charlie, earlier I asked if you want to go back in the sea, we both know that you do and that it can and will be achievable, but you also need to know that you're not wrong. Your fear is not misplaced, sharks can be scary, and the sea is not your friend, they can both be dangerous, even deadly. Your fear is perfectly rational you just need to learn how to manage it.' Although he nods in agreement he doesn't seem convinced.

'Mmmm.'

A thoughtful pause and then his next question.

'Has a shark ever scared you?'

This question is one I've been asked countless times and I'll give him the same response I've given countless times before. 'Not scared me Charlie but caused me to be cautious. After all, a few species of shark are known to be unpredictable and dangerous. The need to be wary and vigilant is advisable at all times when sharks are around, even those known to be passive demand respect, I was buzzed by a blacktip once and it didn't half spook me!'

'But how could you go into the sea, a shark could have been right there, and it might have been one of the ones you were nervous about.'

'The best way to answer your question is to say that Beth and I spent hours, days doing our homework, researching dive destinations and the oceans we'd be plunging into. Knowing where we were going enabled us to predict, with considerable accuracy, the fish life we could expect to see. Species of shark tend to be region specific, in order to steer clear of a particular species we simply avoided those destinations. One of our trips saw Beth and I diving in Palau, a scattering of over three hundred islands in the western Pacific Ocean. It was there where we met Dan, a disgruntled accountant from Bristol, who'd left the UK eleven years before to set up home in this tropical paradise. He developed a love for the archipelago, particularly the underwater world, developing an eager interest in discovering more on the connection between fish spawning and moon cycles, fascinating and inspirational. By the way, the wonderful by-product of travelling to dive destinations around the world are the interesting people you meet along the way. It was Dan who told me something that helped me think of sharks in a whole new way. He revealed that in his early diving days he too was fearful of sharks until he began to compare them with dogs. Dogs are inquisitive and friendly animals but there are some that can be aggressive or exhibit bad behaviour, sharks are no different. Most sharks will ignore you and go about hunting for fish. Having said this if we can have a bad day maybe a shark can too! You like dogs don't you so maybe this could help you.'

'I like dogs. I mean I really like dogs. I love Pepper. So, I get it. Some dogs scare me when I'm on my bike in the street or park but only if they're off the lead and start running at me or chasing me. I know most dogs are good, so I suppose most sharks are good then. Which sharks were you scared of and are any of them in the sea here?'

'I'm terrified of great white sharks Charlie, as are most of my diver friends. I'm nervous of hammerhead, bull, and tiger shark, as they are known to be unpredictable and aggressive. Other than that, I'm not scared. No need to be anxious here as none of the four species I've mentioned are found in British waters, not yet anyway! Climates and fish numbers are changing and will impact on our sea in ways as yet unknown. We do have over forty species of shark in these waters, including the fastest shark, the shortfin mako, clocked at 80 kilometres per hour (kph), (50 miles per hour/mph), rare but they're here. The second largest shark in the world, the basking shark, is found here too and thankfully in greater numbers, often sighted off the coasts of the Hebrides, the Isle of Man and Cornwall during summer months. These giants of the sea pose no danger to humans as they feed on a diet of plankton, the tiniest of life forms. Interestingly, angel sharks used to swim in British waters too, and in large numbers, but the rise in commercial fishing and seabed trawling put paid to them, they're now unbelievably rare.'

'So, no shark has attacked a person here, around this coast?'

'I didn't say that. There have been a couple of incidents of sharks biting fishermen when they were caught up or tangled in a net. Can't really blame a shark for trying to protect itself and acting on instinct, must be terrifying to be dragged up out of the water and plonked on a boat.'

'I get that. It's good to know there have been no attacks. I bet you're glad you never dived with a great white or the other three aren't you? That would have been really scary.'

'I've never dived with a great white Charlie and am thrilled about that. Never wanted to, not even from inside a protective cage which some of my friends have done in Mexico and South Africa. It was just a no-go for me! If I'd seen a great white during a dive I'd have been terrified and wanted to exit the water as soon as possible. Not everyone thinks the same though, an American dive instructor friend of mine has dived with great whites many times with and without a cage. She maintains they are shy. I trust her and know what she told me to be true, but I still couldn't have entertained it. That pointed snout emerging out of the dark heading my way would have triggered that duh dum, duh dum music from 1975, oh my ears would have been ringing! I'm glad I never saw one. As for the other three, well I have!'

'What! How could you? I don't get it. You said you were nervous of them. You said they're unpredictable and aggressive. How could you get in the sea knowing they're there?'

The day is turning out to be very different to the one I'd anticipated but I'm enjoying the opportunity to reminisce. It's strangely cathartic and comforting to share my memories, hopefully it may also be helping me move on in some way. I'm more than happy to tell this boy of my most incredible shark encounters, when I swam in the oceans with my big three, the hammerhead, the bull, and the tiger.

HAMMERHEAD

'Skipping down the steps from the aircraft my first impression of San Cristobal, named after St Christopher the patron saint of travellers, was the intensity of the heat! After two sleep-deprived days travelling on what felt like our own personal crusade, we finally touched down in the Galapagos, the epitome of dream destinations lying in the Pacific in 60,000 square kilometres (23,000 square miles), of ocean, six hundred miles off the coast of Ecuador. The twenty-one islands and associated islets and rocks became a UNESCO World Heritage site in 1978, deemed to be historically, geographically, biologically, and scientifically significant. The Galapagos were named after the giant tortoises that live there, the language of Ecuador is Spanish and translated into English, galápago is tortoise. The desire to dive here had weighed heavy for years, who wouldn't want to explore the underwater world of this ecological niche, a place like no other. Charles Darwin, the famous naturalist and biologist must have felt the same. He set off from the Galapagos on September 15th, 1835, aboard HMS *Beagle* on a five-week cruise to explore the rich tapestry of life found here. There are species of mammals, reptiles, birds, fish, sea creatures and insects not found anywhere else on the planet including Darwin's finches, Galapagos fur seals, marine iguanas, and the giant tortoise. It was mind-blowing, I felt as if I was following in Darwin's footsteps, in itself incredible but our fundamental reason for going was to dive with hammerhead sharks.

'Visitors to the Galapagos can be left in no doubt how seriously the locals guard this special place regarding themselves as proud custodians of this unique wildlife sanctuary, collectively revered as their pride and joy; the flora and fauna must be preserved for future generations. As we weaved our way through the airport we were bombarded with conservation posters and leaflets, wildlife was sacrosanct, nothing was to be disturbed nor taken home, no living thing, no pebbles, or shells.

'In arrivals we were greeted by our overly enthusiastic cruise director and dive guide, Andres Jorge, "AJ" for short, he wasn't difficult to spot, towering above the crowd, his tanned muscular physique, honed and toned in the gym complemented by long dark curls flowing over his shoulders made for an impressive specimen. His colouring and looks inherited from generations of Spanish ancestors who'd settled in the Galapagos back in the early part of the nineteenth century. He stood out and we weren't the only ones to notice, plane loads of passengers passed by and enjoyed the distraction too! He was fit! Banks of porters jostled anxiously at the exit waiting to pounce on tired tourists and assist them with their luggage in exchange for a small fee. It was pretty daunting being surrounded by strangers grabbing at your personal possessions, but we needn't have worried. AJ took charge and within moments had them running this way and that, throwing dive bags and suitcases into vans to be driven away and not seen again until you entered your cabin a little later! Anyone who's ever met AJ will never forget him. Some people leave lasting impressions, draw you in, possess qualities sadly lacking in others. They have that thing, whatever it is and he had it by the bucket load!

'After brief introductions and meeting other guests, we squeezed into a small minibus which deposited us at the sea lion-strewn harbour five minutes later. It was here, in Puerto Baquerizo Moreno, the islands' capital, where we would board the steel-hulled live-aboard, *Ocean Blue*, our home for the next ten days. The coast road, wide and uncluttered, was constructed of multicoloured paving slabs and bordered by equally broad pavements. The absence of traffic seemed to suggest the road was more of a statement than a necessity but the large numbers of tourists clinging to pavements were in keeping with the space on offer, many were spilling off the kerbs to avoid the congestion. Shops, restaurants, and hotels, constructed from an eclectic mix of wood and stone, ran along the length of one side offering unrivalled views of the promenade and waterfront on the other. The narrower back streets, home to the six thousand locals, lacked colour. Land iguana, a species of lizard, darted across the roads like cats do here. The anticipation was palpable as was the stench of sea lion urine, acrid in the extreme. No amount of nose holding or pulling T-shirts up over faces could keep it at bay. Hardly surprising, sea lions were everywhere, swimming in the bay, sunbathing on hot pavements and lazing on bus stop benches. They were held in such high regard, respected, and afforded every courtesy, never touched, or urged to move on and could go wherever they pleased. In order to board the boat we had no option but to giant stride over rows of sea lions choosing to sleep on each of the ten stone steps heading down from the street to the pontoon. My nostrils breathed a huge sigh of relief as we motored out of the harbour on the start of our 400km (250 miles) journey north.

'*Ocean Blue*, 34m in length, was strong and stable, and needed to be where we were heading, the waters were wild. With six cabins below deck and four on the upper level, all equipped with en-suite facilities, this motor boat offered a degree of comfort for twenty passengers. Beth and I were fortunate to have been allocated a cabin up top affording us spectacular views of the ocean, morning, noon, and night. The sundeck was on the top deck, a retreat where we'd spend hours chilling with a cocktail or beer after finishing diving for the day. The strict policy of no alcohol when diving is adhered to by every dive boat I've been on the world over, diving demands a clear head. Mid-ships housed the lounge and dining areas which, to maximise space, doubled up as the bar, shop and briefing area. *Ocean Blue* had been designed well and was more preferable than staying in a hotel on land. Land-based dive operations necessitate early morning jaunts from hotel to harbour to board smaller day boats with their barnacle-encrusted hulls, chunky masts and scruffy decks that can only carry you to dive sites a short journey out to sea or along the coast. A live-aboard enables you to travel further distances to more remote dive sites, places the day boats simply can't reach in a day!

'The first evening was spent unpacking, participating in the necessary safety drills, and preparing equipment for dives which would start at the crack of dawn the following morning. AJ brought the evening to a close with a presentation, "The Diversity of Life in the Galapagos Islands". He mentioned turtles, golden cownose rays, red-lipped bat fish and red- and blue-footed boobies but they paled into insignificance when he uttered the word I'd been longing to hear, hammerhead. Apparently our dreams may come true on dive one! Although I was desperate to see them, it didn't make jumping in with them easy. Guess what, I didn't get much sleep that night, some things never change! The engines roared until the early hours, racing us to our first destination, *Isla Darwin*, or Darwin's Island as we call it in English. The boat eventually fell silent at 02:17, I knew the time as I was still awake. The only sounds I could hear were the rolling waves crashing against the hull, a sobering reminder that we were out in rough waters. The swaying eventually rocked me to sleep soon after 03:48. If I told you I was scared I'd be lying, what I felt in those dark moments was sheer terror. I couldn't stand being afraid but there was nothing I could do about it. Sharks drifted through my dreams as they undoubtedly swirled in the sea beneath the boat, haunting my sleep, speeding through the depths to spiral down before disappearing, dissolving like grains of sugar in hot tea. The dream ended abruptly. Always did. The sharks swerved away, and I'd crawl onto my beach and wake up exhausted.

'Breakfast was at 06.00. My mouth felt like the bottom of a birdcage! Having no saliva made chewing difficult; it was all I could do to swallow a morsel of toast. I sipped water in the hopes of stopping that feeling of nausea, I was sick with anticipation. Part of me wanted to stay on the boat but Beth was having none of it and jollied me along. The first dive was always the hardest challenge for me, and it was looming large. AJ delivered the morning briefing where we were assigned to one of two groups after which we proceeded to the dive deck at the stern to change into our gear. Final checks were made, we climbed into our dinghy and the driver opened the throttle blasting us across the water to the dive site. The magnitude of the situation was clear, we were about to plunge in at Darwin's Arch, that proud stone structure and iconic symbol of the Galapagos, a 43m natural rock arch rising up out of the ocean a mile off Darwin Island out in the open ocean. I was bobbing on the waves of history, if only they could talk! Darwin had opened his eyes on this very vista 180 years before, baring changes to the landscape from erosion of course. Unfortunately, no one will ever get to see it in person again Charlie, after years of pounding by ferocious waves, natural erosion has caused the top of the arch to plunge into the ocean. Only two columns of rock remain. To get an idea of the majestic grandeur of Darwin's Arch you could visit the 50m man-made Arc de Triomphe in Paris or if that doesn't float your boat, Dorset's natural 61m Durdle Door arch near Lulworth may have to do. Both bear an uncanny resemblance in their own way!

'The waves pounding relentlessly into the rocks at the base of the arch were hitting with such force the roar was deafening. The thundering waters were as powerful as any orchestral crescendo I've heard! Never mind Camille Saint-Saëns's, *Carnival of the Animals*, this was Charles Darwin's, *Symphony of the Sea*! We were in a dinghy at the mercy of a tempestuous sea, being battered by waves that seemed to delight in bulldozing us up and down with such ferocity, the sea flooded in to just below our knees. None of us were in any doubt of the power of the ocean in this desolate place, if anything were to go awry here we'd be in trouble. My empty stomach rumbled queasily. There was no going back now. Buddy checks were completed in those last few minutes before entering the water; I checked Beth's gear and she mine. We donned our fins and mask, and I strained every sinew to pull myself up onto the side of the dinghy then waited patiently for her to join me. The strap on her mask needed adjusting delaying her momentarily but enough to cause my anxiety to build and, me to hyperventilate. As soon as she sat beside me AJ started the countdown, "Three, two, one, go," and the group rolled back. In that split second of freefall, before hitting the water, I held my breath praying the water would catch me and not the jaws of a giant shark! Relief washed over me seconds later when we descended beneath the hurly-burly of the surface to enjoy the calmness underneath. The crystal-clear water enabled me to see a seabed of rippled sand 30m below. My eyes were out on stalks, scanning through the blue, hunting for hammerheads. It never ceased to amaze me how the ocean surface can be a thundering squall but the second you sink down even just one or two metres, the underwater world transforms into serenity personified. AJ gave the thumbs down signal to descend, we deflated our BCD and started sinking, the plan was to get down to just above the bottom and wait. My body tingled with anticipation. Time ticked by; nothing. It didn't take long for disappointment to seep in. Maybe we'd be unlucky and not see a hammerhead! That's when it happened. A huge shark swam out of the darkness maintaining its position close to the sand, its shape clearly identifiable, a hammerhead, it couldn't be anything else. A fully grown hammerhead can be 6m in length so this one at 4m wasn't bad for a first sighting. I heard someone yell and realised it was me, although it was less of a shout and more of an emotional release. And yes, you are able to make sounds even with a regulator in your mouth! I couldn't help it and thankfully only did it once, not wanting to be the unfortunate soul to scare it away and face the wrath of a boat full of disgruntled divers. I couldn't move. The fish continued towards me, nonchalantly rolling and swaying from side to side. For such a large fish it moves with grace.

'The characteristic T-shaped head has scientists and marine biologists in a quandary as to why it evolved the way it did, and as yet no definitive explanation exists. Theories vary. Some believe the shape improves the hammerhead's vision, their rolling swimming action with the eyes positioned out to the side enables the shark to see above, below, and behind at all times. Others believe having eyes safely out to the side affords the hammerhead better protection when hunting. Stingrays, a favourite prey of the hammerhead, hide on or under a sandy seabed, once the hammerhead locates a ray it dives head first onto it, pinning it to the floor with no chance of escape. For me, the T-shaped head is reminiscent of the sweeping front wing on a Formula 1 racing car, aesthetically elegant it serves to streamline the vehicle, reduce turbulence, and promote down force, essentially preventing the speeding car from taking off. I wouldn't be at all surprised if engineers had studied the physical features of hammerhead sharks when creating the innovative front wing. If the T shape makes a significant contribution to the movements of a car, maybe it does something similar for the hammerhead. It certainly wouldn't be the first time sharks have influenced the design of man-made objects, engineers in the automobile and aeronautical industries have studied shark skin and the efficiency with which sharks move through water and tweaked designs accordingly. Analysing shark skin has impacted improvements to waterproofing, repelling and thermal protection in both the sporting and fashion industries. Sharks have been swimming in our oceans and bathing in our seas for over four hundred million years, 150 million years before dinosaurs roamed the earth and considerably earlier than humans who only stepped in 200,000 years ago. We are wise to study sharks and learn from their longevity, a species which has survived the test of time could teach us valuable lessons. Sadly though, sharks seem not to be respected enough, wouldn't it be ironic if in the short time humans have lived on earth, our legacy would be to oversee the extinction of this fish species! It would be criminal. Be in no doubt, humans threaten hundreds of thousands of species with extinction, animals and plant life, some scientists fear the actual figure is closer to one million! Speaks volumes and a highly likely result unless we change our ways but don't get me started on that contentious topic! I'll leave that for another time! Back to the dive!

'The hammerhead was closing in but at the last minute changed course to avoid bumping into me. Do you hear me? To avoid me! It swam by in ghostly silence to disappear into the dark. It reappeared moments later and headed back my way. Edging ever closer this extraordinary specimen seemed curious and I had everything crossed that it was not intent on attack. It stopped 2m away and appeared to scrutinise me. Sharks' eyes are often described as emotionless, I have no idea who first said this, but I beg to differ, they should have looked deeper. That day I lost myself in those inquisitive, intelligent eyes, he even rolled forward as if to get a better view. We stared into each other's eyes and shared a moment. I had no idea what he was contemplating but I was sending him muted messages of love, telling him I meant him no harm. The shark's movements, invisible to the naked eye, brought him level with me before he casually rolled away. Turning to Beth, the urge to thumb my chest was overpowering and my heart pounded in time with my salutation. She nodded and we exchanged high fives. I wanted to cry out and hope that hearing my voice would in some way persuade the shark to turn round and return but we became distracted by a sudden tapping. AJ was using his stainless-steel pointer to strike his scuba tank, the metal-on-metal sound reverberated through the water sounding similar to when a percussionist strikes a triangle in an orchestra. The repeated clanging successfully focused our attention. AJ was pointing at a shiver of hammerhead weaving their way over the sand, five then twelve more but beyond them were hundreds, too many to count, stacked high and swimming in the same direction. My straining eyes could barely make out faint flicks of grey and silver as they disappeared into the dark. I couldn't believe my eyes and wondered why they were in such large numbers, where they were going and why were they choosing to go together? As if the moment needed any more excitement two dolphins dived down from the surface, twirled amongst us, and shot off faster than a speeding bullet, blink and you'd have missed them. Incredible. We began ascending, taking longer than necessary, reluctant to leave. Hammerheads swam below us, their grey bodies easy to distinguish against the lighter coloured sand of the floor. The dive had already exceeded expectations, I couldn't have wished for more, but we were in for another treat, hard to believe it could get any better, but it did! AJ fell silent then started striking his tank for a second time and this time his repeated pointing, nodding and general jerking around suggested there was something else and I wasn't wrong, a special visitor was out in the dark and heading our way. I shook my head to let him know I couldn't see what he wanted me to see but he responded with more enthusiastic nodding which told me to keep looking. That's when a monstrous shadow glided calmly into view, a 7m whale shark, the largest fish species in the world had chosen this moment to cruise by. With a mouth 1.5m wide and over three hundred teeth, these gentle giants of the shark family have a bluish grey colouration on the upper side of the head and body which is dotted with columns and rows of white spots, the underbelly is white. This huge fish moved with graceful elegance propelled along with effortless flicks from its enormous tail. The encounter, though fleeting, was magical. We watched until it disappeared into the distance and AJ signalled for us to ascend to perform the safety stop.

'Air we breathe is 78% nitrogen, 21% oxygen and the remaining 1% is a mix of other gases including hydrogen and carbon dioxide. Divers breathe the same mix from a scuba tank, but the air is compressed, squashed and the moisture taken out. Above the water nitrogen is easily breathed out but underwater the pressure is higher and in that environment nitrogen is dangerous and can become poisonous. Nitrogen needs time to be released from the cells before divers leave the water, it's vital to ascend slowly to enable this process to occur. Divers should perform a three-minute safety stop towards the end of every dive to prevent them becoming ill and only after completing the safety stop did we pop our heads up out of the water. I was elated and couldn't wait to tear my regulator from my mouth and scream with joy. I felt that same exhilaration as I had when my eyes fell on my first bicycle on a Christmas morning oh so long ago. I can still see it, a blue frame, white tyres, and a red bow decoratively tied to the handlebars. Father Christmas had stood it next to the tree in the lounge, the Christmas lights twinkled bouncing rainbow sparkles on the steel. The moment I set eyes on that bike was when I first knew what happiness was.

'Human beings breathe on average 20,000 breaths a day, ripping my regulator out and inhaling that first one filled my lungs with air the likes I'd never inhaled before, beautifully crisp and fresh. We bobbed there at the mercy of the strengthening waves. I remember looking up at the sky and squealing, giddy with relief. The world was revealing its secrets and I was so incredibly thankful. I wanted to go back down immediately and return to my paradise but the empty tank on my back prevented it. I put my face into the water wanting to reconnect with this special place, to relive the memory, to see something, anything and was flabbergasted at what I saw. I thought my eyes were playing tricks on me, the floor was moving. I tried to make sense of what I was seeing. Then it hit me, the sand was covered and I'm not exaggerating when I say this, covered with schooling hammerheads, moving and manoeuvring to avoid bumping into each other. A potentially aggressive and dangerous fish was proving to be quite the opposite. Without doubt I'd lived through the most incredible hour of my life. Spending time with such impressive creatures was humbling and left me feeling stronger and more vulnerable in equal measure. Strange but true. Sixty minutes earlier I'd rolled back into the ocean full of fear and trepidation but had surfaced to a world that would never be the same again. I'd faced my fear, stared it in the face and literally looked it in the eye. It changed me and I've never changed back. People can live an entire lifetime never experiencing precious connections with the natural world, they don't know what they're missing.' I stopped. Charlie puffed out his cheeks.

'That was awesome.'

'It really was. Telling you about that day and it's as if it happened yesterday. I loved it and my hammerheads. Ten days later and we were disembarking in Puerto Baquerizo Moreno having completed thirty-two dives. The Galapagos is extraordinary, an untouched slice of paradise, blessed with more than its fair share of nature's wonders, so much so it should be the world's eighth wonder! I will never forget the extraordinary Galapagos.' I pause a while and am reminded of an incident I'd long tried to forget, secreting it away into the recesses of my mind until this very moment, a tale that's demanding to be told.

'I won't forget nearly dying in the Galapagos either!' His eyes dart my way. I like this boy so he needs to hear what I've got to say, it may help him to not make the same mistakes I did, could even save his life one day!

'It was scary, the scariest episode of my life, the closest I've come to shuffling off this mortal coil and interestingly was something I'd never feared! You spend hours, days, months, years in fear of a particular something, wasting energy, worrying unnecessarily for it to never come to fruition but you can be sideswiped by something you never even saw coming. It's nothing to do with a shark either, before you start speculating.

'*Ocean Blue* had moored off the coast of Fernandina, the furthest west of all the Galapagos Islands, a rocky volcanic terrain devoid of plant life but blessed with an abundant marine iguana population, the purpose of our visit that day. These fascinating reptiles have made Fernandina their home and gather in their hundreds to bask on the black lava rocks lining the shore. This unusual creature is only found in the Galapagos, and we dived in one of the bays to see them foraging for algae 5m under the water. Darwin saw them but didn't care for them, disgusting imps of darkness was the note he'd made in his writings. Admittedly they do present as threatening, 1m in length, dark-bodied with pointed spines running down their back and sharp hooked claws at the end of stumpy limbs. They have the appearance of Godzilla, the lizard from the film of the same name, only immeasurably smaller thank goodness. The producers of that blockbuster undoubtedly took inspiration for their beast from the harmless marine iguana. I find myself agreeing with Darwin though, they're not endearing, not in the slightest. The spines remind me of the Mohican haircuts a handful of patients would style for the holidays, mostly boys your age Charlie. The sides of the head are shaved to leave a tall central strip which is often dyed blue or green but only for the summer holidays. The children are forced to cut it short at the start of the autumn term as most if not all schools had banned that punk look. The educational establishments obviously don't believe in the powerful benefits attributed to long hair!

'After the dive we returned to the boat and were offered the opportunity to snorkel along the shoreline to get closer to fur seals, flightless cormorants and Galapagos penguins that were lazing on the rocks. Fur seals are covered in a soft brown fur and are the smallest of the eared seals, flightless cormorants have wings but can't fly and Galapagos penguins are the only penguin found north of the equator. Not being a strong swimmer, I'd only attempted to snorkel a couple of times in my life, I didn't enjoy swallowing seawater with almost every breath! The water was a cool twenty degrees, so we were advised to wear wetsuits to keep the cold at bay. One of the guests, an experienced snorkeller, suggested we wear a two-kilogram (kg) weight belt, we'd be marginally heavier so could sink below the surface with relative ease to view iguanas underwater should we so wish. Taking his advice on face value, we duly donned our belts, grabbed our mask, fins and snorkel and jumped into the dinghy. It whizzed us a short distance to drop us nearer to shore. Sliding awkwardly over the side I landed with an almighty splash causing seawater to rush down my snorkel and into my lungs! Great start! Spluttering and swimming to the shallows with that salty solution swilling around in my mouth was sickeningly unpleasant and not to be recommended. The plan was to stay in the water, kneel on the sand and creep close to shore to snap shots of the wildlife. The water was freezing so half an hour was deemed more than enough time to accomplish our goal. The minutes raced by, and we assembled to swim back to the dinghy as a group. Attempts to set off were repeatedly thwarted by a sudden surge of powerful waves pounding the shore forcing us back. Ten minutes we tried and eventually set off, but I immediately got into trouble and wasn't the only one. The waves were low but stronger than any I'd experienced. I tried jumping and diving through them but made no headway. The waves were coming in thick and fast leaving no time to snatch even the smallest breath before the next one hit and the water quickly became too deep for me to touch the bottom. Leanne, a fellow guest started screaming for help and her husband, Steve, swam to her aid. Santiago, her dive guide, came to help and she needed both men to hold her up out of the water. Things were becoming serious. I attempted the crawl, my strongest swimming stroke but my flailing arms thrashed wildly and were not helped by a weakening kick, it's tiring fighting waves stronger than you are! I was getting nowhere! Well, that's not strictly true, I was going down! I'm known for having a fire in my belly but right there and then torrents of water were flooding down my trachea and oesophagus to extinguish the flames and put my fire out! Knowing Santiago was a stone's throw away I tried calling for help but my voice was choked and that's when it hit me, I was going to die. I was drowning. Before taking, what I seriously considered was my last breath, I took one last look at the sky and started sinking, floating peacefully to the bottom of the sea. The last thing I remember was Santiago screaming my name. Then I was gone. I sank, helped on my way by my weight belt! In those last moments I felt warm and weirdly calm and in the same breath disappointed and exhausted. They, whoever they are, say that your life flashes before you in those final moments before death. My life didn't but then I didn't die! Since that day I've often wondered about that, what rushes through the minds of people and animals in those last seconds before death, what do they think about? Looking into the dark despairing eyes of cows staring out from between the slats in the sides of lorries charging up and down motorways to deliver them to abattoirs, they are surely contemplating something, I'm sure of it! I can no longer look into those eyes. One day I'll crash my car overtaking a lorry load of animals as I'm forced to look away and hold my hand up to protect my prying eyes. Bulls, repeatedly stabbed by cruel matadors and suffering terrible pain taking time to bleed to death, must know they're dying as they sink to their knees that last time. How these misguided matadors can look into those eyes and deliver the final cut is something I'm proud not to understand. My heart bleeds for this majestic beast. Cruelty at its finest! I suppose we'll all find out one day what happens in our final moments but not live to tell!

'Just when I thought my number was up, two heroic arms reached down under the water to rescue me. Steve pulled me up and saved me. He tugged at my weight belt releasing it to sink to the bottom of the sea. Taking the belt off hadn't even crossed my mind. Only four of the group made it back to the dinghy, the rest of us were forced back to shore to wait for the rolling waves to subside. Steve struggled to carry me and ended up dragging then rolling me out. It was like a scene from one of those shipwreck movies when a survivor crawls from the sea to flop face first onto a deserted beach. When the director goes in for a close-up the exhausted castaway lifts their head to reveal a face covered in sand, coughing and retching mouthfuls of seawater before face-planting back down. I lay there dishevelled but relieved. What a sight we must have made. The waves pushed an unfortunate couple onto razor-sharp rocks causing cuts to their hands, knees, and feet as they crawled to safety scattering cormorants and forcing iguanas and seals to make way and drop into the ocean. It was the stuff of nightmares, without the shark of course! One chap was throwing up, another was searching in the shallows for his GoPro camera and three women lost their masks and snorkels. Maria, a Peruvian woman who'd lived by the sea her whole life told me she'd never experienced waves so strong. *Ocean Blue's* captain set the emergency procedures in motion and with the help of the crew, ropes, life rings and a calming sea we were safely ensconced back on board within thirty minutes. There were genuine tears of relief all round! That night we celebrated our survival with cocktails and sashimi and exhausted we slept soundly in our beds.

'A couple of years later I was at home watching *Planet Earth II: Islands*, the infamous episode when venomous racer snakes chase a newly hatched iguana along a beach in the Galapagos. The gloriously wonderful naturalist, broadcaster, and writer, Sir David Attenborough, narrated the clip in his usual inimitable way. It didn't click at first, but it was only on that self-same beach on Fernandina where we'd washed up! Having seen how many snakes slithered out from the rocks on that beach it was utterly remarkable that the hatchling managed to escape and us too for that matter. Imagine what could have been, surviving a near drowning only to be killed by snakes! Lucky lizard and lucky us! I will always count myself lucky to have survived, not once but twice that day!

'You'll remember this story won't you Charlie? The reason I've told you about it was to sow a seed in your brain. That day in the shallows we didn't need additional weights to help us sink, we were only ever waist deep in water with no need to go deeper. Swimming back to the dinghy and that belt became a dangerous accessory, one that I had forgotten in the panic. That belt was no help it only served to pull me down to drown. I doubt I'll ever snorkel again but if I do I'll be weight belt free. Promise me you'll remember what I've told you.'

He nodded and then with a glint in his eye, 'Awesome can you tell me about the bull shark?'

BULL

'This dive took place in Fiji, a group of 333 islands in the South Pacific 2000km (1250 miles) north of New Zealand, in 1.3 million square kilometres (500,000 square miles) of ocean. We landed on Viti Levu, Fiji's largest island, completely shattered, a journey of twenty-four hours plus an eleven-hour time difference will do that! Before boarding the live-aboard we'd booked a resort on the south coast to give us time to get over the inevitable jet lag. Thankfully, the resort proved perfect. Neatly nestled in lush tropical gardens affording views over a beach littered with palm trees and beyond that a crystal-blue ocean lapped the shore. That first evening we wandered aimlessly along the coast in search of a bar or restaurant to soak up a couple of hours and ease weary bones. Our walk was thwarted within minutes, blocked by the mouth of a river spewing its murky contents into the ocean causing the path to cut inland. The water's earthy tones a reflection of the deluge we'd touched down in earlier and the litres of rain running into the river from the volcanic terrain above. We continued along the path in the hopes of finding a bridge. A short amble along the river and we found one located in front of a dive centre which proved too tempting and enticed us in. We never did cross that bridge.

'We'd done our homework and knew bull sharks frequented Fijian waters but as solitary hunters the chances of running into one on a dive was relatively rare but if we did we'd made the decision we'd cope. The dive centre was affiliated to the marine biology department at a local university and the divers were proud to support the students. Being a key player in bull shark research enabled the dive centre to offer a unique opportunity, guaranteeing dives with large shivers of sharks! As strange as it sounds they aroused our interest. No dive centre makes guarantees unless they're extremely confident of delivering on their promises, refunding cash to unhappy customers never goes down well.

'Unpredictable and dangerous, bull shark get their name from their strong physique, adults are stocky and can be 3m in length. They look huge compared to other shark species and females of the species are particularly massive. If you were to cuddle one, though nobody would, your arms wouldn't make it even a quarter-way round, they are the oak trees of the oceans. A dive was planned for the following morning and as luck would have it there were two spaces! Forty minutes after walking through the door and we'd signed up. Bull sharks frequent warm, shallow waters where rivers spill into the sea, they're diadromous. Do you know what that means Charlie?'

'No, I've not heard that word before.'

'The word comes from the Greek and describes fish that can swim in both salt and freshwater. Female bull sharks are able to swim hundreds of miles upstream, up freshwater rivers, to give birth to their young. The pups migrate downstream to spend the best part of their lives in the ocean so in salt water. The dive centre couldn't have been more perfectly located. Walking back outside, the fading light bounced off that river of swirling chocolate causing me to squint. The waters ran brown from November until the end of the rainy season in April. Tropical plants thrived along the banks on both sides, and I couldn't help but hunt for bull shark fins poking through the foliage and was relieved not to spot one.

'After a predictably restless night I woke feeling apprehensive, my stomach in knots. Bull sharks are apex predators at the top of the food chain and potentially lethal. Ten divers had signed up to dive and would be accompanied by six guides, an exceptionally good ratio, which tells you something. We'd arranged to meet at the dive centre at the unearthly hour of 05:15. I hate mornings, particularly early ones but it's at sunrise when the underwater world starts stirring, sea conditions are generally calmer, and visibility is at its best. We squeezed into our wetsuits and clutching fins and masks in trembling fingers trooped outside just as the heavens opened forcing us to dive for cover under a timber-framed gazebo whose inadequate thatch did little to shelter us. I hadn't anticipated Fiji being wet, windswept, and cold, a tropical paradise the likes of Birmingham and Sheffield hey, who knew! We stood there shivering, having to endure a lengthy briefing which was delivered by Tata, the owner and his words did little to warm the spirits. "Do not" and "you must", were the theme of the day. "Do not swim away from the group, do not make sudden movements," and, "You must obey instructions given by guides." I was itching to shout, "I do not want to go! You must leave me behind!" In an attempt to distract myself from proceedings I scanned the surroundings. The centre was considerably larger than the reception building we'd ventured into the previous night. A series of smaller thatched huts ran alongside the now swollen river and judging by the puddles growing at our feet, the thatch was in much need of repair. The huts were home to a shop, café, rental equipment storage, changing and shower facilities, a classroom for teaching dive courses and "Grog Bar", a place overflowing with rum cocktails. Business was good, the centre popular the world over, a reputation for delivering on the bull shark with an excellent safety record will do that! Those of us diving that day were testament to that, we were an eclectic bunch from the UK, the US, Germany, France and Australia, the world and our oceans are vast, but diving connects us.

'Tata was born on Viti Levu in the shadow of Mount Tomanivi, Fiji's highest peak, appropriate as he was a man-mountain who single-handedly built his dive centre, a staggering feat considering the number of buildings involved. He reminded me of the powerful rugby union players from the Pacific Islands Rugby Alliance squads I'd enjoyed watching on TV and was blessed with sculpted features, a stocky muscular body, short afro curls and a beautiful smile. The whiteness of his teeth accentuated the blackness of his skin. He was one of the beautiful people, and strong. The thirty hardwood beams, supporting the roof where we sheltered from the storm, were the size of large trees. This impressive man had felled and carried an entire forest to build his dream.

'Before his six children came along he and his wife lived in the same traditional *bure* his ancestors had occupied for generations. Tata was the youngest of three brothers, who all followed in their father's footsteps to become fishermen. He loved being on a boat out in the open ocean sharing precious time with his father and brothers, but deep down fishing didn't excite him, and he knew it wouldn't be the legacy he'd pass on to his children. What did excite him were the stories divers told of sharks that patrolled off the coast, their tales made the underwater world sound magical, but it was the cash flashed about by those divers in bars at the end of a day that really sparked his interest. He wanted more from life, for himself and his wife, more than the meagre pickings fishing would provide. He wanted to be his own boss, be self-sufficient and build his own business. He knew he needed to find a way to tap into the riches tourists brought with them to Fiji in their wallets but the how eluded him until a casual conversation with a stranger in a bar changed everything. The day had started like any other with no hint of what was to come. After a morning of fishing for the elusive red snapper, a fish popular with the tourists so paid well, his father had a hunch to venture further west, and they got lucky. The money they made from that one haul would support their families for a month, elated, the four men bounded into their local and celebrated into the early hours. They downed enough bottles of Fijian Gold beer to sink a ship! His father and brothers staggered home leaving Tata to drink one last bottle. He got chatting with an American guy perched at the end of the bar, a despondent diver and marine biologist, who'd come to Fiji to count bull shark populations. He was finding his ambitions strangled by the escalating cost of it all and was at the point of jacking it in and returning to California. In order to stay in Fiji, he needed a cheaper place to live and someone who'd take him out on a boat and not charge the earth. Three beers later and the deal was done. Tata built that boat and the guy ended up moving in with him and his wife before children were even a tiny speck on the horizon. He'd found his escape from a life of fishing and a secure future when the university created a marine biology course and more scientists arrived. The need for a dive centre to support the swell in diver numbers became essential so Tata built that too. Fifteen years on and Tata and his employees offer daily dive trips for tourists and research scientists, supported by the university and funds brought in from students around the world with a passion for the sea.

'A nudge from Beth helped focus my attention. Safety was paramount, I needed to listen. Tata sketched the dive site on a whiteboard, and we planned the dive, the times, the route, and the safety procedures. As time went on I started shivering and was unsure whether this was the thought of the sharks or the chill in the air, truth be told it was likely a combination of the two. We would drop in, swim down to the seabed, stay close to the reef and remain in one location to watch the sharks. The bulls would be swimming along a wide sandy channel. Tata's descriptions made it sound as if we'd be watching a bull shark motorway from the safety of the pavement! No one attending that briefing was left in any doubt of what to expect. The usual consent forms were signed absolving the dive company of any blame or responsibility in case of incident or accident then we made our way to the boat. Boardwalks sodden under puddles of rain had started steaming, the wood sizzling dry in the searing heat. *Orion*, a name meaning the hunter, was the 14m, twin-engine power boat charged with safely cradling us three miles out to sea to the dive site. Fingers crossed it would bring us back in one piece! Lacking the usual comforts associated with a live-aboard, zooming over shark-filled waters in such a worryingly basic vessel did nothing to soothe the nerves. A basic galley and toilet occupied the open cockpit at the bow. A thin canopy, offering shelter from the sun and rain, barely covered bench seating that ran down both sides of the boat to the stern. Space was at a premium, taken up with clanking scuba tanks, dive bags and the essential tea urn and biscuit tin. Boarding *Orion* and loading the equipment caused the vessel to sway erratically and knock against the jetty unbalancing already unsteady occupants. We were at the mercy of the torrent of water rushing down from distant hills. It was all we could do to shuffle along to find a spot, sit down and stay put. That the boat was unsteady whilst securely moored was concerning and I found myself secretly praying she'd cope with conditions out in the open ocean. So, there we were, eighteen of us crammed into a space better suited for ten, we shoved our bags and towels under the seats, and we were off!

'Dince joined us on the boat, a young marine biologist working at the university. Originally from Thailand she had studied for her degree in Australia and fallen in love with sharks, bull sharks in particular. Four years after qualifying she arrived in Fiji to study the bull shark populations and made it her forever home after falling in love with a Fijian dive guide working at Tata's dive centre. She squeezed her tiny frame into a space next to me and we became acquainted during the time it took our boat to cut through the waves to the dive site. Part of a team of scientists, she regularly attended dives to gather data and spoke with an extraordinary insight into the importance of shark populations in maintaining healthy oceans. Scientists, marine biologists, and charities wanting to protect sharks, regularly collate data and crunch numbers to inform future actions. Statistics seem to reveal that the more we learn the less we understand so the more we need to learn. The reason Dince joined the boat that November day was to gather data on bull shark migration. Quite simply she counted the number of sharks that showed up. She'd made thousands of dives in Fiji and was able to recognise individual sharks, observe routines and note unusual behaviour. Recording numbers helps inform the health or otherwise of the bull shark population in the South Pacific. Interestingly, at the time of our meeting, her results revealed that a small percentage of bull shark remain close to their place of birth, a handful more circled the waters around Fiji, leaving the majority to travel huge distances, thousands of miles across the oceans to the other side of the world. The numbers showed this but could not be explained. Dince had shrewdly invested time on building relationships with local fishermen and including them in a catch, tag and release project. Juvenile bull sharks were caught up in the rivers and had measurements taken. The date, time and location of the catch was recorded, a satellite tag attached to the dorsal fin before the fish was safely returned to the river. The tags sent data to orbiting satellites and from there to Dince's team of scientists enabling them to track the fish as well as inform on mating sites, birthing locations, and feeding hotspots. Tagging enabled considerable amounts of data to be collated without causing the shark distress. Dince used the data to determine whether sharks were adequately protected and if not, how marine conservation areas could be enlarged. The decision to involve fishermen is a clever one, getting locals on your side will go some way to stopping overfishing and the unnecessary killing of sharks. Even taking small numbers can threaten a species and damage local reefs. Joining forces with locals also means they too have a stake in keeping shark populations healthy. Sharks attract tourists who spend money in hotels, restaurants, bars, and dive centres which in turn supports local employment and economy. Shark tourism is a lucrative business suggesting that this fish is worth more alive than dead!

'Sharks have yet to reveal all their secrets. The proud morning shrill from male birds signalling their search for a mate and a protecting of territory is understood. We know why birds sing. Sharks, on the other hand, swim silently through our seas and oceans disclosing very little. Progress is being made in many areas, but gaps remain in our understanding of shark migration, breeding, hunting, the senses including the electro sensory system, communication, brain function and the age-old quandary, why some sharks attack. The more we learn about sharks, the more we understand, the better we can protect them, contribute to their survival, and help maintain healthy oceans. Sharks are at the top of the food chain and are crucial in maintaining other populations of fish within manageable limits. Without sharks our coral reefs will deteriorate and become unhealthy. Sharks rule the reef and if hunted to extinction the ripple effect would be disastrous, other large fish, particularly grouper, ordinarily hunted and eaten by sharks, would grow in unregulated numbers. In turn the increase in grouper numbers eating fish, octopus and crustaceans would harm the natural balance that sharks help to maintain. Species of fish could be killed off forever. We need sound coral reef structures around our shores to protect coastlines from crashing waves, storms, and flooding. Reefs function as a first line of defence. Taken to extremes an island or coastline devoid of reefs could result in the loss of human life. Nothing hunts sharks except orca, other sharks and humans and it's humans that pose their greatest threat. What we do know is that sharks need protecting, numbers are in decline and humans kill over one hundred million sharks a year, think of that Charlie, one hundred million! Many believe the actual figure to be three times that, hard to imagine hey? I know you're scared of sharks; I was too but honestly they should be the ones fearing us, not you and I of course, I mean humans in general.'

Jane sounds cross. My history teacher, Mrs Hurst, we called her Hursty, got like that when she talked about the challenges for Britain and Europe in the 1930s. She started speaking really fast and had tears in her eyes. When I told me mam about her she said she was 'Passionate and good for her!' I guess Jane is passionate. Passionate about sharks. Passionate about them not dying. I should have listened to Hursty, might have understood why she was passionate about the 1930s. I haven't got a clue what she was going on about half the time. She was feisty. Bit late now. Got Mr Dyson next year, he's dull. I hope it's not too late for the sharks. Sounds bad.

'Do you know, Charlie, you can buy shark meat in Asia, Africa, Australia, North and South America, and Europe and don't get me wrong, I'm not for one minute suggesting that sharks deserve to live any more than cows, chickens or pigs do. What I am saying though is that animals and fish, all living creatures, deserve a quality life and a quality death and this should be in sustainable numbers to ensure longevity of the species. We, humans, as apex predators ourselves, have, in my opinion, a duty to treat life, any life, with respect. Shark meat is popular in Asia, and it is here where a meal on a menu has rung the death knell for millions of sharks and continues to do so. A meal whose main ingredient is considered a real delicacy, costs a fortune, and is obtained by unscrupulous fishing operations concerned only with accumulating cash at the expense of compassion. Sharks are caught, the fins cut off and collected then the fish, still alive, is chucked back in the water to sink to the bottom of the sea to inevitable death. Blood from the wound attracts predators, which the shark is unable to evade, without fins it can't swim so whilst slowly suffocating it's eaten by scavengers. If that's not cruel, causing unnecessary suffering, I don't know what is! In its weakened state the shark has zero chance of survival, and this incredibly sought-after ingredient is sliced and diced to create a soup! Shark fin soup! Barbaric brutality for a soup and why are sharks finned in their millions and treated so abominably? The answer lies in tradition, status, and money. Shark fin soup, a recipe originating centuries ago during the Song, Ming, and Qing dynasties, was eaten by wealthy Chinese and Vietnamese families. In truth shark fin offers nothing to the meal, no flavour, and no nutritional value. Although illegal in many countries, shark finning continues thanks to unscrupulous fishing in international waters, including those of the Pacific Ocean. A delicacy obtained by a cruel trade threatens the extinction of an entire species, indeed vast regions of our oceans are already devoid of them. I'm reminded of my first diving trip to the Philippines, where we expected the waters to be buzzing with sharks but didn't encounter one, not one. White and blacktip reef shark, named for the respective markings on the dorsal fin, used to live in those waters as recently as ten years ago. A consequence of no sharks was an eerily quiet reef, no small fish or usual reef dwellers zipping about, even the corals were jaded and dying, it felt strange, unnervingly so. Not all the waters of the Philippines are the same, thank goodness. The Philippines are bounded by four seas, the South China Sea to the north-west, the Sulu Sea to the south-west, the Philippine Sea to the east and the Celebes Sea to the south. Beautiful regions such as Tubbataha, Anilao and Dauin, are bursting with life and full of sharks, I should know I've dived them all!

'Education and public outrage is helping to reduce the numbers of finned shark and consumption of this soup has declined but we still have a long way to go to restore the balance. Shark fin soup still appears on menus in popular tourist destinations such as Singapore as well as in other parts of Asia, and it's pricey. Believe it or not, even in the UK, which banned shark finning in its waters in 2013, and where governments support stronger controls, you can still import 20kg of shark fins for personal consumption.

That's twenty-five dead sharks! You can't cross the border with meat, cheese, or the humble potato but shark fins are good to go! Makes me mad! Makes my blood boil. It has to stop. Loopholes in legislation must be plugged! Shark finning must stop. As my love for sharks has grown so has my desire to help them, they need safe havens, to be protected in sanctuaries. Large swathes of our seas and oceans should prohibit fishing, any fishing, allowing our underwater world to live in peace, recover and thrive. Shark sanctuaries only cover 5% of our oceans which is a tiny drop in the ocean isn't it? There are 440 species of shark and a third of them are close to extinction! You say sharks are scary, but those numbers are scarier don't you think?'

'It's horrible. It's like the elephant tusks and rhino horns isn't it?'

'Yes it's the same only different. Elephant and rhino are poached for traditional medicine under the mistaken belief they miraculously cure illness. Poachers must have a black hole in place of their soul if they ever had one that is! How people can be so savage is beyond me!'

'Yeah my mate Adam is always banging on about ivory, his mam's an activist and says chewing finger nails would have the same effect! She says we should start a rumour that poacher's teeth are even better, it would soon stop poaching wouldn't it!'

There's no getting away from the gory details. If Charlie's anything like me, images of dying sharks will play on his mind. I can't talk about diving with bull shark without talking about how the experience affected me. From that day in Fiji, I see things differently, with a more critical eye and I'm not just talking about sharks. I scrutinise how people treat each other and how we treat the creatures we are privileged to share this planet with. Being kind is easy or should be! It's incredible how a twenty-minute conversation all those years ago sparked a passion within me that continues to burn today. I've just laid it on with a trowel and it may be prudent to change the mood a little.

'It's not all doom and gloom though Charlie, around the world charities and trusts exist with the sole purpose of protecting sharks but we must do more. The world is at a crossroads, we must act now to turn things around. We're the first world population to understand the impact our lives are having on our oceans, and I've not even mentioned climate change yet! Water makes up 71% of the Earth's surface, only 29% is land. Hindsight's a powerful thing. Let's hope we can turn the tide on our destructive practices so future generations are able to look back at our actions with pride not despair. Sharks make my soul soar and contemplating oceans without them is depressing, and at times an overwhelming feeling of helplessness consumes me. I feel completely at the mercy of others. If it were up to me shark finning would already be banned and this disgusting practice would be confined to our dim and distant past.'

Jane's gone quiet. She sounded a bit cross. Sad too. 'Are you all right?'

'Too many of my cherished memories are of diving with sharks. The struggle to embrace a future without them breaks my heart and at times proves too painful to bear. I'll never dive again, not with Beth for sure, but I don't really want to talk about that now if that's okay. I just can't. I can't go there right now Charlie.' We share a silence, a moment to mull things over I guess. He speaks first, softly, this boy is astute and steers the conversation back to happy times.

'You haven't told me about the dive. What happened, you must have seen a bull shark. Did you see more than one?'

'Oh yes, the dive, sorry, I've been preaching a bit haven't I! Okay, back to the dive. Where was I? Oh yes, on the boat. Trepidation tingled through my veins, jumping into the water with bull sharks was asking a lot of my nervous system. The enormity of what I was about to do was sinking in and it was considerably more terrifying than dropping in on hammerheads I can tell you. Only twice in my life have I experienced such dread, the kind that strikes terror in your heart and can still make your stomach somersault years later. The first time I experienced it was after agreeing to jump out of a Cessna at the end of a parachute in Peterborough! During my first year of dental school, in a moment of weakness, I'd taken a dare, the sort of dare you regret the second the words leave your lips. Six of us squeezed into a hold barely big enough for four and I would jump last! The plane took off. Our instructor advised we look up, words which instantly had us leering out of the window at the ground disappearing below. My heart skipped a beat when I clocked how high we were and where I'd be falling moments later. At two thousand feet the instructor slid the door open and one by one we were beckoned forward. My turn came round far too quickly! I crawled over, parachute on my back and dangled my legs over the side. We were in the clouds and the cold wet droplets soaked my face. I jumped! Flashbacks and jolting awake at two in the morning has been a part of my life ever since! The second time I experienced major butterflies was that day in Fiji, racing over the ocean to arrive at the dive site. The engine fell silent, and I took another death-defying leap of faith. Extreme sports, including diving and parachuting, are dangerous and nerve-wracking especially for first timers or those with a nervous disposition. It requires mental steel and an adventurous spirit to jump out of a plane or into dark waters where sharks roam. Anyway, I'm a tad impressed that I managed to do both!

'The mood on the boat became sombre in those final moments before entering the water. Nerves almost got the better of me as I awaited my turn. Thought it was just me, it wasn't until we climbed back on board an hour later that I discovered the truth, the rest of the group had felt the same but hadn't let on, not wanting to appear weak. When it was my turn to jump I shuffled to the stern, never did manage to smash the "walking backwards in fins thing" and instead waddled awkwardly to the back of the boat. Standing there, looking down at my blue Seac fins dangling over the edge, my eyes fell past them onto the dark grey beneath. Adrenaline launched into my bloodstream and sent impulses around my body leaving me flush with anticipation. Should have taken a leaf out of my parachute instructor's book and not looked down! The strength of my character was surely tested in those final seconds and I'm proud as punch I managed to persevere. Last-minute adjustments were made to my BCD and weight belt. Several stray strands of hair were slipped out from under the edges of my mask to prevent seawater sliding down them and finding their way to drip into my eyes during the dive – salt doesn't half sting and there's nothing you can do once you're down there. I took one last deep breath, inserted the regulator into my mouth and took a giant stride off the boat. Falling, for what felt like forever, I plunged feet first into the cool waters expecting the hit from a shark lying immediately beneath the surface. Thankfully, it never came, and I bobbed back up to the surface to join the others. Only after the boat had emptied of all divers did we receive the instruction to descend. Staying together we arrived on the seabed beside the sandy channel described so accurately in the briefing and were directed to our position in front of the reef. The water was teeming with fish, a fish soup I approved of! It was reassuring seeing so much life around, a shark surely wouldn't be interested in little old me with all this fresh fish fodder. We didn't have to wait long!

'A gigantic female bull shark, larger than I'd ever imagined, came cruising along the channel close to the sand. One, then two, then eleven more, thirteen in total, unlucky for some but not for us, not that day! Their size and shape was impressive. It was as if we were sitting in front-row seats at one of the best cinemas in town. The sharks came closer to hunt fish from the huge numbers schooling directly in front of us. The majestic female made silent, invisible movements to her fins in such infinitesimal proportions they were invisible to the naked eye. Without warning she changed direction, accelerated, and struck like lightening to take fish. I was closer to her than I am to you now, close enough to see her pupils roll back to leave sockets of white and her jaw thrust out for the kill. I'm not exaggerating when I tell you she was close, she swerved to avoid bumping into me; I loved her for that. That was the closest I've ever been or wanted to be to this finely tuned eating machine. I swallowed. My throat was sore. Breathing compressed air, with the moisture taken out, gives you a sawdust dry throat, nine minutes in and I was parched and dreaming of a cold beer in the Grog Bar. Bizarre how easy it was to be distracted even when death is staring you in the face! Over the next ten minutes sharks came in to feast from their fish buffet. Not once did they want to nibble on a side dish of our limbs, they weren't interested in us, not one bit or should I say bite! Although that wasn't strictly true, one shark, a young male, swam along the line of divers, something he'd probably done many times before, to tease us a little. As he drew level with me he turned his head and looked me in the eye. I held my breath. Time stood still as I awaited his next move, but he calmly swam away. Cheeky!

'The team of guides were professional throughout and having them there gave me a sense of security. Maybe it was a tad misguided to feel secure in this environment, but I'll be forever grateful to those brave boys! The experience was mind-blowing. The safety stop was memorable in itself, surrounded by white and blacktips and a couple of the marginally larger grey reef shark. If I asked you to imagine a shark, any shark, you would probably describe a grey reef, classically grey with a broad snout and dark eyes.

'Reaching the surface was thrilling as was the sun on my face and a view of that brilliant blue sky. Beth's urgent call to hurry back to the boat snapped me into action, bobbing on the surface in a shark-infested sea is not the safest place to be! Under the waves the shark discriminates information and chooses not to eat us, on the surface messages are less clear. Splashing about up there may confuse the shark, remember, most shark attacks occur at the surface. I didn't want a bull shark to mistake me for something it might want to eat, I'd done the dive and I am glad I did it but I was ready to get out and sooner rather than later. Within minutes we were safely ensconced on the boat. We'd enjoyed a sea temperature of 28 degrees Celsius and were beginning to relax in 30-degree heat, but a slight breeze made me chilly. A celebratory biscuit washed down with an unusually sweetened tea helped warm cold bones. Hunger pangs and stomach rumbles are common after diving, four more biscuits and they'd gone. Breathing compressed air, diving in salt water and being in a hot climate are all factors drawing moisture from our bodies, to avoid succumbing to dehydration divers need to drink more than the usual amounts of water. The atmosphere on board was electric. The divers were ecstatic to have witnessed such a spectacle and survived it! Even Tata was giddy. To see him exude such elation, at a spectacle he witnessed on such a regular basis, was a joy to behold. His mood was infectious. Coughing to draw our attention, he took great delight in producing an ornately carved box from his bag, holding it high for his audience to inspect, his movements and gestures similar to those of a confident magician performing a slick trick for the umpteenth time. His trinket, no bigger than a matchbox, remained shut as he revelled in the moment, pausing with poise to increase the drama. Cautiously raising the lid, he peeked inside, teasing us by shutting it immediately, only to open it again. Reverently he tipped the box of bits onto the table for us all to see, his prised collection of shark teeth! He sifted through the canines searching for the one he wanted, finding it he held it up, 2cm in length, a flat blade with serrations running down both sides, it tapered to the point. There was no mistaking it, minutes ago I'd been close enough to execute a dental examination on hundreds, maybe thousands of those pearly whites to know one when I saw it, the tooth of a bull shark. Time for his grand finale, he held up a sheet of A4 paper and we, the obedient audience, played our part, oohing and aahing on cue as he ran the tooth down the length of the sheet, slicing it neatly in two. It wasn't a struggle; he didn't put any pressure on the blade, the tooth cut through the paper like a knife through hot butter. Tata had performed a show of sharktacular proportions!'

'That's amazing. I didn't know the teeth were as sharp as that! Makes sharks scarier. You're brave. I can't imagine doing the things you've done. Which shark do you prefer, the hammerhead or the bull?'

'Ooh, that's a tricky one Charlie. On reflection I'd rather share the ocean with hammerheads, they're striking, graceful and often in large schools which makes for spectacular encounters. Bull sharks are powerhouses but too dangerous for me to enjoy in the same way. Shark attacks close to shore are made by bull sharks and often wrongly attributed to the great white, my nemesis. I'm glad I have dived with both species, but I haven't told you of my tiger tale yet and that was the best of the three.'

'Can you tell me about it? Please.'

And there's me thinking he'd be wishing to return to the sanctity of his pool and leave me to devour my thriller. Reflecting on one's past is spiritually uplifting, and I consider myself fortunate to have an eclectic mix of treasured dive memories that merge to make up my dive life. My tiger shark, my one and only tiger, I loved it! I loved the live-aboard, the dive and the destination. My paradise of endless sunsets and blue horizons. Where blue meets blue during the day and the stars dip their twinkly points into the ocean at night. Palau.

TIGER

One-sided conversations with ashen-faced patients nervously gripping at the arms of my dental chair was something I got used to over the years. My trusty chair stood proudly in the centre of my surgery from day one and was still there forty years later as I closed the door on my career for the last time. The first patient to lie back and enjoy its superior comfort was a young mum who, after dropping her little ones off at the primary school nearby, walked in without an appointment at 9:05 on day one. I'd foolishly convinced myself no one would come! Her family subsequently signed up and remained loyal patients to the last. The chair supported hundreds of patients over the years, including many families from that same school. Most found its supine position comforting, a place to lie back, relax and unwind whilst I tinkered with their teeth. Nervous patients struggled to even walk in the door and a small proportion of them were frightened of the chair, struggling to sit in it never mind be treated. Calm or stressed, thankfully enough patients sat down and held onto those arms to provide me with a good living. I'm genuinely grateful to them all, as were they for my attention to detail and care. Patients' contributions to my attempts at nerve-calming conversations were hindered by the usual occupational hazards: mouths crammed with cotton wool rolls, probing instruments and rotten teeth. They were rendered impossible when I needed to shape openings with my ear-piercing drill! Sadness coursed through my veins on that final day as the key clicked the lock shut for the last time. That's when it hit me, I'd treated my last patient, years of working with loyal and trusted colleagues had come to an end but it was when my eyes caught their final glimpse of my chair that my tears started to fall. How an inanimate object can become such a poignant symbol of a career ending and a new life beginning escapes me, but that chair was my constant companion sharing in my highs and lows. I felt terrible leaving it behind.

Today is different, today Charlie and I are able to speak freely, and the time has come for me to tell him my tiger tale. 'Time with the tiger was fleeting but astonishing nonetheless since it was unexpected. I mentioned Palau a little earlier but didn't tell you how historically special this place is, the crystal-clear aquamarine waters wash over a dark past. Reefs teeming with fish are a graveyard to lives long since lost, the resting place for Japanese and American sailors, pilots, and their crew, sunk or shot down amidst fierce battles fought during World War II.

'*Palau Blue*, our 38m, teak-timbered live-aboard was luxurious. Six en-suite cabins, hot water on tap, a team of cooks treating us to the best of Palauan cuisine and comfy sofas awash with cushions, all went a long way to support weary divers at the end of a dive day. Best of all though, it had a cracking coffee machine! Add an exceptional crew into the mix and you have the most comfortable of dive boats. A powerful engine whisked us to dive sites off the beaten track but other than that we sailed those sacred waters. Creaking timbers, fluttering sails and waves gently lapping against the hull are more pleasing to the ear than a constantly humming engine.

'As far as incredible dive sites go, Palau has more than its fair share, including the world-ranked number one, Blue Corner, and an intriguing site whose roots remain firmly embedded in the early 1900s, the aptly named, German Channel. At the beginning of the twentieth century Palau was controlled by the Spanish who, in their wisdom, chose to sell it to Germany! The Germans, in their wisdom, chose to bomb a reef to create a shortcut for boats transporting phosphate from the southern island of Angaur to Koror in the north. Phosphate is found in guano, the excrement of sea birds and was used to make fertiliser and gunpowder. During a volatile period in world history the phosphate became a valuable commodity to the Germans so bombing a reef was deemed appropriate to speed the process of manufacture. German Channel exploded into existence and become a popular spot for manta rays. Sharks have five gills. Manta have five gills and are therefore considered part of the shark family. The bluntnose sixgill and broadnose sevengill sharks are the only exceptions to the rule although more may exist, swimming in the depths of our ocean yet to be discovered, who knows?

'Manta have flat, diamond-shaped bodies, usually black and white in colour with two sizeable triangular pectoral fins, spanning between 5–9m which they flap like wings, earning them the affectionate title "big birds". Two cephalic lobes, akin to large paddles, help funnel plankton-rich seawater into their large mouth, these large rays diet on microscopic organisms. Our crew jovially referred to German Channel as a "big bird car wash"! Beth and I had already enjoyed a glorious ten days aboard and were making our last dive at German Channel before disembarking the next morning. The mood on the boat was electric, I'd never seen a big bird before and I wasn't the only one, fins crossed one would fly by!

'After rolling in we gently drifted down to the sandy seabed dotted with coral bommies.' The boy's quizzical expression suggested he needed the word 'bommie' clarifying. 'We live in houses in villages, towns and cities. Fish and sea creatures thrive in coral reef communities. It's where they hunt from and flee to when they are hunted. Just as our towns and cities are colourful, vibrant, and busy places, so are coral reefs. Our homes and buildings are made of stone and wood. Coral reefs are living animals, generally found in warm, shallow waters where the sun's rays are able to pierce through to reach them. The all-powerful sun sustains life on land and below the waves. A coral bommie buzzes with life and can be many metres tall, it's part of the larger reef structure but stands alone. The largest bommie I've explored was 7m tall and 5m wide and covered with an assortment of multicoloured soft and hard corals, animals that deceive you into thinking they're plants, swaying in the current with polyps that look like flower heads. An allotment of gardens at the bottom of the sea! An abundance of brightly coloured tropical fish darted in every direction keeping low to the coral surfaces. Rows of brown, big-eyed crescent-tailed fish surrounded the bommies, hovering immediately above the sand as if on sentry duty guarding the base. A tan-coloured moray eel gaped out of a hole, mouth opening and closing, spiky teeth at the ready to ambush a tasty morsel. Without warning it rocketed out, 4m in length, it slithered snake-like over the sand before disappearing under another bommie close by. Colourful slugs called nudibranchs, shrimps, crabs, and a multitude of miniscule life forms too tiny for the eye to see make their home on or in a bommie, all coexisting and spawning in this bustling metropolis. Manta rays are known to cruise slowly over a bommie to enable small fish, cleaner wrasse, to shoot up from their dwellings to nibble at parasites living on the manta's teeth, gills and skin. Manta cannot remove the unwelcome parasitic guests by themselves and have to rely on the cleaner fish to do the job for them. German Channel is awash with bommies making it a popular cleaning station for manta. Cleaner fish cleaning manta and there you have your car wash!

'We'd been instructed to roll in, swim down and kneel on the sand 10m from the largest bommie. If manta showed up we were to stay put, not approach them, or make any sudden movements to startle or cause them to feel threatened and so leave. Manta may choose to come to us but under no circumstances were we to encroach, disturb or interact with them. They are inquisitive but shy creatures and don't take kindly to divers speeding at them. Diving is about observing wildlife in their natural environment. After getting down I waited as instructed, scanning in every which way in the hopes a manta would make an appearance. Time ticked by, five, ten, fifteen minutes, no manta. I shuffled on my knees and noticed Jules, our wonderfully enthusiastic dive guide and marine biologist from Seattle, fist-pumping. She was looking down into the depths at something we couldn't see but judging by her reaction, soon would. Sure enough, seconds later, not one but two winged beauties soared into view and swirled loops over the bommie. They flew away but returned time and time again. It reminded me of when I watched *Swan Lake* at the theatre except this was *Manta Ocean*! When the manta had been cleaned to their satisfaction, they flew away over the sand and disappeared into the dark. Jules instructed us to fin slowly in the same direction, not to chase, just to follow, maybe we'd come across them at a bommie nearby.

'A grey reef shark accelerated past but stopped close to a cluster of small rocks, holding itself almost vertically in the water, swishing its tail fin slowly from side to side to remain in that position. Jules signalled for us to watch, it too was being cleaned, an unexpected surprise. We breathe using our lungs. The shark's respiratory organs are the gills. Some species of shark, the whitetip for example, are able to rest on the seabed, remain stationary and are able to continue pumping water through the gills to breathe. Others, including the grey reef shark, must keep moving to enable water to flow over the gills in a process called ram ventilation. We were close enough to see inside the shark's open mouth and what happened next was truly astonishing. An incredibly brave or exceedingly stupid cleaner fish swam into the shark's mouth and picked at the teeth. The shark's mouth stayed open until the wrasse swam out! It would appear that good oral hygiene is as important to a shark as it is to humans, not least me! Makes sense though, without teeth sharks would struggle to eat and ultimately survive. At least humans have the ability to prepare food, cut it up or liquidise it, something the shark cannot do. It was an unusual sight to behold and made me wonder about the first wrasse to swim into a shark's mouth – why wasn't it eaten? The shark must instinctively know somehow that the wrasse helps maintain healthy teeth. It would appear that sharks need to visit the dentist in the same way we do! The shark continued to fin and maintain its vertical position for twenty seconds or so before needing to swim then it would return moments later to be cleaned some more, booking back in for a repeat appointment! What an astonishing spectacle, the shark was literally coming in for a scale and polish! It took two minutes for the wrasse to clean the set of fourteen top and thirteen bottom teeth. Not even my wonderful dental hygienists could have cleaned teeth at that pace. If the shark had sat in my dental chair the same service would take anything from thirty minutes to an hour and we only have five more teeth in our full set. I'm not sure I could have persuaded any of them to stick their hands in a shark's mouth though, they weren't paid enough! Fish are fast and brave!

'The dive had already surpassed the others on this trip. I couldn't believe we'd been so lucky, but it wasn't over yet, not by a long way, other surprises were just around the metaphorical corner. I was startled by a manta flying in from behind swimming so close to me it eclipsed the sun. I froze to the spot as it swam over me, plunging me into darkness, the ray needed to make invisible adjustments to one wing tip to flick it up to avoid touching me. I hadn't encroached, the winged wonder had come to me, sought me out from the crowd. It seemed to hang in the water scrutinising me with large kind eyes before swimming away. Those eyes were huge windows to a beautiful soul. The rest of the group finned slowly in the same direction, hoping to catch another glimpse. Jules, Beth, and I were intent on doing the same but a miniscule movement on a bommie caught my eye. Two octopuses were moving their arms curiously in the crevices searching for crabs or snails. These normally shy creatures were not put off by the three of us gawking at them. Beth swam closer signalling for me to join her, but I beckoned for her to join me; we were there to look for manta after all.

'Beth nodded. I turned to go and there, less than 5m away, was a tiger shark, level with me in the water and heading my way. The wide, rectangular mouth made identification easy. I couldn't contain myself and let out an impulsive yell, not a scream of fear or a cry for help, rather an outcry, a shout from deep within that had to be released. My body tingled as if electricity were streaming through my veins, transfixed as the shark closed in. I'll never forget that jawline, the measured back, and forth motion of the tail and the immense size of the fish, it was massive, well over 6m long and potentially deadly. These magnificent specimens roam the oceans alone. It studied me with dark emotionless eyes, eyes that revealed nothing. My unintentional outburst startled the shark enough for it to turn away and in so doing reveal the vertical stripes along the dorsal surface that give the shark its name. The body is blue with a lighter underbelly which serves to camouflage the shark when it hunts. The tiger swam slowly at first then one flick of the tail and it was gone. The interaction lasted less than sixty seconds but left me stunned, speechless. Jules, Beth, and I ascended to perform the safety stop. I made fist pumps, Beth gave me a high five and Jules raised her hands out in front of her and moved the fingers as if they were claws, the claws of a tiger. It was her first sighting of a tiger too! Moments later and the other divers assembled alongside and the three of us gloated a little, nodding furiously whilst using our hands to demonstrate the claws of a tiger, a tad cruel really, and they couldn't hide their disappointment. Returning to the live-aboard, we reflected on an astonishing dive, being in the presence of such a creature and living to tell was a privilege and yes, I was relieved to have survived it. What had played out down there had been the shark scenario plaguing my thoughts and filling my dreams with dread for decades. That tiger shark was the only one I ever saw in the flesh and a memory that will stay with me forever. Our last night aboard was celebrated in a style befitting such an occasion, a beach barbecue with beer and fireworks. We absolutely did save the best till last that day.'

'You're so brave and strong to go in there with a shark that scares you.'

'You're right about that Charlie and that should tell you something.'

His ensuing silence told me one of two things. He had no clue what point I was trying to make or did and was pondering on it. 'Charlie, I've lived on this planet long enough to have experienced a lot of good times and sadly some not so. Life impacts on a person and events can and do change you for better or worse. Bad experiences can be hard to get through and can leave mental scars which take time to heal. Life is short and how you live it is up to you. In a funny sort of way life is like diving, with its ups and downs and I've had my fair share of safety stops I'll tell you! I've tried to be pulled forward by my dreams and not pushed back or held down by my fears.' I'm holding back and not revealing the whole truth. I can't. I'm struggling. People should never be fooled by a person laughing, smiling, and saying all the right things, these behaviours can mask a multitude of worries and anxieties. Everyone has their own challenges. 'Don't get me wrong Charlie, diving is a dangerous business and there were moments when I was worried for my safety and count myself fortunate to have made it out!'

MAELSTROM MADNESS

'My father's substandard carpentry skills caused me to be nervous of the dark for decades. Night times were a chore. As a child I wouldn't go into my bedroom, never mind get into bed, without my bedside lamp on. As a young adult I developed the habit of sleeping with a television on and it worked a treat, still do it now on occasion when I'm feeling restless. In my teens my parents would often go out two or three times a week, to meet up and play cards with friends, leaving yours truly to babysit the siblings. I'd take advantage and stay up late in the hopes the anxiety would stay away but when my weary head hit the pillow, panic inevitably jumped in there with me! Creaks and noises from the garden below my window filtered through the brick and glass and into my imagination which ran wild. I now know that hundreds, thousands of children and adults suffer with the same affliction but when you're fourteen you think you're the only one.'

'I feel like that, I do, every night at home. I hate it. I hate feeling scared. I don't feel so scared here; I think it's because we sleep in one room. At home I have to keep getting up and checking under my bed, behind my curtains and in my cupboards. I've started opening drawers as well. I don't even know why I do it or what I'm checking for. I think it's to know nothing's there.'

I feel for this wide-eyed boy, bless him, his fears are very real. It surely must reassure him in some way to know that others, like me, have felt or feel the same. 'Night diving is something thousands of divers enjoy; some even prefer diving at night to day diving! When I first heard about night diving I couldn't believe or understand it, who does that, who goes underwater in dark oceans! Crazy people, they had to be, and I intended steering well clear of that peculiar pastime, there'd be no diving in the dark for me or even close to sunset. I was certain of that!

'Beth and I had joined a live-aboard in the tropical paradise that is the Maldives. Comprising 90,000 square kilometres (35,000 square miles), the Maldives is the lowest country in the world, located in the Arabian Sea within the Indian Ocean some 1000km (620 miles), south-west of India and Sri Lanka. With over a thousand coral islands, turquoise waters, and average yearly temperatures in the high 20s, the luxury hotels in the Maldives are popular with tourists, honeymooners in particular. Divers love this destination too, large pelagic species including manta rays and whale sharks swim in those waters as well as the usual sea critters and reef dwellers. It was the abundance of sea life that had tempted us, and our trip planned to coincide with the plankton bloom in Hanifaru Bay on the Baa Atoll. Whale shark and manta choose to gather there in huge numbers to feed and spawn which attracted growing numbers of divers wishing to witness the spectacle. During 2011 the number of dive boats and divers crowding into the bay made it dangerous, propellers and surfacing divers don't mix! Restrictions were imposed in 2012 by marine park aficionados who implemented a diving ban leaving snorkelling as the only way to view these magnificent creatures and then only in a timed slot. At that point I hadn't been to the Galapagos, had I been I certainly wouldn't have jumped in! We were promised hundreds of manta but we were unlucky, only five showed up during our one-hour slot. Disappointment engulfed the boat. Tim, our inexperienced cruise director hailing from Brighton on England's south coast, was equally disheartened and feeling the pressure of not delivering on his promise. Not learning his lesson, he promptly reassured us with another! A foolhardy gesture, at best naive, he promised that the following evening we would do a night dive of epic proportions; there are no guarantees anything will ever show up! His assurances were greeted with wry chuckles but also a ripple of excitement, from the other guests, not me! I wasn't going on the night dive so didn't pay much attention to what he said but the rest were left in no doubt, the night dive was not to be missed. I gave it some thought, less than a millisecond and confidently announced it was not for me. My decision was received with incredulity from the guests, even Beth was flabbergasted, and she understood my misgivings. That night, after dinner, Tim took me to one side and spelt it out in words of one syllable, "You're going on the dive tomorrow or I'll chuck you in myself!" My protestations fell on deaf ears. He wasn't having any of it! Beth's tough talking finally convinced me, "You're here and you may never return to these shores again. You should do it, just think how proud you'll feel afterwards. It's going to be awesome!" That was it. I was going. Tim was delighted and set about teaching me the necessary etiquette for diving in the dark whilst Beth set about charging our underwater torch batteries. It is pitch black down there at night so a torch is a vital piece of kit, two in fact, should one fail, a scary thought!

'Moonlight is subtle, even once a month under a full moon, no amount of sunlight reflecting off the moon will penetrate the blackness under the sea, not enough to benefit humans anyway. Fish have night vision as do many underwater creatures. Creatures that inhabit the deeper depths of our oceans rely less on light having adapted to living a life in the dark. It's the same as if we were walking down a country lane at night, an absence of street lighting would see us struggling to find our way, our eyes adapt a little but owls, dogs and a host of other birds and animals see far better than we do. Sea life, including corals, use moonlight to behave in remarkable ways, to spawn, hunt, migrate and luminesce. Bioluminescence, the chemical reaction which occurs in creatures and plants to enable them to produce light, has been the subject of much research but scientists admit there is more to know. All very interesting of course but I wasn't concerned with any of that on the boat, all I could think of was what lay in store after plunging into the dark.

'The usual hand signals are not feasible on night dives for obvious reasons! Tim taught me how to signal okay by circling the letter O with the beam from my torch pointing to the floor, reminiscent to what children do with a sparkler on bonfire night. Protocol dictates that night dives usually occur in shallower waters, no deeper than 15m, should a diver get into difficulty there's no danger of them drifting down a drop-off to disappear into the depths. Night dives tend to be 45 minutes rather than the usual hour, without the sun's warm rays it's colder at night for the divers and the guys sitting in the dinghy waiting for you to surface to transport you back to the live-aboard. Other than that, a dive is a dive, and the same rules apply. Plan your dive, dive your plan. Tim instructed me to drop in and follow him.'

'But how do you know who to follow when it's dark?'

'Good question Charlie and I was concerned about that as well. The next morning, I woke up anxious and with a head full of questions. Before getting in the water, I discussed my worries with Tim. He told me to focus on what he'd be wearing, focus on what stands out as it would be picked up from a fleeting flash from a torch. He told me he'd be wearing pink fins and on the underside he'd scrawled, "follow" on the left and "me" on the right fin in white paint. He assured me he'd be diving in the classic prone position so the message on the fins would be easy to spot as I followed along behind. The dive was scheduled for 18:30. I couldn't believe I'd signed up and would be dropping into the abyss in no time at all. Tim called a briefing at 18:00 and his opening gambit was how thrilled he was that everyone was doing the dive, something unheard of previously. He made such a big deal of it there was no way I could back out after that!

'Our night dive would take place at the Alimatha Resort on the Vaavu Atoll, a popular holiday destination for Italians. Dive sites close to the shore are known as house reefs and we would be jumping in at "The Jetty". Story has it the kitchen staff would wander down to the jetty and dispose of food scraps into the sea. Fish would swim in from miles around to feast on the snacks. Never knew fish liked munching on pasta, pizza, and spaghetti! Apparently the fish continue to frequent the site even though feeding them there has not been common practice for years. Fish must have good memories! We'd drop in under a small wooden jetty. Only at the end of the briefing did Tim mention the word sharks! Great time to tell me!'

'So, you were going to dive in the dark with sharks?'

'Oh yes and remember he guaranteed we'd see them! I found myself hoping this was another promise that would fail. Seeing sharks when you can see them is one thing but seeing sharks when they could be anywhere your torch light isn't, wasn't what I'd signed up for! The plan was to go down and stay in one place, Tim's exact words were, "Sit back and enjoy the show." In those final seconds before boarding the dingy Tim gave me a get out of jail card, if I hated it down there I could exit the water at any time. Great, I could surface alone in the dark above hunting sharks! I didn't know before entering the water but so concerned were Tim and Beth that I'd freak out down there they planned to surface with me. Under a fading light we disembarked the live-aboard at 18:10, the dinghy raced over the waves arriving at the jetty fifteen minutes later. Clutching my torch, we dropped in at 18:30 and it was dark.

Torches are turned on before you hit the water, you don't want to be fumbling for a torch underwater in the dark. I was anxious, my senses were on stalks. Beth and I signalled okay to each other, my light beam lighting the sandy floor a short distance below, illuminating a seabed scattered with small bommies. Anxious fingers fumbled for the deflator button and dump valve; I had no desire to remain at the surface! We sank into the black, the darkest dark I'd ever known, no matter how hard my eyes strained to see, there was nothing but black. When it's dark and you're outside you can still make out a distant star, the shape of trees or clouds drifting by in the moonlight. If you're at home and the lights are off your eyes adjust and you are able to make out shapes of familiar objects. This was not like that. The dark was one shade of black pressing in on me, closing in. I remember blinking and instinctively rubbing at the front of my mask in the hopes of seeing something, anything except black. I had to focus on the beautiful beam from my torch, my line of light showing me the way, my glorious lifeline. We got down and hovered a metre off the bottom and waited. Suddenly something crossed in my light, from left to right, hugging the sand and then another and another, yellowish, grey and brown in light hues, sharks were arriving in huge numbers, and I recognised them instantly, their long body, broad head and longer-than-average tail giving them away, nurse sharks. An unusual namesake suggesting a caregiver! A sensitive shark! Unlikely! Why they were bequeathed a compassionate name remains unclear. Some suggest the origin lies in the sucking sound they make, resembling that of a nursing baby when they are hunting octopus, a favourite prey. For me, I think the name is more likely to have been derived from an old English word, "hurse", meaning, "floor of the sea". Nurse sharks are generally found on or close to the seabed and on that dive I literally lost count of how many were weaving over the sand in our direction. Speaking of old English words, a particular favourite of mine is "grubble", meaning to stumble around in the dark. I was certainly "grubbling" about on that dive! I have to say that at the time I was relieved they were nurse sharks as I considered them rather docile, not known to attack, but I was in the dark and there were lots of them, so I remained cautious. It was only later Tim informed me that nurse sharks are fourth on the list of shark species known to attack humans, so after the big three! Pondering on this I reached the conclusion this must reveal more about the victims of attack than the shark. Nurse sharks are prone to resting on the seabed in restricted spaces, under shipwrecks and in caves. Approached by a diver, the shark may feel threatened or cornered and defend itself. On the night dive the sharks were swimming freely, edging closer and choosing to move amongst the divers. Our group were in an orderly line with me at one end. I shone my light to my right and a shark was right there swimming silently by my side, hunting but not for me. The hunt was in full swing!

'I aimed my torchlight towards the floor at my feet and was shocked, marble rays had joined the party, huge specimens, two to three metres in circumference, grey and dotted with black spots, some I'd earlier mistaken for bommies. During the day marble rays are known to lie flat to swim or rest on the bottom but not at night, not when they're hunting. A hungry marble ray enveloped a small bommie searching for fish, crustaceans or shrimps that live there, it pressed its circular edge down and lifting its central body up creating suction, sucked prey from the nooks and crannies where they were desperately trying to remain hidden. I was observing a whole new behaviour. Poor little things had no chance of escape, after feeding until satisfied, the ray lifted itself off the bommie and headed my way! It swayed forwards and back in time with the swell in the water and I hoped it would swim on by, but it didn't. It stopped directly beneath me, and I mean within touching distance, throwing itself over a bommie it started to feed. I froze, my heart in my mouth, any sudden movement may have startled the ray and I was in the firing line, one whip from that venomous tail and

I could have suffered a terrible, possibly deadly wound. Earlier I compared sharks to dogs, and remember rays are related to sharks, in one regard however dogs and rays are not the same. When a dog is pleased to see you it wags its tail, the opposite is true with a ray. A wagging tail can kill! I didn't know it then, but Tim's eyes had narrowed to fix on me, he was concerned I'd startle and shoot for the surface, but he needn't have worried, I didn't move. To tell you the truth, I could hardly breathe so keen was I to remain locked in position. I wondered if the ray even knew I was there, Tim assured me it would have but had no reason to feel threatened by my passivity. I was able to stay down for the full forty-five minutes and would have stayed longer if allowed. My first night dive, nurse sharks everywhere and over twenty marble rays. It's funny Charlie but being down there in the dark with sharks was not scary, far from it, in fact it was enthralling.

'After a warm shower Beth and I sat on the top deck with a beer reflecting on how I was able to dive in the dark yet struggle at times to walk down a street at night or even settle down to sleep in my own bed. We concluded the answer must lie in an ability to focus the mind. I had found an inner determination to concentrate on the positive and shut out the negative. I had trained my brain. Since that day I managed to complete over a hundred night dives and although I was never truly fond of them I'm proud I was able to do them. Night dives are offered on most live-aboard trips, and I got into the habit of asking cruise directors to give me the nod when there was one not to be missed then that would be the one I'd do, you're rarely disappointed if you only do the best.'

'So, night dives scared you the most?'

'Not really. I remember another memorable dive in Palau that tested my nerves and we witnessed something truly special but were caught by surprise. I continue to count my blessings to have made it out in one piece. We had already dived two dives on the same site and Jules suggested we do our third dive there too and as it was the same day I naively expected the conditions to be the same. Remember this Charlie, always expect things to change, nothing stays the same, certainly where our seas and oceans are concerned. Jules had analysed the conditions and during the briefing said we'd be dropping in on a falling tide with a ripping current and as such might see some action. She wasn't wrong! We dropped in and spent the first twenty minutes revisiting sections of the reef we'd explored previously, checking out creatures we'd spotted earlier in the day. Jules then moved closer to the drop-off beckoning us to follow her out into the blue. Turning to look back at the drop-off, the cliff face disappeared down into the depths some sixty or so metres below, a sheer wall of rock vanished into the black. A tapping sound filtered through the water and when you hear that you turn to check who is hitting their tank and more importantly why. It was Jules and once she had our attention she pointed down. Scanning the black I couldn't see anything except black! Then, approximately 30m below, a grey reef shark emerged out of the dark closely followed by others, swimming in diamond-shaped formation: ten, twenty, thirty, forty and still more kept coming. I lost count at 180 and can only estimate the shiver to be in excess of three hundred strong. Never seen so many in one go, never will now! The sharks were swimming calmly keeping movements to a minimum, a small sway of the tail was all my eyes could distinguish. Gently jockeying for position, they remained tightly packed and avoided bumping into each other, if only commuters on the London Underground would exhibit such an awareness and respect for each other! Just when I thought we'd had the treat of a lifetime in the blink of an eye something happened to change the mood leaving me tense, scared, and feeling vulnerable.

'My brain registered a flash of white 20m ahead, level with us in the water, then three more. The speed my brain was processing what my eyes were seeing was too slow to keep up with the action. After this perceived time delay I was finally able to make sense of the movements. The shiver had shot to the surface and when I say shot, I mean at the speed of a bullet, one second they were 30m below swimming serenely and in that same second the shiver were at the surface. The flashes of white were four stragglers, the slowest sharks, trying to keep up. The speed those sharks swam was mind-blowing as was their instantaneous change of behaviour. We were in the midst of a feeding frenzy! The grey reef sharks had shot to the surface to strike and feast on their favourite prey, an enormous school of needle fish, swimming directly below the surface. Each successful strike resulted in more frenetic activity, sharks frantically vying with each other for scraps from the remains. The sharks, who'd been the epitome of calm, were swerving, attacking, stealing fish, and tearing at flesh, a whirling dervish fighting for food. Funny how your mind works, during those moments of carnage, I found myself contemplating the hordes of shoppers on black Friday or those stockpiling loo rolls in the midst of a crisis and giggled. The sharks ate until the last needle fish had gone, devouring the lot in less than two minutes! Jules raised both arms and fist-pumped in celebration. At the surface she told us she'd never witnessed such a spectacle, we were one heck of a lucky group, lucky with the tiger shark and lucky to survive a feeding frenzy to die for!'

'That sounds scary. Awesome but scary. So, was that the scariest thing?'

'Again no.' I pause giving myself time to think. This boy is hung up on the scariest and on reflection the scariest diving incident has to be one from Indonesia a few years back. 'We were on a transition cruise, embarking at Sorong on the west coast of West Papua heading to Ambon, a journey of 464km (288 miles) south westerly via Koon Island. We had dived in the Pacific Ocean in the Ceram and Banda Seas Charlie, a region blessed with magical underwater landscapes and colourful reefs equal to any on the planet. The seas surrounding Koon are home to hammerhead sharks and it was here when I feared we wouldn't surface to see the light of day and end up in shark heaven!

Diving at sites around the island, we'd had close encounters with four shark species, whitetip, blacktip, grey reef, and the hammerhead. Fortunate to see so many, we christened each site, shark city, shark city one, shark city two, you get the idea! Ranga, our local guide, suggested we dive our morning and afternoon dives at the same site but drop in slightly further along the coast each time as the current would change, in his words, "It will be ripping, and the sharks will love it!" The plan was to drop in, get down and drift with the current over the reef close to the drop-off and see more sharks. The dive would end where the reef curved at the pinnacle of the island, we would then follow the slope up until we reached a sandy plateau where we'd make our safety stop. Ranga emphasised the need to round that corner, if we continued to drift in the same direction, we would go over the drop-off where the currents were dangerously unpredictable, and we would be pushed down. The briefing was concise, we anticipated no problems, we would dive the plan. The morning dives were a breeze.

'Dive three! Same routine. We set off on the dinghy and dropped in closer to the drop-off. At least that bit went well! The second we went under it was obvious that the current was stronger than any of us had anticipated, even Ranga was caught out. It was the strongest current I'd ever dived in. Ranga had checked it only moments before, but the sea is unpredictable and can change in a second, it certainly did that day. It was ripping. Beth and I were shooting along at great speed, covering the ground so fast for every metre we were descending we were shooting along ten, maybe more! I desperately tried getting down but struggled to kick or even maintain a good dive profile, I was all arms and legs. Somehow I managed to make it to the reef though much closer to the corner than expected or indeed desired. The current was so powerful even the small fish had taken to hiding. There was no time to take my hook out to secure me in position, I had no choice but to grab onto a rock with both hands, if I hadn't I would have continued to drift helplessly. I looked for Beth, her arms and legs flailed as she sought to join me on the reef, but she just couldn't gain control and shot past above me. Beth was in trouble. She wasn't strong enough to combat the force pushing against her. If I didn't act she risked going over the edge! Being closest to her it fell to me to act and act quickly. I let go of my hold and shot off, not in the usual prone position, I was supine (on my back), enabling me to keep an eye on her whilst we both zoomed towards the drop-off! I let the current push me beneath her where I might have an opportunity to grab for her BCD, but she remained frustratingly just beyond my reaching fingertips. Time was running out; I would only have one more attempt to reach her. With every ounce of strength, I surged upwards, and my hands brushed her jacket and I managed to take hold. Determined not to let go, I pulled her down to the safety of the reef where we both held onto a rock for dear life!

'Ranga later revealed, whilst witnessing our precarious position, he'd considered our options for a safe exit and concluded we had two, slim, and none, and slim was risky! He contemplated instructing us to crawl up the reef on our hands and knees, do the safety stop and get the hell out but deemed this impossible, we'd run out of air before reaching the surface. Our only option, option slim, was to let go! We would go over the edge and down the drop-off. Of course, we knew nothing of this plan until Ranga signalled for us to release our grip on the rock! We had to put our trust in him so obediently followed his instruction. The force of the current had increased to three knots, possibly more, a force too strong for Beth and I and we shot off out of control. Kicking proved fruitless, as weak as a feather at the mercy of a powerful wind. Looking into the current the water pressed against my mask with such force the pain in my forehead was excruciating, it felt as if my neck would snap. A horrid thought in the midst of a crisis!

The pressure pushing against the breathing regulator in my mouth caused it to go into free flow, to continually let air out! Great hey, I had no control over how much air was disappearing out of my tank and I was heading towards the abyss and certain death! That is honestly where I thought this would end. My demise was moments away and it was terrifying. Sure enough, we reached the drop-off, went over, and straight down. I checked the dive computer on my wrist and although I was kicking to ascend as if my life depended on it, I sank from 20m to 31.7m in an instant. The carbon dioxide bubbles I was breathing out were going down with me before coming back up and hitting me in the face helping to make the whole episode completely disorientating! I couldn't even tell you if I was descending head or feet first! I checked my dive computer again and it was showing me at 18m, great but before I could celebrate I was back down again to 34m! This was scary and added to the mix I was becoming tired. In those seconds I focused on the small things, on trying to make a right decision, that one choice that would make a difference and get me out. Ranga suddenly appeared by our side and indicated for us to swim away from the drop-off, to kick and keep kicking, we obliged and without warning the current disappeared, we'd managed to swim out of it, to escape its clutches. What a difference five or six metres made. We rounded the corner and swam back to the reef, easy now that we were on the protected side. The sloping reef functioned as a barrier preventing the force of the current from hitting us, it was as if we were hiding behind a wall. I felt numb and my face tingled with adrenalin. It was only later on the boat that I had the opportunity to reflect on events and remembered the sharks! They hadn't even crossed my mind during the confusion and chaos. We'd been down in the deep, surrounded by sharks but hadn't seen one! What a show we must have given them. Bet they hadn't seen that before! We were at the mercy of the sea, in grave danger, in those mad moments nothing else mattered other than surviving the maelstrom.

'As I sit here now, I'm content to have mastered my fear of sharks, dentists, and dogs. The dark proved a harder nut to crack but we have made our truce. I'm able to sleep without the need for a light on most nights, even manage to make it down the garden to collect logs for the log-burner after night falls without having to keep checking over my shoulder. I have to make a dash for it but – hey!'

A yell from Matt cuts the air, time for Charlie to return to the caravan. A quick glance at my mobile shows 16:34, time flies when sharks join the party, the afternoon has raced by. He jumps into action, obediently tucking his bits and pieces into his satchel. Matt and I exchange a look and he discretely nods to the caravan. Covert signals are useful above and below the waves! I confirm my attendance with a nod. Packed and ready to go the boy pauses.

'See you tomorrow. I liked your shark stories. Bye.' He walks a short distance but stops, turns and with a sparkle in his eye adds, 'Ta-ra shark lady!'

Cheeky little fellow but his cheery farewell makes me smile. He's a good lad. Although it's getting on I want to read a little and soak up the last of the rays. This morning I'd felt anxious but am heartened by how the day has panned out. Reminiscing has been a therapeutic process, cathartic. Sharks will swim in my mind for the rest of my life, what a blessing. No, no, not now, why? In an instant the heartache that's been kept at bay chooses now to prod. No, no, I refuse to go there! Attempting to distract my thoughts I make a quick check up the hill just in time to catch Charlie disappearing inside his caravan. His youthful legs have carried him to the top in less than half the time it will take me later. I slide the switch on my kindle, looking forward to sinking into my thriller before I too must attempt the summit.

A FEAST OF SURPRISES

Surprise tea has been a thing in the Parker house forever. Mam isn't a good cook. It's not a secret. She admits it. I know it, her friends know it, my friends know it. When I have friends over we have a takeaway or surprise tea. She tells everyone she hates cooking! Mam's motto is, 'Food doesn't have to be fabulous, just get it down your neck!' She's never been a food fan. She hated meat as soon as the first slice of beef hit her tongue. Liver and onions. Grandma made her liver and onions. 'Leather and onions', Mam called it. She chewed it until her jaw was sore. She couldn't swallow it, so she stuffed it into her cheeks, and it stayed there until the meal was over. She could eat a whole roast dinner with two pouches of meat crammed in her mouth. Grandad called her hamster chops and the nickname stuck. She'd spit the meat on her empty plate when she'd finished, drove Grandma crazy. We don't eat meat; us boys never have. Mam says the animals deserve better, a decent life and us not eating them saves their bacon! Mam doesn't want animals to die for our scran when there are plenty of other foods we can eat. We eat loads of jacket potatoes with cheese, quiche, and coleslaw. We love it. Her mushroom, marmite and mustard pasta is legendary. That's two meals she's got down. Sometimes she watches those cooking programmes on the telly on a Saturday morning and she tells us she's inspired. Then she goes into the kitchen to invent a new, never-eaten-before-by-anyone-on-the-planet pasta dish. Never eaten before for a reason! Jamie Oliver has a lot to answer for. She watched one of his fifteen-minute meal programmes once and invented fig, aubergine, and avocado spaghetti. Jamie didn't weigh a thing, so she didn't either. It took her ages to chop the bits and chuck them in a bowl, she found a jar of dried herbs in the cupboard she'd had since she went to uni and threw half of that in too. She mixed it up then the frying pan came out. After washing the cobwebs off she started cooking. Three hours later, sweat dripping off her head, she dished up. There was loads left when we'd finished, it was rank. She knew it, we were all starving so me dad went to the chippy, and we had cheese pasty and chips, awesome. She was shattered and cross, 'Fifteen minutes my arse! That's three hours I'll never get back! That Oliver's a cheeky blighter. Never again!' Like all good northerners she had a brew and told us she was done with cooking, and we'd be having surprise tea tomorrow. I remember feeling great about that!

Surprise tea is not a surprise. It's a surprise if we don't have one! We have one most days and it can be for any meal, not just tea time. If we're good we are rewarded with one, if we're bad it's a punishment! The good ones are bits and pieces me mam picks up at work in the reduced section. Can be anything, cheese pies, rolls, quiches, cheese and onion bakes, red pepper dips, pitta bread, houmous, tortilla chips, stuff you can rip out of the packet and put straight on a plate. Mam says food tastes better when you eat it with your hands. The bad ones are leftovers from the fridge and cupboards, stuff well past the sell by date and have to be eaten before the rot gets worse and the hairs get longer! Yuk. The worst surprise tea ever was when Harry and me chucked stones across the street at the latch key kids opposite, Scotty and Stef or scratch and sniff as me dad calls them! Their mam and dad never got home till way after school chucked out, so they'd go home on their own and let themselves in and wreck the house or roam the streets looking for trouble. Their house is a tip, and the garden is like a landfill site. I've only been in their house once and it was disgusting. I had to wipe my feet on the front door mat on my way out! Throwing stones is never a good idea unless it's into a lake or the sea, I know that but that day, what was right and wrong wasn't in my head and anyway they started it! When we'd chucked all the stones from our garden we started using clods of soil the size of cricket balls and just as hard. Our front garden is full of them in between the weeds and convolvulus that me mam insists is a wild flower! It was a laugh. It was great until Harry hit Stef smack under her nose. She screamed so loud the whole street came out. Surprise tea that night was cottage cheese, two weeks after its sell by date and blue on top, soggy cucumber, and mushy brown avocado. Disgusting. Mam said us boys needed to learn a lesson. She knew we didn't like any of that stuff, especially the avocado. She tells everyone a story from when I was a two-year-old nipper. She said she asked me if I wanted avocado for lunch and plonked a bowl of green slime in front of me. I picked my spoon up and took a mouthful. She said my eyes rolled back in my head and my whole face grimaced, love that word! I was retching and spitting the stuff out and then I started crying. I told her, 'I don't like cado.' If me dad's around when she's telling someone he chips in with, 'Yeah, ya face looked like a bag of spanners lad. You thought she said, have a cado, you called it cado for years after that!' I've never lived it down! Dad got me with lychees too. He said, 'If you like cheese, you'll lychees!' Say it quickly, lychees – like cheese! I bit into one expecting cheddar but instead got slug-like goo! Yuk. Dad's funny in his own head! We shouldn't have been punished that night. Harry should have got a prize for being so accurate, he aimed at her and hit her smack where he'd been aiming. Would have been worse if he'd hit a car or a window. Dad should've rung Yorkshire County Cricket Club and got him a trial!

Mam's planning a surprise tea tonight and it's going to be a good one, maybe the best yet. I've spied crisps, cheese rolls, vegetable fajitas, falafel, coleslaw, salad, jacket potatoes, bowls of sweets and cheese and pineapple on sticks. Mam says good surprise teas must always have cheese and pineapple on sticks. I think the pineapple should stay in the tin, yuk! She says her best ones have a whole hedgehog, half a grapefruit covered in tinfoil with the sticks stuck in it! It's tradition in our house. Mam says, 'Cheese and pineapple on sticks makes everything better.' None of my friends like it. Nathan once got the stick stuck in his filling. That'll teach him for breaking his promise not to tell my mates about the aquarium incident. He broke his tooth. Karma they call that. Revenge I call it. Mam loves the cheese on stick thing. She says they take her back to when she was a little girl and Grandma did them. Grandma started surprise teas. She hates cooking too. When me mam talks about surprise teas she smiles and then her eyes get all teary. I guess they made her feel special. It's like having party food every day. I get it. I feel it too. The special thing about surprise tea is the surprise at the end, well of the good ones anyway. The pudding. They keep it secret, but I know what we're having tonight. I saw a cake and pots of ice cream squashed into the freezer. Better get changed and help get the stuff out.

At the ripe old age of 62, I wasn't relishing having to wash in a communal shower block. It has never been my thing and never will. They're of a type, white wall and floor tiles laid in the 1940s or '50s, cracked and barely held together with black grout, originally white, worn and stained from overuse and under-cleaning. It doesn't end there, random hairs blocking plugholes, doors that won't shut, ice-cold water warming only a degree even after the hot taps have been running for ten minutes, toilets that won't flush, no toilet paper or if there is, it's IZAL, the non-absorbent tracing paper, unpleasant and harsh! Not to mention clusters of spiders and their cobwebs all cloaked under that formidable bleach stench. No, I wasn't looking forward to showering in a room so completely unfit for its intended purpose. I'm guessing the Sea View shower block will be exactly this and things won't have changed since family camping holidays back in the '60s.

Dawn and Ken Brown, my parents' best friends and their five children, would join us at a campsite by the seaside in Rhyl, North Wales during the summer holidays. I can only imagine how the neighbouring campers must have felt watching two cars pull up and the ingratitude of children spilling out. Oh, they were great days, mostly taken up with endless games of cricket played on a patch of grass the size of a postage stamp. Keith, the youngest of the Brown boys, would scream he wasn't 'weddy' whenever he was bowled out and would refuse to leave the wicket until his father finally ordered him to make the walk of shame when he would howl the place down, well he was only three. One August bank holiday, Ken squeezed his mum into the back of an already overloaded Vauxhall Viva. The car was bulging at the seams, would love to have been a fly on the window in there. On one occasion I remember we were following them down the A55 when the back door flew open, and the frail old woman fell out. She rolled down the road across the white lines into the path of a bread lorry which swerved so as not to hit her, and she finally came to rest in a lay-by. I can only imagine the headlines in the local rag, 'Woman on a roll!', 'Life crumbling... almost toast!', 'They risked it for a biscuit!', 'Loafing around on the hard shoulder!' She proceeded to pick herself up, dust herself down and hobble back to the car where she was bundled back in as if nothing had happened. At the time the mood was a tad sombre at the thought of what could have been but as she survived to live another day it became a topic of much hilarity. Still makes me chuckle when I think of it.

The washing facilities at that site were appalling, our parents needed to resort to bribery to convince any of us to use them. Promises of staying up late, watching television and midnight snacks did the trick. We'd be safely ensconced in one caravan watching a Beatles or David Essex film, while the parents played cards and drank wine in the other. Good times. You could have knocked me down with a feather half an hour ago when I stepped into an impeccably clean and modern shower block, how things have changed! Not a cracked tile in sight, the floor and walls covered in a stylish ceramic tile, grey in colour, secured in place with a charcoal grout and the room light and airy. Vases of freshly cut wild flowers adorned the windowsills, hand wash and cream dispensers stood invitingly beside immaculately clean basins. Spacious changing cubicles, lockers, hairdryers and hot powerful showers completed the look. No smell, no hair, no blockages, and no spiders. Ten minutes under those pounding jets was the tonic I needed to reinvigorate tired legs after that hill climb, I left feeling as fresh as a daisy. Sea View had certainly moved with the times!

Sitting beside Dory and there's not a cloud in the sky, I'm enjoying my sea view whilst sipping a cool glass of Pinot Grigio before popping next door. Time to call Mum. After the usual exchanges the inevitable silence, a period of quiet lasting long enough to become awkward and forcing the call to end prematurely with the customary, 'Speak to you tomorrow, bye, love you.' The loss of a son is a pain that's everlasting, the loss of a brother the same. It's beautiful here, the smell of the sea wafts in on the breeze under the falling sun. I sip my wine, lean back in my chair, close my eyes, and relax. I justify my wine as part of my five a day, grapes are fruit after all! When the weather's warm it has to be a white or rosé. I'd packed a couple of reds to pop on cooler evenings. Life feels good right now. I can hear Charlie's parents barking orders next door. The time has come for me to set about preparing my gift for the birthday boy, can't turn up empty-handed. Scrabbling through my half-unpacked bags my fingers find my small token, small enough to fit into the palm of my hand. I stare at it and am reminded of where and when I first held it. It only took seconds to wrap, kitchen roll and sellotape come in handy! I slip the package into the pocket of my jeans and am nearly ready to go. The trickle of footsteps on gravel suggests the arrival of guests, gulping down the last of my wine, I pop the glass inside, grab a cold Cotes de Provence from the fridge, pick up my chair and head over, time to join the party!

I'm greeted by a chorus of hellos. Matt, beer in hand, introduces me to everyone and sets about organising drinks. They've put on quite a spread, shame about the cheese and pineapple hedgehog thing though, can't stand the fruit but it's an old-fashioned hors d'oeuvre which reminds me of back then, I can't think about that right now, can't let it in. As he introduced me to his wife Sam, I am reminded of a Sam I met in a chaotic boarding queue at Tenerife South-Reina Sofia Airport a few years back. Having purchased priority boarding, Beth and I were legitimately weaving our way through a throng of economy passengers who'd jumped the gun and were blocking our path. Two rather rotund women were refusing to budge. Beth asked if they were in the priority queue to which one replied, 'No, jog on, we're all going on the same plane, it won't go without you.' Jeered on by her gormless sidekick and toothless wonder, 'You tell 'em Sam!' That's when I waded in, 'We have paid for the privilege, we're not pushing in.' Sam, with a face like a bulldog chewing a wasp, came back at me in a particularly aggressive tone, 'Doesn't get you anywhere, what's the point, what a waste of money,' as she scanned the assembled throng for affirmation which didn't come. My smug reply hit like lightening, 'Well, it gets me in front of you two mermaids!' We then squeezed past the astonished pair and boarded the plane. Remembering this makes me smile, made many of my fellow passengers smile too! Sam's face was a picture, a Picasso rendered speechless!

Nicki comes to sit beside me and we immediately get chatting. It's funny really how some people feel the need to spill intimate details of their lives to strangers upon first meeting, her opening gambit is to tell me how she first met her husband, Steve. He was caretaker at the school where she taught and the moment she set eyes on him she knew. He was gorgeous and she made excuse after excuse to have to see him which was easy as they were often the only two people left in the school building past 15:45. That makes perfect sense to me, I can't comprehend why anyone would want to set foot in a school unless they were a child and forced to. I wouldn't be able to escape fast enough. Nicki raves about the good old days and how disillusioned and disappointed she'd become when systems and routines changed. She bemoans the curriculum, the hours of unnecessary paperwork and the endless assessing and testing which she deems unnecessary. She's on a roll and starts slating pushy parents and lambasting governors, both groups purport to be passionate about primary education until their child leaves for secondary school and they never cross the threshold again. As far as I'm concerned teachers aren't paid enough to work all the hours God sends to give a piece of themselves every time they step into a classroom to spend the day with screaming kids!

Conversation inevitably turns to me. Her first question, what do I do? Experience has taught me to exercise a degree of caution before plunging in and revealing my profession to strangers and I contemplate telling her I'm a driving instructor. No criticism of driving instructors intended but that's normally a conversation stopper! What's left for them to say, 'You're brave, bet you've had loads of crashes,' followed by a forced laugh! It's preferable to 'I hate dentists,' which 99% of strangers retort upon discovering I'm a dentist and infinitely preferable to what they do a little later! When I least expect it they ambush me with, 'Can I just ask you about this,' opening their mouth to show me the rotten tooth they need free advice for! A tooth they haven't cleaned since crawling out of bed that morning. A tooth covered in spinach and chicken from the quiche they've been chewing on. Lovely! Oh, the ever-present joy of halitosis! Present company persuades me to be truthful. Sure enough, within seconds Steve chips in with, 'Maybe you could tell us if Molls Polls over there really does need braces?' Upon hearing her name, the child in question rushes over sucking on a lolly! Should've gone with driving instructor!

'Birthday boy o'er there says he called ya shark lady. Don't know what ya been telling him but he's not mardy anymore. He were bogeyed this morning. So, shark lady, ya gonna tell us a shark story tonight?'

'Maybe later on if you're good.' My response makes him laugh. 'I want to get to know everyone before I scare them to death! I've been telling Charlie stories most of the day. I'm sure he's tired of hearing my voice.'

The evening flew by. We chatted, laughed, ate, and drank while the children busied themselves playing. I discovered that Sam, like me, was originally from Chester, born at the City Hospital and brought up in Upton, a suburb near the zoo. It's a small world, I was born in Upton, at home in Alwyn Gardens and before I could walk we'd moved to Hoole, another suburb, where I later attended my first school. Sam told me that her dad would sneak her under a fence to gain free entry into Chester Zoo, emerging in the zebra enclosure and have to run like the wind to avoid a kicking! My dad did that with us too and there was us thinking we were the only ones! Us northerners are a good bunch, love saving the pennies! Being a little longer in the tooth, I consider myself a good judge of character and I like to think I know a thing or two about people, I was in good company. 'They are the salt of the earth,' Mum would say. I almost didn't notice Charlie sidle in to sit at my feet.

'I told me mam and dad about your sharks.'

'Ey up lad, ya got a friend there shark lady. He's hooked on ya sharks ya know. Thought ya might have scared him to death, thought he wasn't keen on 'em, seems I was wrong, he likes 'em don't ya. They're ya favourite aren't they lad.'

Poor boy, studying his face it seems obvious he's embarrassed by these teasing remarks. Blinking back tears, Charlie folds his arms. My silence affords Matt time to plough on with his size 9s!

'Not scared of 'em at all are ya soft lad! Maybe we'll have a dip in the sea tomorra lad hey? Come on lad, let's get this cake eaten so we can bump ya.'

Charlie gazes at the floor. I feel for him and can't understand why Matt persists in throwing teasing remarks around to hurt his son. Cake lightened the mood all round, a delicious treat smothered in devine dollops of ice cream. Whoever invented salted caramel ice cream deserves a medal, that's going in my trolley on my next visit to Waitrose. We sing the obligatory, 'happy birthday' when Matt grabs his son restraining him in a headlock enough to render him helpless! Charlie squealed, forced a laughed and tried to pull away but Steve jumped up to help Matt with his quest. Between them they proceeded to give him the bumps. From the look on Charlie's face, you could tell he wasn't enjoying the experience. Who does? What's to like about being thrown into the air hoping you're caught before hitting the deck. It's degrading and at worst painful. Humiliation over, time to present Charlie with my gift. Fishing it out of my pocket it remains concealed within tightly clutching fingers. Only now do I worry if it might not be appropriate for this twelve-year-old boy. Too late they cried! We'll soon see when he opens it! I hand it to him, keeping it securely within the palm of my hand as people do when they have a spider secreted inside. 'For you Charlie, hope you like it. I think you will.' My words belie my true feelings. I can feel my teeth clenching and the muscles in my face tensing as he tugs at the tissue. Several additional unnecessary layers of sellotape have him struggling. The time it takes to open a present somehow adds to the excitement but ten minutes later and the need for scissors was a tad excessive! Eventually, peeling back the layers, his prize fell out and landed in his hand. He stared at it.

'What ya got lad?'

His dad's question was a genuine one, he was intrigued.

'This!' Only one word but his cheery response and huge smile suggest he was more than happy with my gift, holding it up for his father to see. Having originally been presented to me by Tata in Fiji, it felt right to pass it on. After disembarking *Orion* after that memorable bull shark dive, Tata handed the tooth to me, whispering, 'For luck!' One quiet afternoon in my dental surgery, I drilled a hole through the root end and threaded a black cord with securing clasp to enable it to hang from my neck. I wore my home-made necklace on dive trips, my good luck charm. Not known for sporting jewellery, my trinket box only contains two other chains, a hammerhead, and a manta ray, both small silver pendants affirming my love for sharks. My decision to gift Charlie my shark tooth was impulsive but correct, joy was etched on his face.

'It's great. I love it. It's that bull shark tooth isn't it, the one he cut the paper with?'

'Yes and it continues to be razor sharp, so take care.'

He rushed inside bringing back the obligatory paper and delighted in demonstrating what would become his party trick! His eagerness was endearing.

'That's extremely kind of you Jane.' Sam declared softly. 'He loves it, thank you.'

'Yeah, we buy him shark stuff every year and he's not keen on 'em are ya poor baby! He likes that tho don't ya? If ya were Pepper ya'd have two tails and be wagging 'em both wouldn't ya lad! Cheers shark lady. Ya made a young lad very happy.'

Matt lunged for Charlie and managed to grab him, holding on, he started pulling him onto his knee, ruffling his hair and tickling him. 'Not too keen on sharks are ya lad?' He then made as if to bite his shoulder. Charlie says nothing but his face speaks volumes, his eyes narrow and he's pulling to escape this unwanted attention. Matt is humiliating his son and the boy seems close to tears. I know nothing of their relationship but assume Matt is sniffing out a known vulnerability for a reason I can't fathom, maybe in some power play or to stroke his own ego. Oh, I don't know but what is clear is that this attention is resented. I come to Charlie's rescue.

'Would you like me to tell the children about one of my shark encounters?'

'If ya fancy it, yeah. Ya wanna hear a shark story don't ya kids? I know Charlie does, don't ya lad. He loves sharks don't ya son, his favourite aren't they lad hey, hey? Think ya know already he likes coming here to the seaside don't ya? Ya like being at the seaside don't ya, to be at the side of the sea but not in it, hey lad!'

Matt's playing his son like a fish, but his incessant teasing isn't reeling his son in, quite the opposite, it's keeping his son at bay, pushing him away. Although I intend this metaphorically, Charlie confirms I'm right when he moves to stand behind his mother, who jumps to his defence.

'Leave him alone Matt. For goodness sake it's his birthday party, enough now, get everyone a drink sweetheart, come on, glasses are empty.'

The encounter is good-natured, but I have sympathy for the boy. No wonder he's not divulged his fears to his father, if he were to open up and reveal how sharks are crippling him, the teasing could become relentless. Or would it, I don't know Matt well enough to make those leaps in judgement, but Charlie has, for whatever reason, chosen to conceal his feelings from his family. Matt laughs and leaps up to fulfil Sam's request.

'Come on lad, sit yaself down. I'm only teasin' ya. I'll fill ya glass shark lady and ya can try and calm this lot down before bedtime. Come on boys and you, Molls Polls, time for a shark story.' He growled like a dog, interesting that he too likens sharks to dogs!

The children run over and sit down falling silent with expectation. Earlier Matt had mentioned a word, 'hooked', it triggered a memory. Funny how words can do that.

'One of my shark dives took a surprising turn. Would you like to hear about it?'

The children's squeals leave me in no doubt. I'll tell them of a dive we made in South East Asia in an area known as the coral triangle. We dived in the Flores Sea in the Komodo National Park. The sun-kissed reefs in this part of Indonesia are awash with over two thousand species of fish and some of the richest coral reefs in the world. Diving here was a privilege and I loved every minute of it, well that's not strictly true, I certainly didn't enjoy the dive at Castle Rock with my blessed hook!

HOOK, LINE AND SINKER

'I hadn't been diving many years when Beth, my dive buddy, suggested we do a trip to Indonesia. We'd booked ten days aboard the live-aboard, *Tranquillity*, a sail boat not dissimilar to *Palau Blue*, the boat I was telling you about earlier Charlie, except larger in every respect. A live-aboard is a floating hotel that transports you long distances to dive sites far out in the oceans, you eat, drink and sleep on it; you live aboard! *Tranquillity* was 55m long, luxurious, and spacious, the perfect vessel to home eighteen guests. The outdoor dining area took up the entire width of the stern on the middle deck. The canvas ceiling, criss-crossed with white LED rope lights, made it feel as if we were eating under the stars even when it was overcast, or the heavens opened.

'On the morning of the third day, our Spanish cruise director and dive guide, Isabella, Issa for short, gave the briefing and I sensed a shift in tone as she spoke of reef hooks. At that point I hadn't heard of reef hooks never mind used one, so she had my undivided attention. She made it very clear we couldn't go on the next dive without one! I didn't have one but luckily for me they sold them on the boat; fancy that! We'd be diving at Castle Rock, a dive site just off the coast of the uninhabited island of Gili Lawa Laut with its grassy hills and deserted beaches, a picture-perfect paradise. The plan was to drop in at a pinnacle, a mountaintop, immediately below the surface. Our dive was set for low tide when the pyramid-shaped summit would be poking up out of the water making our entry point clear. A rigid hulled boat (RIB), a strong dinghy, would whisk us the short distance from the live-aboard to the dive site. Issa's briefing emphasised the need for us to get down to the seabed as fast as we could and once down we needed to stay down! You sit on the side of the RIB, roll back and race down head first as fast as your fins will take you, dropping close to the summit in a similar way to how a parachutist leaps from a plane, only falling much slower!

'She jotted down the major points on a whiteboard:

- 'Roll back from the dinghy – do not hang about on the surface.
- 'Fin down quick.
- 'Hook on.
- 'Give the inflator hose a couple of gentle squeezes to put a little air into your dive jacket so you hover off the bottom. Sea creatures don't want you lying on them or the place they call home!

'Issa emphasised her final point, anyone failing to make it down to hook on was in danger of being washed away with the super strong current common at the site. At worst we'd end up in Australia! If we did find ourselves at the mercy of the current we must surface immediately and get picked up by the RIB. The severity of the situation I found myself in was crystal clear and I was determined to get down, hook on and watch the show!

'The hook, made out of stainless steel, is 10cm long and is attached to a 2m line which you clip onto the front of your BCD, that's the jacket you wear when you're diving. When you're in a strong current you secure the hook under a rock, ledge or in a crack and it helps to keep you in one place. Boarding the RIB that morning was a trial, swelling seas and a blowing gale helped throw me into my seat. My knuckles strained, with every ounce of strength I could muster, to keep hold of the safety line, the rope that ran around the sides of the bobbing boat. I held on for dear life! My head was full of anticipation and riddled with fear for what may lie in store! What if I didn't make it down, where would I end up, would I be the only one to miss it, would I be swept away, would I be alone? Many questions but no answers. All aboard and we were off on our stomach-churning journey across an angry sea. Five minutes into the ride Issa advised us to begin making final checks so when we arrived at the dive site we'd be ready to heave ourselves up onto the side of a RIB, not an easy task when you're constantly moving, rising, falling, and turning. The RIB resembled one of those sick-inducing waltzer rides at the fairground from my teenage years. You'd just get used to a certain rhythm when you'd be randomly jerked into another. We were at the mercy of the sea with a 20kg scuba tank on our back which proved tough I tell you. Out of the water the tank feels like you're carrying a seven-year-old child on your back, underwater it's as light as a feather, thank goodness. My knees were buckling but somehow I found the strength to stand up and sit down without falling. I was poised and ready.' I meet Charlie's stare. His unblinking eyes are fixed on me. I'd love to know what he's thinking.

Jane is brave. She must be. I don't get it. She makes diving sound exciting. Amazing. I could never do what she does. I'm not brave like her. I look at me dad. He's listening. Not making any cocky comments now is he. Never listens to me. That's why I don't tell him anything. He's mean to me. I want to scream my head off at him every single day. Dads are supposed to be mates with their boys. Nathan always bangs on about how cool his dad is. Why isn't me dad like that with me? I don't get it. It's not fair!

'So, there I was, tense and dry-mouthed, sitting at the edge of the RIB waiting to roll back, gulping at the air. Time seemed to stand still until Issa filled the silence. Speaking softly but with a quiet air of authority she gave her final stark reminder, "Don't hang around on the surface, get in, get down and hook on. Ready?" Then, with a glint in her eye she added, "*Quieres ver tiburones?*" We exchanged confused glances before she translated the Spanish, "Wanna see some sharks?" My heart was thumping when she calmly instructed, "One, two, three go!"

'It started well! Rolling back, I hit the water, spun round to face down, and finned as if my very life depended on it! It did! It felt as if my heart would pop! Kicking furiously with every ounce of strength my legs could muster I promptly arrived on a rocky ledge 28m below. Since that day I totally understand how an Olympic sprinter feels after crossing the finish line and could have easily collapsed with exhaustion and vomited, not recommended with a regulator in your mouth! The force of the sea pushing against my mask was intense, pressing the rims into my eye sockets with such force I was convinced I'd have permanent red rings around my eyes and come up looking like a clown, ugh, perish the thought! Bubbles of exhaled air normally float gently to pop at the surface, not this time, no, this time they were shooting behind me, my hair too. It was as if I were standing in a gale-force wind, straining forward to avoid being blown to oblivion. I'd got down. Phew, the sense of relief was overwhelming. Now I had to hook on. My fingers fumbled unsuccessfully to unzip the pocket on my BCD that concealed my lifeline. Panic flooded in; I couldn't even open the pocket never mind retrieve the hook! I fully expected to be swept away at any moment but needn't have worried, as if by magic, Issa appeared by my side, she took charge, retrieved my hook, and secured it soundly under a rock. I wasn't going anywhere. With a quick press of the button on my inflator hose she added a little air from my tank into my BCD, serving to make me buoyant and I promptly lifted off the bottom. Her small frame might fool some into thinking she lacked strength, not me. It never ceased to amaze me how those who dive professionally develop superhuman qualities, superior muscle strength and an ability to streamline their bodies to move as fish do in challenging currents. Currents that left me floundering like a flounder at the end of a line!

'Both Beth and I had made it down. We were hooked onto a rocky plateau near the edge of a drop-off, a steep cliff that disappeared below. There was no reef to speak of, no colour, no fish, it appeared devoid of life. Well not quite. There were sharks, blacktip, whitetip and grey reef sharks, I started counting and lost count at seventy. I was hanging in the water at the end of my hook, like a kite flying in the wind, watching sharks zip by. Sharks patrolled in every direction, some buzzed close by; others kept their distance. Watching individuals swim the same route time after time, turning to ascend or descend in the exact same place, I realised sharks are creatures of habit, who knew? You learn things every day and I loved learning more about sharks. They gather at the same place, at the same time, every day before going their separate ways to hunt once darkness falls. Castle Rock was obviously a popular meeting place. White- and blacktip sharks swam close to us, maybe curious. Cautious grey reef sharks kept their distance, swimming in the open waters beyond the drop-off. Sharks swam up from the ocean depths, moved silently in the currents only to disappear back down. There was no attack, not even a threat of one. We remained hooked in position for fifty minutes and then the end of the dive loomed large.

'My trusty sliver of silver had secured me safely in situ, but it was time to unhook and return to the surface. Issa made no mention of deflating during the briefing. I'm certain I'd have remembered that little detail. Deflating, depressing the same hose as before to let the little bit of air you'd put in your BCD back out before unhooking. No, she hadn't mentioned it or if she did, the word hadn't made it as far as my ears! Issa gave the signal to unhook, curving her index finger and thumb to form a c shape and moving her hand backwards and forwards a couple of times. She held up three fingers to show the count back from three to one to enable us to unhook at the same time, a safety precaution ensuring no one gets left behind. Imagine the horror of being stuck on a hook at the bottom of the sea! The current had picked up and was raging. Issa counted down and we unhooked.' I leave a pause to increase the dramatic effect and the ensuing silence is telling. They're hooked! I wasn't!

'I later found out that everyone else deflated their BCD before unhooking allowing them to sink a little and drift away together as a group. Having less air in your jacket helps you maintain a position closer to the bottom to help you find places to hide from the current until you reach slacker waters, or the current subsides. That way you can control the speed of your ascent, ascend as a group, perform the safety stop and exit the water together. There's truth in the adage, "safety in numbers"! Being alone down there is never a good idea and unfortunately that's precisely what happened to me! I flew off, soaring upwards as if shot from a cannon. The air in my jacket was making me as buoyant as a balloon! I knew I shouldn't ascend too fast, going up quickly is dangerous. I needed to stay down and was frantically trying to let the air out of my BCD to halt my progress but was all fingers and thumbs, caught in the current, shooting along out of control, like tumbleweed at the mercy of the wind in an old western. Somersaulting backwards, I eventually managed to hold the inflator hose above my head long enough to press the deflator button but in my haste emptied all the air out of my BCD and dropped like a ton of bricks to the seabed, landing heavily on rocks behind a huge boulder. I took a moment to catch my breath and that's when it hit me, I was lost at sea, alone, separated from the group, with no idea where I was, where I should go or even what to do!'

You could cut the tension with a knife. I'm really getting into the flow of things now. Sam can't help herself, 'Crikey Jane, what on earth did you do? Can't even imagine how you must have felt!' Looking at the sea of shocked faces staring at me takes me back to my infant school days. Wearing that cruelly coarse tweed uniform, sitting cross-legged on that classroom floor for hours on end, bare legs exposed to bugs in the rug and itchy bites scratched red raw. That rug, fraying and worn out, tired like Mrs Cope our poor teacher. Bored out of our brains, we did everything but listen to her ranting and rambling. Lessons were a chaotic mess. She excelled in her incompetence and cope she most certainly did not. The obedient children sitting on the grass at my feet are making my anecdotal exchange easy.

'Okay, where was I?'

The question, intended as rhetorical, was immediately answered by Charlie's enthusiastic shouts, 'Stuck behind a boulder at the bottom of the sea!'

'Thanks lovely, yes, I tried lifting my head above the boulder, but the force of the water pushed hard forcing me back down. Every time I tried to escape the same thing happened, I was trapped and alone with no way out. I was like a leaf at the mercy of the wind. I'm not averse to my own company but down there I was increasingly desperate to see another human, anyone. Dark thoughts started running amok in my mind. I couldn't shake the sickening vision of my boulder being my headstone. I felt sick. My nerves were shredded, and panic had well and truly set in as the reality of my position sank in. Realisation hit. I was alone in a shark-infested sea and no one knew where I was to come rescue me. I knew I was minutes from death, twelve to be exact, that's when the air in my tank would run out. This would be the day I'd die. When I'd opened my eyes on that May morning I never contemplated that was the day they'd close forever. Some sad souls know the moment death will strike and for others I'm guessing, it comes as a bit of a shock. I will never take the simple acts of breathing and blinking for granted anymore. Thoughts turned to my mother, who would tell her and what would they say? I was moments from drowning, being swept away, eaten by sharks, or most likely all three. It was pretty sobering I can tell you.' Forcing a smile, I am aware of the shock etched onto the faces staring back at me, it may be prudent to move on, death and the frailties of life aren't the best topics at a birthday party! Time to change the subject! 'But you know what? I got out, if I hadn't, I wouldn't be sitting here with you would I?'

'What happened?' Young Eric's question shows he's listening!

Not wanting to give it away too easily I decide to tease them a little. 'Well, what do you think? How did I get out of that, maybe a dolphin swam down and I hitched a lift or maybe a passing mermaid carried me up in her arms? What do you reckon? Mmm, no? Anyone want to hazard a guess?' The ensuing silence tells me to put them out of their misery. 'The answer isn't exciting but none the less effective, bubbles!' The word was greeted with quizzical looks from the ensemble.

'Bubbles!' Charlie could hardly contain himself. 'Bubbles, how? How did bubbles help you?'

'Bubbles, Charlie. My bubbles. The air I'd been breathing in from my tank went into my lungs and the carbon dioxide leaving my lungs was breathed out into the ocean. We don't usually see the carbon dioxide we breathe out, it's an invisible gas but we do see our breath on icy days and when diving. The bubbles float through the water until they find their way up to the surface and they are visible to anyone in the vicinity. My bubbles were a life-saving beacon, a shining neon sign, as good as an arrow pointing at me for everyone to see! The air I'd been gulping in and exhaling during those desperately frantic minutes was responsible for saving my life, oh and Issa of course, who'd witnessed everything. The first I knew I would live was when Issa popped her head round my boulder and signalled the okay sign. Okay? Was I okay? No one could comprehend the relief. She held out her hand and pulled me up. Her movements inspired confidence, she was as strong as an ox, I held onto those life-saving fingers so tightly, no way was I letting go until I made it out.

'We joined the rest of the group at the pinnacle, 5m below the surface, where they'd been diligently waiting for me and performing the safety stop. Just when I thought it would be plain sailing, the sea had other ideas before setting me free. Without warning the strengthening current pulled me down and there was nothing I could do about it. I couldn't hold on and plummeted down an invisible waterfall back towards the bottom of the sea. Desperate not to become separated from the group for the second time that day, my fingers scrabbled for Issa and miraculously managed to grab her calf and cling on! We spiralled down and in the blink of an eye we had sunk down to 18m. What a picture we must have made, me flailing behind her like a fish at the end of a line. A couple of kicks from her powerful legs and we were back at 5m. To this day I tell anyone who'll listen that Issa saved my life twice and in about as many minutes! I held onto her leg during the safety stop not letting go until reaching the surface. Getting out of the water was a joy, the fresh air filling my lungs liberating. Issa had a story to tell as did I. The crew found it hilarious and would lunge for my leg at every opportunity! Strange isn't it, you'd think after a scare like that I'd be put off diving for life but far from it, I kept going back for more!'

'That's one heck of a story shark lady can't understand why ya do it, ya call that fun! Ya a braver sausage than me, ya'd never catch me swimming with sharks nor any of my lot! Moral of the story is, don't do it!'

Matt's comments elicit a titter from the group. If I'd been given a pound for every time I'd heard those words I'd be a wealthy woman! I'll give him the same response I've given countless times before, let's see if that wipes the smirk off his face!

'If I can do it then anyone can! Diving is dangerous but so is crossing the road and we do that every day. People get hung up on how dangerous sharks are and yes eighty or so unfortunate souls are attacked every year, which is, of course, horrendous and five or six people will die. Those last few moments of suffering must be unbelievably terrifying, truly horrendous to contemplate. Attacks are often on swimmers or surfers splashing at the surface which may fool the shark into misinterpreting them for something else, maybe a seal. The curious shark comes in and takes a bite, realising its mistake it retreats affording the majority of victims the chance to escape and get out of the water. It's awful, there's no disputing it, a tragedy and a terrible shock for the family and friends but most sharks pose no threat.' Thought that would shut him up but he's not having any of it.

'Nice try shark lady but it'll take more than that to convince any of us to go down there with 'em! Whatever floats ya boat I suppose!'

Not sure why but his sarcastic tone niggles me. Time to deliver my punchline, 'Okay, yes, sharks kill, they do but what about horses, deer and cows, they kill too?'

'What about 'em? Ya not seriously trying to tell me they're like sharks are ya?'

His inane idiotic guffawing is getting to me!

'Give o'er shark lady, yeah, blokes down our way always dying of cow bites, ya very amoo-sing. Only thing a cow bites is grass, great lawn mooers they are! Dying from a cow bite would be headline moos! Got plenty more where these came from!'

Does he know how unfunny he is? He's standing there triumphant, believing his infantile quips have proved some point or other. The younger ones find him funny. I find him irritating. I stifle a yawn! Charlie's frowns reveal he's not sold on his father's humour either. The muscles in my cheeks are tightening. I'm not known for suffering fools and am finding it a struggle to contain myself where Matt's concerned. Hackles raised, I diplomatically choose to repeat my question but this time address only the children. Charlie jumps in.

'Cows and horses don't kill like sharks. Cows are dull creatures. All they do is eat grass, stand and stare at you or lie down and stare at you. Horses are marginally more interesting, and deer are harmless. None of them are scary. They're scared of us.'

'Of course, you're right Charlie, they don't kill like sharks, but they do kill! Every year, across the globe, cows kill around twenty-five people, horses about the same and deer kill hundreds.' Now I've got Matt's attention, not saying much to that is he! The children's ears have pricked up, I've hooked their interest. I have no idea why, but I feel driven to defend sharks! 'Horses, deer and cows kill many more people than sharks do but it's sharks that get the bad press! I'm not suggesting for one moment that horses, deer, and cows intend to kill, incidents are the result of accidents, but they kill all the same. Horses throw riders or kick out when frightened. Destrier horses, now extinct, were war horses belonging to knights in medieval times and were trained to kick and kill during battles. Deer jump out when drivers least expect it and cows charge or trample, the average weight of a cow is 720kg, only 150kg less than a small car, when that hits you it's a lethal weapon! What I'm trying to say is that other animals cause people to die.' I pause for effect and to give myself time to consider the next question to reinforce my point. 'Come on then kids, here's another one to get your brain into gear. One creature kills more humans than any other, anyone care to take a guess?' Not needing to be asked twice, the children chime in with, lions, tigers, hippos, elephants, killer whales, scorpions, jellyfish. 'No, come on what could it be?' Eric can't contain his frustration.

'Tell us! Tell me!'

'I'll give you a clue. There are 195 countries in the world and this animal lives in 190 of them, including ours. Dogs, foxes, and snakes are Harry's contributions. 'Sorry Harry, one more clue before I tell you, okay? Here goes, it's tiny.' Birds, bees, wasps, ants, spiders, after which, the group fell silent. Flies was Eric's final guess, which was greeted with howling from both families.

I waited a while before coming to his defence and putting them out of their misery. 'Mosquitoes. The tiny but deadly mosquito and the word, "mosquito" is Spanish for, "little fly"! Eric, you are correct, well done!' No one's laughing now but a great big smile is plastered across my face. Turning to Matt, I'm eagerly awaiting a stream of his mosquito jokes, strangely none are forthcoming. I guess mosquitoes just aren't funny! 'Mosquitoes spread disease but not all mosquitoes, only the females of the species. They buzz down and stab you with a needle like proboscis in their mouth on the hunt for protein that's found in blood. It's only the females that do this as they need the protein to encourage their eggs to grow! Most of the time we don't feel a thing, a parasite in their saliva numbs the wound so they can suck our blood at leisure, without us even knowing and it's a parasite in the saliva that gives us malaria killing over half a million people every year. Imagine if sharks did that! No one would get in the sea ever again! Swimming, diving, even paddling would be too terrifying. Another half a million people die from dengue fever, encephalitis, and yellow fever, also transmitted by mosquitoes. They're tiny but big killers yet people don't fear them in the same way they do sharks. We protect ourselves with a spray which helps blow any worries away. They should play that, duh dum duh dum, shark music when a mosquito flies by, adding an ear-piercing scream should it land on a baby! Of course, there's something else even more dangerous than mosquitoes and that's humans of course! Half a million humans die at the hand of other humans every year, making us our own worst enemy! Humans kill at least one hundred million sharks every year making us their worst enemy too! I haven't even mentioned the number of deaths to humans from falling coconuts, popping champagne corks, people chucking themselves off ladders or falling icicles. All kill more humans than sharks do. I'm not saying that sharks don't kill, they do but so do everyday things that we don't fear. It's about proportion and perspective. Sharks killing humans is a mere drop in the ocean.'

'Wow, awesome,' is Charlie's response, 'I never thought of it like that. I feel sorry for sharks now.'

I like this boy.

'Right my boys, time for bed. Come on you two. Harry. Come on Eric. In you come and I'll make your hot chocolate. Charlie, as it's your birthday bash you can have a little longer.'

Sam's request is met with a series of tuts and sighs. No child likes bedtime, especially on a holiday. Tantrums and tears are common in infants, so it comes as no surprise when Eric lets rip venting his frustration, bursting into tears, kicking, and screaming as his mother struggles to carry him inside. Harry gets up and duly trots after them. Charlie disappears inside, only to come straight back out clutching his treasured guitar, an Eko made in Recanati, which he's thrilled to tell me is in Italy and the city of poetry, you do learn something every day. He sits at my feet to play a beautiful rendition of, 'Junk,' written by Paul McCartney back in 1968, a particular favourite of mine. Hearing this soulful tune tweaks memories of Greg. I'm about to succumb to the past but luckily for me, the two younger boys choose that moment to appear in the doorway in their pjs preventing my mood plunging. Eric has calmed, his emotional outburst is reduced to a quiet sobbing whilst clutching a threadbare dragon, another hand-me-down or dearly loved plaything. The way he's hugging it and rubbing it against his face suggests the latter. Hot drinks arrive for the children who come to sit calmly at my feet to drink them.

'Look at 'em, never sit with me like that! Think you're a bit of a hit. If ya keep stum boys, she might tell ya a quick bedtime story. What do you say shark lady, fancy working ya magic on 'em again.' Throwing me a wink he continues, 'If ya can keep 'em quiet, especially me little Shadow here, ya can come round every night!'

Matt's a resilient fellow, I could grow to like him if only he were kinder. 'Seeing your dragon Eric, reminds me of a place where real dragons roam.'

THE ISLAND THAT
TIME FORGOT

'Dragons aren't real, they're only in stories.'

Not wanting to crush Charlie's confidence or contradict him in front of his father, I need to tread carefully and choose the right words. 'I'm afraid they're very real Charlie but not the fire-breathing dragons you read about in fairy tales. Our reason for travelling to Indonesia was to dive but the landscape through which we sailed was breathtakingly beautiful. Komodo National Park consists of twenty-nine volcanic islands, each one a picture postcard, rugged and hilly, covered in long grasses, woodlands and deserted beaches, the likes Robinson Crusoe washed up on. I'll never forget surfacing from a dive a stone's throw from the shoreline of Rinca, one of the larger islands and bobbing there waiting for Agung, our cheeky RIB driver, to zoom over and whisk us back to *Tranquillity*. As he brought the RIB alongside he dropped the ladder and started laughing and yelling, "Komodo dragon, Komodo dragon coming!" I hadn't got a clue what he was talking about, but he was obviously finding something hilarious. Laughing is infectious and within seconds we were all giggling away; the world needs more of that! Anyway, a little while later as

I was getting out of my dive gear, Issa and I got chatting. I needed to know what Agung had found so funny. That's when she told me that Rinca Island is home to the Komodo dragon, the largest lizard on the planet and deadly. Three thousand dragons live on only five small islands in the world, four of them were close by, Rinca, Komodo, Gili Montang and Gili Dasami, the fifth, Flores, is further east.'

Eric is sniffing quietly but his sobbing has subsided. His tears trickle down his face carving rivers of soily streaks on his cheeks. Sam bends down and lovingly kisses each eye. 'Salty kisses will make it better sweetheart.' She pulls a tissue from her pocket and dabs his face, a job he completes, wiping his nose on his clean pyjama sleeve!

'Komodo dragons are 3m in length, with a flat head and round snout, similar in size to that of your dog Pepper. The mouth is obviously of interest to me, and a dragon has a forked tongue and sixty jagged teeth, each one over 2cm tall. Their skin is scaly, and they get about on four stocky legs with long claws at the end of webbed feet. The tail is the same length as the body and a powerful weapon. They are similar in size and appearance to crocodiles so it's hardly surprising locals refer to them as, "land crocodiles". They hunt buffalo, deer, pigs and goats, creeping up on them to take a bite then leaving them to die before returning to eat them.' The animal actually suffers a slow, painful death before the dragon returns to feast. The conundrum challenging scientists for years was what killed the animal and it wasn't until 2009, when a team of scientists, led by Bryan Fry at the University of Melbourne in Australia, discovered that dragons have venom glands, and the toxicity of the venom prevents the wound from clotting. In a nutshell the prey bleed to death! Might not be pertinent to go into too much detail before the boys go to bed, could hinder a restful sleep! 'Dragons have eaten humans too, maybe those fooled by how slow they move. Appearances can be deceptive. Dragons can pick up the pace when they want to hitting speeds of 20kph (12mph), which is similar to that of the average human. Caught a few people out that way! They're fast hey?'

'Bet Usain Bolt could beat one in a race.'

'You're probably right there Charlie, he's been clocked running at 44.64kph (27.8mph), but I wouldn't want to be chased by a dragon even if I were him. If he can run faster than other humans then maybe there's a dragon that can run faster than other dragons! I was relieved we weren't on the island, drawing confidence from being in the sea some distance off shore. Any confidence I had drained away when Issa pointed out two dragons swimming powerfully towards the live-aboard, their strong tails pushing them through the water at speed. Needless to say, I was horrified.

'Komodo dragons live for around thirty years and in that time they get used to live-aboard boats anchoring in their bay and learn to swim for food scraps thrown overboard. Clever dragons! Knowing they could swim was terrifying, but Issa recounted an incident so shocking it gave her nightmares. A RIB packed with divers had drifted close to shore to enable guests to snap shots of dragons sunbathing on the beach! By the way, the collective noun for a group of dragons is "bank". Whoever chose this word missed a trick. A fire of dragons would have been exciting, better than a boring bank! A collective noun which someone did nail though was "flutter" for butterflies although this beautiful insect should be called flutterby not butterfly!

'Where was I? Oh yes, Issa's story... the RIB was bobbing in the shallows when an inquisitive dragon entered the water and swam over to the boat affording the delighted photographers wonderful close-ups. All was going smoothly until the creature started circling the boat, using its forceful tail to speed up with each circuit. Without warning it propelled itself up out of the water coming to rest in the RIB which cleared the vessel of passengers in a heartbeat. Picture the scene, a sea of thrashing arms and legs fleeing in pure panic.

The dragon, rather than chasing them through the water, chose to remain in the RIB proud as punch at the chaos he'd caused! He must have loved that RIB, he chose to lie there for the rest of the day basking in the glory, he'd found his very own sunbed! Without the RIB there was no diving, so guests were confined to barracks! It wasn't until the sun sank below the horizon the dragon flopped back into the water and the crew retrieved their precious boat. Beth and I were sipping a sundowner on the sundeck when it dawned on me what could have been, surfacing from a dive to be eyeballed by a dragon! That would have been scary hey?

'Imagine the fear when Issa announced we'd be touring the island the following morning! It's not every day you have the opportunity to walk with dinosaurs so although apprehensive I was determined to go knowing I'd regret it if I didn't. Fear wasn't going to get in the way to stop me.' Shooting Charlie a look we share a smile, we both know that was for him.

'Boarding the RIB that next morning not exactly itching to go, it was with much relief that we rounded the bay to be dropped off onto a newly constructed boardwalk and not the beach. The scent of freshly chopped wood filled the air and the sturdy path served to strengthen my resolve, erected on stilts, the walkway lifted us a metre off the ground, the ground where the dragons would be. Feeling nervous and vulnerable the boardwalk gave me a feeling of security, a false feeling of security maybe but it helped all the same. I had chills I can tell you, especially when we were not met at the dock and had to start our trek alone. Our group comprised ten guests and two staff with eight guests giving in to fear and remaining on *Tranquillity*.' Another glance at Charlie, this time our eyes don't meet, his head hangs down, but he must know that was for him too.

'Impenetrable gorse bushes, dense and sharp, lined the route on one side, shrub land and swathes of sandy soil the other. The heat was intense. Monkeys trooped by, running and playing in the sand as the path wound its way over dry streams one minute and muddy swamps the next, we were walking an eerie landscape. We continued under an impressive stone archway carved in the shape of two opposing dragons standing on hind legs, the front legs meeting overhead to form the arch. What a greeting! Rounding a bend, we were shocked to be confronted by row upon row of hundreds of small wooden crosses, painted white and neatly dug into recently cultivated ground. From our elevated position we could appreciate the vastness of this spectacle. Walking through this graveyard, this burial ground for countless victims of dragon kills, proved sobering. I couldn't help but question the decision to bury these sad souls near the entrance in full view of visitors although it did serve as a stark reminder, we were in dangerous territory. As if I needed it! Imagine my embarrassment upon discovering the crosses were markers identifying newly planted trees!

'A short time later a couple of rangers greeted us, awaiting our arrival in a small clearing beside a sizeable log cabin, a cabin erected on stilts to discourage prying dragons. A sign on the door proclaimed, "Komodo National Park – Indonesia, World Heritage Site", and that's when it dawned on me, how truly privileged we were to be in this unique setting. Twelve buildings lined the path, homes for scientists studying the dragons and for brave locals who'd chosen to settle there! Imagine that, how could you ever feel safe?

'We gathered together beside an ominous display of buffalo, pig, and deer skulls, staked like trophies, which proved distracting. Hearing the rangers insist we stay on path, stay together, follow instructions, and remain at least 4m from a dragon, refocused the mind. No way was I going that close! Obeying the rules was vital to ensure our safety but they fell short of guaranteeing it, should an emergency arise both rangers would be armed which helped to ease my fears somewhat. Armed my foot! No gun in sight, no, a forked stick!

'The plan was to trek up the hill, in whose shadow we were standing, we'd be following a sandy trail, winding through a forest on the hunt for dragons. We would be rewarded with a view to die for! The intense heat had me reaching for my water bottle, I was parched. Being ushered along and not wanting to be left behind, my bottle remained unopened in the depths of my rucksack. What I saw next sent shivers down my spine, a dragon of enormous proportions ambling towards us along the walkway, slow and steady as if out for a Sunday stroll. He had us leaping left, right, and centre, and what did he do? Plodded past without a care in the world! Then following along behind him another and another, reminiscent of the buses in Birmingham, you don't see one for ages then three arrive at once! Patiently waiting until the dragons had moved on we hopped back onto the path and made our way to start the climb. We came upon a bank of seven dragons lying spreadeagled on their stomachs, legs awkwardly splayed out to the side, sleeping by more cabins. Crazy hey? You come out of your front door, and you have dragons in your garden!' Oh, here goes, Matt can't contain himself.

'Ya know why the dragons were sleeping in't day don't ya? So, they can fight knights!'

Ignoring the groans, he laughs. My body stiffens at the stupidity of his remark, he's such an irritating man, but more than that, he'd interrupted my tale when I was in full flow. Struggling to keep my irritation in check, I throw him a wry smile and plough on.

'According to Rinos, our guide, cooking smells drift on the wind tempting hungry dragons, who huddle at the foot of the stairs in the hopes of snaffling leftovers, no wonder the buildings were built on stilts, won't be long before those clever creatures learn to climb stairs! I found myself staring into the shaded spaces beneath the buildings searching for dragons, and sure enough dark shapes were there waiting to pounce! You could never drop your guard living there.

'Our hill climb proved steeper than expected, the path difficult to navigate, sandy and dry underfoot. Dappled sunlight streamed through the trees, fallen branches blocked our way, natural objects thwarting progress. Leaves littered the floor, brown and burnt from an unforgiving, ever-present sun. Birds pecked amongst the debris on the hunt for insects. A journey predicted to take an hour, took two! What a challenging environment the dragons and locals call home! Arriving at the summit dense woodland gave way to knee-high grassland and we were greeted by a sight worthy of the climb, an ocean view in every direction and green sun-drenched hills dotted with trees. A much-welcome breeze blew up there helping to cool our hot bodies and make ripples in the grass, pushing it to rise, to fall and sway in waves. Spying *Tranquillity* anchored in one of the bays triggered the imagination making me wonder about travellers who'd sailed these waters over the centuries. Imagine going ashore for fresh water or to gather much-needed provisions, what a terrifying surprise lay in wait for those intrepid explorers! Setting foot on a land, seemingly transported back in time to an island time forgot.

'After shooting an album of photos we started the descent, our route taking us down the other side of the hill. We hadn't walked far when we stumbled upon a dragon, sleeping under the only tree growing at the top, an ancient timber which had stood proud and alone for decades. Branches leaned landwards, blown there by a relentless wind. Transfixed by the architectural beauty of this lonely tree, I almost stepped on the dragon, his tail hidden in the undergrowth and the body draped amongst the thick tree roots criss-crossing our path. I genuinely believed him to be part of the tree, brings a new meaning to, "getting to the root of the problem"! Gingerly skirting round we continued our journey with renewed vigour. Reaching the bottom, Rinos stopped beside five holes dug into the ground, similar in size and shape to a badger sett, a dragon nest. A dragon enters one of the holes and lays around thirty eggs, the other four holes are decoys, sneaky these dragons! Once hatched, the little ones race out to disappear up the nearest tree to avoid being hunted, and the creature hunting these baby dragons, other dragons! Unbelievable!'

Sam catches my eye, she's tapping her wrist, bedtime. The children have finished their drinks, Eric's eyes are heavy. Sam swoops in and cradles her little one into her arms.

'Time for beds kids, Jane can we wrap it up please?'

'Of course, I'd finished really, we'd had an incredible morning with dragons. We got down the hill in one piece, retraced our steps along the walkway, jumped into the RIB and there you have it, my dragon adventure; a day I lived to tell!'

'Right, come on Harry, you too.'

Sam goes in with her two and Nicki and Steve take this as their cue to say their goodbyes. Matt and I set about packing away the chairs and tables then I too make my leave, truth be told, it had been an enjoyable evening.

'See ya tomorrow shark lady.' Matt's cheery farewell before disappearing inside with an armful of cans brings a smile to my face. He's a good fellow really just at odds with his boy, shame. Charlie disappears inside but appears at the door reiterating his father's words. Shark lady, the nickname makes me smile.

'Sleep well Charlie, have pleasant dreams tonight. Don't let the bedtime sharks bite!' We exchange smiles and I wander back to my camper.

REFLECTIONS

There are times in your life when you remember where you were when you heard extraordinary news. An example would be Freddie Mercury's untimely death in 1991. Driving to Birmingham Dental School for a lecture, something I did throughout my career, circumventing the St Chad's, Queensway roundabout in the city centre, the newsflash aired on the radio. News so shocking, I almost crashed the car! The memory remains strong, the details clear, it was 07:30, an unusually warm November morning and I was wearing black trousers, white blouse and a black jacket, appropriate attire in light of Freddie's demise!

Another example comes from the summer of 1977. I was enjoying a well-earned holiday after surviving a particularly tough year at dental school. I'd spent the day shopping in town and enjoying lunch with friends. We were back at my place playing cards after dinner, when a stunned Reginald Bosanquet delivered the news on ITV's *News at Ten*, 'Elvis is dead.' I even remember the date of this one, August 16th, the day before Greg's seventeenth birthday and it is to my brother that my thoughts now turn.

It was September 12th last year and I'd gone to visit Mum, we were enjoying a coffee in the lounge when the phone rang. She wandered into the kitchen to answer it. I don't know which is worse, being the bearer or receiver of bad news, either way it was obvious Mum was hearing distressing information, her voice faltered with each response. Putting the phone down, she stood motionless with her back to me, her head bowed, a moment I knew not to intrude upon. Turning and with tears in her eyes, she spoke with a steely determination. 'Greg's had an accident on his motorbike. He's in hospital, in Aberdeen. I must go to him. He's in a bad way.' Hearing the news took my breath away, I remember gulping air into my lungs as tears ran down my cheeks. I was numb. I trudged into the kitchen to hug Mum. Turning on the cold tap, I held my hands under the soothing flow then lifted the cool pool to my face. Snatching sheets of kitchen roll, I pressed them to my face to stop Mum seeing the pain etched within and to stem the flow of water dripping shady patches onto the grey tiles at my feet. We hugged, exchanged words of comfort, and set about making plans. No one knows how they'll respond when a crisis hits, drunken conversations with friends sometimes touch on the 'what if', though no amount of forethought helps when emergencies strike, instinct kicks in and you act, we both did on that fateful day anyway. Although a few snippets linger to be forever chiselled into the recesses of my brain, the remains of the day are a blur. I must have spoken to Sarah and Rosie and Mum almost certainly contacted Dad who just so happened to be away on business. We probably ate at some point, and I must have booked us onto a flight departing Manchester the following morning. Soaring through the skies for ninety minutes, trapped with thoughts of Greg, agonising over how the complexities of our relationship had served to push us apart for years.

Two years my junior, we were inseparable as children, playing together from dawn till dusk but all that changed in our teens, the years ticked by, and our relationship broke down. We lost the desire to communicate with each other, he ignored me and I him, neither of us were to blame it's just the way it was. Attending the same secondary school only served to polarise the problem, a reflection of our drastically different approach to lessons and friendship circles. I worked hard, toed the line, any line, as did my friends. Truth be told, I didn't really fit in, holding teachers in too high regard and as a result overeager to please them. School was nothing more than a necessary chore I was unable to enjoy. I was that awkward child on the periphery of everything, poor Greg even more so. He struggled. Literacy was never his strength, but he excelled at maths and science. He was in the thick of things, bad things, fighting with other boys and confrontations with teachers. The struggles he faced in the aftermath of the accident would prove tougher than any schoolboy scrapes. Greg was in a fight for his life, a fight he never saw coming, a fight he wouldn't win.

Walking into the ward that first morning it was painfully obvious how Greg was suffering. Struggling to breathe, nurses were in the process of administering oxygen, the pain in his chest and legs hard to bear, his mind and body numbed with medication. Over the weeks Mum, Dad, Sarah, Rosie, Stephen, and I took turns to stay in local B&Bs so as to be close to the infirmary. We even investigated the possibility of taking on a rental property affording us more of a base with options to extend the agreement should Greg's treatment persist. He was not going to be left alone. That was the plan. Whispering motivational words through gritted teeth, emotions hidden behind fake smiles, are only truly understood by loved ones wishing they didn't. Watching someone you love fading away is a pain like no other, there was nothing we could do to stop it, like watching leaves falling from a tree, withering, and perishing before your eyes. The end is inevitable. Words shared during his last days on this earth were desperately positive, holding onto the belief that oozing buckets of goodwill would be enough to pull him through. How naive. At one point he found some fight and turned a corner, it gave us hope but two hospital-acquired infections saw to that and the end of him. After a traumatic six weeks, a time of unbelievable heartache, events reached their tragic conclusion. Greg left us at the tender age of sixty, far too early, what a tragedy. I honestly thought my siblings and I would grow old and be there for each other until our bodies grew tired and the five of us would become creaking doors that would eventually close for the last time in our dotage. It would go in order of age, me first, then Greg, then the three little ones. As I said, naive! Naive and devastated. In his final moments he and I stared into each other's eyes, a brother, and a sister. The love was there; I could feel it and see it in the depths of his pained eyes. I know he felt it too. It remained unspoken but it was there all the same. That's when I knew it had never left, had been simmering beneath the surface a lifetime. His final words I will never forget, 'I can't die Janey I haven't seen the world yet!' I never said a word but that's when I made him the promise to see it for him. The day after Greg died Beth phoned, kicked me when I was down and snatched that promise from me. Broken promises are disappointing but failing on this one will haunt me for the rest of life.

Lying here consumed with regret, I pray Greg wasn't. Wasted times. Wasted opportunities. Since that dark day, in that horrible hospital, regret has set up home in my heart. Oh, how I wish I'd made every second count, made every memory special but most of all I wish I could go back. Mum continues to maintain a strong faith; her life revolves around the church and if anything, her beliefs are stronger now than they were before. She has always turned to God when death struck. As children we were encouraged to have a faith and cherish living a moral life. We were staunch supporters of the local Sunday school, attended services, youth club evenings, summer fates, carnival parades, bonfires, and Christmas services. The church and worship were at the centre of our universe, but it was during Greg's final minutes when he shuffled off this mortal coil when I prayed real prayers for the first time and came to understand the meaning of despair.

These are the thoughts thwarting my sleep this night. My insomnia puzzles me, having had a lovely day and an abundance of fresh air should have had me dead to the world, excuse yet another pun, it would appear I'm full of them! I'm also profoundly overtired. My brain, mind and aching heart have other ideas. I tug at the pebble hanging from the cord above my head, turn on my reading light and reach for my kindle. Time to read.

'How's ya day gone lad? Ya like ya party?' Dad rubs my head and pummels me. I squeal and kick my legs to get away. No matter how much I struggle, I can't get up. I want to get away from him but he's too strong and won't let me. 'Stop it Dad. I don't like it!' He takes no notice and keeps grabbing at me. He's tickling me, I hate that. I squeal again but louder. That will stop him. I know what happens next.

'Shush you two. Eric's just gone off. Harry's nearly gone. Come on. They're shattered. Quieten down now. Stop it.'

Mam gives me dad one of her glares and I know better than make a noise now. He won't.

'Oi lad, ya mam's chucking me daggers o'er there. If looks could kill I'd be six foot under!'

He laughs a proper belly laugh. The beer's given him Dutch courage.

'I mean it Matt. Come on love, give it a rest!'

That'll stop him. He knows she's had enough. He leans into me and whispers in my ear.

'Go on then Sharkbite, tell me, have ya had a good 'un?'

I nod. He pulls me closer. He rubs the top of my head and pulls me to him but this time it's cute and it makes me want to curl up with him. I lean on him a bit. We lie there and say nothing. Used to love being with me dad. Bedtime was something me and me mam did. It's different since Harry was born. Mam spends more time with the young ones. Sometimes wish I was an only child but not for long. She gets Harry to bed and then it has to be Eric's turn. I don't get a look-in. I miss Mam's stories. Miss being with me mam. Miss it loads. Don't love bedtimes anymore. I hate them. I spend ages trying to get to sleep when Dad goes down. No wonder teachers moan about me being tired all the time. It's his fault not mine.

'I missed ya on the beach today lad.'

Listen to him trying to be nice. He's lying! Makes me mad. He doesn't miss me, but I miss being there with Harry, Eric, and me mam. Suppose I even miss Dad sometimes, but only sometimes! My bottom lip is wobbling a bit. Better not say anything. He'll notice. He's a good bottom lip detector. And great at teasing!

'I like ya shark lady friend. She's okay she is. Thought her stories might scare ya some but ya seem okay.'

I'm not talking to him about it, but I have been thinking about that too. Dad's stories scare me. Jane's don't. The way she talks makes sharks sound exciting. Knowing more about them is good. I don't know why but it is. Dad's gone quiet. I'm not saying nothing. My head's full of stuff I don't understand. It's bedtime in a minute. I'm a bit scared but not as scared as I was last night. Here's Mam. She squeezes between us. She puts her arms around us both. I like it when me mam holds me.

'How are my two big boys then, all right you two? No more fighting? Well, come on, tell me how's my boys? Can I get you a drink darlings?'

I shake my head. I've had enough. I'm tired. Dad gets up.

'Allow me my sweet.'

He's trying to talk posh. He bows and goes to the fridge. Surprise, surprise he grabs a beer for himself.

'Wine Sam?'

She nods. He pours her out the last bit of the bottle and me and Mam snuggle. She whispers in my ear.

'You look tired love. Why don't you get into your pjs and get yourself to bed? Tomorrow's another day.'

I want to talk to her. I want to tell her how I feel. How scared I am but I don't know what to say. I can't do it. Can't find the words. Weird. I love words but saying the words I want to say is really hard. I stare at her.

'You all right love? Mmmm? Anything the matter?'

'No. I'm okay.'

'You sure? Something's up. What's wrong Charlie? You can tell me. What is it? Tell me. You can tell me anything, you know that don't you?'

I nod but I can't say it. I wish she could read my mind then she'd know. It's bedtime. Bedtime. That's when I'm frightened. Too scared to lie in my bed in case my eyes close before I'm ready. I'm scared of the dark and the night-time monsters that swim in my dreams. Shark dreams. Nightmares. Must keep my eyes open. I'm frightened to shut them. Stay awake. Stay awake. I must stay awake. Stay awake so the dreams don't come. I don't want to sink under the waves again. Not tonight. I don't want to drown. I'm tired. Tired of being chased. Always tired but too tired to sleep. If she came up at bedtime, she'd know. She'd know how scared I am. She'd see me. She'd know I sneak a comic under my pillow when I get home from school, and she'd know why. She'd see me chucking stuff on the floor to protect me. Anything that makes a noise, a crunch, warns me if something is trying to sneak up on me. She'd see me peeking through the curtains again and again. Got to get the curtains shut tight. They have to meet in the middle. The join has to be perfect. No cracks where they can watch me. She'd see me checking under my bed. She'd see me looking in the cupboard. She'd see me sliding the door open and shut, open, and shut, checking it and checking it again. She'd see me lying there waiting for me dad to go downstairs. She'd see me zooming to the door and open it, so the hall light comes in. I like the light. It helps me see my way out. My escape route. But she doesn't come. She doesn't see. Mam doesn't know.

I go and get my pjs. My duvet and pjs are scrunched up at the bottom of my bed where I left them this morning. Mam doesn't make our beds, we have to do it ourselves and if we don't, she doesn't. I sneak a look under my pillow. The superhero saving me tonight is Tin Tin and his trusty sidekick Snowy. I go to the toilet, turn the light on and close the door. I get my pjs on in a flash. I sometimes forget to brush my teeth but being with Jane today has helped me remember. The hum of my Oral B is really loud. I have to stay in here for two minutes while it cleans my teeth. Every boy and girl should have an electric toothbrush though. My teeth would be really bad if I brushed them with a normal brush. No way I'd stand there for more than ten seconds. I sit down on the toilet lid. I hate how long it takes. It's taking ages tonight. I stand up and look in the mirror. I stare at the face staring back at me. Something's different. I look into the eyes. Something inside is different. I don't know. I close my eyes then peep to see if the face in the mirror peeps too. It does! I wink at the face, and it winks back. I like this game. My bull shark tooth is dangling down. I lean forward and make it swing. I close my eyes. I yawn. Yawning with an electric toothbrush in your mouth isn't cool. Spots of spit and toothpaste shoot out of my mouth and splatter the mirror. A dribble trail of whitish goo runs down my pjs. I wipe it away with my hand, but it doesn't get rid of the stain. The shark on the front of my pjs has a white blob on top of his dorsal fin. It makes me smile. I've turned my shark into a whitetip! This makes me think of Jane and that makes me smile. The toothbrush stops. Time for bed.

'Night,' I whisper, don't want to wake my brothers up.

'Night sweetheart, sleep well, see you in the morning darling.'

'Yeah, sweet dreams Sharkbite!'

Can't help himself. I climb up and pull the duvet over my head. I lie there. Man, it gets hot under here. I kick it down the bed. I can hear Mam and Dad whispering. Don't know what they're saying. I like hearing them talking, it helps me relax. I can hear Harry breathing above me. He's fast asleep. I can't hear Eric. I stare at the wooden slats above me. I close my eyes.

A bed just short of five foot long and two foot wide is uncomfortable at the best of times. Trying to hold a kindle, never mind read one, whilst squashed in the foetal position is proving hopeless. Hands and arms ache trying to balance the electronic device in a million and one different ways. Resting it on the pillow next to me makes managing the controls impossible. After ten tortuous minutes I concede defeat and throw the blessed thing down the bed. For goodness sake. My fingers are suffering with kindle fatigue. No fun getting old. Holding anything for more than five minutes causes my arms to twinge, my palms to tingle and the knuckles on the fingers of both hands to ache. Working during those last eight years I'd become aware of escalating pain in both hands and upon hitting sixty it became excruciating, almost too much to bear. As a dentist I performed countless examinations and X-rays, restored decaying or fractured teeth with fillings or crowns and of course performed surgical extractions. Not meaning to blow my own trumpet but I was a bit of a whizz when it came to wisdom teeth extractions, so adept was I at removing them, patients remained blissfully unaware of the moment the tooth actually left the cavity. During the last three years I chose to continue my professional development, undertaking a course in dental implantology, a firm believer of the adage, 'you're never too old to learn'. An artificial titanium tooth root is inserted into the patient's jaw bone for the bone to integrate around. Once integrated, an abutment and ultimately a ceramic crown or bridge is placed on the top. Replacing missing teeth with implants is not new but it was new to me. I gave up a day a week, a Saturday of all days, to attend lectures at Birmingham Dental Hospital and honed new skills and techniques at the dental practice of a colleague. My working weeks were long and weekends short serving to add strain on already sore hands. Whichever way you cut it; a dentist relies on their hands. The eventual diagnosis of trigger finger in both hands as well as Greg's untimely demise focused my retirement planning. Then there was Beth.

Beth, my best friend, and dive buddy, to whom I'm eternally grateful for introducing me to the magical underwater world, that's gone too. There'll be no more of that now. Thoughts of her choose this moment to make their appearance and drip in to flood my mind. This is turning into a long night! Beth's scenario is not the same as Greg's, not by a long shot, she's still alive. It began when I noticed a tremor in her left hand but only Beth knows how long it had been going on. Nineteen months ago, after diving in the Similan Islands, an archipelago in Thailand, the two of us were sharing a taxi from the airport. She was on her mobile chatting with Andy when I noticed the shaking and I became transfixed with the rhythmical movements of her hand, but something instinctively stopped me mentioning it. I'd almost forgotten about it until we met up a few months later, she came for the weekend to allow us to plan our next trip and there it was again, her hand resting on the side of her chair gently jerking back and forth. She seemed unusually distracted and distant. By the time she left for home I was out of my mind with worry. It wasn't until she phoned to talk to me the day after Greg died, she revealed the extent of her illness. She started speaking and I misinterpreted her awkwardness as a struggle to find the right words, it's not easy knowing what to say in times of grief. After the appropriate words of comfort, she came right out with it, she had Parkinson's disease. She cried. We both did. Our conversation lasted nearly an hour as she revealed how hard life had become for her trying to get through the days on so little sleep. We discussed her diagnosis, symptoms, and prognosis. I thought the conversation had drawn to a close and was about to put the phone down when she said the words that took me off my feet, sideswiped me and changed my life forever. 'I know people with Parkinson's can dive Jane and that it doesn't affect everyone in the same way, but Andy and I have made a decision. It's hard Jane. It's hard for me to say it to you.' She left an inordinately long pause then, voice faltering, she delivered her punchline, words I never saw coming. 'My diving days are over. I can't face the journey. It's too much. There will be no more diving for me. I can't do it anymore. I'm sorry Jane. Sorry.' I broke the silence telling her we'd catch up soon and hung up. I put my mobile on the charger and fell into my armchair. Everything stopped. I sat there stunned, speechless. There followed a period of silence so quiet it rang in my ears. My emotions got the better of me, I cried then cried some more, the grief slipped out of my eyes and rolled down my cheeks. Upon hearing of a death, the death of a family member, a friend, a friend of a friend, a person on the news, a stranger, I have a reputation for crumbling. Since Greg's death my tears weigh heavier. Greg died, my dearest friend was suffering with a progressive disease, and we'd never dive together again. I'd never dive again. In those two days my life changed.

The death of a loved one stays with you forever, a pain that never dies, a grief that lives on. It remains inside you, waiting, waiting for a trigger, a moment, a word, an object, a song, a piece of music, a smell, anything with which you have an emotional connection, something to remind you and take you back. A white feather, the number 304 from the gate post in Hoole Lane and the Welsh Rugby Union team singing the national anthem, 'Hen Wlad Fy Nhadau' ('Old Land of My Fathers') are triggers guaranteed to get me every time. But other things can ambush me without warning, often when least expected. I'd heard people say grief comes in waves and counted myself lucky to make it through a huge portion of my life not understanding what that meant, I do now. When tragedy hits a metaphorical wave crashes into you and you become immersed in a sea of grief. You sink into an ocean to drown in the depths of despair. You doubt you'll survive it. During this time, you cry and wail like never before. You barely function but function you do. Weeks and months go by, the waves continue to roll, some crash into you but not as often or with the same force as before. The odd rogue wave can strike with such power it wipes you out, hitting you as hard as that first one but over the months the waves ease giving you time to catch your breath between them. I know the waves will hit, will wash over me but I also know I'll come up for air and make it through. Beth's call and a wave crashed, the floodgates opened, and grief trickled out. I agree with psychiatrist Dr Colin Murray Parkes who first used the phrase, 'grief is the price you pay for love'. Friends have reassured me that somewhere in the region of 18 months' time I'll wake up one day, shower, eat breakfast, go out, return home, eat dinner, watch TV, climb into bed and only when my eyes fall heavy will I realise that that was the day, the first day when Greg didn't cross my mind. The first day thoughts of him stayed away. I'll cry myself to sleep but will wake slightly stronger. From that first day, the days will get easier. I'm counting on them being right. I know grief and I have barely begun our journey together, but I have to believe I'll get there. Today I let grief in. Greg and Beth, I love them both and always will, don't think I knew how much until her call came to change things.

Not sure if it's the scientist in me but I'm highly organised, clinically so and function best when in control. Once a career in dentistry had been decided upon, each step in achieving my goal was meticulously planned, the university, the degree, the practice, my home, my life, all mapped out. Holidays were treated in the same efficient fashion with nothing left to chance. Greg's death and Beth's illness sparked a chain of events causing my life to spiral out of control, to turn upside down and throw me into the unknown. A whirlwind of emotions swirled within. In light of these new developments, my future had to be re-evaluated with less desirable choices. It's late and I should be sleeping but my mind is busy, time for tea. During the day it's got to be Darjeeling and once night falls chamomile, here's hoping its soothing and calming properties do their thing!

Boooom! Tin Tin and Captain Haddock's 'blistering barnacles' stayed under my pillow and there were no nightmares! Yessss. Wow. First time forever! I'm out of bed in a shot. I'm dressed in a flash. Stick my hand in the biscuit tin and I'm up and out.

Thankfully, tea's sleep-inducing qualities are not a myth and I slept a solid five hours. The sun rose early, forcing me to follow suit, finding it impossible to stay in bed once awake. Sleep and I have waged our own private war with each other for forty years, a battle I constantly lost. I earned the reputation of being a night owl and would often crawl into bed, two or three hours after the witching hour only to wake, like clockwork, four hours later, eyes sore and gritty. Never have been, nor ever will be, a morning person. Friends joked I must be allergic to work, allergic to pollen as it turns out. Suffering with dry eyes for most of my life, it came as some relief to eventually discover it was hay fever. Respite on holidays wrongly reinforced a work-related condition. Plants exude different pollen in different climes. My eyes obviously prefer pollen in Indonesia and Thailand! This morning my eyes are clear and fresh even though I cried more than I wanted or indeed anticipated yesterday. After breakfast I stroll to the end of the beach and back taking in the sea air. Upping sticks and moving to live by the coast may help me, might need to give this some serious consideration, the breeze wafting in over the sea helps blow my troubles away. Today will be a beach day. I drop my bags onto the sand and set about making myself comfortable.

Today will start like every day here, me running. The rest of them are in the caravan. Harry will have to wait for Eric. They'll be ages. At the top of the path, I stop and look out to sea. Man, I feel great.

I look down at the beach. Bit of a surprise, Jane's down there. Why is she on the beach? Boom, I'm off. I'm not stopping till I get to her. I'm going to win and will be the champion!

He's full of the joys of spring this morning. 'Good morning Charlie. How's things? You're bubbly today? Did you enjoy your party last night?' Before giving him the chance to respond I continue. 'Hope you slept well?' My question expects a mixed response and I'm pleasantly surprised to be wrong.

'Yes thanks, great and no nightmares. The sharks didn't come.'

He's jumping about full of the joys of summer. 'That's wonderful. I was concerned that all that talking about sharks may have resulted in bad dreams and I'm thrilled it didn't.' Maybe hearing about my shark encounters helped him in some way. His fingers fiddle with the shark tooth dangling from his neck. That he's wearing it vindicates my decision to bequeath it to him. 'You like your shark tooth then? You didn't sleep in it did you?' He nods. 'You're lucky it didn't scratch you while you slept, it's still sharp you know. Maybe you're a shark boy after all hey?' A smile creeps across his face.

'Yeah I'm a shark boy or "Sharkbite" like me dad calls me. I can't believe I didn't have a bad dream. I love my shark tooth. Thanks.' I liked her shark stories. She's been down there with them. Lots of them. Different sharks. Close to them and she's never been bitten. Wonder what she's doing over here. I hope she comes to the rocks again. 'Are you staying here today, on the beach I mean?' I'm worried she's going to say yes. If she does I'll be sad. I want us to go on the rocks so we can talk some more.

'Thought I'd give the beach a go today Charlie, is that okay? Do you fancy spending some time here until your family come down? I need to think for a while and catch up with myself. Maybe you could do the same.'

I nod but it's not true, I really want to shake my head. 'Suppose so. I'll stay until Harry gets down.' I'm trying not to let her know

I'm not happy about it. I wait for her to say something. She doesn't. I'll just sit here and dig in the sand with my toes and fingers. I like it when it's quiet. I don't feel so scared today. I look at the sea and think about how things used to be. I don't know if I'll ever go back in, but I feel better.

The two of us, relative strangers, a boy in his teens and me, a woman in her sixties, sit together and stare out over the sea. I'm reflecting on my past and looking into a future I can, as yet, not see. Maybe he's doing the same. Somehow I feel stronger today. I hope he does too.

DANCING TO A
DIFFERENT TUNE

Charlie digs his dirty-nailed toes into the soft sand. The heat streaming from this glorious Northumberland sun promises another scorcher. Temperatures are set to escalate towards the end of the week with Friday promising to be the hottest day of the year so far. Higher ambient temperatures during spring and summer months are not reflected in any significant warming of the Atlantic waters lapping our shores. The hotter the sun, the warmer the air, the cooler the water, freezing to excruciatingly cold is how it feels to me. Wild swimming groups love nothing better than jumping into lakes and seas to swim, even when it snows. Respect to them but it's not for me. The number of times I've swam in these waters during the last forty years can be counted on one hand. If scuba diving in cold water had been my only option, I wouldn't have taken to the sport. It didn't matter how many times friends sang the praises of dry suits and their thermal insulation; I wasn't falling for it! No, wild swimming is a club I'll never join! It won't come as a surprise to you, but there'll be no swimming for me this week.

Older bones and joints don't like staying in the same position for long, sitting, lying down, or standing for lengthy periods is fine while it lasts but as soon as you move, the need to hobble and limp to straighten is the norm. When you pulled faces as a child, your parents warned, 'Be careful you don't stick like that.' The same applies to the skeletal integrity of a 62-year-old retired dentist! I need to get up and stretch stiff legs. As I rise, the boy follows suit, and we head down to the water's edge. I brave it and tentatively dip my toes in the water. Icy-cold water ripples between my toes and over my feet causing me to shiver, blooming heck it's freezing. Another step further in brings the water up to just below my knees and I've reached my limit. Paddling, though tough, is a therapeutic process. The chilling temperatures take your mind off everything else, anxieties and woes float away on the trickling tide. Swimming in seas as cold as this takes courage and there are generally two schools of thought on how best to enter the water, the short or the long game. Greg was an advocate of the short game, running like the wind from way up the beach and not stopping until the water's lapping at your waist then dive under head first. I, on the other hand, play the long game and when I say long, I mean painfully long and slow, sometimes taking thirty minutes or more until fully immersed! Taking an eternity to get in and not being able to get out quick enough to avoid freezing into a block of ice! There is of course a third option that both Charlie and I will opt for today, to stay on the beach! He's been quiet this morning so startles me when he starts speaking.

'I like the softer sand up there on the beach. We play games on it. This hard sand is wet and great for digging and building. Mam told me when I was little I got upset when the sea came in. I tried to build walls and dig trenches to stop it. I didn't want the waves to make the soft sand wet. I thought it was drowning.'

A school of silver bait fish dart swiftly at my feet hunting through the shallows. Jerking a foot towards them they zip away maintaining their safe distance. Fast fish these slivers of sprat. 'Look Charlie, the fish.' His feet remain firmly planted on the sand, but he's interested enough to strain his neck to see them.

'Sprattus sprattus!'

'I beg your pardon Charlie?'

'Sprattus, sprattus! That's the Latin name for them. I love saying it. Sprattus sprattus. I get some in my pool sometimes. Don't think they like it much. They swim round in circles like crazy trying to find a way out. I try and catch them to help them, but they won't let me. They move too fast.'

'When I used to dive Charlie, it was a privilege sharing the ocean with massive schools of barracuda, jacks and my favourite, trevally, especially the golden or orange-spotted varieties. Hovering weightless close to a school as it moved in unison, spiralling like a tornado, movements synchronised as if choreographed. Fish are not alone in this type of group behaviour, birds do it too. Spectacular starling murmurations swoop over country landscapes at dusk before the birds roost for the night. I've seen all three lanes on the M40, just south of the A34 to Oxford, brought to a standstill by a sight too good to miss. Scientists have more to learn about these formations. It seems obvious that being part of a larger group, making co-ordinated, instinctive movements, deters or distracts predators. There's got to be truth in the adage, "safety in numbers". Watching the sprat swimming this way and that, head in my direction but turn and zoom away at the last second, reminds me of the Galapagos trip and without doubt, the most beautiful dive I've ever made.

'On the last full day of any live-aboard holiday, the number of dives tends to be limited to two, not the usual three or four. The first will be taken early, at 06:30 or 07:00, and the second around 10:30. Returning to the live-aboard after the second dive, kits are cleaned to within an inch of their life. Fresh water rinses remove corrosive salt crystals which, if left unchecked, can expand to damage seals in your breathing apparatus, limiting the life of this expensive piece of equipment. Once washed, the kit is laid out on the decks or hung from the rigging to dry in the sun. Only when each item is bone dry do you pack it for the flight home. Travelling to dive destinations around the world involves one, two or three flights, sometimes even more than that. Dive kits are heavy and expensive to transport on aircraft, wet kit is heavier, more costly, making the drying process vital in keeping costs down. Limiting the number of dives on the penultimate day leaves more time for kit to dry. Keeping flight costs down is only one factor in taking fewer dives, health and safety is the most important consideration mainly avoiding decompression sickness commonly referred to as the "bends". Yesterday I talked to you about oxygen and nitrogen, well when you dive nitrogen is absorbed into your blood and reverts back to gas as you head for the surface. Diving protocol suggests you ascend slowly enabling the nitrogen time to come out of the blood and leave the body through your lungs. If you ascend too fast the nitrogen can bubble in your blood, in the same way a fizzy drink fizzes in a bottle when it's shaken, not good if your blood were to do that is it? When you exit the water there's still nitrogen in your blood which also needs time to come out. Boarding a plane and taking to the air results in a reduction in cabin pressure so flying too soon after diving has a similar effect on your body as ascending from a dive quickly. Your blood can bubble on a plane just as it can bubble on the surface of the sea! That's the bends! Symptoms start with a headache, sickness, or dizziness and in worst case scenarios result in death. Professional dive agencies recommend leaving twenty-four hours between the last dive and the first flight, divers must remain vigilant on every dive.'

I'm not convinced Charlie understands the technical aspects of diving or needs to but before his eyes glaze over and I lose him completely, I'll cut to the dive. 'Anyway, it was the penultimate day of our trip, the day before disembarking and consequently our last opportunity to dive. Beth and I were the only two guests not flying home on the Monday so when AJ asked if we wanted to join him on a third dive, we were bursting to say yes! AJ wanted to go back to the site we'd dived after breakfast, to repeat the dive but venture closer to the drop-off. The other guests were knee-deep in washing, rinsing, and drying and were understandably green with envy when they learned what we were up to. As we boarded the dinghy, they waved and smiled through gritted teeth, christening us "The Three Musketeers"! They weren't wrong, we were up for adventure. This third dive held something special in store, I could feel it. We'd be lucky, good things come in threes. So that was how Beth and I found ourselves racing over the ocean on a hot Ecuadorian afternoon for one last dive.' Pausing, I sneak a glance at Charlie who's walking behind me, his toes in the water. I stop, he stops. He looks at me. We exchange smiles.

Following Jane with my feet in the water is great. I don't feel frightened right now. The water's cold. I like the way my feet sink into the sand. I'm chilled. I don't understand everything Jane says. I don't get the nitrogen bit, but I do get diving's dangerous.

'We were familiar with the topography at the site having dived it a couple of hours earlier but that didn't stop AJ delivering a briefing on route. For the third dive the plan was to descend to 20m immediately above a rocky outcrop, where we'd seen turtles, schools of jacks and two inquisitive sea lions spiralling up out of the depths to play a while. We would then move to where the rock narrowed to a point and jutted out over a drop-off. AJ had seen a manta ray there three trips ago and was hoping we'd see it. We were hoping too, what a wonderful treat that would be before saying goodbye to the Galapagos. AJ was careful not to make any promises and emphasised we weren't diving in a zoo, there are no guarantees but there's always a chance. Hope is good but it's good to keep your hopes in check. You just never know!

'I count myself fortunate to have travelled to many far-flung places and dived with people from around the globe, many who have become friends. Occasionally guides will offer divers the chance to repeat a dive, something divers aren't generally keen to do unless sightings are exceptional then everyone wants to jump back in! A turtle, school of jacks and two sea lions would not have been sufficient incentive to tempt anyone, except Beth and I, we would jump in just in case! We just made a habit of saying yes when asked and were thrilled we did on that day; we were in for a treat.

'During our descent, a friendly sea lion blew bubbles in our faces, curving his torpedo-shaped body with lightning speeds, he whirled energetically amongst us. Unfriendly as it turned out, choosing to nip AJ's shoulder before shooting to the surface. We drifted to the drop-off in the current. Entering the water at 14:57, the first shadow emerged out of the dark at 15:04, dead ahead and heading our way. Squinting through the gloom to try and make sense of what I was seeing, we were surprised as two more shadows appeared followed by another four. As they neared I could make out flicks of white enabling me to identify the species, we were in the presence of eagle rays, and they were on route to give us a glorious fly-by. As if that wasn't enough, the seven were joined by a further six! Thirteen! Unlucky for some but not for us! The rays were swimming in red arrow formation in perfect diamond symmetry. AJ instructed us to keep low to the rock and make our way slowly to the edge of the drop-off. I could hardly breathe. The rays were swimming gracefully just off the point, turning through the water to form a swirling column, a fish tornado! Each ray moved using their two triangular wing-like pectoral fins in a way that suggested they were flying. Gliding up towards the surface they swirled back down to the point before heading off into the dark. Up until that day I'd considered myself fortunate to glimpse one eagle ray and blessed beyond belief to witness an aggregation of three. Previous encounters had been with smaller-sized individuals too and this was off the charts. These were huge specimens, the largest eagle rays I'd ever seen, and we were close, close enough to study them. The top of their body was flat and dark blue with too many white spots to count, the underside white with two sets of five gills. Their white head protrudes to a snout and at the other end they have a slender black tail over 1m in length. The two relatively large pectoral fins enable them to glide and jump through the water. Humans have pectoral muscles, "pecs", which connect the chest to the shoulder and upper arm, you see Charlie we have more in tune with fish than we think! Each ray had a 2m wingspan and was 2.5m from the snout to the tip of the tail. Being in the company of thirteen majestic specimens for that two-minute encounter had already escalated the dive to the realms of the extraordinary. Imagine how my heart tingled seconds later when they reappeared, gliding towards us against the current to swoop over our heads, affording us a perfect view of their underbelly. One ray was so close I needed to duck to avoid its tail brushing against my face. The tail had the appearance of a whip with venomous spines at the top end near the pelvic fins. The tail is what enables the ray to defend itself should it feel threatened or under attack, a hit from the tail can inflict a serious or deadly wound. As I watched these beautiful creatures swoop and dip, it had completely slipped my mind that eagle rays are stingrays, large stingrays! Eagle rays are generally shy of divers and offer no threat as long as they are not threatened. We were in no way aggressive, so the rays were comfortable and edged ever closer, it was breathtaking. I even had the crazy notion they were attempting to communicate with me in some way, which of course they can't, not with humans anyway. Whatever the reason, they were certainly checking us out. The ray at the front of the diamond positioned itself directly in front of me and stopped, its wings barely moving whilst we shared a moment. It was a thing of beauty, we held each other's gaze, something few divers have had the privilege of experiencing. Motionless we stared into each other's eyes, I wondered if it could read my mind. It stayed there, suspended in saline, waiting as his twelve companions congregated behind and once assembled the group moved away only to return moments later. I never expected to see such a thing in my life and without any shadow of doubt it was the best Sunday school I'd ever attended! Their rhythmical movements created sequences that seemed choreographed, as if the rays were performing a dance and moving to an invisible beat only they could hear. I was reminded of a performance by The Royal Ballet at the Royal Opera House in Covent Garden, London. Lights dim, the conductor waves the baton, the orchestra start playing and the dancers spring into action, dancing with their hearts, their feet in perfect synchrony. The finely balanced rays moved with pointed wing tips to pirouette into position, creating an arabesque, chassé or perhaps more fittingly, a fish dive! This was a concert I didn't want to end but end it did, and all too soon.

'Time had come to ascend and leave the dancing birds of the sea behind. We ascended slowly, moving over the rock to where we'd perform the safety stop. At a depth of 12m, sixteen whitetips swam up from the drop-off, it was astonishing. A couple of confident juveniles approached, their curiosity getting the better of them, but our bubbles spooked them, and they darted away. The shiver moved over the rocks beneath us, twisting and turning, keeping close to the stone. It was mid-afternoon so too early for them to be assembling for the night hunt, but then this was an exceptional dive, we'd come to expect the unexpected. What a wonderful grand finale! We exited the water at 16:12 after an unforgettable dive, a dive lasting seventy-five minutes, the longest of the trip.

'As the dinghy whizzed us back to the live-aboard the atmosphere on board was electric, buzzing with excitement having shared in such a unique experience. We had witnessed something incredible, and we knew it. AJ was elated and gave us an impromptu dance performance, gyrating and throwing his hips, hip-hopping his way down the dinghy. It felt less like a dive and more like an adventure, an adventure penned by Alexandre Dumas, the French author, in arguably his most famous novel, *The Three Musketeers*.

Written in 1844, Dumas described the adventures of D'Artagnan in seventeenth-century France and a world of romance, swashbuckling heroes, secret encounters and daring escapades. Yes, our dive was equally exciting. As the dinghy roared across the ripples we gave a roar of our own, "*Un pour tous, tous pour un*", "One for all, all for one", we were indeed musketeers!'

Meandering along the shoreline I find myself riddled with regret. I've made my last dive and it's not fair, it wasn't my time to stop. Retirement planning began in earnest when I hit fifty and top of my list saw me travelling to a number of exotic dive destinations around the world. The plan had always been to retire to live, not retire to wait to die. To do more of what I love but there will be no more long-haul flights. No more live-aboard evenings under glorious sunsets in the company of like-minded souls. I'm left empty, bereft of emotion and looking out over a cold, grey sea that mirrors the desolation in my heart.

'On the last dive of any trip Beth and I would perform a safety stop ritual, our goodbye to the ocean, waving and blowing kisses, that day we blew thirteen. At the time I doubted I'd ever see such a thing again, now I know that to be true. Over the years, saying goodbye had become increasingly difficult, we weren't getting any younger and the final time we'd bid farewell was beginning to loom large. Bobbing on the surface that day, I looked down at the seabed and sent silent messages of love and thanks towards our earth's core, our planet's heart. Our beautiful oceans, seas and turning tides are the heartbeat that washes through my veins to restore balance. My vitamin sea!'

She's gone quiet. Don't know what to say. Mam says if we can't say anything nice we shouldn't say anything at all. I'm thinking about Salt. 'Saying goodbye is hard and can make you sad. I used to have a guinea pig. She was white so I called her Salt. I loved her. One day she stopped eating and me dad said she was sick. The next day she was worse. I held her and she fell asleep. I remember stroking her head and saying goodbye. I loved Salt. You love diving. It's the same. If I could have Salt back I would. You should dive again, you could, nothing's stopping you is it? You loved it and you miss it. You can't just give it up. I don't know much about diving, don't know much about anything really but I do know that you loved it. You shouldn't give it up because you're getting older. Anyway, you're not old. Go. You have more life left. It's what you want isn't it?'

'Charlie it's about Beth, we were close.'

'Well, you can still see her can't you? You don't have to dive with her to see her you can just pop there and go out for lunch. Mam does that all the time with her friends.'

I'm struggling to suppress my exasperation. 'Close', shouldn't be surprised that he took that word literally, assuming I meant geographically close. Shouldn't be frustrated with him, he's a young boy and most of my colleagues would have made the same inference, dentists are not known for their emotional resonance or empathy! 'Beth and I were close, dear friends, someone I trusted, trusted with my life, the only dive buddy I've ever had, I wouldn't have dived at all if it hadn't been for her and as she can't go, neither can I!'

'If you can't go with her then make other friends and go diving with them. You want to. You should. I went to Beavers and to Cubs. My friends went up to Scouts, but I still had to go to Cubs. It was strange at first, hard, but I got used to it. I just started playing with other kids. Mam says I shouldn't let anyone, or anything stop me from doing what I want, as long as it's not something bad. You'll have to do what me mam tells me to do. Ask yourself the question, what do you want to do? Only you can decide.' Saying these words to Jane makes me miss my brothers and me dad. Life has changed and I don't like it. I've been forced out of the water, and it wasn't my fault. I want to go back. Go back in. We used to have fun and I miss it.

Hearing Charlie say these words makes me miss my friend Beth and diving. Life has changed and I don't like it. I've been forced out of the water, and it wasn't my fault. I want to go back. Go back in. We used to have fun and I miss it. Diving has given me cherished memories. Charlie's an astute young fellow with more insight than I've given him credit for, a special boy oblivious to how his words have impacted on me. Sometimes children possess wisdom beyond their years and this boy is an old soul.

WATER OF LIFE

Love 'Fishy Fry-day'. Love it. This week's gone fast. Too fast. One day it was Saturday then it was 'Fishy Fry-day'. The chip shop is in the village. Normally I look forward to it. We all do. Scoffing pasty and chips from newspaper, what's not to like? The vinegar and grease wash the news off the pages and the ink sticks to our fingers turning them black. Doesn't bother us one bit. Ted, the man in the chip shop, says 'It's the best thing for them grubby tabloids, no news in 'em!' 'Lying rags', me mam calls them. She says something similar about politicians too. Thinks it's funny a group of owls is a parliament, 'Nothing about that lot in Westminster is wise!' Me parents are funny! I swear our mucky fingers grab at the best cheese pasty and chips in England, probably the world.

From our caravan park there's only one road that goes down the hill into the village. Terraced houses line the street but only on one side. Each door is painted a different colour. They look great. When the houses get to the bottom they stop. Then there's a pub, a café, an arcade, a newsagents, and our chippie. After the chip shop the houses carry on up on the other side of the hill and at the top is a farm. On the other side of the road, opposite the shops is a harbour and a shop that sells fish, crabs, lobsters, pots of cockles and mussels, everything from mackerel to monkfish and it stinks! We don't go in there. The place hasn't changed since I first came here but me dad says it was different when he came here as a nipper, the tourists have trashed it. Doesn't look trashed to me and anyway we're tourists. Mam says ignore him; it's been the same for centuries. I didn't know the Georgians played pinball!

The five of us squeeze onto our bench in front of the harbour. It's full of empty fishing boats. It's always full of empty fishing boats. The boats are berthed along the harbour walls, some singly but most are double banked. There must be a lot of fish in the sea round here. When the sea moves, the boats move, rattling the rigging. The mooring rings in the floor by our feet jingle and jangle. The fisher folk hang nets over the sides of the boats to dry. The air stinks of fish. Mam says the fish is the lifeblood of the people here. Us tourists never see the action; it all happens too early while we're asleep or having breakfast. She says you can go to any fishing port up and down the coast and you'll see the boats but rarely see the work that goes in. Marauding seagulls prowl on the decks like the scavengers they are, eating scraps rotting in the sun. I love those words, marauding and scavengers. That's what seagulls are, always on the prowl. The scraps don't have much time to rot. The birds get in fast. When they've picked the decks clean they jump onto the rail round the boat and rock up and down. I know what they're doing, they don't fool me. They're watching and waiting to pounce on a boy who doesn't eat his chips quick enough! They're not getting mine tonight. We'll have an ice cream and then walk back along the front to the car.

I won't forget this week. Shark lady's going tomorrow. Her shark stories have changed something. I don't know what and I don't understand why they have but they have. I'll miss listening to her and talking with her. She's told me of places I'd never heard of and a world I never knew existed. I'll miss her. I always sit in the middle in the back of the car. I have to, I get car sick. Even in the middle I feel sick. I do tonight. My belly aches. Probably the chips or the small roads winding about but it feels different, it feels like it's something else. The first day of term last September, Hursty forced me to stand for school elections. She wanted me to be on the school council and go for pizza with our head, Mr Ames, every other Friday. Pointless! I don't even like pizza, surprising for a veggie but I don't. Don't like Ames either so double didn't want to do it. Trouble was nobody wanted to do it. What's the point, it's fake? It just looks good to the parents and the governors! The kids have no power, not really. Hursty knew I'd cave once she talked to Mam. Mam loves stuff like that. She's so proud of me. She's one of those old-fashioned parents. She was 'Miss Perfect' at school, a goody two shoes and did whatever the teachers told her. She was so perfect they made her head girl. When I went home from school and told her about the council, she already knew. Hursty had phoned her and that was it. It was no use telling her I wanted out of it. She was excited and said she'd be my campaign manager! She made me write my speech but kept telling me what I could and couldn't say. I wanted to sack the music teacher, but she didn't let me put that in. But it was my speech. It's what I wanted to say because it was the truth. People don't like the truth. The music teacher deserved sacking. How can anyone not like Bob Dylan? She doesn't let me play his stuff or my stuff. I told me mam that if I can't say she should be sacked then I was going to say she should have a pay cut! She banned that too! The next morning, I tried to get off with a fake illness but me mam wasn't having any of it. At morning assembly, the whole school piled into the hall, and we had to read our speeches. When it was my turn I couldn't find my speech. I'd forgotten it, accidentally on purpose! Thought Hursty would let me off! She didn't and told me to make it up. I started with, 'So the dog ate my homework,' which got a laugh, and I was off, winging it. Don't know what else I said but they elected me to the council. Oh, I do remember promising to fight for kids' rights and not having to do homework at weekends. The biggest cheer was when I said I'd pump the governors for more cash to give teachers a pay rise, even music teachers! The hall roof nearly came off. I'm a bit of a celebrity at school now. The teachers and kids love me! My stomach feels like it did that day when it was my turn to speak. Mam said it was nerves. Yeah I'm nervous but I don't know why. Or do I? I don't say anything, just sit quiet. Eric falls asleep as soon as the car starts going up the hill and Harry's looking out the window. Eating makes you tired. When we get back to the caravan I'm going to bed.

Dad carries Eric in and puts him to bed. Mam's sorting us a hot drink. I take my chain off, that shark tooth isn't going to bite me tonight! My head hits the pillow and bam, I must have gone straight out, I didn't even get to drink my hot chocolate. First time this week I didn't sleep well and now I'm awake and it's really early. The rest are still in bed. Mam, Harry, and Eric are asleep. Dad's snoring. Mam probably had a 'Fizzy Friday' Prosecco or three when they got back, great sleep juice! No idea what the time is but it's light out. I lie in my bunk and look up at the slats. I didn't have a shark dream, not had one of them since last weekend. I can't lie here. Want to get out. I grab my shorts and T-shirt from the bottom of the bed, whack them on, take a handful of biscuits and open the door. I stand on the top step. Weird, but I don't want to jump and run this morning. I walk down the steps. Halfway down I get a stab in my leg. I forgot about my shark tooth. I unzip my secret pocket and put it on. My head feels heavy. My body feels heavy. I don't want to say goodbye, I hate saying the word. Come to think of it I don't like saying hello either. Both involve hugging adults. Why do adults insist on hugging and kissing? My favourite Aunty Susie does high fives. Love that. Love her. When relatives try and hug me I stand back, pull away and bend my head as far from theirs as I can. It works most of the time but if I'm unlucky and they get to me, I get slobbered halfway down my neck. Yuk! Yep, high fives or shouting from the other side of the room work for me then legging it!

I'm going to see what Jane's doing. I've still got a weird tummy. I stand on the grass outside her door and twiddle my shark tooth. I notice my fingers. Man, they're disgusting! Makes me smile. I lied when I told me mam I'd washed them last night. I lick them and wipe them on my top. Wow, now that is disgusting. Newspaper print and stale fry-up is not a good breakfast combo and can't be good for you. Suppose I better make a bit of an effort. Before I knock I'll wipe my hands in the wet grass under her steps and dry them on my shorts. Great now I've smeared black stains on them, classy! I take my cap off, run my hands through my hair and push my fringe out of my eyes. Cap on and I pull my T-shirt to straighten the creases to complete the look! I'm rocking it! Mam never irons a thing, an idiotic faffery she calls it. I'm ready. I knock and step down. Nothing happens. Awkward. I knock again, a bit louder. Still nothing. Think it's obvious she's not in. Maybe she's gone to check out. I'll hang around and wait. From the front of her van I can see the beach and the rocks and there she is, sitting on my stone by my pool! That's it, I'm running. Think I'll aim for a personal best. Ka boom!

'Hi Charlie, good morning. Thought I'd come down here one last time before I leave.' He's out of breath and flops down next to me exhausted. 'I was pretty nippy Charlie until my right knee seized up a few years back, even crawled my way through three half marathons, couldn't do it now, would probably have a heart attack or fall and break a leg!'

'I came to find you to say goodbye. I went to your van and saw you. We haven't sat here all week have we? Not since the first day. I'm going back up to get my bag and then I'll come and sit with you if that's okay?'

'Ah that would have been lovely Charlie but I'm about to head off. I only wandered down here to say goodbye to the sea.' I pause.

His chin falls to his chest and he's chewing at the inside of his cheek, he's troubled. My attempts at jollying him along with a nudge and a wink fail to have the desired effect, quite the opposite in fact. He slides away and avoids making eye contact. My time here has exceeded expectations, meeting this wonderful boy and the conversations we've shared have been the icing on an unexpected cake. During our time together I've had the opportunity to reflect on a beloved past and am ready to embrace the future with more optimism. Bold decisions are required. My camper van adventure, although barely a week old, has transported me to new places, geographically and emotionally and moved me in ways I could never have foreseen. I was a shadow of my former self when I arrived in Northumberland nine days ago, weighed down by life, grieving had taken its toll and eroded my self-esteem. Life was a heavy burden. I was consumed by grief, worn down and worn out. Even with an abundance of supportive friends and a loving family, life was overwhelming. I was lonely, alone, facing a future on my own and drowning in self-pity. That's how it was. Many poor souls suffer with invisible illnesses, depression, and anxiety, struggling through days in pain and silence. I'm not depressed. I know that. I count myself as one of the lucky ones, but even happy souls can dip into pools of sadness that prove difficult to escape from. Today is the day I reached a decision, just now in fact, sitting here on Charlie's stone staring out to sea. I will follow my dreams and no longer allow fear to hold me back. I'm determined to live whatever life I have left to the fullest. I owe it to Greg to fulfil the promise I made to him. I'm content and it was Charlie who initiated that.

'Come on Charlie, I need to make a move, walk back up the hill with me won't you? I've a long drive ahead and would like to get there for lunch. I'm spending a couple of days with an old friend.' Charlie remains silent but stands up. Together, side by side, we walk over the rocks one last time. No words are spoken nor needed. Arriving at the top I disappear into the confines of my camper to retrieve what I'd prepared the night before. I hand the envelope to my young friend who accepts it with a newly found smile. 'Open this when I've gone will you? Have a great time next week. I'll be thinking of you. It's been wonderful spending time with you and your family. Your mum and dad aren't up and about yet are they so please tell them I said goodbye. I really hope we meet again Charlie to share more stories of my life under the waves. Bye, Sharkbite!' We share a smile and I climb into the driver's seat, wind down the window, throw him a wave and I'm off. I stop before the bend and he's still there. One more wave for luck then I'm gone. Onwards and upwards to my next adventure!

She's gone. I watch until she drives round the corner. I want to cry. Not going to though. I don't want to go back to the beach yet. I'm going back inside for a bit. Everyone will be up now. The door must be open, I can smell breakfast. Toast, the smell of toast is great. I'm going to have some. Warm toast and salted butter, love it. Wonder what we're having for tea. Surprise tea would be good. Walk in the door and me dad grabs me.

'Hey lad was that ya shark lady friend I saw driving off? She gone then?'

'Yeah. Mam are we having surprise tea tonight?'

'If you like, love.'

'Worrying about ya stomach. Not missing ya shark lady friend much are ya!'

I get away from him and sit down. I look at my envelope. It's one of those large ones me dad hates. He won't use them; they make him cross. He says they're 'Damn expensive!' He gets mad every time he has to send more than a letter or a card. He never pays for proof of posting, parcels, or tracking. Squeezes everything into a small envelope and puts it under a book to flatten it. Doesn't matter how heavy the letter is a second-class stamp goes on it and he hopes for the best! No wonder half our stuff doesn't get where it's going! It was okay until he applied for a job. He squeezed the forms into a small envelope, whacked a second-class stamp on and blamed the post office when he didn't get an interview. The post office is hardly going to let him be a postman doing that are they! This envelope's thick. 'She gave me this.' I hold it up so they can all see.

'How exciting, wonder what's in it, open it sweetheart so we can find out.'

Mam sounds as excited as me. I don't know it yet but what's inside will make a difference in the hours, weeks, and years to come. I rip the envelope open and tip out what's inside onto the table, a £20 note, a small card, and a letter.

'What's all that about Charlie? I'm intrigued, read the letter.'

Mam's not the only one. I stare at the letter. Man, Jane's writing is hard to make out. Dentists and doctors are the same, rubbish at writing. Writing writing that's impossible to read. Writing writing. Sounds weird that does. It's like painting paintings and cooking cooking! My brain thinks weird stuff sometimes. I read it so they can all hear.

Charlie,

As you read this I'll be well on my way along the infamous A1 heading north to Edinburgh and beyond. Feel like Buzz Lightyear writing that! I'm going to spend time with a friend before continuing north. I intend hugging the coast roads and stopping wherever and whenever the fancy takes me. The £20 is for pasty and chips on Friday. Your parents have been so kind, spoiling me with food and wine, it's the least I can do.

'Ah how lovely is that it's such a kind gesture. Been good company for you too hasn't she? Actually, she's been good all round. I've enjoyed spending time with her, she's interesting.'

Mam's right. Never met anyone like her.

'Get on with it lad, keep reading it will ya!'

Wish he'd leave me alone, the letter wasn't for him anyway!

If you and your family ever come down to my neck of the woods then please pop in, my address, email and phone numbers are on the card. I will treasure our time together Charlie, you have left a lasting impression on me and helped me move on. Keep in touch!
Lots of Love,
Shark lady x x x

I stare at the letter and see the PS's. I'm not going to read them out loud. Dad will only start on at me and want to know what she means.

'Stop frowning lad, if the wind changes ya face will stick like that.'

I'm going out before he has a chance to read them. I fold the letter and shove it in my pocket and I'm out the door and running. I want to read the pages on my own so I'm not stopping till I get to the beach, when I do, I sit down and read.

PS Charlie, you're stronger than you think. You can do anything if you put your mind to it. We've chatted about some of your teachers and although you're not fond of a few of them, there's always one who's worth their weight in gold. Talk through your troubles with them! If you struggle doing that just know there is always someone there to listen to you, me included!

PPS A teacher at my secondary school once told me something that has stayed with me all my life, 'We all have persevering muscles, we just need to discover them!' I have found mine and am about to use them! You will find yours. Josie and Mia found theirs! If I'd had another day with you I would have told you about them, our time ran out, but their story is poignant and worthy of telling.

Here goes... A few years ago, I dived in Mexico, in the 60,000 square miles of sea known as the Sea of Cortez or Gulf of California. Beth and I were staying at a hotel in La Paz, the city of peace and coastal capital of the Mexican state of Baja California Sur. La Paz is known for the Malecon, a 5.5km (3.4 miles) seafront promenade, adorned with sizeable bronze statues sited at regular intervals, statues that depict that which lies at the heart of this community, its connection to the sea; a mermaid swimming alongside a dolphin, a giant oyster shell complete with pearl, two hammerhead sharks chasing up towards the sky, a life-size fisherman standing in a paper macramé boat and a leaping whale are only a handful of the sculptures you meet along the way. Works of art on a walk of art! Ornate metal benches line the walkway, white in colour keeping them cool under the searing sun as well as affording their occupants glorious views over the sea. Locals and tourists meet here to reminisce, eat ice creams, or drink beer whilst enjoying sunsets not bettered anywhere in the world. The pavement widens halfway along the promenade to encompass an equally ornate bandstand, a centrepiece, resembling those built in Victorian times and seen in parks throughout England.

Landing at Manuel Marquez de Leon International Airport, I was struck by the intense, desert-like heat and the desolate sandy landscapes. Our driver put his foot down, on some inner mission to make the ten-mile journey in record time, and successfully deposited us in La Paz less than 12 minutes later! The absence of traffic a godsend! After checking into our hotel, we strolled along the Malecon to take in our surroundings and benefit from the refreshing sea air. Feeling peckish we happened upon Steinbeck's, a thatched taco restaurant overlooking a state-of-the-art marina, a vibrant space. Newly varnished hardwood decking took *you past quaint shops, art galleries, restaurants, and bars. People spilled outside to sit under colourful awnings and sip cocktails. Music filled the air which enhanced the mood and drowned out the symphony from seagulls swooping for scraps behind fishing boats returning happy tourists and their catch to port. We were seated at a long table outside amongst colourful pots of cacti and other tropical plants. Sitting with strangers was not my idea of fun but communal eating and being part of this community was actively encouraged and I have to admit, the energy was electric. I couldn't help but fall in love with the place. What's not to like? Palm trees, swathed in rope lighting, lined the path snaking to the entrance, made for an impressive spectacle. The twinkling lights reflected from the tall trunks into the turquoise waters at our feet to form a magical display. Inside, candles flickered on dark wooden tables, and seascapes, boat prints and wildlife watercolours decorated sand-coloured walls. It was warm and cosy. What better way to christen our holiday than sipping a margarita, that quintessentially Mexican cocktail, under a setting sun. Then mother and daughter, Josie and Mia, joined the party! I noticed Josie immediately and I wasn't the only one, staff greeted her as an old friend. This diminutive, blue-eyed brunette came bounding along the boardwalk, daughter in tow. She was a seriously stylish 38-year-old beauty. Her long hair framed a tanned complexion suggesting she wasn't a tourist but a local. Looking lovely in linen shorts and shirt, she completed the nautical look with deck shoes and an air of confidence. The waiter showed them to our table and the only empty seats in the restaurant. They were seated opposite us. I instantly became transfixed by this effervescent woman; her enthusiasm was infectious. She lit up the room! Mia was quieter, though no less endearing, a 12-year-old probably somewhat in the shadow of her dynamic mother.*

Originally from Lee-on-the-Solent, 8km (5 miles) west of Portsmouth, Hampshire, on England's south coast, Josie moved to La Paz in 1998 to study marine biology. She met the man of her dreams, a fellow student, and they both returned to England in 2003 to marry. He originated from Southampton so that was where they chose to settle. Twelve months later they welcomed baby Mia into the world. Sadly, the marriage failed to stand the test of time and after the divorce, the heartbroken mother upped sticks and moved back to La Paz taking Mia with her. In that part of the world air temperatures soar to 30 degrees Celsius during the summer months and remain above 20 during the winter. Equally attractive are the sea temperatures, peaking at 29 and not dipping below 20. There's no creeping into the sea when you want a swim like back home. No shivering. No suffering. No freezing water lapping at your thighs while you stand there, losing the feeling in both feet, waiting for the water to feel marginally warmer than ice! Josie's words not mine, but true all the same! Josie was determined to raise Mia in a more temperate climate. The pursuit of a better future was the thread she weaved to create the tapestry of her life, the fabric of her being.

The decision to return to Mexico had been an easy one. She'd missed friends, the food, the climate, and the warmer waters she'd studied and knew so well. She spoke of her hopes for Mia and wanting her to thrive in La Paz, a vibrant city with its mix of traditional and cosmopolitan lifestyles. Most importantly she wanted her to learn Spanish, a language popular the world over, particularly the Americas. She secretly confessed to daring to dream that Mia would love the sea as much as she did and enough to want to follow in her footsteps and study marine biology, a subject Josie loved so much.

Back in La Paz Josie continued where she'd left off, studying whale shark aggregations, and gathering data to ensure protection of the species. Hearing her mention this was exciting, we'd travelled to Mexico to swim those warm waters with the world's largest fish. So passionate was she about the legacy she could leave behind for future generations, she lectured at the local university and gave talks in a local secondary school. Funny isn't it, within minutes of meeting someone you end up telling them your whole life story! Ring any bells?

Having been brought up in a coastal community with miles of pebble beaches and sea views, Josie had always dreamed of owning her own boat. Finally realising her dream, she named her pride and joy, Kino. Her 15m sailboat was one of over a hundred yachts, speedboats and fishing vessels neatly moored in the marina. I was intrigued by her choice of name, and she delighted in revealing its connection to John Steinbeck, the American author who'd found himself drawn to La Paz back in the 1940s. Steinbeck fell in love with the harbour town, so much so, he chose to stay there to write The Pearl, a heart-wrenching tale of man's greed. A fisherman dived for oysters in the hopes of finding a pearl to fund a doctor to treat his sick son, the victim of a scorpion sting. The fisherman's name, Kino! He does indeed find a pearl, an enormous specimen, naming it, 'The Pearl of the World'. A find of such proportions stirred jealousy and greed within the local community who conspired to steal it. During a brutal brawl Kino's son is killed. The story ends with him tossing the pearl back into the depths of the Sea of Cortez. It begged the question, why choose to christen her boat after this sad tale? Her answer will stay with me, 'Kino was a good man, a man who loved his son and I, like him, would do anything to protect my daughter,' then with a twinkle in her eyes, 'And anyway, the pearl is still out there waiting for me to find! There must always be hope, hope for life, hope for a better future and hope that people can change.'

The two of them proved wonderful dinner companions and it was during the meal that they shared a colourful account of a remarkable tale, the likes of which I'd never heard before! They had recently returned from a three-week sailing holiday following a route they knew well having made it many times before. Heading north, they kept to the west, past Isla del Espiritu Santo towards the small rocky island of Los Islotes, home to a two-hundred-strong sea lion colony. Conditions were near perfect, the sea calm to moderate, visibility excellent and a generous breeze filled their sails. Apparently a 15-knot wind pushing in the direction you're heading is desirable. When winds allowed they sailed, when they dissipated they used the motor. Josie stressed the importance of arriving at prearranged mooring points in good time, to this end they hugged the coast to benefit from the protective shield it provided. Sailing out in the centre of the gulf would render them vulnerable and at the mercy of dangerous swells. Tropical storms hit the area between August and November and the El Norte winds blow from November to March, turning the calm sea into raging rollers. In those months, Mia was of the mind, the Sea of Cortez should be renamed, 'The Sea of Storms'!

They loved their trips and Josie made them sound idyllic. They would jump in and swim with playful sea lions, snorkel alongside whale sharks, watching as they gulped gallons of nutrient-rich water. Dolphins, often in huge pods, would swim by and show off, leaping and spinning. Humpback whales would breach, blow vapour from their blowhole then disappear into the depths with a final wave of the tail. Listening to her I understood why Jacques Cousteau referred to the Sea of Cortez as 'the world's aquarium', it holds many treasures.

Josie planned stops along the way, places to eat on crystal-white beaches under pristine blue skies. After mooring up for the day, Josie romanticised about afternoons and evenings playing cards, reading, and sharing stories as the sea swallowed the sun. She would sip Corona, the traditional Mexican beer, with the customary lime slice wedged in the neck of the bottle and relax under a blanket of stars. The only other place I've seen a sky full of stars was in the Maldives. It's so sad that our English skies fall victim to light pollution, we don't see the half of it! A sailor's life sounds simple yet intoxicatingly addictive.

On the day in question, they'd moored in a picturesque bay alongside a deserted beach where they planned to have breakfast. Mia, her kayak full of provisions, headed over to start setting up. Josie would swim over after making a quick repair to the sail. Mia wandered along the beach in search of unusual stones and shells, and that's when she spotted it, a huge piece of driftwood washed up on the shore. As she went to investigate, something happened to stop her dead in her tracks, the wood moved! She tried to make sense of what she was seeing and deduced the wood must be a sea lion, but it was larger than any sea lion she'd seen before. She confessed to feeling a little scared but made the unusual decision to venture closer to get a better look! As she stepped tentatively along the sand she confessed to being troubled, something about the sea lion wasn't right. She couldn't put her finger on it until she was almost upon it and then she knew. It was lying on its back; the two pectoral fins were sticking out to the side and its caudal fin was flat on the sand! A sea lion has flippers, this wasn't a sea lion. Mia was standing beside a shark! She screamed to alert her mum. You should know

Charlie that Mia was scared of sharks, even a shark lying on a beach. On hearing her daughter's cries, Josie looked over at what she too assumed to be wood, wave-carved wood she called it. Never heard it called that before, loved that! Only when she zoomed in with her binoculars was the object's true identity revealed and it wasn't just any shark, it was a great white! A fish just short of 2m, a juvenile but a great white all the same. Assessing the situation, she deduced it must have been caught out by the receding tide and left high and dry on the sand! Contemplating their options, she devised a plan of action and before leaving Kino grabbed a rope and bucket.

Josie described looking into those black eyes and forming an instant connection with the stricken fish. It was helpless and she felt its pain. It would certainly die unless it got back in the water. She thought it might already be too late for it. She gave the tail a couple of strong tugs, but it wouldn't budge. Hardly surprising, juvenile great whites can weigh anywhere in the region of 150kg. Mia needed to help if they were to free the shark but knowing how scared she was, of sharks in general and great whites in particular, Josie wasn't sure she would. But help she did, and this is where the rope and bucket came in. Josie secured the rope to the tail. Mia filled the bucket with water and poured the life-saving contents over the shark to prevent the skin drying out in the heat. As you know sharks need to extract oxygen from water flowing over the gills to breathe. Tiny breaths are better than none. Sharks need water to sustain life. We all do!

With the rope secured to the tail, they both took hold and attempted pulling the shark down the beach, lying 4m from the water's edge meant they didn't have far to go! Getting the shark in the shallows would allow the waves to support and rock the shark enabling it to move into deeper waters. The difficult bit, the bit they were scared of, was untying the rope *once it was time to let it go. They had to be out of the water before the shark submerged. Imagine a scene reminiscent of a tug of war, Josie and Mia on one team, the shark on the other. It seemed to take forever but eventually the shark slid slowly down the sand, gathering momentum there was no stopping it and it plunged into the water with a resounding splash! Mia hopped out immediately and Josie untied the rope careful to maintain a safe distance from that mouth and its rows of sharp teeth! Up to her waist in water she didn't fancy losing a leg or two! The shark remained stationary, so Josie struggled but managed to turn it over onto its belly and point the snout out to sea, but it still didn't move. It was lifeless. They spoke of feeling helpless and desperately sad, the shark had been out of the water too long and all their efforts had been in vain. Luckily, they were wrong! The shark must have been exhausted or suffering from shock or both as without warning it suddenly flicked its tail but astonishingly swam back towards the beach! It was disorientated and trying to beach itself again. Luckily, the water was too shallow and prevented it making any headway. It did make as if to go but for a reason they couldn't understand turned and headed towards the beach for a second time. Maybe the waves were proving too powerful for the shark in its weakened state, and it didn't have the energy to combat the force pushing against it. Time ticked by. It would move then lie still. Then out of nowhere it gave a fiercer flick of the tail and was gone, never to be seen again. Josie couldn't get out of the water quick enough.*

They were brave hey? Great white sharks have a bad reputation, known to be aggressive so I was interested to learn why they chose to intervene and help it. They could so easily have left it to fate. Not so easily as it turned out! Josie did admit contemplating sailing away but couldn't, that decision would have gone against every natural instinct. Those few metres from shore to sea meant life or death for the shark and it was a journey it couldn't make on its own. Josie couldn't leave a defenceless creature to die. The fact that it was a great white merely focused the mind. Though vulnerable it still presented a level of threat. Too close to those teeth, one flick of the snout and either of them could still have become the victim of an attack and have suffered a nasty or deadly bite. Had Josie been bitten out there in the middle of nowhere and miles from a doctor, she could have bled to death leaving Mia stranded alone. Another boat passing by would have been a miracle. At that time Mia was unable to sail on her own. By the time we met the plucky pair in Steinbeck's Josie had already started teaching Mia the skills she'd need to enable her to sail single-handed should an emergency arise.

Both were brave but it was Mia's behaviour that intrigued me the most. How someone so timid and nervous of sharks would help to save one, let alone get in the water with one, beggared belief. She claimed to have acted on instinct. She spoke of being scared and that it would have been easy to leave but she knew she had to help. She told us about finding the strength and refusing to let fear get the better of her. She was fully aware that if she had, the shark would certainly have died. Her mum could not have done it without her. Had she turned the other cheek and not helped, she would have felt guilty later and not been able to forgive herself. Her mum had brought her up to treat people and animals with respect; to care for those who are weak and to leave the world a better place. She knew she had to be strong. She knew she had to fight the fear. Mia didn't overthink the situation and dwell on the dangers, she just acted and did the right thing and as a result the shark swam to freedom to live its life in the water.

Passing the time with the two of them, whilst sitting under the stars breathing air infused with the scents of the sea, served to elevate our meal from the ordinary to the extraordinary. Spicy fish drizzled with a tomato and lime sauce, with a side of cooling guacamole, never tasted so good! Saying our goodbyes, Josie threw her arms around me and planted a kiss to both cheeks in customary Latin American fashion. After the sun slipped below the horizon, lights from the bars and restaurants lining the boardwalk sparked into life, bathing the boats in the marina in an explosion of colour bouncing over the water. Standing at the water's edge, the moon and I found ourselves reflecting into those dark waters, the moon lit the ripples on the surface while I stared down beyond them into the depths, searching, wondering how many great whites were passing beneath those hulls. These thoughts would usually trouble me at the start of a diving holiday but not that night. That night my head hit the pillow and I was rocked to sleep in an instant, dreaming of sharks but in a good way! The rest of our trip sped by in a whirl. One minute we were heading to Mexico, the next checking in for our flight home. I had seen the best that Baja had to offer. Stunning scenery, incredible wildlife and made two new friends along the way, friends I will treasure and maybe sail the seas with one day. I remain in awe of them both, their outlook on life and their bravery. As for Kino's pearl, that remained elusive, lying in its fictional salt water resting place for someone else to find, or maybe not!

'Charlie, Charlie, come on lad, I was wondering where ya'd got to. We're going crabbing on't rocks over here, ya coming?'

Dad makes me jump. He's at the bottom of the hill. Harry and Eric are halfway down. Eric's kicking his ball and Harry's hanging around as usual. They'll be a while yet. I love crabbing. Dangling crab lines into pools waiting for that tug. It's not as easy as you might think for vegetarians to catch crabs. We don't do ham or bacon. Dad and I experimented with other bait. Standing for ages waiting for them to take cucumber, gherkin or the dreaded cado but they wouldn't. Don't blame them, ghastly green gunge the lot of them! At the end of one summer there was a right stink in our caravan. Dad put it down to us having a dead rat underneath. I hoped it was a seagull! He crawled under there searching for it but had no luck. He was beyond thrilled when me mam found an open pack of green cheese in Harry's drawer. No idea how it got there! I'm sure I'd have remembered putting it in there at the beginning of the holiday when I'd lost at scrabble! Who knew it would take two weeks to find! Harry's clothes stank, ha! The crabs loved that stinky cheese. It was me who came up with the idea of trying Pepper's dog food. Perfect. Crabs obviously love smelly stuff, the smellier the better, weird seeing as they don't have noses. A bloke at the aquarium told me scientists discovered crabs wave hairy antennae to smell with. Dad reckons a pair of his socks would go down a treat! Me and me dad are expert crabbers and competitive. But I want to finish this first.

'Come on son it'd be good to spend time together. Hurry up Harry and Shadow want to spend time with ya. I could do with Shadow following ya and giving me a break. What do ya say? Come on. We're going o'er there onto ya rocks. Can't say no to that can ya? Come on lad, I've got ya bucket and line. I miss ya lad!'

He misses me! The way he said it sounds like he does. He sounds different. 'Coming! I'll be there in a minute Dad.' He's on the rocks. He's using our buckets to balance. Better be quick. I want to sit on my stone at my pool.

PPPS Charlie, you've helped me come to a decision. I want to look back on my life without regret. If I don't return to the oceans and dive again I'll regret it for the rest of my life. Thanks to you the light at the end of my tunnel burns brighter. I intend to retrieve my 'to do list' from the bin and start ticking them off. I will fill my passport with immigration stamps from Indonesia, the Philippines, and the Galapagos but the very next flight I'm boarding will land in Mexico, you know where!

Earlier in the week you asked me what I really wanted from life and now I'm asking you the same. Don't look back with regret Charlie, your whole life is ahead of you, live it. Embrace it. Look further, dream beyond what you believe is possible. Make each and every memory count. Let's both dive into good memories. If I can, you can.

The water's cold. Take a deep breath and go for it. Remember millions of people swim in our seas and oceans. You've thrown pebbles into the sea haven't you? Who hasn't! When the pebble hits there is a splash followed by ripples in the water, one then another and another. Life is just the same, some pebbles can cause ripples that last forever! Spread joy Charlie!

Fingers crossed I find the pearl!

Take care and see you soon Sharkbite ☺

Lots of love Jane… Shark lady xx

I stare at the paper, that blank sort of stare kids do in lessons, that daydream stare that winds teachers up, yeah I'm doing that. Staring but not taking anything in. Jane has talked about a new world and it's in my head. She has left a mark. I can feel it like my brothers fingers, prod prod prodding at me. Her stories are bugging me but in a good way not a bad one. I sit but not for long, I fold the letter and put it in my pocket. Time to be the crab catching champion. I'm up and running. Running to get there and show them how it's done. Who knows what happens to words we read or hear? Who knows where they go? Do they stay in your brain somewhere or drift around until, for some unknown reason, they hit a nerve? Don't suppose we'll ever know but her words are in my head as I race along the beach. I squeeze next to Dad, he's on my stone. It's my stone and I'm going to sit on it. I drop my orange line into the water and boom I've got one. Easy. Hurry up Harry and Shadow are at a small pool closer to the beach. Dad and me say nothing just drop our lines in, hold them until we catch one then drop the catch in our buckets.

'Dad.'

'Mmmmm?'

I want to talk to him but don't know what to say. 'I want to tell you something but... but... I'm scared.' I'm whispering. I can't believe I'm going to tell him. 'Dad, I...' This is hard. My throat is tight, and my mouth is dry. I can't help it; I start to cry. Oh no I didn't mean for that to happen! Dad's noticed. He puts his arm round me.

'Hey up lad, what's up? Don't cry son. Tell me. What ya scared of?'

I can't. The words won't come out. I turn away and wipe my eyes with the back of my hands to try and stop the tears. I stare into my pool. Dad's into one. He reels in his line. He drops the crab in his bucket and pulls me to him.

'Charlie, what is it? Ya can tell me. I want ya to tell me. I'm ya dad. Ya can tell me anything. Anything. I mean it. Tell me. I love ya son.'

He's not said that before. The way he said it sounds serious. Think he means it. He sounds strong and it makes me feel strong. I look at him. Look into his eyes. They are watery. We stare at each other. I cry. He holds me and kisses the top of my head, and it hits me. Hits me like a bolt of lightning. He does. He loves me. First time in ages I know it. He does. Me dad loves me. He's there for me. I can tell him. Tell him about the aquarium, the shark, the sea, the night-times, all of it. I stop crying. Things are changing.

NOT ANYTIME, ANYWHERE

13:14, The Beach, Northumberland

Matt and his sons had been crabbing in the rock pools since 12:07. Fishing for crabs was a much-cherished pastime, a family tradition through four generations of Parkers. Matt's three boys spent hours dangling legs and lines into pools, their gear modern, colourful, and efficient, reels with handles to encourage the speedy winding of a much-prized catch. Matt's gear was of a more traditional nature, from nature, a thirty-year-old stick and string! This cherished heirloom reminded him of a treasured childhood and holidays at the seaside with a man he was proud to call his father. Matt ached for his sons to hold him in the same regard and relished opportunities to be alone and bond with his boys. Sitting beside his eldest was particularly pleasing, he'd feared for the child of late, sensing a shift in, what had previously been, a close relationship. Father and son were drifting apart, and no amount of cajoling, persuading, teasing, or humour helped heal the ever-widening gulf, the boy would simply clam up or distance himself. Matt believed he was failing as a father, and it was eating away at him. The harder he tried the worse things became. Bedtimes were a particularly tense affair. The dejected father would close the door, trudge down the stairs, and discuss the latest behaviour update with Sam and run through their options. They had already tried encouraging Charlie to join clubs, make new friends, family days out, weekends away, treats, involving the school and tough love but they had all failed to achieve the desired improvements. Both parents were hoping their decision to spend longer on this summer holiday would snap him out of his mood and miraculously restore the fractured relationship. One week in and the distance between them remained.

The two younger boys were sitting beside a smaller rock pool, the elder of the pair revelling in the independence entrusted in him by his father. The days the four of them huddled round the edges of one pool, relegated to the past. Harry was delighted to be separated from his big brother as it offered him more opportunities to catch a coveted crab. Charlie was a skilled crabber, and no one stood a chance of catching one with him around. Distracted by the amount of successful strikes Charlie was enjoying, Harry devised a plan to drop his line on the other side of the pool and for reasons only known to him, opted to crawl around the inner edge amongst the slippery clumps of seaweed.

Matt was troubled and his worries were not eased by his son's latest admission. What could possibly be scaring him? What Matt said to his son in the forthcoming minutes could hold the key and turn things round, but Matt's perceived inadequacy had chipped away at his own confidence. He doubted his ability to support his son and was distracted from the crabs, racking his brain on what to say to coax his son into divulging his worries without shutting him down or pushing him away. Matt understood the importance of the conversation they were about to embark on but the words, like the crabs, eluded him.

A piercing scream cut through the air at 12:21, carried on the prevailing breeze into the ears of the father to startle and break his contemplations. A series of desperate cries followed by urgent appeals for help and Matt was on his feet.

'Daddy, help me, help me, I can't get out!'

Matt threw his stick into the bucket and sped over to the pool. The gruesome sight greeting him caused his heart rate to soar, his son Harry was neck deep in the water bathing in a blood bath! The amount of blood in the pool suggested a deep wound. Matt understood the urgency of the situation, the need to get Harry out was crucial. Matt needed to assess the extent of the injury and prevent him going into cold shock, his son was already gasping for air. Anyone getting into difficulty in cold water runs the risk of their condition deteriorating unless extricated immediately, the risk of hypothermia or death is very real. Eric sat sobbing on the stone, his little legs dangling over the edge, toes hovering above the water. His rosy wind-blown cheeks drained of colour at the sight of the scarlet-stained waters at his feet, the tears dripping from his chin, making miniscule circles in the pool of red.

Matt stepped down the side of the pool, his plimsolls immediately disappearing beneath the surface so focused was he on reaching his boy. His position was precarious, his feet straining every sinew to fight against the slippery soles in his struggle to maintain balance on tiny ledges and sharp edges. He couldn't afford to splash down as he stretched to grab his boy who remained tantalisingly beyond his reaching fingertips. Clumsily circumventing the inner edges of the pool, he managed to manoeuvre closer to take hold of Harry's T-shirt and pull him through the water. Blood poured from a gash under Harry's left foot as Matt pulled him out, a wound requiring more than TLC, a plaster and ice cream! The concerned father feared an operation may be on the cards or at least stitches, he could see bone! Anxiously cradling his son, he barked instructions over to Charlie.

'Harry's cut his foot. He'll be okay but it needs looking at. I'm taking him up to Sam. The pair of ya stay here, look after Shadow, don't worry, it's not bad, Harry will be all right. Ya mam will be down in a bit, or I will. Put ya stuff away Charlie and get over here. Come on lad, I'm off.'

His panicked cries confirmed that bystanders to an accident or those who come upon the aftermath of a traumatic event can suffer from shock in a similar way the victim or victims do and it's a condition that should not be underestimated. Trauma trickles out to touch those on the periphery, especially if the victim is a family member or a loved one. Charlie could feel emotions stirring but kept a cool head. Matt could be forgiven for doubting his son's ability to handle the crisis, but he needed to give his boy more credit, he was savvy enough to hear panic in his father's voice and more than able to act accordingly. He released the crabs back into the confines of the pool and watched as they made their bolt for freedom, scurrying to hide in invisible cracks and crevices until the next time they were tempted out by the foul-smelling Pedigree Chum! Even during the hiatus, he gained immense satisfaction knowing he'd caught more crustaceans than his father and couldn't restrain a whispered boom!

Eric, still blubbering by the pool, watched his father set off towards the hill. Charlie grabbed both buckets and reels and gingerly picked his way across the rocks to join him. He had a sure-fire plan to comfort his little brother. They would go to the beach. Football would achieve his goal!

'Hey up Shadow, come on, stop crying, it's okay. Harry will be okay. Mam and Dad will sort it. Let's go and play footie. You can be The Blades and I'll be Liverpool. We'll have two goals, and you can kick off.'

These words instantly had the desired effect, Eric stopped sobbing.

'Charlie, Harry's got an ouch. A bad ouch. On his foot. Blood. Lots of blood.'

Charlie gave his brother a reassuring hug then hand in hand, the two boys headed over to the pitch! The match would kick off in 14 minutes.

Football was another treasured Parker pastime passionately enjoyed by all members of the family. Father and youngest son supported Sheffield United, their local club, affectionately known as The Blades, a name harking back to the city's historical links with the steel industry. Mother and both older boys were ardent Liverpool fans. Matt never hid his disappointment of Charlie's choice of team. From the moment Sam announced they were expecting their first child, Matt had fantasised of Saturday afternoon outings to Bramall Lane where they would meet up with his mates, enjoy the match and scoff a half-time pie. Their relationship would flourish, and his son or daughter would develop an undying bond for the club and the two of them for each other. Sam, football crazy, selfishly supported her boys' allegiance to Liverpool. By rights she should have supported Chester, being born there but as her father had been brought up in Wrexham, North Wales that became their club of choice. At secondary school, peer pressure persuaded Sam to re-evaluate her allegiance and support one of the four big clubs in the north-west of England, Manchester United, Manchester City, Everton, or Liverpool. There was only one for her. She justified her, out of the blue, decision to turn red, citing Liverpool as the team of a generation, a decade, with more than their fair share of great players, Clemence, Hughes, Rush, Hansen, Smith, Heighway, Fowler, Owen, her list was endless. Legendary managers added fuel to her argument, Shankly, Paisley and Dalglish to name only three. Liverpool won most matches and trophies but none of the family fell for it! Her love for Liverpool lay with legs! Steven Gerrard's legs to be precise! She oohed and aahed over his luscious limbs since the day the eighteen-year-old player made his debut at Anfield against Blackburn Rovers on November 29th,

1998. He is her hero, and she never tolerates a word said against him.

Charlie, bestowing Eric with the honour of kicking off, proved too tempting an offer for the youngster to resist, football was his life, as was the adulation in which he held his big brother. His yearning to be included in games with both brothers consumed his days and the youngster never got used to the regular rejections or the resulting frustrations that inevitably boiled over inside him. Charlie and Eric arrived on the pitch at 12:48 and set about demarcating the goalposts with buckets and reels. Charlie shot a look up the hill in time to see his father set foot on the summit, his legs buckling under the strain of the burden on his back. The significance of Harry being carried by his father wasn't lost on Charlie; the injury must have been far worse than he'd been led to believe by his protective parent.

The match kicked off at 12:54, the Sheffield striker sprinted towards the Liverpool goal as fast as his little legs would let him. The Liverpool keeper was dancing about theatrically, arms and legs akimbo, waiting for the shot. Eric bore down on the goal and took his best swipe at the bouncing ball. The goalie dived dramatically in the opposite direction, leaving an empty net for Sheffield to take a 1–0 lead. The young striker couldn't believe his luck! It was the first time he'd ever scored against the more experienced keeper and to celebrate his success he rolled down the sand, delirious with joy. The goalie smiled a secret smile, he wasn't perturbed in the slightest, one goal would be the limit of his generosity, Liverpool would win the game as sure as eggs is eggs! Before Liverpool kicked off to restart the match, the sound of a revving car drew the attention of both boys. Father and son were departing for the hospital with some urgency, leaving a tearful Sam behind. She took a moment to compose herself before turning to acknowledge the players with a cheery wave. Her anxiety levels were on overdrive, one of her brood was suffering pain and it tugged at her heartstrings. Funny but that morning she'd woken up with a feeling of doom and gloom which hung over her like a cloud and needed lifting. She believed she was blessed with a sixth sense and the feeling of dread confirmed an inner inkling of Harry's injury. Whether she did or did not, she'd experience a feeling far worse on this fateful day! But right there and then, watching the car drive away, she was focused on being with her boys on the beach, just the tonic she needed to help worries float away and time to fly. Calling to them she attempted reassuring that all was well, and she'd be down in a jiffy, words they never heard, words that drifted away on the breeze.

The match continued at 13:02, Liverpool one nil down but with time on their side immediately equalised. Minutes later Liverpool went 2-1 up, the tide had well and truly turned! The Sheffield United player's resilience was commendable, but his young age didn't evoke any sympathy from Liverpool who were growing more determined with every kick and shooting from further out. The strengthening breeze started playing havoc with the ball, swirling it one way then another. The Liverpool striker was in his own half, the ball at his feet, taking aim he let fly. His foot connected with the ball so sweetly, he could feel the goal in his gut. He watched as it looped towards the target but before crossing the line a gust of wind caused it to swerve and hit the defender's elbow just inside the penalty area. Hand ball! Penalty to Liverpool. The striker rejoiced and couldn't help gloating as he placed the ball on the imaginary penalty spot, choosing to disregard the whimpering protestations from his younger opponent.

'It's not fair, I'm the goalie. I saved it Charlie! I'm the goalie!'

Both boys knew he was right, but Charlie was already focused on the penalty kick. He would take a long run-up and strode off towards the halfway line, Liverpool legend Charlie Parker was already celebrating being 3-1 up. This kick was going in, he knew it. Turning to face the goal he stood strong, Ronaldo-esc, legs apart, chest out and proud, he was confident and ready. He was kicking against the wind so this would have to be his strongest kick yet. At 13:11 the striker sprinted full pelt and let loose an almighty strike, even he was surprised at its strength. The ball flew with pinpoint precision towards the goal and would bend into the top corner. Boom! The moment the ball left his foot Charlie turned and hared off down the beach in triumph. Running, he pulled his T-shirt up to hide his head, stretched his arms out to the side, mimicking a World War Two Spitfire and elaborately weaved over the sand. To add insult to injury he sang a chorus of his favourite football ditty, 'Championes, championes, ole, ole, ole, championes, championes, ole, ole, ole.' His elaborate celebration culminated with a misjudged knee slide, something he instantly regretted as he head-planted into the sand face first! 'Boom.' He spat out a mouthful of sand and rolled onto his back to admire the sky and take in that winning feeling. He needed to blink out sand and dust himself down. Sand gets everywhere, it was in his eyes, ears, mouth and nose, all mini sandpits of irritation requiring the intervention of his shirt. Standing he turned to tease his brother, blinking through grains of sandy tears made locating him a tad tricky. He scanned the pitch, nothing, the path up the hill, still nothing. His eyes fell on the sea, nothing, well, the ball but no brother. Where was Eric? It was 13:14.

The ball had flown past the goalie's flailing arms and into the goal, the lack of net and the swirling wind carrying it onwards and upwards. The young keeper turned in hot pursuit of his beloved ball which soared higher, curved down, bounced back up, floated over the shoreline before coming to rest on the surface of the water well beyond the shallows. Not stopping to contemplate the possibilities, Eric entered the water. He'd waded in without a care, focused only on retrieving the ball, it was his and he wanted it back. He stepped tentatively towards his prize, too young to realise that each step caused a momentum in the water, pushing the bobbing ball further out to sea beyond his reach. The sloping sand beneath his feet was taking him in and deeper. His feet began to slide and sink, the small yet powerful waves pushing against his thighs making him increasingly unstable. Within seconds he was waist deep in the water and found himself being lifted ever so slightly off his toes. One more step and the ball was his. The ever-present swirling turbulence of waves had ploughed a trough and raised ripples in the undertow, without them he would have undoubtedly succeeded in his quest, but it was not to be. He would disappear beneath the surface in 6 seconds time! Six, five, four, three, two, one, the wave hit him in the chest and knocked him off balance. There was no splashing. No shouting. No witness. Eric slipped silently under the water at 13:13.

Sam cleaned the mess left behind by the bleeding boy, rinsed the blood-soaked towels, packed lunch into Matt's rucksack and changed to go down to the beach. The sickening sight of blood was making her nauseous. She poured herself a fizzy orange and gulped it down. Sparkling drinks always calmed her upset stomach especially on Saturday mornings after fabulous 'Fizzy Fridays'! Grabbing a handful of biscuits, she gave a cursory scan round the caravan and satisfied all was well stepped out, locked the door, and turned to take the air. It was magical how troubles dissipated in fresh air, ebbed away as certain as tides turned. Matt and Harry would be back soon, and all would be well. Reaching the top of the path she scanned the beach and a shocking scene presented itself, Charlie standing on an otherwise empty beach.

The mother's reaction was immediate as it was powerful, a gut-wrenching scream no squall could suppress, followed by desperate cries, 'Eric, ERIC! Where are you? Charlie where is he? Where's your brother? Charlie!'

Frantically scanning the terrain, her eyes were drawn to the sea, her brain trying to make sense of what she was seeing. Yellow. She could see yellow. A yellow ball bobbing on the water and a shape under the surface! A shape in the water, a familiar shape, a shape she had cradled, a shape she loved. His mother's bloodcurdling screams sparked Charlie into action, he started running, instinctively knowing what his brother had done and where he had gone. The wind could not waft her words away, delivered with force enough to ring in Charlie's ears.

'Get him. Get your brother. Eric's in the water. Charlie help him. Now! Charlie, you have to get him out!' His mother was hysterical, frantic and he knew she was too far away to save her son. Reaching the water, he felt paralysed by fear. What should he do? What could he do?

His mother's cries were coming thick and fast, as relentless as the waves washing at his feet. The boy scoured the surface of the water hunting for shark fins, their absence failing to reassure but he had no time to weigh up his options. He knew what he had to do. He had to go in. Taking that first step into the water was difficult but he took it all the same. Wading in, within seconds he was up to his waist in the cold swell, his eyes searching the surface but unable to penetrate the grey. He would have to go under. Two deep breaths and he dived head first, the frothy water gurgled over his face and in his ears. The water was cold. Pain shot across his forehead, the cold hurt. He returned to the surface, gasping for air, pushed hair from his eyes then instantly back down into the underwater world he feared so much. Eyes open searching, the salty water stinging. A feeling of panic engulfed him. His strokes were frantic and ineffective. Gulping a mouthful of the sickening solution forced him up again. Spluttering and coughing he plunged straight back down. A flash of red. What was that? Red. Eric's shorts were red. He lunged for the red his desperate fingers brushing the fabric but remaining frustratingly beyond his reach. Up for air and immediately back down. His eyes searching through an eyewash of pain, a burning fire these salty waters could not extinguish. He was in up to his shoulders having to stretch on his toes to push himself forward and deeper. Desperation washed over him as he frantically darted one way then another, the water under his chin and there it was again, a flash of red ahead. He jumped forward and sank beneath the surface to take hold. Yes, he had him! He felt elated but that feeling of relief vanished almost as soon as it hit, the body in the water wasn't moving, merely swaying at the mercy of this cruel sea. Getting his brother's head above the water was vital but Charlie was struggling to get any leverage, his feet couldn't touch the bottom, he was floating out of control and in danger of drifting out to sea! The situation was critical. Determined to keep hold of his brother, Charlie used every ounce of strength to spin round and jump forwards, digging his heels into the ever-moving floor he pushed towards the shore. He was consumed with a sinking feeling and thwarted by sinking feet but driven on by the love in his heart, he managed to drag his brother out and drop him on the beach. It was 13:16.

Sam, a helpless bystander, numb in horror at the unfolding spectacle, was running and continued running until her legs gave way, her lungs weak, too tired to take a breath. Reaching the bottom of the path she fell, dizzy and light-headed, her mouth dry, her chest tight. The shocking sight greeting her at the water's edge caused her blood to run cold and a chill to shiver across her skin. Eric's lifeless body slumped motionless on the sand. Frozen to the spot, her heart ached of love, her head full of dread but spurred on to save her baby she found the strength and launched into a frenzied sprint across the sand. Arriving with them she could not contain her anguish any longer, sinking to her knees, her misery poured out, the tears flooded down her cheeks. She cradled her treasured boy, squeezing him to her chest, her tears dripping onto his pale young face. There was no response. Nothing. The boy lay there, curled in her lap, his lips blue, his body cold.

'Eric, please!' The distraught mother shook him, gently at first then with more urgency. 'Eric, come on! Please! Oh God! Please!'

Time stopped and an eerie stillness smothered the shore. The sounds of the sea, the wind and the seagulls were drowned out by the silence. Death had descended from the heavens to snatch her child, a child the mother wasn't ready to sacrifice. Her frantic cries were all she had left.

'Eric, wake up! Come on. Eric! Eric, I need you. You must wake up! Eric!'

She fell quiet. She kissed his pale cheek and buried her head on his chest, the realisation dawning, she'd lost him, he'd gone, her baby was dead! The agony of despair rushed through her veins, flooded into her blood, and poured into the depths of her soul causing her to let go an animalistic howl of deafening proportions, a roar of grief from deep within the pit of her stomach. His mother's haunting screams frightened Charlie who had never heard nor seen his mother so distressed. It was as if he were a non-participant in a dream, a bad one, where the action was in slow motion. He noticed her bleeding knees, scratched raw by the gritty sand but she couldn't have cared less. He found himself wishing his father was there, he would know what to do! His mother lacked control, shaking, and sobbing then unconstrained wailing. Then a cough. A cough! Wait! A cough! A cough! Eric coughed! It was 13:18.

A thrilling development, a glorious cough told the mother her child would live. There followed a cacophony of coughs and spluttering spit followed by more sobbing and wailing but this time from the distressed infant not the relieved mother. The glorious sound of his crying triggered a memory in Sam, a maternity ward, a slapped behind and the first time she'd heard her beautiful boy cry. Hearing the sound on the sand was overwhelming.

'Eric, my darling boy, you're okay, you're okay now. Come on sweetheart. You are going to be okay!'

She was reassuring him and convincing herself, her tears of joy spilling over her eyelids and down her forehead as she looked to the heavens and whispered her thanks. Charlie sat shivering beside them, clutching his knees to his chest in his quest for warmth, his face tingling with the shock. Eric took time to compose himself, cold, he too started to shake. Sam knew they needed dry clothes and the warmth only the caravan could provide. Adopting a bright and breezy tone she urged them to their feet.

'Come on you two let's get you up the hill and these wet clothes off. You'll be warm as toast in no time and then we can find you a little something!'

Sam jollied them along whilst they trudged up the hill, caught up in what could have been. After hot showers, a change of clothes then it was hot chocolate all round topped off with a generous helping of marshmallows. The equilibrium was restored. Within the hour the wind strengthened, clouds thickened, the air grew chilly and the sea choppy. The change in weather hadn't gone unnoticed by Sam, drawn to the window she contemplated how lucky they'd been. A boy wading into the water under the current conditions would sink and become invisible to a mother and a brother, hidden beneath white-capped waves to drown in a dark sea. Sam was cherishing this time with her beloved boys and finding it impossible to contain her joy, squeezing and kissing Eric at regular intervals, much to the boy's disgust! She tentatively steered the conversation to the importance of adhering to family rules and not chasing balls into the sea but most of her words were lost on Eric, too young to comprehend the sequence of events or consequences of his actions and too distracted by his toy farm to care, but Charlie understood. It wasn't until a little later when the grateful mother shifted her attention to her firstborn. She gazed at him lovingly, awash with thankfulness. He'd withdrawn to the sofa to read so Sam took the opportunity to snuggle next to him, pull him to her and whisper in his ear.

'Do you know what you did Charlie? Do you know how important what you did was? Charlie, you saved your brother. You went in and I know how hard that was for you to do. You went into the sea and got him out. He would have been lost. He'd gone under. You saved his life Charlie, my brave boy. My strong brave boy.'

She held him and kissed the top of his head. Charlie did understand the importance of what he'd done, it hit him in a wave of emotion, he couldn't believe he'd found the strength or courage to go in. He smiled; he'd found his persevering muscles. Thinking back, once he'd made the decision to go in, sharks did not enter his mind, the water had gone over his head and he'd dived under, in that moment nothing was as important as saving his brother. Charlie had not let the fear in. He cried. It was 14:28.

The car pulled up at 14:37 causing Sam to rush outside. Both parents needed to help Harry into the caravan and settle him on the sofa. The events of the day had left the boy subdued, he'd been given an injection of lignocaine to anesthetise the area and eight stitches to oppose the edges of the wound. His foot, understandably painful, protected with an adhesive fabric dressing with strict instructions to keep the area clean and stay out of the sea for the rest of the holiday. Sam brought Matt up to speed on how Charlie had averted disaster and how their family lived to fight another day. At 14:54 Matt chose to make a quick turnaround to the hospital to have Eric checked out for secondary drowning in case water had got into his lungs and as all was well they arrived back at Sea View in time for surprise tea. Surprise teas were made for days like these and this one would be a cracker with every treat thrown in. Matt was incredibly proud of his son, 'chuffed to bits' to be exact. It wasn't until Sam was putting Harry and Eric to bed and father and son were sprawled in their usual spot on the sofa that Matt remembered Charlie's words from earlier.

'Hey son ya were trying to tell me something before when we were crabbing, do ya want to tell me what it's all about?'

Charlie took a moment of contemplation before responding and when it came he spoke with a new-found confidence.

'No, you're okay, I'm good. It's all good.'

'No worries Sharkbite, ya know where I am if ya need to talk. I love ya son.'

Hearing his father speaking these words, Charlie knew them to be true. His father loved him. He really did. He couldn't remember hearing his father saying these words with any sincerity before and in that moment Charlie knew he loved his father too. He didn't need to tell his father anything, things had changed. Charlie had changed and the boy knew it. Charlie could not be certain what the future would hold but he knew whatever happened, whatever he chose to do, he would be seeing it with different eyes and feeling it with a different heart!

The Parker family would never forget the traumatic and joyous events of that day, relishing opportunities to tell their own version of Harry's cut, Charlie's heroism, and Eric's near drowning. Remembering that day made Charlie smile, he was proud he had saved his brother but for him it was more than that, he would be forever grateful to the white-haired shark lady and the impact she'd had on him. He cherished that holiday, the summer he turned twelve, when two strangers shared stories, became friends and their lives changed. The day he didn't let fear win.

'Hey lad, time for a story hey?'

Dad and me are on the sofa. He pulls me to him but in a kind way. He loves me and I love him.

'Ya were great today lad. What ya did and how ya saved ya brother. I know ya not keen on the water lad so to do what you did and go in was brave. Me chest is bursting lad. I'm so proud of ya.'

We sit there chatting then me mam comes over. We all talk for a bit, but I'm tired.

'I'm tired, I'm going to bed.'

'Okay love. Are you okay darling? You feeling okay?'

Mam sounds worried.

'What happened with Eric this afternoon has probably taken its toll on you darling. Sleep well. Tomorrow's another day.'

She stops and looks at me. She strokes my cheek and whispers in my ear.

'Are you sure you're okay love? We are so proud of you munchkin.'

'I'm okay. I really am. I'm fine. I'm just tired. I'm going to bed. Don't worry.'

It doesn't take long for me to do my teeth and get into bed. My fingers search for the book that I shoved under the pillow before tea. It's not a comic that will save me tonight. I don't need a superhero to protect me. Tonight, I'm going to find out what happens to Sonja and Marco in the next chapter. I read for a bit, but my eyes are heavy. I look up at the wooden slats under Harry's bed. Mam's right. Tomorrow is another day. Tomorrow I'm going in. I'm going in with Eric. I'm going in with them all, well not Harry, not for a while, not till he's allowed but I'm going in. I know I will. I'm ready and strong. Time to trust and try!

'Night Mam. Night Dad.'

I close the book.

EPILOGUE

Words, I love them. Quizzes, crosswords, new words, word facts, word games, songs. Anagrams are a recent discovery, jumbling letters from a word to make another word or two. It blew my mind when I noticed that the two words, 'the eyes', make 'they see'! 'Elvis' becomes 'lives'. Elvis lives! 'Impossible' becomes 'I'm possible' and my favourite, 'teachers', becomes 'cheaters'! Ha!

I'll think of a word, any word. Pizza. Yes pizza. That's a word. It makes me think of food. A food I don't like. Strange for a vegetarian not to like pizza. What's not to like? Margherita pizza. It's so easy for vegetarians to like and eat. It's just cheese and tomato plus you can chuck on your favourite vegetables. Great. But not all vegetarians like vegetables. Not all vegetables anyway. I mean, who likes tomatoes? Real tomatoes with the skins on. They're like slugs. Yuk! Tomato sauce is great. Tomato in beans is brilliant. But real tomatoes. Disgusting! How are you supposed to eat them? And yes I do love cheese but slimy cheese with tomatoes lurking everywhere, no thanks! Mam tried to get us to eat sun-dried tomatoes twice. Sun-dried! Sunburnt more like. I gave her a bit of lip about it, so she made us a surprise tea with Margherita pizza with tons of sun-dried tomatoes on. Completely cremated they were. It took me ages to get the skins off them. She wasn't best pleased with tomato skins all over the table and floor. They stick to everything, could use them instead of 'No Nails'!

Another word. Night. I'm not keen on night-times. I have trouble sleeping and spend ages checking everywhere in my bedroom. I have a light to make the night bright. Night is dark. Dark is not my favourite thing. Black. Midnight. Night is scary. I'm going to work on bedtimes when I get home.

Another word. Clown. I used to like them, thought they were funny when they chased each other and bumped into things or fell over. Mam and Dad have never taken us to a circus. They refuse but I've seen them on TV. They don't agree with animals being kept in captivity and used for our entertainment! I agree with them. Nathan, or Spike as I like to call him since the cocktail stick incident, told me about a film with a clown in it that sounds horrendous. Halloween a few years ago and there were tons of kids walking round in pjs and clown masks. I'm never watching that film, ever!

Pizza. Night. Clown. Words that make me think things.

One more word. Shark. I know how this word makes me feel. Scared. Terrified. Frightened. So scared I can't go into the sea. Those eyes. The sharp teeth. They swim in my mind. I only ever saw a real shark once, in an aquarium and that was enough. That did it for me. Ruined things, the beach, holidays, swimming. Jumble up 'scary sharks' and you get 'sharky scars'! Except that was how I used to feel. Don't feel like that anymore. Thought I'd be scared of them forever, but I was wrong. I now see sharks with different eyes. I've heard stories about them. I've learned about them and see them like Jane sees them. Through her kind and caring eyes. She looks at them differently and because she does, I do. I know I have work to do before I swim like I used to, but I know I can do it. I will do it. Knowing this makes me happy.

The word shark makes me think about a big fish. A fish that has lived in the oceans for millions of years. A fish that is being hunted to extinction. A fish that is being treated cruelly. A fish that has sharp teeth and a pointed fin on its back and is perfectly designed to do what it has to do, to hunt fish. A fish that helps to keep the oceans and seas healthy. A fish that protects our coastlines and reefs. The scariest thing about sharks is not the fish itself but oceans without them.

Charlie.

Strength is found within us all
Waiting, strong for fear to call
Knocking our door to make us fall
Grasp that nettle, that thing that stings
Hold it, squeeze it, the pain will thin
Stop that fear from creeping in
Drip, drip, dripping under your skin
Seeping, sinking, don't let it win
Worries are never as bad as you fear
Open your mind, your coast is clear
For you to dive, to take the plunge
Be where you want, it's time to change
Carefree you'll be and free from strife
Dive and swim in your own water of life

What you fear isn't the shark, it's what comes next.
Staying out of our oceans and seas will suppress the fear but it will
be there the next time you face your demon.
The fear is whether you go in or stay out.
All fear is the same.
Don't let the fear in.
Don't let the fear win.

Sharks swim in rivers, seas, and oceans.
Sharks were here before us.